the Duchess Inheritance

JORDINIA: BOOK 2

C.K. BROOKE

a 48fourteen Publishing Trade Paperback

BOOKS BY C.K. BROOKE

The Duchess Quest
Jordinia: Book 1

The Duchess Inheritance
Jordinia: Book 2

The Red Pearl

The Duchess Inheritance, Jordinia: Book 2. Copyright © 2015 by C.K. Brooke.

Edited by Denise DeSio. Cover by Amanda Matthews of www.amdesignstudios.net.

Library of Congress Number: 2015905232

ISBN-13: 978-1-937546-40-3
ISBN-10: 1-937546-40-3

For you, my readers:

the only joy greater than writing is the gift of your readership. Thank you.

the Duchess Inheritance

JORDINIA: BOOK 2

West Halvea

•Kempei
•Dekantor

THE NEW REPUBLIC
OF JORDINIA

☀ Pierma

HÄFFSTROM

•Omar   • Pikosta

• The Garden Palace   ☀Vündtgen

• Solomyn

THE KINGDOM OF
THE BAINHERD PLAINS

•Pon
Castle

•Bearn   Yuwelyn Bay

THE KNIGHTS' FOREST

Hopestone Bay

HEPPESTONI

Beili
•

THE MALEILAN SEA

The Great Continent

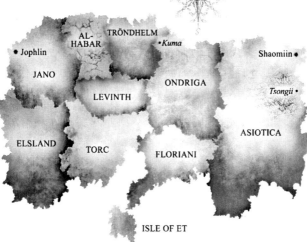

THE
CONTINENTAL
SEA

TRÖNDHELM

AL-
HABAR

• Jophlin

•Kuma

Shaomiin •

JANO

ONDRIGA

Tsongii •

LEVINTH

ASIOTICA

ELSLAND

TORC

FLORIANI

ISLE OF ET

EKIANIC OCEAN

EAST
HALVEA

CONTINENTAL
SEA

WEST
HALVEA

GREAT CONTINENT

MALEILAN
SEA

Part 1

INHERITANCE

1

COSMITH

THE VILLAGE INN'S FRONT DOOR burst open, and a young woman bounded forth. Jon Cosmith's heart trembled to see Eludaine Ducelle jogging toward him, her short black hair delightfully disheveled. But she darted straight past him to the ebony stallion, Spitfire.

With affection, she threw her arms around the beast's neck. "Dear Spitfire, if only I could keep you for myself," Cosmith heard her whisper. "But Bos and Selu must take you home now." She lifted her head, catching the man watching her. "One of my fondest memories of you is riding together upon this horse," she admitted shyly.

He grinned at her. "My fondest memory of you did not take place upon any horse."

"*Jon.*" The young woman blushed, although the corners of her mouth were upturned.

He was pulling her into his arms when their companions' voices drifted nearer. Regretfully, Dainy slipped from his hold and made her way toward them, joining in their chatter.

"Your hat, Cosmith." Seluna Campagna tossed the familiar brown cowman's hat across the threshold. He reached up and caught it.

"And your satchel." Boslon Visigoth held out the tan bag, and Cosmith thanked him, receiving it.

"Well." Selu craned her neck to look up at the giant. "Time to say goodbye to the Emperor's children, then?"

Cosmith started. This was a rather odd way of referring to Macmillan and Dainy, although the violet-haired woman was entirely accurate. He was simply unaccustomed to the notion that Marley Macmillan and the Duchess of Jordinia shared the same father: Jordinia's former Emperor, Dane Ducelle. Not to mention, Cosmith now knew that he and Macmillan shared the same mother.

He wasn't one for farewells, so he lingered by the borrowed steeds—Storm, Folly Silver, and Spitfire— whom Bos and Selu planned to return to their owner in southern Häffstrom.

Dainy squeezed Bos around his enormous middle. "It's not goodbye forever," the giant assured her. The girl wiped her eyes, and Cosmith watched her, longing to take her into their room and comfort her as soon as the others were gone.

"That's right." Selu smiled. "You'll certainly be invited, should there be any," she cleared her throat, "upcoming *celebration* of sorts."

At first, Dainy beamed at the insinuation of Bos and Selu's matrimony. But slowly, her fair countenance fell. "Oh. Well, I'm not sure if we'll be around here for much longer." At their curious expressions, she reached into the folds of her frock and extracted the silver triangular key they'd recently unearthed. "This was in the little box we found in my treasury vault," she divulged. Selu held the object up to her oblong eyes.

"Jon thinks it's from Asiotica," explained Macmillan. "We intend to travel there, and find what it goes to. Dainy's inheritance—"

"*Our* inheritance," she corrected him.

He smiled at her. "Our inheritance," he amended, "may not be lost, after all."

"You're going to Asiotica?" Bos and Selu appeared taken aback. "But when?"

"I know not." Dainy shrugged. "Perhaps soon!"

The giant frowned. "I should accompany you. It shall be a tremendous voyage from here to the Great Continent. You'll need a grander escort than merely Cosmith and Macmillan." The other two men glared up at him, indignant, but Bos only grunted. "No offense."

"Oh, no." Dainy shook her head at once. "I'll not make that mistake again. Uncle Pascale did not live to see his wedding day, because he insisted on escorting me here first. Nay, you mustn't come with us, Bos. Stay here, and begin your life with Selu."

Bos made to object, but Macmillan asserted himself. "You know full well the Duchess shall be perfectly safe with me. I am her brother, after all."

Selu placed a hand on her partner's hulking arm. "We must heed Macmillan, dear," she reminded Bos. "As Dainy's elder brother, he speaks for her now."

At this remark, Dainy furrowed her brow, while Cosmith—Dainy's intended—slowly clenched his jaw. He had not thought of that…

Bos reluctantly relented, and at last, he and Selu departed with the horses. Pulling down his hat to shield from the sun's glare, Cosmith hitched his satchel over his shoulder and turned back to the inn. They were still exhausted from the journey behind them and the trying events of Dainy's uncle's betrayal and her subsequent rescue in the previous days. All they wished to do was rest in preparation for their next voyage. Which, Cosmith noted, had better be soon, before autumn should fall, bringing hurricanes with it.

Although the sun still shone, he led Dainy to their rented chamber. Patiently, she waited as he pulled down the shades and slid off his boots.

The door rolled open behind them, however, and Macmillan stepped in, yawning and stretching his arms. "Can you believe my feet *still* hurt from walking through the Bainherd Plains?" He collapsed onto the mattress unceremoniously, hazel eyes staring up at the rafters. Dainy cast Cosmith an uncertain glance.

"Mac." Cosmith beckoned him.

The lad looked up, puzzled.

"Is it not time you rented your own room, brother?" suggested Dainy carefully.

Macmillan looked between them, eyes narrowing. "Oh," he said at last, an unpleasant smirk creeping across his features. "I see what you two are intending. And I'll not hear of it." He lay back on the bed, sprawling out his limbs with a contented sigh. "You are not to lie with my little sister again, Cosmith. Not on my watch."

Cosmith tensed.

"This isn't funny, Mac." Dainy frowned.

"I'm not jesting," he contended. "You heard Selu. As your elder brother, I speak for you now. And I say you two may not share a bed until you're wed." He shrugged. "It's only proper."

"Unbelievable," muttered Cosmith, as Dainy looked to him imploringly. Flustered, he steered her back to the door.

Macmillan sat up. "Where're you going?"

"The Duchess and I have better things to do than hang around with you," Cosmith snapped, guiding Dainy from the room.

2

SELU

IN THE RURAL VILLAGE OF Solomyn, Häffstrom, Selu and Bos found a quiet farm for sale, resting peacefully between two streams, with brown hens strutting through the tall grasses and a milk cow lowing in the barn. The wooden house was sturdy and comfortable, a fine place to share a simple, peaceful life together.

With a portion of the gold winnings that Cosmith and Dainy had generously given them, they purchased the property. Each day, Bos felled trees and crafted furniture from the wood. Selu marveled at his capabilities, never having realized her beloved was such an artist.

On their first night in their new home, she made to share his mat. But Bos gently pointed her away. "We are not yet wed."

"What do you take me for? A virgin?" She laughed. "You know I'm a widow. Not to mention…" Her voice faded at the dark memories of her youth in Jordinian prison, where she and her mother had suffered the rebel soldiers' abuses.

"Still," he insisted. "It is not right."

"We've shared a mat before," she argued. But even as she spoke, she knew that occasion had been different, as nothing of an intimate nature had transpired between them.

Bos smiled, blue eyes glowing. "I shall build us a bed for our wedding night," he promised. "Which," he reached into his pocket, "may be as soon as you wish."

Selu's breath caught to see the delicate wooden bracelet resting in his enormous palm, as he lowered himself onto both knees and presented it to her in the traditional way. He slipped the band around her left wrist, and Selu admired the meticulous rose- and leaf-like designs carved in the wood.

Examining the base, she noticed he'd etched a succession of runes, spelling out two unfamiliar words: *Hazja Lænde*. "What does this mean?" she asked, brushing her thumb against the foreign engravings.

"It is Old Jordinian, meaning *eternal love*. Do you like it?" He suddenly looked apprehensive. "I made it myself. If you prefer, I could buy you someth—"

"It is the most magnificent nuptial bracelet I've ever seen." She took the brawny man into her arms. "And I'd not trade it for the world."

He wrapped her in his mighty embrace. "Write to your mother, then. Invite her to be a witness to our matrimony, and to live with us here in Solomyn."

Selu could not restrain the single tear that leaked from her eye. This was a kindness she'd not anticipated. She nodded against his massive shoulder, overcome with gratitude.

3

BET

"WHAT'S THE WORD TODAY, BETINE?"

The older woman scowled. "Don't look so cheerful, Carlo."

The boy laughed. "It's that bad, then?"

Bet Toustead handed over the parchment she'd torn from Capitol Square. Carlo looked merely amused, blond curls falling over mischievous blue eyes. "An article about lumber shortage? And this is newsworthy *how*?"

Bet sighed, rolling up the parchment and swatting his head with it. "Are you such a fool, boy? Jordinians are already hungry and cold. If wood becomes a commodity, things are only going to worsen around here."

The young man chuckled darkly, indicating his fellow urchins peddling stolen wares in the streets. "It can't get much worse." He shrugged. "And besides, is there not the entire Knights' Forest from which to harvest plenty of wood?"

"And you think the other nations of West Halvea shall simply permit us to seize the forest for our own?"

Bet shook her violet head. "Mark my words, Carlo Di-Gyle, there's going to be another war."

"Over wood?"

The woman tucked the post into her ragged skirts, following him down an alleyway as he stalked a half-eaten pear. "Without wood, how will Jordinians light their hearths, cook their meals, warm their homes?"

"I expect they'll have to cough up more coin for their resources," muttered Carlo, picking up the abandoned fruit. "Which leaves even less for the likes of us."

"Exactly," said the woman, relieved he was finally catching on. She declined as he offered her a bite of pear, although her stomach groaned.

"But onto some real news, Bet." The boy spoke with his mouth full. "What's this I hear about Marten Hoste visiting Häffstrom last moon? Something about the Ducelle girl—?"

"*Shh!*" Bet glanced over her shoulder, fearful. "Do not say that name here. Are you mad?"

Carlo took another bite of pear.

"Besides." She tightened the ragged shawl about her bony shoulders. "That is just a stupid rumor."

"Heard from your daughter lately?"

Bet shook her head.

"Well, I'm off," the lad decided. "There's got to be an odd job somewhere in the grand capitol city of Pierma this morning."

"No picking pockets," Bet advised him.

Carlo grinned impishly.

The woman glanced around to ensure no one was watching before swiftly tracing a circle on his brow. "May the Eternal God bless and keep you today," she murmured. "May you find wages to earn, bread to eat, and shelter under which to take rest this night."

Carlo embraced her, and Bet watched her young friend round the dingy corner.

4

DAINY

DAINY BADE THE TAILOR FAREWELL, clutching her bundle as she departed the dressmaker's shop. "Thank you, Mac," she sang.

At Jon's suggestion, their mutual half-brother had exchanged his gold bars for coins, and given a bag to each of them. Dainy had finally purchased a new wardrobe, and was thrilled to no longer have to wear the pink frock and wooden shoes she'd been borrowing from Hessian Gatspierre's maids.

Dressed comfortably at last, she made off down the narrow streets of Omar Village, arms interlinked between Mac and Jon. As they strolled, she noticed Jon studying the horizon. "What is it, my love?" she asked him.

He looked thoughtful. "The autumnal equinox cannot be far off."

"Ah." She nodded. "The rainy season." She had, after all, been raised by the seashore on the coast of the Beili Dunes, and knew the equinoxes brought the rainfalls with them.

"You mean hurricanes?" Mac spoke from her other side. "Is it a bad time for sailing to the Great Continent, then?"

"Not if we leave soon." Jon by-stepped a group of small boys as they ran past, chasing after a rolling hoop. "It'll take nearly two moons to reach Asiotica from Häffstrom's coast."

"Then what are we waiting for?" Dainy beamed, steering her companions through the jostling crowd as they passed an aromatic patisserie. "Why not head to the coast?"

"I daresay," grinned Jon, appraising her. "But my little firecracker is becoming quite the adventurer."

5

KRAMERIK

"GOOD MORROW, CAPTAIN. THE USUAL?"

Captain Hans Kramerik nodded as he took his seat by the bulletin, glancing up to read the latest posts. The waitress shortly returned with his hot cup and saucer. "And I added a shot of honey, just how you like." She gave him a friendly pat on the shoulder before bustling off.

Kramerik grinned, unfurling his maps. His men had been loading cargo onto his freighter since dawn, and he planned to set sail that evening. The portside café in Pikosta was always his choice location for rest and review before a long journey ahead.

At somewhere around his third cup of tea, he began to doze. At the jangling of bells above the café door, however, he jolted with a snort, just in time to see three new patrons stepping inside. The captain looked down and straightened his blazer, resuming examination of his maps.

"Spectacular," one of the newcomers was saying abrasively. Kramerik glanced up again to see a black-haired lad confronting his companion, a sturdy-look-ing fellow wearing a cowhide hat. "We ride all the way to the coast, and there isn't a single passenger ship at port."

Curious, Kramerik watched as a pretty girl with a curvy figure remained by the door, looking between them uncertainly.

"Where else would you have had me take us?" snapped the man in the hat. "A port is a port. How was I to know—?"

"Good morrow," the waitress interrupted cheerily. "What can I get you three?"

"A tall whiskey," declared the hatted man.

"Jon," chided the curvy girl, though her voice was rather bell-like and pleasing to the ear. "It's only noon."

"Just a pitcher of water, please." The black-haired chap slumped down into a chair, and the others took their seats across from him. "What now, then? The furthest any of those ships is headed is only to East Halvea."

"You don't know that." The other finally removed his hat to reveal a head of tousled brown hair and a rath-er handsome, if unshaven, face. "We didn't interview every single captain."

"Might as well 'ave," grumbled the first, as the waitress returned with three glasses and a pitcher.

The comely girl spoke again. "Perhaps we ought to take a boat to East Halvea, then," she suggested evenly, pouring her companions a drink. "And maybe someone can carry us to Asiotica from there."

At this, Kramerik rose, bumping the table in his haste. "Excuse me."

They turned.

"Forgive me, but I couldn't help but overhear... You seek passage to Asiotica?"

The youths nodded.

"My merchant vessel is set to leave for the Great Continent this eve," Kramerik informed them. "She is small, but I've a spare cabin or two for extra passengers. I should be happy to have you aboard."

"You're sailing to Asiotica?" asked the black-haired bloke.

"No, but we're docking in Jophlin. At least that would get you onto the Continent."

"How much?" inquired the other man, brown eyes intense.

The captain shrugged. "Four gold apiece? An even dozen for the three of you?"

They nodded, their expressions considerably brighter. "That is reasonable," agreed the brown-haired man, standing to his feet.

"Hans Kramerik, Captain of the S. S. *Evangela*." He shook their hands.

"Jonwal Harrington Cosmith." He gave Kramerik an impressively firm handshake before swatting the other lad on the shoulder. "This is Marley Macmillan. And the lovely lady is his kid sister." He indicated the lass. "Miss Macmillan," he introduced her, after a slight pause.

The girl blinked. Kramerik took her fair hand in his weathered one, holding it to his bristling beard. He couldn't help but delight in the simple pleasure of kissing her hand; although, of course, he was old enough to have sired her. "Delighted to meet you, Miss Macmillan."

She gently released his hand.

"Well." Kramerik straightened. "Meet me at port before sundown, then. Oh, and gentlemen?" His grin was rueful. "I'd suggest one last good, square meal. Unfortunately, my galley chef is not the finest."

6

DAINY

"NOW, REMEMBER," JON ROLLED DAINY'S trunk in one hand, hauling his own in the other, "you are *Miss Macmillan*, savvy? We cannot inform anyone of your true identity throughout our travels."

"But Hoste said I shall have amnesty anywhere I go, outside of the New Republic," Dainy reminded him, recalling their conversation with the Jordinian leader.

A shadow passed over Jon's handsome features. "I do not trust Marten Hoste."

Beneath the setting sun, the trio greeted the captain of the *Evangela*. Although small compared to the other ships in Pikosta's harbor that evening, the freighter was new, and certainly the largest vessel Dainy had ever boarded.

"She runs on *col*," Captain Kramerik explained, guiding them past the quay and up the boarding ramp. He proceeded to describe a rocky sediment, which had recently been discovered in the eastern mines of the Great Continent. Jon and Mac were fascinated, wishing to know everything about this col, where it was found, how it was mined, and how it was burned to heat a boiler and propel a steamship.

"It's the latest technology," Kramerik proclaimed. "Cutting edge. The wave of the future, I tell you!"

"She's a fine freighter, Captain." Jon stepped onto the main deck, offering a hand to help Dainy up. He glanced at the whitewashed walls and waxed planks, nodding approvingly.

"What sort of cargo does she haul?" inquired Mac, following Kramerik to the cabin deck.

"Textiles." The mariner smoothed his beard. "Wool, cotton… In fact, we're en route to Jophlin right now, to retrieve an order of silk. And then to the Isle of Et, to deliver several cases of leather."

"You're all over the map, aren't you?" mused Jon, stroking his own bristling chin.

"Speaking of maps," piped Dainy, and Kramerik gave her an appreciative glance over his shoulder. "I should like to see one. I know little of geography."

"I'll draw one for you," Jon offered.

But the captain laughed. "I've maps aplenty, dear Miss Macmillan. You are welcome to all of them."

Dainy beamed. How fortuitous that she and her companions had not only found passage, but managed to stumble directly into the path of such a warmhearted captain.

They came to a small hallway, where she suddenly shivered at the long row of narrow doors. It was all too reminiscent of the treasury in Omar, where she'd recently spent one horrifying afternoon locked inside of her vault.

"Well!" Kramerik rubbed his hands together. "How delightful to have you aboard. I do appreciate your business."

"As we appreciate your service." Mac bobbed his head as Kramerik opened their cabin doors.

Dainy made to reach for her trunk when the captain placed a hand on her shoulder. "Any time you wish to peruse my maps," he told her, "my quarters are just across the way. Please, do not be shy." He then departed to oversee his crew, leaving Dainy and her companions to acquaint themselves with their new lodgings.

The young woman stepped into a small, tidy cabin. After sliding her trunk beneath a fold-out cot, she fingered the triangular key in her skirt pocket to ensure that it remained safe. At the sound of approaching steps, however, she looked up. Her pulse quickened to see Jon, penetrating eyes staring her down as he strolled up to her, taking her by the waist…

"Cosmith," snapped Mac. "Our room's over here." He pointed next door.

Jon shrugged. "For now."

"Huh?" Mac frowned as Dainy raised an eyebrow.

"So long as we're in Halvean waters, Macmillan, your brotherly authority is relevant. But soon as we pass the coast of East Halvea…" Jon smirked, removing his hat and tossing it onto Dainy's cot. "Such patriarchal customs shall no longer apply."

"What d'you mean?"

"He means," said Dainy, forming a smile of her own, "that once we sail out of Halvean territory, I may share my cabin with whomever I wish."

"No," said Mac flatly.

"Yes," countered Jon and Dainy.

Mac dropped his voice. "Have you two no shame? What will Kramerik think? What of his crew?"

Jon laughed. "Who cares?"

"I care!" snapped Mac. "My sister is a duchess, Cosmith. Not one of your many whores."

A chill coursed through Dainy that had little to do with the breeze. She suddenly found she could look nowhere but down at her shoes.

Beside her, Jon stiffened. She trembled at the tickle of his breath against her cheek as he whispered, "Excuse me, darling," and proceeded to pull Mac from the cabin, slamming the door behind them.

Though secluded, Dainy could clearly overhear their every word. She turned away, knowing it was wrong to eavesdrop, but they were making no effort to conceal their voices.

"*What in hell is the matter with you, Macmillan?*"

"She may be smitten with you, but the fact remains, you are an incurable womanizer."

"Do not make me strike you…"

Mac ignored him. "So, if Dainy means more to you than just another notch in your belt, you will prove it. Which means you'll keep your over-practiced hands off of her, and respect her for once."

"Respect her? Good God, man, I *love* her. D'you think I've ever felt this way for a woman before?"

"I'd imagine you'd have lost count of all the women before."

Dainy leaned against the door, her heart hammering. Why, but could there be some truth to what Mac was saying?

Indeed, Jon was the only man she'd ever loved. But was she not merely the latest in a lengthy procession of maidens he'd already seduced? The thought made her stomach churn. Exactly how many other women had come before her, anyway? And who was to say that, in time, he would remain satisfied with just her, when—heaven knew—the man could have any girl he desired?

Mac spoke again, as though reading her thoughts. "So how does the Duchess compare," he asked scathingly, "to your long line of conquests?"

Dainy was startled by the emotion in Jon's tone as he responded, "There is no comparison."

Her breathing slowed, and she lowered herself onto the cot. Jon's hat remained there, and she picked it up, hugging it to her chest. His voice had reduced to a whisper, though she could still make out most of the words. "...A second chance? I am not the man I once was."

"All I see is the same arrogant rake who always gets what he wants," muttered Mac. "And people do not change."

Dainy listened to her brother's departing footfalls until her door bowed open again. Jon took a tentative step inside, looking uncommonly somber. Slowly, she rose to her feet, still clutching his hat.

"S'pose you heard all that." Awkwardly, he rubbed at the back of his neck. "Look, Dainy... you are all that matters," he blurted. "You ought to know. An hour here, an eve there with a complete stranger never meant a thing to me—"

"Jon," she interjected, her heart softening even as it thrummed uncomfortably. "Listen. I... I can overlook what has come before me," she gathered her breath, "so long as none come after." She eyed him carefully, hoping he understood.

He came forward, taking her face between his hands. "There is no before or after. For me, there is only you."

Dainy remained still but for her lashes, which flickered shut as he leaned in and brought his irresistible lips to hers.

7

MONTIMOR

PIERMA HAD CERTAINLY CHANGED. MONTIMOR could hardly believe it was the same capitol he'd once known. The formerly bright and bustling streets were now filthy and dull, poverty littering every corner. Although, it wasn't much better back home in Ferro, either.

At the startling clopping of hooves, he glanced up to spy a mail rider approaching on an old gelding. The rider slowed before a crowd of peasants, brandishing a scroll aloft. "Betine Toustead?"

Montimor gave a start.

A curly-headed lad nodded to his fellows. "Oy, he means Bet." He looked up at the rider. "Try Capitol Square. She's always reading the bulletins there."

The rider turned his horse around, and Montimor hurried after him around the next block to the Square. His jaw nearly dropped to spot the bone-thin, black-clad woman perusing the postings at the wall.

"Comrade Toustead?"

Montimor noticed her violet hair looked stringier

than ever. "I am she," she confessed warily.

"A message for you."

"From whom?" Bewildered, Bet reached up and received the scroll.

"The postage is from Häffstrom. Good day." The rider steered his gelding back to the road.

Montimor watched as she tore through the wax seal and unfurled the scroll, lips pursed as she made out the runes. After a moment, she rolled it back into a cylinder and gazed into the street, a faraway look on her narrow face.

Montimor stepped out of the shadows. "Who do you know in Häffstrom, Bet?"

She startled. "Do I know you?"

"You mean, you do not recognize me?" He stroked his moustache.

Bet Toustead squinted at him, her features contorting in shock. "*You,*" she gasped. "But how—" She pressed a hand over her mouth. "Where the devil have you *been*?"

"It's a long story." Montimor frowned. "Where is she?"

Bet glanced down at the scroll in her hands. "Oh dear," she breathed, eyes wide.

8

KRAMERIK

THE S. S. *EVANGELA* CROSSED the sprightly waters of East Halvea the following week, the first quarter of their journey to Jophlin, Jano complete. It was a humid evening when Hans Kramerik spotted the pretty maiden standing alone at the stern, watching the dark waves disappearing behind them. She smiled politely as he approached, a simple white dress hugging her shapely figure and reflecting the lantern light.

"Do you fare well, Miss Macmillan?" Kramerik joined her at the rail. "Is your cabin comfortable?"

"All is well, Captain. I'm still amazed at how fast your freighter travels. I've never sailed on a col-fueled vessel before."

"And on what sorts of vessels have you sailed, my dear?"

She shrugged sheepishly. "Just an old fishing boat."

The captain surveyed her. "May I ask what brings you all the way to Asiotica?"

She hesitated, and Kramerik instantly regretted his

question. Of course, it was none of his business. "Oh, just some family affairs," she replied.

He nodded, glad she did not seem to take offense at his prying. "Well, at any rate, I'm delighted to have you aboard," he said softly.

But he was unsure whether she'd heard this last utterance, for she abruptly changed the topic. "The *Evangela*." She repeated the ship's name. "That is lovely. Did you come up with it?"

"Aye, she's named for my late wife."

Miss Macmillan frowned, plainly embarrassed by her gaffe.

"It's been a long time," Kramerik assured her, "and my grief is well behind me."

She did not speak again, and Kramerik rued her silence, until he raised a weathered palm to his brow, suddenly remembering. "But I've neglected to show you my maps! Would you like to come to my study and review them? I can show you our route, and the countries of the Great Continent—"

Her green eyes brightened and she nodded, proceeding behind him to his study. Upon the desk before her, the captain outspread his parchments, tracing their route and explaining the diverse nations of the Continent. All the while, she listened intently, poring over his scrolls and drilling him with clever questions. He admired her, wishing for the company of a damsel so curious and lively on his every voyage.

And yet, Kramerik reminded himself, he was no longer a young man anymore, despite how this girl had begun to make him feel. Surely, she'd only consider him in a fatherly way. For his features were aging, his beard graying, and his lifetime of sorrow and experience had likely surpassed her young reckoning. But could a man not hope?

Carefully, he set aside the map they'd been studying. "How old are you, Miss Macmillan, if you don't mind me asking?"

"I have seen eighteen springs," was her earnest reply.

"Ah." He heaved a wistful sigh, gazing through the glass-paned door. "My daughter would've been close to your age by now." He reached for the water pitcher and poured a glass. "Had she survived her birth, that is." He handed her the glass, and she took it, looking sympathetic.

"That's how I lost Evangela, my wife." Kramerik seldom spoke of these matters, but for some reason, he wished to share his heart that night. "She died in childbirth, as did the babe."

"I'm so sorry, Captain."

"Please, just Hans." He stepped closer as she sipped her drink. "*Eludaine,*" he intoned, the name having been absent from his tongue those many years.

She choked on her water, gripping her throat with a sputtering cough. Alarmed, Kramerik thumped her on the back until she nodded, eyes streaming. "Beg pardon?" she gasped.

"My daughter. Her name was Eludaine." Kramerik removed the glass from her hand. "I christened her after the little Duchess of Jordinia. Although, perhaps you're too young to remember the Ducelles?"

She cleared her throat, her cheeks pink.

"Brutal, what those Jordinian rebels did," he muttered, scratching his beard. "Executing a three-year-old child…"

She swallowed. "Well, Hans," she said his name rather uneasily, though Kramerik reveled in the sound, "it is getting rather late."

He helped her to her feet. "But of course. It's been a pleasure, dear." He took the liberty to pat her shoulder before opening the door. "Would you like me to escort you to your cabin?" he dared offer.

She blinked. "Oh, I'm sure I can make my own way."

Perhaps he'd been too forward, thought Kramerik, watching her depart his quarters under the evening sky. There was still a long journey ahead, however, and plenty of time to get to know each other. He'd simply have to overcome his doubts and seize what opportunities he could, hopefully earning more than just her friendship in turn.

The man gripped his desk, sighing. Then again, she'd only seen eighteen springs. Why, he'd lived her entire lifetime nearly thrice over! And yet, he couldn't help his blossoming affections for her. Perhaps, it was fate that had brought her to the café in Pikosta. It might've even been Evangela's spirit at work, wishing companionship for her former husband at last.

9

DAINY

HER CABIN DOOR WAS CURIOUSLY ajar and a lantern lit when she returned. Dainy smiled with surprise to greet Jon seated on her cot, toying with his belt as he awaited her. "To what do I owe this pleasure, Mr. Cosmith?" she asked fondly, lingering in the doorway.

His alluring grin weakened her knees. "Speaking of pleasure, Miss Macmillan," he purred, "why not step inside, and close that door behind you?"

She giggled. "Where's Mac?"

"The boy has been at the drink with the crew all evening." Jon smirked. "He'll remember nothing of tonight, I assure you."

Pulse pounding, Dainy closed the door as Jon held out his arms to her. With a tremor of anticipation, she stepped into his embrace, pressing her face into his sweet-smelling hair.

"Besides," he murmured, running his hands down the length of her back. "Did you not notice? We've sailed past East Halvea." He planted his mouth hungrily at her neck. "No longer must our dear brother speak for you."

Dainy watched as he dimmed the lantern and turned down the linens. He helped her out of her frock with ease, then unfastened his own clothing. With a deep moan, he lay her down, and shared love with her once again. Dainy closed her eyes, savoring his every exhalation, her heart fluttering with each tender brush of his lips across her body. The cot groaned beneath their weight, the sea around her disappeared; there was only him.

After, the man collapsed at her side, their bodies damp with perspiration. Dainy curled into his hold, resting her head upon his chest and inhaling with the soothing rhythm of his heartbeat. "Please do not leave before I rise this time," she requested quietly.

"Never again," he promised, nuzzling his bristling cheeks into her hair. The two were lulled by the gentle sway of the sea.

10

MACMILLAN

THE URGE TO VOMIT AWOKE Macmillan early. He glanced around to find himself lying sideways in his cot, but had no recollection of getting there. Groaning, he stood, then covered his mouth and raced to the nearest railing.

He was sick for several minutes, emptying his stomach into the sea below. Why had he indulged in so much drink the night before? He grabbed his throbbing head, pitying the hung-over sailors who had no choice but to return to their duties. Thank God he was only a passenger.

Footfalls issued from the captain's quarters. Macmillan looked up to see Hans Kramerik approaching, fully uniformed, his graying hair and beard neatly combed. He paused just outside of Dainy's door. Macmillan wiped his mouth and held up a weak hand in greeting.

"Good morrow," Kramerik greeted him, sounding somewhat nervous. "Has—has your sister arisen yet?"

Macmillan shrugged. "I've not seen her."

"I was... hoping she might join me for breakfast. Perhaps it would be more appropriate if you asked for me?"

Macmillan cocked an eyebrow. Had he heard the old man correctly, or was he still drunk? "Um. I'll ask." He gave Kramerik a strange look before stepping up to Dainy's door and giving it a light knock. There came no answer. "Er... sister? You awake?"

"M-Mac?" she stammered, her voice muffled. "I'm dressing!"

"Oh." He took an automatic step back. "Sorry. I only wished to pass along the captain's invitation—"

She didn't reply, instead giggling and uttering a shushing sound under her breath. Suspicious, Macmillan pressed his ear to the door. "Who are you talking to?"

"What? No one! Go away, Mac."

He didn't budge.

The door swung open at last, and Macmillan's blood curdled to see Cosmith strolling out, wearing a smug grin as he leisurely fastened the buttons of his blouse. Macmillan shook his head in wordless fury.

"We're not in Halvea anymore, brother," Cosmith murmured. "Cap'n," he saluted Kramerik casually, not bothering to buckle his belt as he strode away. Dainy emerged in his wake, slowly retying her sash about her waist with a flush at her cheeks. Gazing after Cosmith's departing figure, she sighed, her expression dreamlike.

Macmillan cleared his throat. "*Sister.* The captain wishes to invite you to breakfast."

"Forgive me." Kramerik turned away, though not before Macmillan saw the disappointment wrought upon his aging features. "I can see your sister is elsewise occupied." He was quick to depart them, fine leather shoes clapping against the shining planks.

Macmillan jerked his head toward the retreating captain. "What in hell was that about?" he murmured to Dainy. His half-sister only shrugged, looking equally confused.

The freighter gave an unpleasant lurch atop an animated wave, and Macmillan fought back another surge of nausea. Cupping a hand to his mouth, he crouched over to appease his roiling stomach.

Dainy smirked. "Have fun last night?"

"Apparently not as much as you and Cosmith."

She pursed her lips.

"I suppose it was my fault." Macmillan straightened. "I neglected my watch over you. I promise, it shall not happen again."

"Mac." Dainy rested her hands on her hips. "While I find it positively *adorable* that you seek to guard me, you need to *butt out.*"

"It is my responsibility to preserve your virtue!"

She groaned. "Jon will become my husband soon enough."

"Oh? Then where's your nuptial bracelet?" Macmillan pointed to her bare left wrist. "It appears he's not given you one."

"Not *yet.*" She clutched her wrist defensively, though Macmillan could detect just a trace of doubt in her voice.

"And why not?" he pressed. "I've given him enough gold."

"I do not presume to know," Dainy sniffed. "Perhaps he is formulating something. Jon always has a plan."

"Or, perhaps he has no need to propose," suggested Macmillan, cornering her at the rail, "since you already permit him free use of you as his little plaything."

"How dare you?" Her mouth fell ajar. "Jon loves me!"

"Jon needs to keep his hands off of you," warned Macmillan. But his sister only pushed past him, the hem of her cream-colored frock billowing behind her.

11

SELU

BOS AND SELU WERE BREAKING bread at dinner-time when there came a knock at the door. A woman stood on the threshold, clothing in rags, hair stringy, face gaunt as ever, but with bony arms outstretched.

Selu embraced her at once. "*Mother.* You received my letter! You made it to Solomyn!" She turned to her fiancé, beaming. "Bos, please meet my mother, Betine Toustead."

"'Tis an honor." Bos bowed his blond head. "Welcome to your new home." Selu noticed her mother take in a slight breath at his tremendous height. It was a common reaction. "We were just about to sup. Care to join us?"

Bet shook her head.

"Mother?" Selu furrowed her brow. "Is something wrong?"

Bet surveyed her, apologetic. She then gestured to the dirt drive, where Selu only just noticed a dusty wagon was parked. "I do not come alone," Bet whispered as a slender figure strode forth.

Selu stared as he emerged up the threshold, taking in the raven hair, the thick black moustache, the charcoal gleam of his eyes. She gripped the doorframe so as not to slump to her knees. But she was seeing a ghost, a dead man alive and walking. She had to be dreaming—it could not be…

He gazed her over. "Hello, Luna."

Selu shivered. Only one person had ever called her that. And that person had died of the gray fever, ten years ago. Or so, at least, she'd thought. "Monty?"

"It's been a long time." He nodded. "You've changed a bit."

"As have you," she replied unsteadily, her neck hot as she grew more painfully aware with each passing second that Bos stood beside her, his hand-carved nuptial bracelet hanging heavily at her wrist.

As though reading her thoughts, Monty craned his neck to look up at the giant. "Montimor Campagna," he introduced himself, holding out a stiff hand.

"Boslon Visigoth," he replied calmly. Selu looked away, her heart breaking. She couldn't bear to see Bos's expression, whatever it was.

Monty addressed her. "I had the fortune of intercepting your mother in Pierma, recently. And now, I've come to take you home with me. If you'll gather your things, we may leave as soon as you wish."

"Home?" Selu's stomach constricted. "To where?"

"To my estate in Ferro."

"Ferro?" she cried. "So that's where you've been?" Her lip trembled. "All this time, Monty, we thought you were dead! The infirmary told us the fever had claimed you! We observed your funeral, dressed in black… We *mourned* for you—"

"My identity was confused with that of another."

"Then why did you never return for me?" Selu demanded. "Know you not that I was destitute?"

"I tried to look for you," he attested. "You must understand, Luna, I was very ill for many moons. The fever had addled my brains. I knew neither that I'd been transferred to a sanatorium well north of Pierma, nor that my papers had been mistakenly swapped with those of another. When I came to, I knew not who or where I was." He frowned. "It took me over a year to recover my sensibilities. When I finally remembered you, I returned to Pierma at once. But you were nowhere to be found."

It had been a long time since Selu had last wept. Yet, that was all she could do now, as her world shredded around her. Of course, it was a miracle that Montimor Campagna, her husband, had survived the gray fever after all, and stood alive before her. But what of Bos, and the new life she was to begin with him?

"I am not permitted back in Jordinia," she declared. "I've been banished."

Her husband's dark brows came together. "What for?"

"It doesn't matter." She wiped her eyes. "The point is, I cannot return."

"Nor can you wed another man, when you are already my wife." Monty indicated Bos, who watched them silently, and Selu's heart tore.

"Daughter," urged Bet. "What is your crime? Montimor can have you pardoned. He practices law now, in Ferro Village—"

"No," growled Selu. "I do not wish to be pardoned, nor to return to that vile and corrupted land."

Her mother's eyes widened.

"Furthermore, I wish to have our espousal severed. You are not my husband, Monty. You're merely a stranger who abandoned me ten years ago." She went to reach for Bos's hand, but the giant gently pulled away.

She braved a look up at him, and saw that he kept his features impressively blank. "To sever a holy union is an unspeakable sin against the Eternal God," he said. "If Mr. Campagna is your lawful husband, then you belong with him."

As a girl in prison, Selu had once been whipped. But the lash had not struck her as severely as his words. Wounded beyond belief, she held her aching stomach, staring down at her feet.

"I should like to leave soon." Monty checked his pocket watch. "Tomorrow, if possible. I've much work to return to."

"Then return to it alone," snapped Selu. Her mother gave her a reprimanding look.

Monty frowned. "I understand you are distressed, wife," he said carefully. "And that is why I shall leave you tonight to reconvene with your mother and say your goodbyes to Mr. Visigoth. But please be prepared in the morning when I return to fetch you."

Shivering, Selu watched her husband turn back down the lawn. She remained silent as his horses and wagon disappeared around the dusty bend.

12

Bos

BOS KNEW LOSS. HE HAD witnessed his parents and kin die at the swords of the rebels when he was a boy, and had tended his dear Aunt Fjeldá when she perished in the fever epidemic. But this was something new entirely. Of course, it carried the same blunt devastation as death. And yet, at least in the face of mortality, Bos held faith that his loved ones awaited him in the Evermore, to be reunited someday.

In this case, however, he was never to see Seluna Campagna again. For he now knew that she did not belong to him, and never had. Nay, he'd been in love with another man's wife, all along. The revelation pierced him with unspeakable shame.

He didn't sleep that night, leaving Selu alone with her mother. Having no appetite for breakfast when the rooster crowed, he went about his morning tasks, losing himself in the methodical milking of the cow, even as Mr. Campagna's wagon rolled back up the dirt drive.

Bos was raking the lawn when he heard her footsteps. He did not turn.

"May we talk?"

At the sound of her voice, he fought the sudden, overpowering urge to weep. Eyes burning, he set down his rake, but did not face her. "There is nothing to talk about."

"Shall we not at least say goodbye?" Her voice quaked. "Please. It cannot end like this."

"What has never begun cannot end."

He winced as she sucked in a breath. "So you will simply pretend as if nothing ever happened?"

"You are a married woman. Our time together has been naught but a sin and a lie."

Selu stifled a sob, and Bos closed his eyes against the sound.

"You truly believe that? I didn't know you to be capable of such cruelty," she spat. "*Typical man.*"

He finally turned to her, chest heaving. "You think I do not suffer as well?"

"How do you suffer?" she demanded. "You dismiss me with little more feeling than a shopkeeper closing his store to customers! Please…" She held out her arms. "Can we not take a moment just to—?"

He stepped back. "No, Seluna. You must go now." He pointed to the wagon in the drive. "Return to Jordinia with your husband." His voice shook. "And may God bless you both, with children and prosperity…"

"*Hazja Lænde,*" cried Selu, flashing the underside of the nuptial bracelet still bound at her wrist. "*Eternal love.* Does that not mean anything to you?"

She was making this far more difficult than he could bear. Of course, it meant everything to him. Bos loved her, and always would. But all the love in the world would not make their union right. Detesting himself, he gathered the courage to lie to her. "Not any-more."

She looked stunned. Taking up his rake, he returned to work, lest he should have to see her cry again.

At last, she stormed away, though not before hurling something small at his back. He did not have to turn to know that the bracelet he'd carved for her lay in the dirt at his heels.

13

COSMITH

MACMILLAN WAS SOUR, THE SEA was rough, and the food was awful, but Jon Cosmith had seldom seen better days in his twenty-seven years. Sharing Eludaine Ducelle's cabin every night left him in awe of her ever increasing beauty, her lengthening raven hair and luminous spirit. She continued to delight him with each passing day until he was simply beside himself with longing for her by the evenings.

He lived for their shared nights, when she became his once more, and the two exchanged love late into the quietest hours of morning. Between the taste of her tender lips, of which he never seemed to tire, the lovely feel of her porcelain skin so smooth against his, and the gentle cadence of her sweet voice singing him to sleep each night, Cosmith was overcome with love.

Faint music from the sailors' strumming rode on the winds one such night, and the man lay awake holding Dainy in her cot, stroking her silky black hair as she slept. He was contemplating arousing her for another round of lovemaking when a knock issued at the door.

"Dainy?" It was Macmillan.

Cosmith rolled his eyes, retrieving his trousers. The girl stirred beside him, but he pressed a soothing hand on her brow, seeing her back to sleep before slipping through the door.

"Damn it, Cosmith," Macmillan exclaimed, plainly dismayed to see him emerging shirtless from his sister's room.

"*Shh.*" Cosmith fastened his belt. "Do not wake her. What do you want?"

Macmillan gasped as a wave disrupted his balance, the cloying odor of rum on his breath. "I told you to keep your hands off my sister," he growled.

Cosmith rubbed his brow, wondering at the hour.

"Where's her nuptial bracelet, anyway?" the young man demanded. "Or do you never intend to give her one?"

Cosmith frowned. Of course he intended to present a nuptial bracelet to Dainy. Only, he didn't wish to give her just any bracelet. Ever since he'd learned they'd be journeying to the Great Continent, he knew he'd find something special abroad for the girl. A one-of-a-kind bracelet for a one-of-a-kind duchess. He was simply waiting to reach Asiotica. And he was not about to let Macmillan spoil his surprise. "It is none of your business," he replied coolly.

"It is every bit of my business if you are merely keeping my sister as your mistress! Stringing her along, coaxing her to your bed, all under the pretense that you intend to wed her…"

Cosmith gaped at him. "Is that what you really think?"

Unexpectedly, the cabin door creaked open. Dainy

stepped out, garbed in a breathtaking nightshift of teal lace, her generous bust barely contained beneath its snug neckline. Cosmith eyed her, inwardly begging Macmillan to go away, wanting nothing more than to return the stunning maiden to her cot.

"Must you two always find something to bicker about?" she lamented. "You are brothers. Why can you not get along?" She continued to reprimand them, but her words were lost to Cosmith as he stared at her, pretending to nod in assent. He'd agree to anything, should it sooner bring him back into her bed...

A sudden, deafening crack rippled through the air. It ended in a loud explosion, whipping up a fierce wave beneath them. Macmillan startled. "What was that?"

Dainy leapt to Cosmith's side. "It sounded like the night when..." Her voice trailed off, but Cosmith knew what she'd been about to say. Indeed, the bang sounded eerily akin to when her foster uncle Pascale's boat had been detonated by dynami.

Macmillan looked to the sky. "Perhaps lightning?"

Cosmith shook his head as another crack shot through the air. This time, something landed near the freighter's lowest deck. It exploded with a *boom*, blasting off planks of wood. Dainy clutched him as the ship jolted. The crew's bellows rang over the night air as, through the parting fog, they spotted a strange vessel encroaching upon theirs.

"What's going on?" Dainy whispered, while Macmillan's face turned pallid.

"My dearest, I once told you I hoped to see you in my clothing again." Cosmith tried to grin sportively. "Now's the time. Quickly, love." He pushed open the cabin door, guiding her in by the small of her back.

"Don some garments from my trunk."

"M-men's garments?"

Cosmith nodded, dropping his voice. "And remember your key. Keep it hidden on your person at all times. *Do not*—I repeat, *do not*—let them have it."

Dainy stared. "Who?"

"You will not like my answer. Now hurry." He closed the door to give her privacy, and Macmillan immediately rounded on him. "Pirates," he snapped, before the young man could speak.

Macmillan's mouth moved soundlessly.

"And with a figure like Dainy's, there's no way in hell that curvy little thing's going to pass for a male. But we must at least try."

"*Pirates?*" Macmillan finally exclaimed. "Are you certain?"

"Looks like it. Why else would someone attack a lone freighter in the middle of the night?" Cosmith grimaced. "There are valuable textiles aboard this ship. And it appears we're about to be looted."

"What do we do?" Macmillan's hazel eyes were stricken.

"First and foremost, we protect Dainy. Disguise her, hide her…"

The cabin door opened again, and Dainy emerged sporting Cosmith's blouse, along with a pair of black trousers. Despite the surrounding chaos, as sailors stormed and shouted across the decks, Cosmith could not help but admire how darling she looked in his clothing. Not to mention, how enticingly feminine her shape still managed to appear.

His eyes lingered on the bulge of her chest beneath his blouse, and he heaved a small sigh. "Wear my vest over that, Dainy. And hide your hair beneath my hat."

"Why am I doing this?" she grumbled, although she knelt down and fished through his trunk for the vest in question.

"Because I'll not have you ravished."

"Ravished?" Her face blanched.

The three gave a start as the foreign ship nearly collided with their freighter, and another deafening blast of dynami sounded from the black waters below. All too soon, the shouting and boot steps above multiplied as the ship was invaded.

Cosmith took the Duchess into his arms. "*I love you*. Now hide." He indicated the space beneath her cot.

He shirted himself, then drew the new sword he'd purchased from the Omar Village smith before their journey. "In the meantime," he murmured, unable to suppress his grin, "I've been dying to use this."

14

KRAMERIK

CAPTAIN HANS KRAMERIK WATCHED IN horror as pirates invaded the *Evangela*. The tattered flag of the notorious *Inferno* rippled in the ocean winds, steadfast through the blasts of dynami that threatened to detonate his young steamship. All too soon, a rough crew of hooligans trampled his polished decks, slashing the sailors and pilfering his precious cargo.

"Please," Kramerik besought them. "You can seize my goods, but do not harm my ship. Cease fire, I beg you."

They only laughed, jeering faces and crooked teeth glinting under the moon's light as they carried his inventory up the ramps. "Is this sod even valuable?" A baldheaded fellow fingered an open crate of muslin. "Looks like a bunch of old rags to me."

"Haul it all," rasped the first mate. "And don't ask no questions."

Kramerik pressed his face into his hands, fearing for his life as his crew valiantly battled their attackers.

"Evening, Cap'n," greeted the *Inferno's* first mate

mockingly, raising a sword to Kramerik's chin. A second sword was instantly pointed at the mate's neck, and Kramerik nearly groaned to see who wielded it.

"Leave my captain alone," growled the arrogant Jonwal Cosmith.

Kramerik was irked. Since that disappointing morning, when he'd witnessed Cosmith emerging from Miss Macmillan's cabin, his tolerance for the man—for both of them, really—had vanished. Kramerik hadn't known the two were a pair. The girl wore no bracelet, after all. She was clearly not the virtuous young maid he'd taken her for.

"I can defend myself," Kramerik snapped. He had his crew; he didn't need the help of some rakish playboy, nor did he wish to give the self-satisfied wretch anything more to gloat about.

"Tell your man to lower his sword," spat the mate, directing his blade at Kramerik's throat, "*or else.*"

"You heard him," muttered Kramerik.

Cosmith lowered his weapon, though he continued to watch them warily. Kramerik wished he'd go away.

"We've heard your request, Captain," the mate leered, breath reeking of stale rum. "If we spare your pretty little ship, what'll you give us in turn?"

Kramerik paused, surprised. Why, though his cargo was already lost, he still had a chance to salvage his ship? He needed only offer something enticing to these rough men... But what?

Not *what*, he realized, but *whom.*

He chewed his bottom lip. Perhaps it was rather malevolent. But Hans Kramerik had endured enough loss in his life. Was it not high time that someone else pay for his misfortunes, for others to suffer instead of him?

"A pretty little ship," he replied carefully, "in exchange for a pretty little girl."

The pirate cocked his head, and Kramerik reveled in the way Cosmith's brow furrowed. "There is a young woman aboard," the captain revealed, "who has no qualms with bedding *coarse men*. I'm sure your crew is in need of a comfort girl, no?"

"Bastard," snarled Cosmith, lunging at the pair of them, but the first mate artfully deflected him.

"And where is this lass?" the mate asked, keeping Cosmith at bay with his blade.

"Her room is the first door to the right on the cabin deck." Kramerik grinned as he met Cosmith's panic-wrought eyes. "Right, son?"

15

MACMILLAN

"*CAPTAIN!*" MACMILLAN PUSHED HIS WAY through the mob as sailors all around him dropped under the pirates' blades. The ship had been plundered, another deck blasted, and by the tilting stern, Macmillan felt fairly sure there was a significant leak somewhere. The *Evangela* was going down, and those remaining needed to abandon ship.

"Captain Kramerik," he bellowed again, when a thunderous roar snapped across the wind.

"Hans Kramerik is dead! I am your captain now."

Macmillan felt as though his eyes would spring from his skull. Kramerik was dead?

"Listen up, you lot of writhing vermin," hollered the captain of the *Inferno*, red hair flailing in the wind. A hush washed over the deck as the eyes of every seaman fell upon him, brawls paused and weapons lowered. "We got what we came for. Now get your arses back on deck. Move!"

Macmillan stared at the enormous red-haired man, unsettled to discover that something looked rather familiar about him. He was quite sure he'd never seen this pirate—or any pirate, for that matter—before. But did the captain not resemble someone whom Macmillan had perhaps recently met?

The crew did not hesitate. They hurried up the rigging, hustling back onto their ship. His stomach lurching, Macmillan saw that Hans Kramerik indeed lay as a corpse, his blazer blood-soaked, moonlight reflecting off of his shiny boots.

Fretful, Macmillan glanced about for his siblings. He'd not seen them in some time. "Jon?" he called into the dark sky. "Dainy?"

"Mac," came a deep hiss behind him. A strong grip pulled his arm. "They took her!"

"They *what*?"

Cosmith hurled himself over the gangway and onto the knotted rope to board the *Inferno*. "Come on!" he shouted, impatient.

Macmillan pulled himself up the rigging. Breathless, the pair threw themselves onto the *Inferno's* withered, moldy deck. Their worst fears were confirmed the moment they spotted the unmistakable silhouette of the Duchess, still wearing Cosmith's hat and clothing, tied captive at the bow. There she stood under the watch of two heavily tattooed black men.

Macmillan turned to his brother imploringly. "How did this happen?"

He'd never seen Cosmith look so agitated. "Kramerik sold us out," he spat, dodging out of the way as more men boarded behind them. "And for naught. They killed him and wrecked his ship anyway. The least he deserved, if you ask me."

"Well, what in hell now?" cried Macmillan, not

bothering to hide the note of hysteria in his voice.

"I am thinking," said Cosmith, his eyes betraying his terror.

The ragged voice of the *Inferno's* captain made them jump. "All aboard?" Without awaiting a response, he tossed a flaming bundle of dynami onto the *Evangela's* deck as it drifted apart from theirs, despite Kramerik's remaining crew. "Enjoy the fireworks, you damned lowlifes."

His men cheered as the whirs and squeals of impending dynami rang through the air, erupting with an ear-piercing crack. Macmillan and Cosmith ducked as they ran, covering their ears while the *Evangela* blasted into a barge of flames atop the dark waters.

At last, they neared Dainy's bound figure. Cosmith's hat was enormous on her, drooping down over her eyes and concealing her face in moonlit shadow. But her short legs trembled visibly beneath his overlong trousers.

"And where is my comfort girl?" came the captain's grating voice, followed by a husky sigh that made Macmillan's skin crawl. The man pushed past them, heavy boots plodding across the ancient deck. His crew followed eagerly, Macmillan and Cosmith hiding among them in plain sight. Macmillan could feel his brother tensing beside him, his jaw settling into a furious clench.

The captain stopped just before her, a taunting smile at his unshaven lips. "Who've we here, now?" He tipped up the brim of her hat, revealing fearful green eyes. He was reaching out to stroke her chin when Cosmith jerked forward.

"I would not touch her, if I were you."

All eyes turned to him. Instantly, a group made to seize his sword and bind his hands. But the captain waved them down. He appraised Cosmith, a ginger eyebrow raised. "And you are?"

"I am of no consequence." Cosmith swallowed. "It is *she* who is of great significance."

Macmillan gaped at his brother. Was he out of his mind? These were the last people to be trusted with Dainy's identity as the Duchess of Jordinia!

The captain smirked. "Go on."

The *Evangela's* flames cast shadows across Cosmith's face. "Never mind," he uttered abruptly. "I have already said too much. If I tell you more," he shot a dark look in Dainy's direction and shuddered, dropping his voice to a carrying whisper, "*she may kill us all.*"

A hush fell over the crowd.

The captain, however, merely grinned. "Well, now you've aroused my curiosity." He traced a long-nailed finger down the length of Dainy's cheek.

"I said don't touch her," Cosmith barked.

Dainy's breaths were quickening; Macmillan could see her chest swelling and falling as her eyes darted fearfully between them.

"For your own safety," Cosmith added, his voice level again. "For this woman is a very dangerous creature, indeed."

Macmillan cocked an eyebrow.

"Dangerous?" repeated the captain dubiously. He laughed, a gravelly, gurgling sound.

Cosmith nodded. "Oh, yes. She is a powerful Heppestonian priestess. Cross her in the slightest, and she will set a binding curse upon you and all your descendants." He looked away. "But now I have said too much."

"Heppestonian, you say?" The first mate snorted. "Ain't no way. Her skin's pale as sheep's wool." The others hemmed in agreement, and the captain's eyes glinted.

Cosmith emitted an exasperated sound, as if the explanation was so obvious. "But of course, can you curs not see it? She cast a spell to turn her skin white." He lowered his voice. "But I've seen her in true form. The woman is ancient, and black as the night."

"If you're trying to make fools of us, boy…"

Cosmith held up his empty hands. "I tell the truth," he contended. "You could ask her yourself," he shrugged, "except she doesn't speak a lick of Halvean."

On cue, Dainy issued a strange grunt, followed by a succession of unintelligible yet musical syllables. The black men guarding her jumped. "Captain," one exclaimed in his deep, accented voice. "Indeed, she speaks Heppestonian!"

The other babbled something at her, the whites of his eyes wide, and Dainy nodded with a coy smirk. "*Hu tu ama,*" she proclaimed impeccably, "*ama ta Beili Dunada.*"

Her captors' mouths fell ajar.

Macmillan was astounded. Why, he'd never known that Dainy spoke Heppestonian! And judging by the look of surprise on Cosmith's features—though the man was quick to smooth it—he clearly hadn't, either.

"What did she say?" demanded the captain.

"She says she's the Witch of the Beili Dunes," the black men whispered.

"*Hu a tu alta,*" Dainy hissed, and her captors

backed away.

The first mate looked disconcerted. "What does she say now?"

"She wishes to be left alone."

"*Mahs!*" screeched Dainy, stamping her foot. The crew jumped.

Cosmith folded his arms, sighing. "Now you've done it," he scolded them, clicking his tongue. "You have angered her."

"*Now,*" translated the Heppestonians. "She wishes to be left alone now."

The captain's grin widened. "Or else what?"

Dainy began to chant rhythmically, her voice rising ever louder with each utterance, just as a low mumble of thunder sounded in the distance. The Heppestonians covered their ears, retreating across the deck. "She curses us!"

"She speaks to the gods!"

Macmillan was nothing short of impressed.

The first mate finally relented. "Captain Mac-Neale," he said, and both Macmillan and Cosmith turned at the name. "I think we ought to leave her be, for the moment."

"MacNeale?" Macmillan blurted, before he could stop himself. Heads swiveled in his direction and Cosmith glared at him, but his curiosity couldn't be helped. "Are you any relation to Ezra MacNeale?" He recalled the redheaded man with whom they'd first begun Hessian Gatspierre's quest. "Of the Bainherd Plains?"

The deck fell silent as the captain stared at him, the only sound the pounding of Macmillan's own blood in his ears.

"Enough of this blasted sideshow," the captain hollered. "Back to work, all of you!" He clapped his hands together, and his crew scuttled off to their various corners like scurrying spiders. "Except you two," he added unpleasantly, pointing between Cosmith and Macmillan.

Cosmith shook his head. "I swear to God, Mac…"

Once the others had gone, the captain dropped his voice. "All right, just who in hell are you two? And what do you know of Ezra?" His amber eyes shot between them.

Macmillan quickly fabricated a name. "I am Eli Walker. And this is my brother, Bill."

Cosmith swallowed.

"Julién MacNeale," grunted the captain, shaking their hands gruffly. His fingers were grimy, his nails brown.

"Ezra MacNeale was…a friend of ours," said Macmillan.

MacNeale cocked an orange eyebrow. "Was?"

"*Is*," corrected Cosmith, glancing at Macmillan significantly. "He is our friend."

Macmillan watched his half-brother. They both knew Ezra MacNeale was dead. Along with the other contenders, he'd burned to death in the forest fire set by the Jordinian assassin, Tolohov Quixheto. What did Cosmith possibly think they had to gain by pretending he was alive?

But the captain's eyes beheld a faraway look. "I hail from the Bainherd Plains," he confided quietly. "And Ezra is the name of my son, whom I've not seen since…" He held his hand to just above his knee.

Cosmith swallowed again.

"He's a man grown now, yes?" MacNeale looked hopeful. "Pray tell, what's he like?"

Macmillan's stomach sank. If the captain were ever to discover that his son was dead, he'd surely kill them for their deception.

"Ezra is an upright man," replied Cosmith. "Decent, honorable." A diplomatic description, Macmillan thought, given that the man in question once had Cosmith captured and nearly killed for stealing.

"Nothing like his dear old Pa, I see," mumbled the captain.

"In fact, he risked his life to protect this very priestess." Macmillan's mind raced as he pointed to Dainy. "Because of her fearsome prowess in sorcery, many in West Halvea wish her dead."

"Thus is why we began a mission with your son," supplied Cosmith, "to deliver this woman to safety on the Great Continent."

"A mission?" whispered MacNeale, fascinated. "With my son?"

Macmillan nodded encouragingly. "Ezra helped to bring her thus far, at great risk to himself. If we don't bring her to the Continent, then all our work will have been in vain."

Cosmith draped an arm over his brow. "Oh, and how disappointed Ezra shall be if we fail him now, Eli."

MacNeale inhaled, folding beefy arms as he looked out to the black sky. The *Evangela* burned serenely behind them like a fallen star. "I abandoned my wife and child long ago," he confessed, the steamship's glowing flames reflecting in his amber pupils. "I take no pride in that, Mr. and Mr. Walker." He sighed. "But perhaps, if I can do one thing… for my only son…"

He gazed up at the stars, though the constellations blurred in the smoky air. "We're not far from Jophlin, the coast of Jano. You understand I cannot dock the *Inferno*; my crew and I are wanted men. However, I can lower a boat once land is in sight, and your priestess can sail to shore." His eyes brightened. "And then, I shall turn this ship around and return to West Halvea, where you boys can bring my son to me."

"B-but," stammered Macmillan, "we intend to accompany the priestess—"

"One of my crew can go with her." The captain waved a dismissive hand.

Macmillan wished to protest, but Cosmith looked down. "Very well, Captain."

Dainy issued a soft whimper, and mumbled something in Heppestonian. Cosmith did not raise his eyes, continuing to speak to the planks. "In the meantime, the priestess respectfully requests she be unbound, and shown to a place where she may safely rest, accompanied by us, her trusty escorts."

"Anything for Ezra's friends." Captain MacNeale drew his sword and cut her bindings. Dainy bowed her head in a dignified manner, sauntering back to her companions.

"*Heron, Scar, Sickle!*" MacNeale stomped down the deck, and three of his crewmen turned. "You're bunking with Jobe and Malone." He indicated Macmillan, Cosmith and Dainy. "Misters Walker and the priestess are to have their own quarters until further notice."

MacNeale swatted Macmillan on the back with a heart-stopping smack. "Get some rest, lady and gentlemen," he entreated them, pointing down to the cabin deck.

16

DAINY

THE MOMENT MAC CLOSED THE door, Jon leapt onto Dainy, eyes ablaze with admiration. "My darling, you were *incredible*." He lifted his hat from her head and flung it aside, proceeding to drench her face with kisses. "I'd no idea you spoke Heppestonian!"

Dainy's pulse raced as she held him, overwhelmed by the safe comfort of his arms after the terror of the last few hours.

"Nor had I." Mac sounded equally impressed. "You put on quite a show back there."

"Do you still have your key?" asked Jon, apprehensive.

Dainy reached into her brassiere and extracted the silver triangle. Both men sighed with relief as she swiftly concealed it again. "Although," she indicated her clothing, "it's too bad my masculine disguise did not work."

"Oh, but it did," insisted Jon. "Trust me, my sweet, if you'd have been wearing that lace nightdress of yours, priestess or not, those disgusting men would have certainly tried to—"

"The point is, you're safe," interrupted Mac, giving his brother an uncomfortable glance.

"For now." Dainy frowned. "But how are we to escape this ship together? I can't be dropped on a rowboat with some degenerate pirate while the two of you sail back to West Halvea!"

"We'll figure something out. In the meantime, I want to hear more Heppestonian." Jon squeezed her playfully. "How do you say 'Jon Cosmith is the cleverest, handsomest, most virile man on the Continental Sea'?"

Mac rolled his eyes, and Dainy smirked. "Sorry, Mr. Cosmith," she cooed. "But that statement would be a lie."

Jon watched her, umber hair falling over his eyes. Dainy brushed it aside. "You are the cleverest, handsomest, most virile man in all the *world*," she corrected him, leaning in to trail her mouth across his.

"Oy," snapped Mac. "I am sharing this cabin too, remember."

"A fate I'd sooner forget," bemoaned Jon.

Dainy concealed her grin. "It's late. Truly, we should rest."

Not bothering to remove his boots, Mac collapsed into one of the hammocks. Some foul pirate had previously slept in it, but the young man did not seem to mind. "Cosmith!" he barked, however, as Jon sidled into Dainy's hammock with her.

"What?" The man nestled up to her, and Dainy felt as though her body would melt against his touch. "*Relax*, Macmillan. D'you think Dainy and I want to be intimate with your ugly face looking on?" He closed his eyes. "Besides." He yawned. "It is damn near impossible to make love in a hammock."

Dainy froze.

Mac snorted. "And you know this from personal experience, I imagine."

Dainy closed her eyes against a current of jealousy, straining to keep her irritation at bay. "Stop, both of you," she commanded, before Jon could issue his retort.

Mac snuffed out the lantern. The tiny cabin now submerged in total darkness, Dainy heard only the men's tired breathing as she rested her cheek upon Jon's taut chest, decidedly clinging to him all the more. "I love you, Jon Cosmith," she whispered through the blackness, entwining her trousered legs with his. "Exactly as you are."

The man relaxed beneath her, his tense arms softening as they held her. Silently, he raised her fingertips to his lips and, one by one, granted a kiss to each, his mouth warm and inviting against her flesh.

Quite abruptly, his grip loosened and he issued a slight snore, exhaustion having overcome him at last.

17

BOS

BOS COULDN'T STAY IN THE farmhouse after she left. Seluna Campagna constantly rounded every corner in his periphery, stalking every doorway, her silken voice and the scent of her sun-kissed skin haunting the lonely halls.

After securing his livestock to the care of a neighbor, Bos departed the town of Solomyn. He'd known all along what he was supposed to do, since the afternoon he'd left his friends in Omar Village. He wasn't sure how far they were, or whether they'd yet made it to Asiotica. But he intended to find them.

For his loyalty, he now knew, should never have strayed unto Selu, but should have remained solely with the Emperor's daughter. With conviction, the giant took up the main road with all the speed that his long legs could carry him. Eludaine Ducelle's image was emblazoned onto his mind's eye. How could he have ever permitted anything to deter him from serving her as his prime priority?

He paid a wagoner to carry him to the sleepy coast

of Charr, Häffstrom. From there, he made his way to the docks, inquiring about work aboard a vessel to the Great Continent. "We can take you to the Continent, for sure," offered a cheery sailor. "But our destination is of little importance; rather, what we hope to accomplish at sea."

Bos raised an eyebrow. "Which is?"

"Jail those bloodsucking thieves," growled a dark mate.

"We are bounty hunters, sir," supplied a boy.

"Pirate catchers," clarified the first sailor. "And you would make a fearsome addition to our ranks." He indicated Bos's size. "What say you? Join our crew, help us round up some buccaneers, and we'll drop you off at the Continent, free of charge."

Bos looked around at them. It was an unusual offer, but there seemed no other passage to the Continent at port. As well, he'd not have to pay any fare. "Aye." He finally shook the sailor's hand. "Bos Visigoth."

"Erig Tessler. Welcome aboard."

WEEKS HAD PASSED SINCE THAT morning, each day proving less eventful than the last. There were simply no pirates to be found on the endless sea, and Bos was growing impatient. Could they not simply admit the futility of their hunt, sail him to the nearest port and be done with it? At this rate, they'd be searching for years before they came across any pirates, let alone captured one. Bos lamented his decision to accompany them. Why hadn't he simply awaited a vessel heading straight for land?

He was sorting through a net of fresh catch when a breeze pulsed at his neck. He glanced up at the sky. All appeared clear, except for a few murky clouds beyond the horizon. A distant grumble of thunder reverberated over the lapping waves, and Bos turned to the boy beside him. "Did Tessler say a storm was coming?"

The youth looked up, alarmed. "Storm?"

Bos sighed, steadying his massive boots on deck as a choppy wave lashed beneath the boat, and another groan of thunder rolled ominously behind the sun.

18

COSMITH

"DROP THE ANCHOR, GOLBAIN! WE are not sailing through this beast!" The breeze howled as Captain MacNeale stormed across deck.

"Yer sure, Captain?"

"*Are you questioning me?*"

Cosmith hurried back into the cabin, only to find Dainy seated in a hammock, her feet brushing the floor as she swung with the rollicking ship. She glanced up as he slammed the door, her face even. "Why, Jon," she greeted pleasantly, "you look so frightened."

Cosmith grimaced. "And you do not."

"Sea storms don't scare me. I've dealt with them my whole life."

"Yes, but surely never in the middle of the ocean?"

"The eye of the storm is the safest place to be," she recited, swinging her legs in opposite directions. "I rather like wearing your trousers, by the way," she added, off-subject. "They're quite freeing. I feel I can do anything I want in them."

Cosmith grinned, momentarily forgetting his anxiety as he watched her rise and perform a little jig on the cabin floor, even as the ship lurched beneath them. "That's right, Dainy," he purred. "You can do anything you want in my trousers."

She threw back her head and laughed. Cosmith loved that about her. Not only was her laughter beautiful, but plentiful. How had he ever obtained such a woman?

"Jon Cosmith, I ought to smack you," she declared. "Although I suppose I walked right into that one."

"Mmm." He smiled, cornering her at the wall as he pressed his weight against her. "And what if I walk right into you?" He enveloped her curvy shape in his arms, lowering his lips to hers, just as a knock issued at the door.

The man stepped back, and Dainy grabbed his hat from his head and plunked it atop her own. The brim slid down over her eyes, concealing her blushing cheeks beneath its shadow. A wise move, thought Cosmith, as the door pushed open and rain splayed inside.

"Erm, Bill?" It was Macmillan, looking like a wet cat with his hair drenched flat against his scalp. He blinked rainwater from his lashes. "The crew wishes to speak with *the priestess*."

Cosmith's chest tightened. "Whatever for, dear Eli?"

Macmillan beckoned them, desperate. "Just come," he mouthed.

Cosmith took Dainy's hand. "Ready to playact again, darling?" he whispered. "You need only continue exactly as you've been doing, and you'll be golden."

She gave a single nod of her chin. Nervous, the men followed her out to the lashing storm, where all hands were on deck.

"Mr. and Mr. Walker." The baldheaded fellow, Sickle, addressed them, keeping a safe distance from Dainy. "We wondered if the priestess was conjuring this storm."

"I know not," replied Cosmith carefully. On the one hand, to declare Dainy responsible would further convince these superstitious men of her powers, ensuring she continue to be left alone. Yet, on the other, if they believed her to be stirring trouble, they might wish to be rid of her, even throw her overboard. The thought made Cosmith ill.

"May we ask her?" inquired the Heppestonians.

Cosmith forced a grin. "Be my guests," he assented, inwardly praying that Dainy would formulate the right response.

He watched as she conversed with them, and their expressions grew oddly sympathetic. At last, one relayed: "She says the storm is not her fault, but caused by a local sea spirit, with whom she's unfamiliar. She will do everything in her power to try and stop it."

Brilliant girl, Cosmith praised her silently.

Dainy began to sing in Heppestonian, and the men were startled by her high, clear voice. A mountainous bolt of lightning suddenly struck the sea beside them, leaving behind a strange singeing odor.

"Her song is angering the sea god," someone cried.

"Nonsense, you idiot! She's enlisting the help of the sky gods."

Cosmith stared at Dainy as the storm around them began to rage.

19

BOS

THE TEMPEST WAS FEARSOME, BUT Tessler insisted on sailing through, much to his crew's dismay. By evening, however, this decision proved to be genius, for behold, anchored in their midst was an ancient ship rocking in the salty mist, withered flags billowing in the mighty wind.

"The *Inferno*," breathed Tessler, eyes nearly welling as he ordered his crew to speed closer. "There's a gold reward on the head of its captain, Julién Mac-Neale!"

Curious, Bos eyed the vessel, feeling a sense of mounting excitement. "A pirate ship, eh?"

"Full speed ahead!" Tessler shouted his orders, gaining on the anchored vessel until they were merely a stone's throw away in the lashing waves. "Right, blast them so they stand no chance of sailing off! Aim for the hold, boys," he roared over the rain-smeared sky.

Before Bos knew it, his companions were chucking flaming bundles of dynami into the water. He ducked as an explosive roar shattered the waves' surface, and jagged scraps of wood rained on deck.

All too soon, the two ships merged, rigging was tossed between decks, and Tessler's crew stormed the *Inferno*, the crashing and ringing of swordplay accompanying the rush of the wind and waves. Bos peered out to the other deck, trying to concentrate over the men's incessant bellowing. He'd never done anything like this before, and had pondered no strategy. He'd not actually expected to intercept a real pirate ship, after all.

Through the jostling sea of heads below, Bos thought he spotted something familiar—Jon Cosmith's hat, to be exact. But the figure wearing it was shorter than Cosmith, and neither did it possess the man's robust shape. In fact, Bos realized, watching more closely, the figure did not appear to possess much of a man's shape at all.

His heartbeat quickened. He was imagining things. The Duchess of Jordinia had simply been on his mind of late, was all. She seemed to be everywhere he'd looked the past several weeks, so overtaken by regret was he to have abandoned her for Selu, in more ways than one.

Another explosion rattled the hull, and the *Inferno* tilted sideways. The cowman's hat was knocked clean from its wearer's head, revealing a crown of jaw-length raven hair. Two familiar figures instantly flanked her sides, and Bos took in a breath. There was no way. It couldn't be…

The girl turned, and Bos saw a fair face mirroring his panic, her eyes strikingly green even from the distance. "Eludaine," he gasped. He cupped his hands over his mouth. "Tessler's men, cease fire!"

But it was too late. Another blast of dynami rocked the *Inferno*'s centermost deck, and the girl was knocked from her feet.

20

DAINY

THE SPACES BEHIND HER EYES ached. That was all she knew. Dainy thought she recognized the voices around her, the sound of rain pelting down outside. They were still in the Knights' Forest, weren't they? In the hollow that Mac had found, the fire crackling at its mouth, and Jon's laughing smile, teasing her…

"…has been through enough already," someone was saying, sounding cross. She recognized that deep voice, although she couldn't for the life of her recall to whom it belonged. "How could you fools have endangered her?"

"We've explained a *hundred* times," came her brother's exasperated sigh.

"Keep your voices down," someone else whispered, cupping her crown protectively. Something about that warm, calloused hand made her shiver. "She needs her rest, for God's sake."

"Too late," said Mac, as Dainy's eyes flickered open.

The first thing she realized was that she wasn't

lying in a forest cave, but in what appeared to be yet another ship's cabin. She then noticed she was wrapped in a pile of blankets on the floor, while three figures hovered anxiously above her. She blinked her eyes into focus, taking in the worried faces of Jon, Mac and—

"*Bos?*" Was she still dreaming? She tried to sit up, but his enormous hand halted her.

"Eludaine." He smiled, scooping her into an unexpected embrace. Dainy was entirely submerged within his massive arms until he released her and settled back on his knees, blue eyes gazing at her in a startlingly tender way.

"Wh-what are you doing here?" she stammered, surprised to hear her words coming out so thick and slow-sounding. "Where's…?" She knew someone else belonged with Bos, but couldn't gather the person's name, let alone the person.

"Lie back." Bos patted her blankets with a gargantuan hand. She obliged, and Jon smoothed back her hair dotingly. She noticed Bos's eyes dimming slightly at the gesture.

"You all right, Dainy-girl?" asked Mac, repeating the name he'd heard her Aunt Paxi use back in Beili— was it only a few moons ago? It felt like years now. The memory made Dainy sad. "Can we get you anything?"

"Water," she croaked. Jon handed her a skin. Thirstily, she drank, noticing a taste of blood in her mouth. "What happened?" she finally asked, propping up on her elbows.

Mac frowned. "When the dynami struck, you fell."

"What about the pirates?" She glanced up at the wooden ceiling. This sturdy, polished ship certainly didn't look like the *Inferno*.

"Most are dead," said Bos in his deep timbre. "The survivors have been captured. MacNeale is imprisoned below decks."

Dainy shuddered at the thought of the fearsome captain. "And whose ship is this?"

"The bounty hunters'," grunted Bos. "These men catch pirates, then turn them over to the authorities for a reward."

He proceeded to explain how he'd met Erig Tessler on the coast of Häffstrom. But something nagged at Dainy as all three men began the blow-by-blow account of their battle with the pirates, complete with who struck whom, who was killed and who was seized, and how many sticks of dynami finally took down the notorious enemy ship. The whole ordeal sounded rather dreadful, and she was glad to have missed it. But still, there was that ineffable something…

Dainy shot upright in her blankets. "Where's Selu?" She peered around the room, as though expecting to spot the woman's lithe figure curled up catlike in the corner at any moment.

Mac looked at his hands.

"Er…" Jon cast Bos an awkward glance. "Selu and Bos are no longer together, Dainy."

Her face contorted. "Why?"

"Her husband lives," shrugged Bos, his voice empty. "She has returned to Jordinia with him."

Dainy could hardly register his words. "I thought her husband died of the gray fever."

Jon shook his head, and Dainy felt heartsick. Selu's husband was alive, and the woman was now in Jordinia, from where Dainy and the others were banished? Would they ever see her again? And poor, dear Bos!

"Bos," Dainy whispered. "I'm so—"

"What's done is done." Bos looked away. "There is no more need to speak of it."

An uneasy silence befell them, and Dainy could scarcely contain her sadness. "I'll never see her again."

"You will someday," Jon patted her knee, "when we recapture Jordinia."

Dainy massaged her sore eye sockets. His words were too much for her at the moment, the idea still sounding as foreign and far-fetched as when her friends had first mentioned it.

"Anyway, Tessler is sailing us to Jano," Bos informed her. "We're only a few days away. There they shall claim their reward for MacNeale, and we may continue our journey."

Dainy quivered. "I can't believe that captain still sails with us. Even if he is locked up."

"And he'll be in for a sorry surprise," muttered Mac, "should he ever find out his son is dead." He scowled at Jon.

"If he knew Ezra had died, he would've had no reason to help us," Jon retorted. "He'd have slashed our throats without a second thought, and taken *her*," he indicated Dainy, "by force."

Dainy closed her eyes to their bickering, leaning back in her blankets.

"Oy." Mac lowered his voice. "It's almost dawn. We should try to get some rest."

Groggy, Dainy watched as the men removed their boots. Bos settled into a hammock, the rope bowing down and touching the floor beneath his heft, while Mac climbed into his own. "I'm sorry you're on the floor, Dainy," Mac added. "But when we first lay you down in a hammock, all the swinging made you—"

Jon waved him down. "Don't embarrass her."

Dainy could already feel the heat rising to her neck. "What?" she demanded.

Mac shrugged. "You were just a little sick, is all."

That was when Dainy noticed Jon wore only his trousers and blouse, his vest wrinkled up and wet-looking in the corner. Her cheeks burned furiously. "I retched on you?"

Jon grinned. "No worries."

Mortified, she pulled the blankets over her face. The man knelt down beside her, prodding her over the covers. "Why are you hiding?"

"Because you must think me foul."

The others laughed. "Everyone vomits, Dainy," her brother informed her.

"And it would take a lot more than that to deter me from you," smiled Jon, sliding under the blankets beside her.

"What are you doing, Cosmith?" asked Bos strangely.

Dainy poked her head out from beneath the covers, while Jon rolled his eyes at the giant. "I cannot sleep without Jon," she professed.

Bos turned to her brother in disbelief. "Macmillan, you are permitting this?"

"*You* try separating them, then." Mac huffed. "It's like trying to keep a fly from the marmalade. I give up."

21

Bos

NOTHING COULD HAVE PREPARED THEM for Jophlin, Jano. Strange crane-like birds the size of dogs, as plentiful as the olive-skinned people, crowded the streets. But even greater than the crowds, the birds and the heat was the noise. Though it wasn't only the groaning of old ships in the harbor, or the abundance of squawking fowl, or heavy wagon wheels rolling down stony streets. Nay, it issued mostly from the Janoans themselves. They were a rather excitable people, voices constantly raised and all of their interactions shouted, not spoken.

"We've only one problem." Macmillan pressed his way between Eludaine and Cosmith. "Our gold went down with the *Evangela*. How are we to pay for food, travel, lodging?"

"I've some coin left," offered Bos, making to hand over his purse. But Cosmith shot him one of his self-satisfied grins, waving the money away.

"You didn't think I'd let us go hungry, did you?" The man smirked, keeping up his brisk pace down the congested street.

"Meaning?" prompted Macmillan.

Cosmith only chuckled patronizingly. Bos felt a sudden surge of indignation as the scoundrel casually brushed his palm against the Duchess's backside before bringing it up to his vest and flashing a velvet pouch at them.

"What's that?" Eludaine looked curious.

"Blue silver," Cosmith murmured.

The others issued noises of disbelief, and Bos's eyes narrowed.

"Not possible," Macmillan decided, and Cosmith laughed blithely. "You do not have an entire pouch of blue silver in your vest, Cosmith."

"I didn't even know that stuff was real," admitted Eludaine.

"It is the rarest metal on the globe, dear girl," boasted Cosmith. "And the most valuable."

"Then how did you come by it?" Bos eyed him with mistrust.

"Nicked it from the pirates." Cosmith shrugged, as though this were an everyday occurrence.

"You stole it?" The Duchess halted, her tone crisp with dismay.

"Come now, love." He grinned wickedly. "Is stealing from pirates really stealing?"

"No." Bos glowered at him. "It is worse."

Eludaine folded her arms, a frown painted upon her delicate features, and Bos was startled by how distinctly regal she looked. What on earth she doing with a man like Cosmith?

"Oh, come *on*," insisted the thief buoyantly. "It would've sunk to the bottom of the sea anyway, had I not salvaged it! At least this way, we can make the rest of our voyage a first-class venture."

Eludaine and Macmillan pursed their lips, though their expressions faltered. Bos only shook his head.

"Now, I know not about you three, but I'm *starving*." Cosmith resumed down the road, and the others had no choice but to follow. "Macmillan, keep your eyes peeled. I want you to find us the finest dining house in Jophlin."

"So long as you're paying the tab," the young man muttered, though not without betraying a small smile.

THE DINING HOUSE THAT EVENING was one of the strangest in which Bos had ever set foot. Everyone sat on the floor, eating atop legless tables, with no utensils. Meanwhile, the food was chewy, tangy, spicy... and mostly shellfish.

Eludaine seemed to be the only one of their party enjoying herself. Having grown up seaside, she recognized most of the aquatic fare. The men watched as she sucked oysters straight from their shells and ate up tiny bulbs of octopi, tentacles and all. They then copied her, valiantly attempting to conceal their grimaces once the flavors settled onto their tongues.

Afterwards, the four spent the evening strolling leisurely through the city, taking in the exotic scenery of rocky hills, narrow crackling streets, and scores of old boats docked in the harbor. Once darkness settled, they came across an enchanting stucco building bearing the runes *Otelía di Joplini*, and flaunting a massive stone fountain in its yard. It was even larger than Hessian Gatspierre's mansion.

"Ah," Cosmith sighed, contented. "I do believe we've found our lodging for the night."

"*This,*" said the Duchess, bewildered, "is an inn?"

A trio of comely ladies stepped down from a nearby carriage, each dressed in close-fitting robes of shimmering pastels, their chocolate hair adorned with jewels. They eyed Cosmith, Macmillan and Bos openly, not bothering to suppress flirtatious smiles and cajoling giggles at the foreign white men.

"Jon?" Macmillan flushed as he gave them a friendly wave. To his very evident pleasure, they waved back. "If you rent us a room here, I should like to take back every mean thing I've ever said to you, and declare you the greatest, most generous brother who ever lived."

Eludaine heaved a pointed *tuh.* "You don't even speak Janoan, Mac."

"He doesn't need to." Cosmith grinned. "Everyone speaks the international language of—"

Macmillan laughed. "Come on, Dainy," he egged at his sister's stiff stance. "Why so uptight?"

"I don't like the forward manner of these Janoan women," sniffed the Duchess sourly. "The whole day long, all the girls here have been mewling after you three like cats in heat."

Cosmith smirked. "And this is bad?"

The expression on Eludaine's face mirrored Bos's own outrage. But the deplorable man only laughed. "Lighten up, sugar." He rubbed her back in a possessory way that Bos did not like at all. "I am only teasing."

Bos was impressed as she flung his hand from her. "Your loyalty to me is no laughing matter," she hissed, her eyes unveiling a chasm of deeper hurt.

"Whoa." Cosmith blinked. "I think you're overreacting a bit, Dainy."

The Janoan lasses turned away, having lost interest, and a doorman escorted them inside the *otelía*. Macmillan let out a deflated breath, while Eludaine stubbornly folded her arms.

Cosmith rounded on her. "Are you really so possessive?"

"I know not," she retorted. "Are you really so oversexed?"

Bos's eyes widened. He was grateful no one else around them understood Halvean.

Cosmith blinked, looking equally surprised by her choice of words. "Never mind." He turned. "We are not having this conversation in public."

"Oh, we are having this conversation." She gripped his arm, dropping her voice. "I've forgiven you your past, Jon, so long as you remain true to me hereon."

The man glanced down at her hand on his arm. "I told you, I was only joking." He frowned. "Perhaps you ought to bridle your jealousy, young lady."

Bos longed to strike him.

Eludaine's eyes narrowed. "Of course," she shot back. "Just like how well you bridled yours when you thought me in love with Mac. At least I don't go around kissing other people at inns when I get jealous."

She stalked off, leaving Cosmith staring indignantly after her.

22

DAINY

THE OTELÍA DI JOPLINI WAS admittedly stunning, flaunting opulent marble pillars, mirrored walls, golden chandeliers and breathtaking frescoes on the ceiling. Dainy had never imagined any inn to be so palatial, and felt strangely guilty to think of her aunts Paxi and Priya, back at their tiny bungalow in Beili.

Of course, Jon paid for their rooms using the blue silver he'd stolen from the pirates, who in turn had stolen it from God only knew whom. The very knowledge made Dainy uncomfortable. Presently, she stood alone on the verandah, overlooking Jophlin's dark port in the hilly distance. She couldn't bring herself to retire to her room just yet. If Jon thought he'd be sharing her bed, he was in for another matter entirely.

"Lots of merrymaking in the hall tonight, sister." Mac's voice sounded behind her. "How about a dance?"

"I'm afraid I am not dressed for dancing," Dainy declined, gesturing to the trousers she still wore. "And I'm a horrible dancer. Remember?"

"You weren't so horrible when you stood on my

feet," came Bos's response, and Dainy turned. She'd not realized the giant accompanied her brother. "Where's Jon, then?" She looked between them. "In the hall, being the life of the party? Carousing with a harem of pretty Janoan doxies?"

She expected Mac to laugh, roll his eyes or commiserate in some capacity. But she was surprised to see him only shrug. "He's around here somewhere, sulking." He gave her an accusatory look, as though she were responsible for this, and Dainy bit her lip in annoyance. Jon was the one who'd hurt her feelings. If the man was so upset, why did he not simply come to her and reconcile? Why was she standing there with Bos and Mac instead?

"You go on, Macmillan," Bos told him. "Find a local maid to teach you some Janoan." Dainy could hear the smile in his voice.

Mac thumped him on the back. "I just might do that, Visigoth," he decided, departing the verandah with a slight bounce in his step.

Dainy looked up at the giant. "You ought to go with him."

"Will you join me?"

"Nay." She was in no mood for crowds.

"Then I am not interested in going, either."

It took Dainy a moment to understand why her chest had tightened with nerves. She realized it was because she was alone with Bos, and he was inching toward her, staring at her in a way he'd never done before. Her brain went fuzzy. She could formulate no words, no actions except to stand there, watching him approach.

"The biggest mistake I ever made," he whispered,

gazing down at her with alarming passion in his eyes, "was not to compete for you as my bride, Eludaine Ducelle."

Her breathing was audible. Had she heard him correctly?

"What are you doing with a cad like Cosmith?"

Dainy swallowed. It was all she could do, swallow and breathe. She'd temporarily forgotten how to do anything else.

"I should've never let that man near you." The giant cupped her cheek with a massive hand, and Dainy's jaw trembled. His palm was so unbelievably warm. "It should've been us."

"Bos," she breathed. "You are distraught over Selu…"

He shook his head, silencing her. "Selu was a mistake."

Dainy looked down. "Selu is my friend."

"The woman is entirely out of the picture. I know not why we still speak of her." He continued to cup her face, his overlarge fingers so foreign and new, so different from…

"Bos." She finally stepped back. "You know I am to marry Jon."

He looked to her wrist. "I see no bracelet."

Dainy sighed. That, too, was another matter which had begun to gnaw at her. Why had Jon still not presented her with a nuptial bracelet? Was Mac right, after all? Was Jon in no hurry to formally propose, since she already freely shared his bed? The very thought made her feel foolish and used.

"This is good." Bos smiled. "I'm glad you've exchanged no vows with that man. It means it's not too late for me."

Dainy did not resist when he stooped down and gently kissed her, his mouth tasting like cold, clear rain-water, his skin smelling of campfire—

"Can you believe, I almost forgot—? *Oh.*"

At once, Dainy pulled away, swiveling around to see Mac stopping short in the doorway. Her entire body rapidly filled with remorse. What had she just done?

Mac coughed. "Uh, Bos, I took off with your room key." He handed the man a piece of metal.

Bos pocketed it. "Thanks."

"Right," said Mac awkwardly. Seeming at a loss for words, he reentered the hallway.

"M-Mac?" stammered Dainy, following after her brother without so much as a second glance at the man she'd just kissed.

Mac stopped, but did not turn.

"Will you please not speak of this to Jon?" she whispered, feeling shamefully ill with herself.

"Speak of what?"

Dainy watched his back as he disappeared down the hallway.

23

COSMITH

THERE SHE WAS. COSMITH HAD been waiting for what felt like hours, beginning to wonder if she'd ever emerge. He stood on the lawn, fondling the *lilía* in his hands, and waved for her attention. His heart leapt when she spotted him and approached him at the trickling fountain.

"For you." He held out the purple flower.

Dainy looked as though she might cry as she took the lilía. Patiently, Cosmith watched her, waiting for her to speak. But she only looked down, holding her flower.

The man cleared his throat. He was not very good at apologies. "It's a beautiful night in Jophlin, no?" He indicated the lantern-lit streets and the bright half-moon overhead.

She nodded.

It was time. Eager, Cosmith faced the brush, beckoning. Out of the shadows stepped three men, holding their strummers aloft and encircling the girl. They began to sing at the tops of their rich voices, strumming their instruments pleasantly.

Dainy's eyes glowed like emeralds as she watched them, the most innocent of smiles overtaking those rose petal lips. When they'd finished the first number, she applauded with delight, and they launched into the next song, this one fairly slower and, Cosmith could tell by their meaningful smiles, with lyrics of love. Still clutching her lilía, Dainy stood enraptured, turning away from Cosmith every time he caught her looking at him, the wistful smile never leaving her face. After their third and final tune, the musicians bowed and strode off down the moonlit lane, tipping their hats as passersby whistled in their wake.

"Did you hire those men to sing just for me?" she asked, her voice full of emotion.

Cosmith nodded. Gently, he took the flower from her hand and tucked it behind her ear. Its purple petals adorned her raven hair, giving her an otherworldly, almost mythical appearance. He sighed at the pristine young face staring up at him. "I know how much you like music. I thought you ought to be serenaded."

Without warning, she burst into tears. "I'm so sorry, Jon!"

He laughed, taking her into his arms. "There, there." He exhaled to feel her sweet form pressed against him. "It's quite all right. I'm sorry, too. How I hate when we quarrel."

But she only cried harder, pulling away, her words unintelligible. "...*terrible person*," she sobbed, covering her face.

He placed a hand on her shoulder, straining to understand. "Who is a terrible person?"

"*I am!*"

Cosmith laughed again. "Dear girl, you could not

be a terrible person if you tried." He examined her, trying to gauge where this strange behavior could be coming from. Women were the most peculiar creatures. "You are travel weary," he decided. "Come." He took her arm. "Let's get you inside."

He led her into the building, and the two climbed the winding staircase to the second floor. Their chamber was the most spacious Cosmith had ever seen, and in the washroom sat a single clawed tub, filled with fragrant heated water.

The sconces flickered on the walls as Cosmith unbuttoned Dainy's blouse, admiring the contrast of her ebony hair against her creamy neck. The little silver key sat tucked within her brassiere, and he slipped it safely into his pouch of blue silver before undressing alongside her.

She went to remove the flower from her hair, but he stayed her hand. "Leave it," he requested. He helped her into the bath and lowered himself atop her. In the warm water, she wrapped her arms around his neck and lay back invitingly, the flower still charmingly garnishing her hair.

The man moaned with pleasure as he slipped within her, basking in the press of her wet breasts against him. "I wake up with you each morning," he murmured, "thinking it impossible to love you any more than I already do." He grinned at the sound of her sweet sighs as the bathwater lapped at their skin. "And I go to bed with you every night, proving myself wrong."

She exhaled his name, tracing her fingers along his jaw as she received his love, and he smoothed back her hair, mindful not to ruffle the lilía. At his touch, she shivered, her eyes fluttering shut.

"You need never question my loyalty, Eludaine." He brushed his lips delicately over her closed lids. "For I am faithful to you, and ever shall be."

24

MACMILLAN

JANOAN WOMEN WERE NOT SHY. Macmillan had danced with several, and done a bit more than dancing with one in particular. *Donatela*—he'd not be forgetting that name any time soon.

"Do we have to leave Jophlin already?" he bemoaned yet again, watching mournfully as the hired carriage rounded the crowded street. "I did not even get to say goodbye."

Cosmith's lip curled.

"It's not funny." Macmillan's chest ached. "Now I shall never see her again."

"Trust me, mate," his brother replied. "That is a good thing."

Presently, Dainy emerged from the otelía, followed by Bos, and Macmillan's frown deepened. In his momentous excitement with Donatela the night before, he had forgotten the kiss he'd witnessed between Bos and Dainy.

His discomfort mounted. He had already promised his sister he'd say nothing about it. And yet, was

Cosmith not also his brother? How could he betray the man?

"Time to leave, then?" Dainy slipped her arms around Cosmith's waist.

"Yes, m'lady. We're looking at a five-day journey to Al-Habar by carriage. Thank God we do not have to walk."

"And from Al-Habar, we pass through Tröndhelm and Ondriga, before reaching Asiotica," she supplied knowingly.

"Very good." Cosmith smiled, flagging down the carriage as it rolled onto the otelía's roundabout. "I see someone's studied a map."

Dainy clutched his arm happily. "How exciting," Macmillan heard her whisper, and he watched her in disbelief. Why, she was truly behaving as though nothing had happened!

The coachman stepped down from his bench, eyes enlarging as Cosmith paid him in blue silver. "Al-Habar." Cosmith pointed east.

The coachman nodded, eyeing them in amazement as he pocketed the money and opened their doors. Macmillan slid across the posh leather seats and sighed, pressing his head against the cool window. He cared not that this would be his first carriage ride. He could only think of the olive-skinned, long-haired dame from whom the vehicle was about to carry him away.

Bos sidled in alongside him, and Macmillan registered a vague sense of surprise that the giant could fit so easily inside. Finally, Dainy and Cosmith sat opposite them. Cosmith immediately stretched out, resting his feet on Macmillan's seat.

"Get your filthy boots off me, Cosmith," Macmillan grumbled, shoving the man's legs aside.

Cosmith didn't budge. "But I'm tired, Macmillan, and wish to keep my feet up." He smirked. "Your sister hardly permitted me a wink of sleep last night."

Bos visibly stiffened.

"Don't be a pig." Dainy elbowed Cosmith as the carriage began to move, and the Otelía de Joplini regretfully dissolved into the distance behind them.

The cabin fell silent, and all became distinctly aware of Bos glaring lethally at Cosmith.

"What?" Cosmith finally addressed him. "Are you bitter because you're the only one of us who didn't get any action last night?"

"Oh, I got some action last night," Bos replied calmly, and Macmillan went rigid. He did not like where this conversation was going at all.

Neither, apparently, did the Duchess. Clearly mortified, she fought to change the subject. "Say, do either of you know any games?"

"In a moment, Dainy," Cosmith dismissed her, patting her knee. He watched Bos with amused curiosity. "For now, I wish to hear what sort of excitement befell our largest friend yesterday."

Bos gave him a mocking smile. "Trust me, Cosmith. You do not."

Dainy looked as though she might cry, but Macmillan couldn't feel very sorry for her. She had, after all, brought it upon herself.

"Fascinating." Cosmith squinted across at Bos. "I'd taken you for the type to be without any experience, if you catch my drift." He dropped his voice to an insultingly low grunt, mimicking the giant: "'*Premarital relations are dishonorable.*'" He laughed coarsely.

"Cosmith," groaned Macmillan. "You're being obnoxious, even for you."

Bos raised an eyebrow. "You think I've never been with a woman before?"

"All right, this conversation is becoming really quite inappropriate," interjected Dainy.

"Do tell," Cosmith entreated Bos cheerfully.

"You truly wish to know about the girl I kissed last night?"

"Bos," Dainy whispered, shaking her head.

"Why not ask her? She's sitting right beside you." The giant leaned back in his seat, folding his arms with triumph.

Macmillan hadn't realized he'd been holding his breath. Exhaling, he could only watch as Cosmith turned to Dainy, his features hardening. There came a brittle silence.

"Care to explain?" His voice was dangerously soft.

Tears streamed down Dainy's scarlet cheeks. "It was just a kiss. It never should have happened."

"You admit it, then!"

"I'm sorry, Jon," she bawled, her chin quivering. "You'd hurt my feelings, and Bos was there, and...it was a mistake."

Cosmith chewed the inside of his cheek. His brown eyes then flashed at Macmillan. "Did you know about this?"

The young man's stomach knotted. He stared back at his elder half-brother, pointedly aware of Dainy's eyes on him, and gave a small shrug.

"I'll take that as a yes," muttered Cosmith darkly, lowering his feet to the floor. "So. Everyone knew, except me."

The tension was unbearable as the four fell silent, listening to naught but the sound of the carriage wheels rolling against the street.

"All right, then." Cosmith scowled at Bos. "Might as well get everything out in the open. Address the ornery blue at our fireside, to steal an expression from Mac."

Macmillan swallowed.

"Why did you kiss my woman, Visigoth?"

"Because she deserves better than you," answered Bos.

Cosmith did not flinch. "Let me make this plain." He leaned forward. "Just because you are heartbroken over Selu ditching you for her husband does not suddenly give you the right to rebound on my intended as her replacement. You took advantage of a vulnerable situation, and I ought to beat you senseless for it; but I'm going to let it slide, because you must be out of your damned mind."

His voice rose with the color in his face. "However, if I *ever* hear of you touching Dainy again, I swear to God, I will kill you."

Bos smirked. "I'd love to see you try."

Cosmith reached for the hilt of his sword, but Macmillan and Dainy restrained him.

"Please stop," Dainy begged. "It was as you said, Jon. Bos is distraught, and so was I. Our sensibilities were not intact. You know I love you." She grabbed his hands and shook them, but the man would not look at her. "I'll do anything for your forgiveness. Please, I cannot lose you!"

Macmillan looked away. He could not bear to watch his sister groveling.

25

Bos

THEY WERE ONE DAY FROM the border of Al-
Habar, the landscape browning with each passing mile.
The last several days had been uneasy as their carriage
journeyed into the desert, with Cosmith's frequent
glowering in Bos's direction, and Eludaine avoiding
Bos completely. As for the two as a pair, they spoke
little. At any rate, they weren't clinging and climbing
all over each other as when Bos had first caught up with
them.

The carriage pulled up to a crowded inn their final night in Jano. Dinner was held in an outdoor dining hall, the dry autumn breeze drifting between clay
columns crawling with colorful salamanders. Cosmith
paid for their rooms, and the four were shown to a table.

The Duchess lingered beside a pillar, admiring the
lizards with childlike fascination, when Cosmith summoned her coolly. "Come, Eludaine. Bread and wine
are being served."

"I'm only stretching my legs," she snapped, although she turned and wove her way back to them.

"I've been sitting in a carriage the last five days, in case you've forgotten."

"Whoa!" One of the wait staff nearly dropped his tray. "Did I just hear someone speaking Halvean?"

They glanced up to see a jovial-looking fellow of middle age. Smiling from ear to ear, he hurried over. "I've not heard my native tongue in ages. Art Boldour," he introduced himself, "of the Sialla Straits, East Halvea."

"We're from West Halvea," Eludaine told him kindly.

"Never been," declared Art Boldour, still smiling. "What brings you lot all the way to Jano?"

Cosmith took a sip of wine. "On holiday."

"Tomorrow we depart for Al-Habar," Macmillan informed him, earning a sharp look from Cosmith.

Art Boldour laughed. "Al-Habar? Why in hell would you want to go there, boy?"

"Just passing through."

"Then I hope you know what you're doing." The waiter dropped his voice. "You know the rules of the Mulleh, right?"

"The what?" Eludaine and Macmillan asked together.

Art massaged his forehead. "Look, I've got to get back to work. But we'll resume this conversation after hours." He shot a look at Eludaine. "It is crucial."

COSMITH SEEMED IN DARK SPIRITS, and did not wish to join the others for a walk after dinner. Instead, he remained at the table, ordering glass after glass of wine. The Duchess watched him with a reluctant expression as she made her way across the sandy yard with Bos and Macmillan.

"Do you still think of Donatela?" she asked her brother.

He shrugged.

"There will be other girls, Mac."

"Perhaps none like her." Macmillan exhaled, looking up to the stars. "How do you know if you're in love?"

"There's a difference between lust and love, Macmillan." Bos stepped between them. "For instance, if you're interested in a person merely because they're physically attractive or charismatic, then perhaps that is only lust."

Eludaine pouted, clearly catching his meaning. "But if you find yourself inexplicably connecting with someone," she asserted, "harboring an affection for them to the depths of your soul, regardless of whether anyone thinks they deserve it…then, I believe, that is love."

Her words startled Bos. For a moment, he couldn't fathom how someone so young had articulated his own heart so well. For she conveyed how he felt for Selu— *had* felt. For he and Selu were never to be, he reminded himself. His last hope was with Eludaine. She was the only other woman with whom he could envision himself, the only alternative to soothe his aching heart.

Bos cleared his throat. "Take this for an example of lust, Macmillan. Let us say a certain young lady is enamored by a certain good-looking man. Do you think that, were this man bigger, or more awkward, or standing at over seven feet tall, she would feel the same for him?"

"No," declared the Duchess, before Macmillan could respond. "Because then he would be you, Bos."

"And I am not handsome, like Cosmith," supplied Bos, making his point.

"To the contrary." She halted in her tracks, staring up at him. "I find you very handsome, Boslon Visigoth."

His face burned. He'd not been expecting that response.

"But I do not love you," she added.

He watched as she stalked away. Sighing, he slowed his pace to keep a distance, lingering with Macmillan behind her range of hearing. "She is stubborn."

Macmillan shrugged. "When it comes to Cosmith, there's never any swaying her. You know that."

"Still." Bos shook his head. "There must be some way to get through to her. It would be a travesty to seat Jon Cosmith on my Emperor's throne. I will never bow to that man."

Macmillan stopped, his freckled brow furrowing. "The devil are you talking about?"

"Have you not figured it out?"

At his puzzled expression, the giant lowered his voice. "If Eludaine marries Cosmith and reinstates her monarchy as Empress, then Jon Cosmith becomes Emperor of Jordinia."

Macmillan stared at him.

"I often wonder if that is not the only reason he wishes to wed your sister," muttered Bos darkly.

"That is quite an accusation." Macmillan frowned. "I know Jon's flawed, but I think he really loves her."

"You were the one to say it. The man cares for no one but himself." Bos waved a dismissive hand. "I took your side last time, Macmillan. What say you? Will you not take mine now?"

Bos wasn't expecting his friend to look so uncomfortable. "Jon is my brother," was all Macmillan replied, resuming his pace along the dark lawn alone.

26

DAINY

THE MULLEH, AS ART BOLDOUR explained that night, were the governing leaders of Al-Habar. And they were very strict, indeed.

"Men and women may not dine together. Women must always walk behind men, never beside. Opposite sexes may not touch in public. This means no kissing, no hand-holding, no arm-in-arm, nothing." He mopped his brow with a napkin.

"May we ride in a carriage together?" asked Dainy, who didn't fancy the idea of riding alone for two days through a strange land.

"That, I believe you may," replied the waiter, and Dainy sighed with relief. "Although, you've robes to wear over that, haven't you?" He indicated Jon's trousers and blouse she still wore from their last night on the *Evangela*.

"Robes?"

Art Boldour's eyes bulged. "Women must be robed and veiled in Al-Habar at *all times!*" He stared between the men, incredulous. "Surely, you blokes were not about to take her over the border dressed like this? Unless you've a death wish for her, bring her into town tomorrow morning, and garb her pretty little hide from head to toe in black."

He continued to appraise Dainy, frowning. "And buy her a long veil. Do not let them see how short she wears her hair. The Mulleh consider it an abomination for a woman to cut her hair."

Dainy and Mac exchanged glances of disbelief.

"Your heads must be covered at all times," Art went on. "Do you fellows have hats?"

"I do," said Jon.

"Good. Make sure you two find one as well." Art pointed between Bos and Mac. "A cap, a bowler, a tea cozy, anything—so long as it covers your crown."

Jon inclined his head. "Many thanks for your invaluable guidance, Comrade Boldour."

"*Comrade?*" Art raised an eyebrow. "Jordinian, eh?"

If you only knew, thought Dainy.

"Well, folks." He sighed. "It's been a real pleasure. But I've got to get home to the wife and young now." Art stood to his feet, shaking their hands. "Good luck with your travels. And please," he insisted, "do be careful."

MAC'S LAUGHTER WAS UNCONTROLLABLE.

"Oh, shut it," grumbled Dainy, tripping on her overlong hem. "D'you think I enjoy dressing like a widow in mourning?"

"You look like you belong in a convent," remarked Bos, amused.

One look in the mirror through the tiny opening her veil allowed, and Dainy had glimpsed all she needed to. She was shapeless, invisible beneath a blanket of black silk, and was already sweating beneath her oppressive veil, which felt more like a headdress.

Jon waited in the carriage. The young woman had to hitch up her robes to climb inside, already missing the freedom of wearing his trousers. But she felt surprisingly hurt that he did not laugh at her comical predicament, nor even so much as crack a grin. Jon was always one to tease; the fact that he didn't now only served to remind Dainy of the painful rift she'd regretfully driven between them.

The ride through Al-Habar was hot and arduous. The villages were squalid and ramshackle, even poorer than Beili, with stray goats in the streets and children running naked down the lanes. Dainy's heart ached for them.

When the afternoon became too monotonous, she and Mac took to the guessing game of truth or tale. So far, she was losing. She kept guessing that Mac told tales, surprised to learn that most of his outlandish stories were true.

As the sun descended, she was still giggling. "Let me get this straight: you and your mother ate cooked beetles in the forest. You once saved her from a swarm of bees by throwing her, fully clothed, into a lake. And on winter nights, you two used to climb trees to speak to the owls."

Mac grinned. "And don't forget how I once saw a

bird's nest made entirely from locks of her hair." They chortled over the visual once more.

"I'm glad you enjoyed such a happy upbringing with my mother, Macmillan," uttered Jon flatly. "Meanwhile, I was left to be brutalized by my father, until I found respite on the streets. But by all means, please, the two of you continue laughing together about it in my face."

Dainy sunk back in her seat, her smile vanishing. The last thing she'd ever meant to do was hurt Jon again. She'd not thought it possible to feel any worse.

27

COSMITH

THE INN THAT EVENING LOOKED neither clean nor reputable. Bearded men with caps over greasy hair lingered shadily in the shadows, with not a woman in sight. Everything was coated in a layer of dust, and the building itself was in a state of crackling disrepair.

"Not here," Dainy was saying, crossing her arms in that maddeningly stubborn way of hers. "I should rather sleep in the carriage."

"We cannot sleep in the carriage," Macmillan told her.

Cosmith looked away. It had been nearly a week since he'd last spoken to the girl, ever since she'd gone behind his back and kissed another man. And of all people, that man was Bos. Too infuriated to dwell upon the matter, Cosmith hurled himself out of the carriage. The others pulled on their new caps and followed, dragging the hesitant black-clad Duchess along with them.

The innkeeper was a small man with an oily mustache. Cosmith held up two fingers to indicate two rooms. The keeper nodded, smiling through jagged teeth, and held out a palm. Cosmith extracted his velvet pouch. He thumbed past the larger pieces of blue silver and Dainy's little key, which had remained there since their first night in Jano, and selected a shard with which to pay him.

The keeper's inky pupils dilated at the sight of the blue silver. He grinned, beckoning at the pouch. He wanted more. But Cosmith shook his head. A night at this inn was not worth two pieces of gravel, let alone two pieces of blue silver.

He did not like the way his host's smile only widened. Suddenly, the man ululated something in Al-Habarian. Cosmith reflexively drew his sword, as two large men bounded toward him.

Bos and Macmillan bolted forward, struggling to restrain them. But Macmillan emitted a howl as one of the Al-Habarians pulled back his arm and twisted it ruthlessly. Cosmith slashed the attacker's cheek, and the man cried out, releasing Macmillan to clutch his bleeding face.

"Jon," warned Bos, pointing to the back of the room.

Cosmith turned in time to see a dark man hurtling a dagger through the air. The weapon was headed directly for his heart, when a shrill voice screamed his name, and a mass of black leapt in front of him.

28

MACMILLAN

"*DAINY!*" COSMITH WAS IN HYSTERICS.

Overcome with panic, Macmillan could only watch as the veiled girl toppled down, his brother struggling to support her, a knife sticking clean from her robes. A stream of blood seeped down to the sticky, filthy floor.

Bos snatched the bundle of bloody silk from Cosmith's arms. Her enshrouded legs draping limply over his burly arms, he spirited her outside, hollering for the others to follow.

"Forget the blue silver," Macmillan panted, wrestling free from their attackers. "We need to leave now!"

"Her key is in there," Cosmith cried, whipping his sword at the innkeeper who'd snatched his pouch.

Macmillan shuddered as he withdrew his knife. He'd killed a man before, and never planned on doing it again. But, just like the last time with the Jordinian spy, Anton Visidair, he had no other choice. Gritting his teeth, he plunged the blade into the innkeeper's skeletal back.

Cosmith pried the pouch from their dying victim's grip as Macmillan yanked out his weapon. The two flew from the inn, the remaining assailants chasing after them.

"Drive!" Cosmith yelled to the coachman, jumping into the cabin with his brother.

Glimpsing the men pursuing them with curved knives aloft, the coachman lashed his horses and drove onward at full tilt. His vehicle was struck by dagger after dagger, but he rode on, knocking over carts and merchant stands, passersby darting from their way. Eventually, their pursuers could no longer keep up, halting breathlessly in the murky streets behind them.

"Oh, God," Macmillan gasped. His sister lay in silence across the seat, her head resting in Bos's lap. The giant had removed her veil, and her face had turned deathly white.

She watched as Cosmith pushed his way to her, threw off his hat and knelt down at her side. He saw the dagger sticking clean from her flesh and took in a ragged breath. "This needs to be extracted." His voice shook.

Wincing, Macmillan turned away. He heard Cosmith suck in another breath, while Dainy heaved a cry of pain. "I'm sorry," Cosmith whispered. Macmillan looked up to see his brother handing a bloody knife to Bos.

Cosmith leaned over the girl, straining to keep his voice even. "Dainy, I need to examine you, all right?"

She gave the slightest of nods, and Macmillan's heart pounded. "Please don't die, Dainy…"

"No one is going to die," barked Cosmith. He tore open her garments, exposing a bloody gash in her right arm. "Needs antiseptic," he muttered. He reached into his vest and removed his flask. Dainy groaned with displeasure as he administered its contents onto the wound. Finally, he ripped a jagged strip from the bottom of his blouse for a makeshift bandage, and began to wrap her arm.

"It's only her arm, then." Cosmith brushed his sleeve across his eyes. "So long as there's no infection, sh-she'll be fine."

Bos was murmuring in Old Jordinian, tracing circles over Dainy's head as the four rocked with the racing carriage. Eyes moist, Cosmith brought his face over Dainy's.

"I've never seen you cry before," she observed in a small voice, reaching up her unwounded arm to stroke his cheek. "It is rather beautiful."

He stared down at her. "Dainy, you took a knife for me," he growled. "Why in hell did you take a knife for me?"

She didn't respond, simply brushing his hair from his eyes.

"You are the person of value here, not I. D'you realize what a waste it would've been to have sacrificed your royal blood for a lousy scumbag like me?"

"Kiss me," she breathed, pulling him in by the back of the neck.

Cosmith shook his head. "You are mad."

"Mad in love with you."

Macmillan couldn't help but smile slightly as he watched his mother's son kissing his father's daughter. Cosmith brushed his fingers down her face, collecting her cheeks between his palms as he moved his mouth over hers.

The carriage wheels vibrated beneath them as they rode into the night, and Macmillan slumped back in his seat, relieved.

29

Bos

THEY MADE NO MORE STOPS in Al-Habar, except for the occasional refreshments. They slumbered in the carriage as Eludaine had initially requested, and rode ceaselessly through the forbidding nation by day. To pass the time and distract the Duchess from her injury, the men entertained her with songs and tales while she reposed in Cosmith's lap.

Her favorites were, unsurprisingly, Cosmith's ballads, of which the verbose man knew far too many, in Bos's opinion. Bos and Macmillan had heard enough of his epic songs in the past; however, they were admittedly less irritating when sung to Eludaine. This was partially because the man omitted the cruder parts for her ears, but also for the way the girl smiled at his lyrics, her laughter trickling like syrup down a maple's bark.

At the border of Tröndhelm, the four bade the coachman farewell and climbed aboard a new wagon to resume the journey east. The desert landscape transformed into rocky mountain range, the oxen pulling them up hills of pines and evergreens. By the time their wagon reached the stony nation of Ondriga, the travelers were exceptionally weary.

"Let's stop here," suggested Macmillan, as they came into a small border village. "We all desperately need food, laundering, baths."

Cosmith sighed, stretching as they descended the cart. "All I wish to do is get piss drunk and sleep an entire day straight."

Bos shot him a disgusted look.

Wandering cattle and wagons full of children passed as they explored the streets of the little village of Kuma. Bos noticed the Ondrigan language sounded rather guttural, unlike any tongue he'd ever heard. On several occasions, he caught Cosmith and Macmillan sniggering furtively together at the locals' speech.

After lunch, the Duchess selected a new frock from the local clothier—a plain white chemise sewn with brown skirts—and eagerly disposed of her bloodied robes and veil. Bos's muscles tensed as Cosmith's eyes shifted hungrily down her figure. The man was simply incorrigible.

Evening fell, and they came across a lodge for the night. Dogs roamed freely through the dining hall, and Bos thought he heard a goat bleating in the washhouse, but couldn't be sure. Cosmith had long since made himself comfortable at the bar, and the others had given up trying to quell his continuous drinking. Frustrated, they left him there and dined apart from him in a neighboring room, only to return and discover him in worse shape than they'd feared.

The man was intoxicated beyond reckoning and had garnered a crowd, with whom he was laughing raucously and sharing more drinks. Eludaine visibly fumed to see several Ondrigan women eyeing him flirtatiously, and sidling up against him to try on his hat.

The Duchess shoved through the gathering, stopping just before him. Her hands shot to her hips. "Having fun?"

"Dainy!" boomed Cosmith, slamming down his mug and leaning in to grab at her. She backed away. "I was wondering where you were. Come an' have a pint with us!"

"No, thank you."

"I think that is enough drink for tonight, brother," said Macmillan carefully. "Is it not time you retired?"

"Nonsense. The night's only just begun!" Cosmith expanded his arms, only to knock over someone else's mug. "Whoops."

Eludaine sighed, taking his hands. "Come on, Jon. Up you get."

But he only turned to the bartender, banging on the counter for more. The barman responded in his guttural language, and Cosmith burst out laughing.

"Do not mock him, Jon!" Eludaine scolded. "You might offend him."

"I'm s-sorry," Cosmith slurred, wheezing with senseless laughter. "Only, it's difficult not to laugh when their tongue is so ridiculous."

She frowned. "Well, perhaps to them, *your* tongue is ridiculous."

"You tell me, Dainy," Cosmith purred, hiccuping. "You would know all about my tongue." He drew the girl in by the waist, stroking his wanton fingers down the plane of her thighs. "Or rather," he intoned devilishly, "is it my tongue that knows all about you?"

Bos's insides curdled, and the Duchess's face

seared scarlet.

"Get your head out of the sewer, man," Macmillan snarled.

"What?" Cosmith laughed again, leaning back on his barstool. "Were we not talking about languages?"

Bos had heard enough. Grabbing the wretch by his collar, he forced him to his feet. "Get your arse up, Cosmith." The man stumbled as Bos clutched his arm with merciless tightness, and Macmillan took up the other arm, dragging him from the scene. Eludaine tailed determinedly behind them.

"You are a drunken pervert," spat Bos, once they'd reached the privacy of the stairwell. "And I know not how the Duchess tolerates you."

"Oh, the Duchess tolerates me beautifully, Visigoth." Cosmith chuckled suggestively. "Don't you, Daisy?" He tripped over a step in an attempt to look back at her. "You boys should see the way she tolerates me." He hiccupped. "Every last throbbing inch of—"

"Shut your filthy mouth, Cosmith," warned Macmillan, "or I will shut it for you."

They nearly had to carry him to their room, until finally dropping him onto a mat. Dutifully, Eludaine removed his boots and tucked blankets about him, when he reached out for her, his expression desperate. "Sleep," she commanded, pushing him back against the pillows.

"Make love to me," he begged, grabbing at her waist. Bos shook his head, appalled.

"You are drunk." Blushing, the Duchess removed his hands.

"But I need you."

"You are drunk," she repeated, smiling as she

backed away. Bos boiled. How could she be smiling?

Cosmith was already snoring by the time Macmillan lowered the shades and Eludaine snuffed out the lantern. "All right, now *I* need a drink," muttered Macmillan, pushing past them and grumbling something about missing being an only child.

Bos was stunned to see the Duchess still grinning to herself as they left the chamber. "This is obscene." He slammed the door behind them. "That is the man you wish to wed?"

"He's intoxicated, Bos. He knows not what he—"

"Do not make excuses for him! He knows exactly what he says!"

"He's doing the best he can! It's not as though he was reared with a better example to emulate. At least Jon thinks only of love when he's drunk, and doesn't become a violent brute. That's at least one significant improvement from his father."

Bos was shocked. "Why do you love him? Give me one good reason."

"Love is not borne of reasons, Bos! I don't love Jon *because* of anything." She rubbed at her bandaged arm. "Rather, I love him *in spite* of everything…"

"What about Jordinia?" Bos demanded. "You would disgrace an entire nation with your mindless compassion for that wastrel? For the greater good, why would you not seek a more honorable partner?"

She surveyed him strangely. "What in heaven's name are you talking about?"

Bos groaned. "You, too, are unaware that whomever you marry shall become the next Emperor of Jordinia, once you reclaim your throne?"

Eludaine blinked. "I find that unlikely to ever happen," she confessed, her voice low.

"We've made it this far," he countered. "If your inheritance contains something of value to help us fight the New Republic, then the recapture of your empire may be more imminent than you think."

"All I have is that little key," she argued, pointing to the chamber, where her Asiotican token still resided in Cosmith's pouch. "We don't even know where it goes! For all I know, it could merely lead to another empty vault."

"None of us believes that," insisted Bos, "least of all the opportunist, Jon Cosmith. Can you not see it, Eludaine? He is using you to become Emperor."

She looked as though he'd slapped her. "You go too far, Boslon." Her nostrils flared. "I think it time you leave."

"I am not leaving you alone with a drunken deviant."

She laughed without humor. "No. I mean *leave*." Her chin tightened. "Go home, Bos."

He stared at her. All his life, he'd been loyal to the Ducelles. His family had died for royalism. Bos had left his nation and sacrificed everything to seek the Emperor's daughter. Yet, there she stood, the Duchess herself, glaring at him stonily, eyes like green ice.

"I have no home," he growled. He turned his massive back on her and departed.

30

DAINY

JON MOANED AS DAINY PRESSED a wet cloth to his brow. "Lay back," she ordered him. "And stop trying to sit up."

He squinted as Mac pulled up the shade. "Was I a complete jackass last night?"

"Worse," replied Dainy lightly, wringing out the cloth into a basin. "You were a swine."

"Speaking of swine," interjected Mac, "have you noticed all they eat in Ondriga is pork?"

"Urgh." Jon draped an arm over his face. "Please do not speak of food."

Mac grinned. "Would you like me to bring up a fat link of sausage for breakfast, brother? Or how about a nice big plate of fried ham?"

"I swear to God, Macmillan, if you don't stop, I am going to come over there and vomit all over you."

"Charming, Jon." Dainy sighed, returning the cloth to his brow. "Really."

He shut his eyes again. "All I remember from last night is Bos looking like he was ready to clobber me."

"Say, where is Bos?" Mac peered about. "I never saw him come in last night."

Dainy looked down. "Bos no longer travels with us."

Jon slowly reopened his eyes, as Mac demanded, "What d'you mean?"

"He left."

"Why?" asked Jon.

Dainy met his eyes. "Because I told him to."

"*What?*" Mac glared at her. "Why in hell would you tell Bos to leave? Where has he gone?"

"Home," said Dainy stiffly. "If he cannot suppress his disdain for certain members of our party, then he may not accompany us."

"*Dainy!*" scolded Mac.

Jon winced. "Do not *yell*, Macmillan…"

Dainy crossed her arms. "Bos was saying horrible things about Jon, all right?"

"That's nothing new," grumbled Mac.

"Yes, but this accusation was particularly heinous."

"Care to share?" asked Jon, his voice soft.

Dainy swallowed. "No," she decided, lifting her chin. "It is ridiculous." But at both men's expectant stares, she relented. "Bos seems to have taken up the absurd notion that Jon is only interested in me so that he may become Jordinia's next emperor."

Mac exhaled, turning away, while Jon reached for her hand. "You are right," he professed quietly. "That is ridiculous."

JON'S HEAD HURT TOO BADLY to continue traveling, so the three remained in Kuma a second evening. "Does this help?" asked Dainy presently, running her fingers through his hair.

"Tremendously." Jon sighed, holding her close, and a pleasant chill coursed down her spine. "But more importantly, how are you healing?" He indicated her arm, where she'd been stabbed. The gash no longer bled, but was still raw and unsightly, and ached every time she moved it.

"It hurts a little," she admitted. "But it's nothing compared to the suffering I'd have endured, darling, had you been struck in my stead."

The mat rustled as he lifted himself over her. Fervently, he kissed her, and Dainy diffused into the pillows, her stomach leaping, gravity disappearing around her… All too soon, he pulled back, hovering above her in the darkening room, his hair falling over his eyes.

"I could live a thousand lifetimes," he whispered, "die a thousand deaths, and still never atone for all the wrong I've done." He kissed her again, just above her lips. "I will never deserve you, Eludaine Ducelle."

She wrapped her arms around his neck. "I will be the judge of that."

Jon surveyed her cautiously. "I confess, it had occurred to me…about becoming Emperor. But I swear," he avowed, "that has nothing to do with my love for you. I only wish for you to regain what is rightfully yours."

Dainy was unblinking. "I believe you."

He didn't seem to hear. "However, if you wish,

you may find someone else. Someone…more deserving, whom you feel might make a better leader than I."

She shook her head, hurt. "Why would you say that?"

"To prove that I am not merely using you—"

"You need not prove anything to me, Jon." She was unable to restrain the tremor in her voice. "I said I believe you. Why would you speak of finding someone else? Do you not wish to marry me, after all?" Before she could stop herself, she blurted tearfully: "Is that why you've still not proposed?"

He'd been about to interrupt, but stopped mid-sentence, taken aback. "No, Dainy," he insisted. "That is not why."

She awaited his explanation, but he only sighed, looking pained. They lay in silence for a time, until he began to circle her knee with his fingers, making to slide his hand up her skirts.

"No, Mr. Cosmith," she muttered, catching his wrist and plunking it back down onto the mat. "Not until I wear a bracelet."

31

SELU

IT WAS NOT A HAPPY reunion. First, Selu had to contend with Montimor's mistresses. There were more than one. After turning away the third woman who'd come knocking at their brick Ferro row home, Selu finally confronted her husband.

"We were separated for years, Luna." He pored through the pile of parchments on his desk. "I'd assumed you'd died in the epidemic, as you had I. I grew lonely. Let us not forget, you were the one I found living with another man."

"Yes, but I had never shared his bed," snapped Selu.

Monty did not look up. "And you expect me to believe that?"

Indignant, she stalked away.

Jordinia grew colder as the moons passed. On several mornings, Selu caught her suit-clad husband shoving aside peasants who approached him on his way to work. Her heart aching for one sooty-faced young mother with an infant, Selu hurried into the kitchen and filled an empty flour sack with milk bottles and other victuals. The mother drew a circle over Selu's brow, blessing and thanking her, before slipping back into the shadowy alley with her baby.

"Why has the price of wood suddenly become so astronomical?" inquired Selu over dinner one evening, dragging her fork listlessly through her string beans.

Monty hardly glanced up from his papers. He always worked during meals. "The north is low on lumber. But you need not concern yourself. We can afford imported wood."

She took a drag of wine. "Yes, but most Jordinians cannot."

"That is enough drink for you tonight." He replaced his reading spectacles over his nose.

Selu bit her tongue. She was a grown woman, who'd lived independently for the last decade. She did not need a man to tell her when she'd drunk enough. Bitter, she stood, flinging down her napkin.

"Where are you going?"

"I'm not hungry." She climbed the stairwell and went into the bedroom, rubbing at her wrist, where the sharp diamonds of her new nuptial bracelet dug into her skin. Frustrated, she wrung her hand free of the oppressive band and threw it at the bureau.

Unexpectedly, the impact from the heavy little bracelet popped open a small drawer, one she'd never noticed before. Curious, she pulled at the silver knob. The drawer merely contained more of Monty's parchments, although these looked rather aged.

With a furtive glance over her shoulder, Selu flipped through the papers, scanning over official-looking documents until something caught her attention.

Heart palpitating, she skimmed down the page. But it did not make any sense. She reread the runes, her eyes narrowing.

"What do you think you're doing?"

She jumped. Her husband's shadow stood in the doorway, silhouetted against the dim light of the setting sun.

Seething, Selu held the paper aloft. "What is this?" she demanded. "Who is this," she glanced down at the name on the document, "*Dawna Rheyes?*"

"Give me that." Monty bounded up to her and snatched the page from her hand. "I am not to find you snooping through my private belongings again. Are we clear?"

"I wasn't snooping." Selu pointed to the paper he held. "That is an official Certificate of Marriage. It is dated two years before we met. Why did you never tell me you were married before?"

"Because it is none of your business."

Her mouth fell. "Are you serious? I am your wife! It is every bit of my—"

The hard back of his hand came crashing at her jaw. Selu gasped, clinging to her face in shock.

"Your ingratitude disgusts me," said the man coldly, folding the old document and tucking it into his breast pocket. "I give you a warm home, fresh food, fine clothing. Yet, ever since I brought you here, you've done nothing but mope between these walls, begrudging my every effort to relate to you, remaining frigid in my bed when I try to fulfill my husbandly role. You will stop this abominable behavior at once."

"What happened to Dawna Rheyes?" said Selu, ignoring him despite her throbbing jaw. "Or should I say, the *other* Mrs. Campagna?"

"Do not make me strike you again."

Defiant, she stared into his black eyes. "I should like to see the certificate of her death, or else your Bill of Marital Severance."

At last, Monty swallowed, looking uncomfortable. "There is none, is there?" Selu slowly grinned. "She still lives. And you are still lawfully wed to her."

At Monty's failure to deny this, Selu nodded knowingly. "Ah," she breathed. "The truth is revealed in your silence, Mr. Campagna. If you were already wed when we took our vows, then our matrimony is nullified."

The man smoothed his moustache.

"So, I am not the first bride you abandoned." She strode to the armoire and opened the double doors, pushing through the garments until finding her traveling cloak. "The only question remaining is why you wished to have me back in the first place?"

"I always intended to sever my espousal to Dawna. If you can wait just a few moons more," he pleaded, "I can acquire a proper Bill of Severance—"

Selu laughed, slipping on her old boots. "Alas, I think I've figured the reason. You read the letter I sent to my dear mother, did you not? In it, I mentioned having recently come into a considerable fortune of gold. Thus is why you sought me, yes?"

Monty exhaled through his nose, his moustache fluttering. "Speaking of your mother," he snapped, "she will be devastated if you leave again. And I'll not continue sending her funds if you do."

Selu shrugged. "Mother is resourceful. She does not need the aid of a pathetic bigamist."

"I can have you thrown back in prison," he threatened quietly, cornering her in the doorway. "I know not what they are, Seluna, but I know you've committed crimes of treason against the New Republic. Should I so desire, I could easily turn you in."

Selu watched him, knowing he was serious. And that was why she had only one choice. "Goodbye, Monty." She pushed past him. She had to flee Jordinia that night.

32

MACMILLAN

WHILE HE SLEPT, HE DREAMED of Donatela, her dark hair falling over his face as she moved above him. Macmillan shivered with the recollection of her touch, the sheen of her olive skin, the unprecedented pleasure of knowing a woman for the first time in the rocky grass under the humid Janoan sky.

Although their union was brief, and afterward she left him, giggling, before he could exchange another word with her, she consumed his every thought. He saw her face in each girl they passed, her brown eyes in the rolling wheels of every passing wagon. He couldn't seem to shake the absurd hope that he'd see her again somewhere along his travels, that she was following him, pondering him as much as he pondered her.

The journey through Ondriga was laborious. As they neared the winter season, the weather became chillier, and Cosmith had to purchase furs for the three of them. Rolling eastbound through yet another village, Macmillan and his half-siblings watched as a distant snow fell, capping the peaks of a faraway mountain range.

"I have now seen twenty-eight winters," remarked Cosmith, staring out his window. "I was born on the first snowfall of the season."

Dainy smiled at him through chapped lips. "Happy birthday, Jon."

The quiet desolation of Ondriga dissipated when their wagon finally crossed into the great land of Asiotica. The villages turned into cities, which became grander and wealthier by the mile, touting strange architecture that steadily grew in enormity and complexity. The natives' skin lightened and their hair darkened, their foreheads widened and their eyes narrowed. Macmillan had never seen people like them.

Asiotica was clearly the most prosperous nation on the Great Continent. Strange carts emitting puffs of smoke rolled past theirs, and so many lights burned in the evening that it was difficult to distinguish night from day. As for the people, they dressed lavishly from head to toe in furs and silk.

"How did this land come into such wealth?" wondered Cosmith, gazing up at the tall structures of stone and metal.

"Look!" Dainy pointed to a tract on the ground as a series of carts rolled along it. "What in the world?"

Cosmith leaned over her to peer out her window. "It appears they've programmed a chain of wagons to run on *col*." He looked fascinated.

"Kramerik was right," remarked Macmillan. "Col is the wave of the future."

Cosmith shot him a look. "Do not speak to me of that abhorrent captain."

"Where do we begin, boys?" Dainy sighed, leaning back in her seat. "Who will know anything about our key?"

"A locksmith," said Cosmith, and Macmillan frowned in annoyance. Cosmith always had the answers, did he?

"But how shall we ask? We don't speak Asiotican," Macmillan reminded them.

Cosmith moaned dramatically. "Are you serious, Macmillan? *Asiotican* is their ethnicity. Their tongue is called *Sen*."

"I didn't know that." Dainy gave her brother a sympathetic shrug as the wagon jiggled down yet another cobblestone street.

They booked rooms at an enormous lodge with a flat roof, deciding to stay in the present city for the time being, until they could figure out what next to do. Neither Macmillan, Cosmith nor Dainy knew how to decipher the strange characters that made up the written language of Sen, bearing no resemblance to western runes, but this did not deter them from exploring.

It was several mornings later when the three made their way down the busy market street, Cosmith wearing that ostentatious hat of his as fast-walking Asioticans and col-powered wagons whirred past. Dainy pointed to a vending cart of some strange baked confection. "I'd like to try that!"

"Macmillan, treat your little sister to anything she wants." Cosmith handed him a piece of blue silver. "Meanwhile, I've some business to attend uptown. I'll catch up with you two in a bit, savvy?"

"Whatever, Cosmith." Macmillan covertly pocketed the money. At this point, he knew better than to ask questions.

33

COSMITH

IT WASN'T AS THOUGH JON Cosmith had never shopped for a nuptial bracelet before. But that had been a thoroughly different matter. The only bracelet he'd ever purchased was not for his own purposes, but as payment to Dainy's foster uncle, Pascale. And that was in the tiny seafront village of Beili, Heppestoni. Here in Asiotica, the jewelry market was its own animal.

Street after street was lined with rows of fine jewelry, and he came across every precious stone he'd ever heard of (along with some he hadn't). He was tempted to snatch a few, just for an alternate form of currency, but resisted the temptation. He wouldn't mar the sentiment of the day's endeavors by reverting to his old ways. Dainy wouldn't like that. And besides, he'd plenty of blue silver left to afford him any bracelet he should want for her.

The man lost track of time as he perused the stands, until something singularly striking caught his attention. He lifted the unusual piece, running his fingers across the smooth green stones. He instantly knew he'd find no other like it.

The craftswoman grinned. "*Jade.*" She annunciated the word carefully, taking in his foreign appearance.

Cosmith flashed her a sizable bulb of blue silver, and she nodded, holding up three fingers. It would cost him three of his larger clusters of the metal. But he cared not. He'd give all the blue silver in the world to present this bracelet to Dainy.

34

DAINY

"*SHAOMIIN,*" GRUNTED THE LOCKSMITH, SHAKING his head and handing back the key.

"What did he say?" muttered Mac.

The old man sighed and reached beneath the desk to extract a worn piece of parchment. Dainy, Jon and Mac leaned over the table, realizing he was showing them a map of Asiotica. He tapped somewhere on the northeastern coast, repeating, "*Shaomiin.*"

"But of course," whispered Jon. "Moon City is the capitol of Asiotica. How could I have forgotten?"

Mac stared at him.

"*Shao* is city, *miin* is moon…" Jon mumbled.

Dainy turned to the locksmith and bowed, hands folded before her brow. "*Xengsi,*" she thanked him. She'd learned at least one useful word in the weeks they'd been there. Steering the two brothers by their arms, she departed the smith's shop, emerging back onto the flurrying road.

"So we must go to this Shaomiin place now?" asked Mac glumly.

"Don't tell me you wish to give up already." Dainy laughed, giving his arm a shake. "We've made it this far!"

"That's just the problem. The further we go, the further I am from *her*."

Jon's features contorted. "Cor, you're not still on about that Janoan broad, are you? That was just a roll in the hay, mate. You have got to get over—"

"I cannot get over her!" Mac was flustered. "Everywhere I turn, I expect to see her!"

Jon snorted. "You knew her for all of five minutes."

"They were the best five minutes of my life!"

Dainy covered her ears.

"Let us return to subject," said Jon, mussing Mac's hair condescendingly. Mac smacked his hand away. "The locksmith seems to think our key belongs in Shaomiin. I say we leave for the Moon City today."

"I second that," declared Dainy.

Jon smirked. "Two against one, Macmillan. You stand outnumbered."

"Very funny," sighed Mac, heading with them for the taxi service.

ON A COL-FUELED WAGON, THEY reached Shaomiin after two days. Horses could gallop faster, but horses had to be rested and fed, and elsewise tended. The wagon could carry them for days on end, so long as it had col to burn.

"Imagine this in West Halvea!" Jon tucked his arm over Dainy's shoulders as they wound through the streets. "Makes you feel as though we're on some alien star, no?"

Dainy grinned, leaning against him.

Shaomiin Harbor was a cacophony of loud crowds, flashing lanterns, ringing bells, tall buildings, colossal steamships and the strangest, most ineffable music Dainy had ever heard, almost resembling the whining of cats. But despite their conspicuous appearances, the three travelers thankfully did not seem to attract much attention; Dainy reckoned the people of Shaomiin must've been used to foreigners docking in their ports.

"This city is huge," called Mac over a noisy gong issuing from a nearby atrium. "How shall we ever find a locksmith?"

"Keep walking," Jon advised them. With a twinge of irritation, Dainy noticed a pair of Shaomiin girls eyeing him. She grabbed his arm, shooting the young women a cool look.

They walked for nearly two hours before discovering a smith's village. Over the snowy cobblestone, they approached a shop with the familiar shape of a triangular key hanging above the door. The noise and glaring sunlight were muted as they stepped inside, but no one was present to greet them.

Jon cleared his throat, and a balding man bustled in. He began speaking rapidly in Sen, but Jon halted him. "*Halvean.*"

"Halvean?" the smith repeated. "My Halvean no good." He shook his head, and Dainy was surprised he could say as much. "Indi," he continued, "speak four tongue." He held up a hand, waggling four fingers. "I get Indi."

Dainy and her companions could only nod.

The man disappeared again, and Dainy watched the corner expectantly, wondering who this Indi fellow could be, and how one person could speak four different languages. The scholar must be very old and learned, indeed.

But she was surprised when the smith returned with not a wizened sage, but a willowy young girl, no older than Dainy herself. Her wispy hair was gathered back like a horse's tail, and she was shorter than Dainy by several inches.

She bowed. "Welcome to Shaomiin." She spoke in an unusual airy accent Dainy had never heard before. "I am Indriel Chow. But you may call me Indi." Dainy marveled at her mastery of the Halvean tongue.

She handed over her key. The smith took it, appraising it with a hum. "We were told to come to Shaomiin to learn more about this," Dainy told Indi uncertainly. "We're seeking the lock it belongs to. We suspect it may go to a treasury, or vault of sorts…"

Indi rapidly translated her words, but the old man shook his head, responding in Sen. "He says this is no treasury key," explained Indi. The locksmith was still speaking when she suddenly laughed. "I'm sorry." She leaned over the desk, pointing to the foreign characters engraved on the piece. "But it isn't a locksmith you require; rather, a tutor in Sen! For the characters tell you exactly where to go."

"What do they say?" demanded Jon.

"One-six-six-one Tsongii," read Indi, returning the key to Dainy. "It is an address."

"Brilliant," whispered Mac.

The locksmith babbled something more, and Indi nodded empathetically.

"What's he saying now?" asked Jon, glancing suspiciously between them.

Indi turned to him respectfully. "He says he's puzzled as to what could possibly be in Tsongii, for the region is only deserted mountain range. There is no civilization there, far as we know."

Mac looked confused. "Well, does he at least know what sort of lock this key might open?"

Indi translated and listened for the smith's response. "He says the only way to find out is to go to the address and see." She shrugged.

Mac sighed. "And how in the blazes are we going to find the address in the middle of some uncivilized mountain range?"

"I can help you," offered Indi. "I've lived in Shaomiin all my life."

Jon brushed her off. "Thank you, but we work alone."

"Wait!" Dainy clung to his jacket. "Indi could be of tremendous value. We cannot read or speak Sen, we know not where we're going—"

"We've made it this far without a guide, have we not?" snapped Jon. "I think we can handle a few more miles and a couple of mountains. Besides," he stroked his vest where, Dainy knew, his pouch of blue silver rested, "we do not need another person to pay."

"I'll help you, free of charge." Indi stepped out from behind the counter, her youthful face peering up at them hopefully. "I am studying to become a translator, and could really use the practice."

"Come on, Jon," Dainy pleaded. It'd been moons,

after all, since she'd had any female companionship.

He finally sighed. "All right."

"Ah." Indi turned to the locksmith happily, uttering something in Sen, and the old man embraced her. "This is my first real job," she explained. "And my grandfather is very proud of me."

35

MACMILLAN

INDI AGREED TO TRAVEL WITH them to Tsongii, although she recommended waiting until after the winter solstice. "You don't want to travel during the Sun Dragon Festival," she assured them, swooping up a spatula of rice from her bowl. "Unless you want utter madness."

"How do you *do* that?" asked Macmillan, frustrated. He'd still not mastered the art of using the strange, flat-mouthed Asiotican eating utensil.

She peered at him from across the table. "First of all, you're holding it wrong. Your thumb goes under the neck, not over."

"Tell us more about the Sun Dragon Festival, Indi." Dainy scooped up her sliced beef with relative ease. "It occurs on the winter solstice, you say?"

"Yes, which is very soon." Indi nodded. "In Asiotican legend, the Sun Dragon King and the Moon Dragon King fight a war every solstice. In summer, the Moon Dragon wins, so the days become shorter. But the Sun Dragon is champion of winter, which is why the days become longer, until their next battle."

"And what occurs at the festival?" inquired Cosmith, leaning back with a cup of rice wine.

"It's a celebration of light, and all the ways it triumphs over darkness. Therefore, there are many candles, lanterns, bonfires—"

"Are there firecrackers?" interrupted Cosmith, with a surreptitious glance at Dainy.

Indi swallowed her mouthful. "Yes, there are all manner of beautiful fireworks over the harbor at midnight."

Cosmith stroked his chin in thought. "Fascinating."

Indi suggested they dress warmly for the mountains of Tsongii. So, after tea, Macmillan, Cosmith and Dainy browsed the markets for heavier furs. Macmillan rolled his eyes as yet another woman batted her lashes seductively at Cosmith from across the stands.

"Is this what I'm going to have to endure the rest of my life?" Dainy huffed, fingering a woolen hat. "Women constantly throwing themselves at you?"

Cosmith chuckled. "Please. She was hardly throwing herself at me."

This only seemed to incite the girl further, and Macmillan braced himself. "Well, I'm glad you're enjoying all the attention," she snipped. "At least that makes one of us."

Cosmith shot her a perplexed look. "I did nothing to prompt her, Dainy."

"Yes, well, you did nothing to discourage her, either," the Duchess muttered, stalking ahead.

Macmillan continued alongside his brother, feeling awkward.

"Eludaine, don't you walk away from me," called Cosmith after her departing figure. "Get back here!" He cupped a hand to his mouth. "Do you hear me? *That is an order.*"

But she only charged on until the man chased after her, stopping her in the middle of the street. She glared up at him. "Who do you think you are, giving me orders?"

"You'd better damn well get used to me giving you orders," growled Cosmith, "if you wish to become my bride."

Dainy glowered at him, and Macmillan held his breath. "In that case, Mr. Cosmith," she spat, "perhaps I do not wish to become your bride."

Macmillan's eyes widened. There was no way she meant that. But judging by the stricken look on his brother's face, the man had clearly taken it to heart.

"Well, I suppose I bought this bracelet for nothing, then!" Cosmith cried. And suddenly, he reached into his vest and flung something green and shiny into the stunned girl's palm. "It is Asiotican jade," he told her, his voice somewhat tremulous. "It reminded me of your eyes. You may dispose of it as you wish." Immediately, he stomped away, pushing through throngs of passersby.

Macmillan was shocked to see Dainy looking positively livid. "*Jonwal Harrington Cosmith!*" she bellowed over the snowy breeze. Her nostrils flared. "You get back here *this instant*, and propose to me properly!"

The man turned and stamped back, his expression fierce. Dainy watched him, her chest heaving.

"I was going to propose to you at the Sun Dragon Festival, on the harbor under the fireworks," he informed her furiously. "But I suppose this cold, crowded street is just as well!" In two fluid movements, he flicked his hat from his head and snatched back the jewelry. He lowered himself onto his knees before her, holding out the token with both hands, his eyes boring into hers. "Be my wife," he commanded.

"Yes," she answered automatically, trembling as he rose and slipped the band around her wrist. She went to admire it, but Cosmith took her face between his hands and kissed her vehemently, his lips visibly pulling and tugging at hers. The girl's eyes flickered shut, and she went limp in his arms.

Passersby gaped at them, and Macmillan turned away in embarrassment. It was proving to be a rather long journey with these two.

36

COSMITH

"TWO CANTEENS."

"Check."

"One matchbox."

"Check."

Cosmith was reviewing the list of supplies for their daytrip into Tsongii while Dainy sat at the foot of the bed, shuffling through their purchases. "One pair of sparkling green eyes, gazing up at me." He grinned, setting down the list.

Dainy smiled back. "Check."

The man stalked over to her, examining the bracelet she wore. He loved the way the exotic band encircled her wrist, professing her to the world as his. "One pair of sweet, succulent lips," he intoned, "that I may kiss whenever the need strikes me. Such as now." He leaned in and pecked her mouth.

She giggled. "*Check.*"

His lips still brushing hers as he spoke, he ran his hands over her chest, and instantly stiffened with desire for her. "Two exquisite breasts, unrivaled in their fine perfection," he murmured, feeling her sigh as he moistened her lips with his tongue. The girl blushed beautifully as she lay down beneath him, just when a knock sounded at the door.

"Damn it, Macmillan," barked Cosmith. "This had better be important." Reluctant, he returned to his feet. Dainy also sat up, regretfully smoothing her skirts over her shapely little legs, when Macmillan strolled in as though he'd been invited.

"Fair weather tonight for the festival," he remarked. "At least, it's stopped snowing. Fancy a walk around the harbor?"

"Erm." Dainy looked to Cosmith. "Perhaps not now, Mac."

"Ah, come on. How about a pint?" He looked between them, hopeful. "Everyone is celebrating. There's music and dancing…"

"We're a bit busy." Dainy gave him an apologetic smile. "Packing," she amended hastily, nudging their satchel with her foot.

Macmillan frowned.

"Why don't you ask Indi to join you?" she suggested halfheartedly. "I'm sure she's free tonight."

"Please." He made a face. "All due respect, but Indi is no Donatela."

Cosmith and Dainy groaned in unison. "When are you going to realize that Donatela was only toying with you, man?" demanded Cosmith. "Any girl who lies with you the hour she meets you, then up and runs off laughing is not exactly serious about you."

"Jon is right," insisted Dainy. But Macmillan only departed them, grumbling.

Cosmith rounded back on his fiancée. "Now,

where were we?" He slipped his hands over her hips.

"Honestly, Jon." She smirked, leaning back beneath him. "You're insatiable."

"You hypocrite," he murmured, aching with pleasure as the girl rolled her luscious mouth along his throat.

The door shot open once more. "Good God, do you two never stop? I was gone for all of four seconds!"

"What *now*, Macmillan?" Cosmith grunted, pointedly aware of Dainy's breasts heaving gently beneath him. The lad mumbled something in response, and Cosmith sighed, impatient. "We cannot *hear* you."

"I said goodnight," the lad snapped, closing the door at last.

"Poor Mac." Dainy frowned at the spot where he'd just stood. "He must be so lonely."

Cosmith rolled his eyes, folding up her skirts to slide his knee between her thighs. "I do not wish to pity our mutual half-brother at the moment."

"Oh?" she teased, trailing her foot up his calf. "Whatever do you wish to do instead, Mr. Cosmith?"

He grinned, bringing his nose to her freckled one. "I think you are clever enough to guess, my dear."

37

DAINY

THE COL-POWERED WAGON CARRIED THE four—Dainy, Jon, Mac and Indi—to the Tsongii foothills in mere hours. The crowd diminished with each mile nearing the desolate mountain range, until the road ended. Mac looked up at the high peaks disappearing into a gray sky. "Looks like snow again today."

"I'm glad we dressed warmly." Dainy clutched Jon's arm as their driver came to a stop, and the four climbed down from the wagon into the biting air.

"What now?" asked Mac, bemused as the driver rounded back in the opposite direction.

"There's a trail," Indi noticed. She led them across the foothills to a dirt path weaving its way through the mountain's base. Following her lead, they wandered for what felt like hours, losing themselves in the bitter cold that seemed to cut them to their bones.

As the sky whitened, the icy air growing more frigid, Dainy had the oddest of recollections: a vague, disturbing sense of standing on hard, cold ground in a similar wilderness, accompanied by the sound of screams, rough hands shoving her against a tree…

"Dainy!" Jon dropped to his knees beside her. "Did you trip?"

She fought to regain her breath. Shuddering, she looked into his worried face, and shook her head.

"You're pale as a ghost." He took her cheeks between gloved hands. "But I forgot, you were raised in Heppestoni. You're not accustomed to this climate."

"It gets cold in Beili," she mumbled as he helped her back to her feet, embarrassed that everyone was watching her. "I'm fine. Let's just keep moving."

They continued as fresh snow fell, first in flurries, soon in heavy flakes. "I cannot gauge the sun's position." Mac sounded anxious. "The whole sky is enshrouded."

"Did anyone bring a tent," inquired Indi, "in case we should have to spend the night out here?"

"Spend the night?" barked Jon, halting. "I thought this was merely a day's sojourn."

Indi looked down. "I did not know it would snow."

"Perhaps we ought to turn back," suggested Mac gently. "We can try again some other time, in better weather."

But Dainy folded her arms. "We've made it this far. Sixteen sixty-one Tsongii has got to be around here somewhere."

Mac shrugged. "It just looks like wilderness to me."

Afternoon wore into evening, and the snow dropped in earnest now, tinted blue in the shadows. Still, they pushed through the stony range, even as their feet ached, frozen in their boots. "Indi, are we lost?" Jon called up to the girl, his shoulders blanketed in frost.

"I've a compass," she replied uncertainly. "We're

southwest of Shaomiin Harbor. Would you like to return now, before nightfall?"

Jon deferred to Dainy and Mac. "It is your decision."

Dainy twisted her lips. "Look. I did not get abducted by pirates, stabbed by Al-Habarian thieves, and make it halfway across the world just to be deterred by a little bit of snow. I'm not leaving Tsongii until we find the lock for this key." She patted her furs. "I care not how many nights we should spend out here."

Jon gave her a faltering look. "My dear, we've not brought supplies enough to last us more than a day in this place."

"So?" Dainy crossed her arms. "We journeyed all the way from the Knights' Forest to Häffstrom without supplies, and we fared just fine then."

"But that was summertime, sister," said Mac, exchanging an exasperated look with Jon. "There was plenty of game and vegetation, running water, warm weather. There was no need for shelter—"

"Pardon my interruption," said Indi shyly. "But there's something you may wish to see."

They followed their guide up a steep hill. "A fence?" Dainy rapped her knuckles against the gritty iron bars.

"If there's a fence, then someone must own the property therein," said Jon, as Mac's eyes widened. "Perhaps this place—"

"Has an address," breathed Mac.

"Seek the gate." Eager, Dainy ran her hands along the bars. But after an hour of chasing naught but a continuous fence, she grunted with frustration. "'Tis as if this fence encompasses the entire mountain range." She pouted, blinking snowflakes from her lashes. "It has to end somewhere!"

Jon sighed. "My darling, we'll not be able to see where it leads for very much longer."

"Did no one bring a lantern?" Dainy demanded, although she was beginning to feel rather guilty for forcing her friends to stay out there on a freezing, fruitless hunt.

"We've some matches," Jon told her softly. "But perhaps we ought to look for someplace dry to stay the night."

Feeling foolish, Dainy could do nothing but acquiesce, following as her brother scouted the area for caverns. Indi said nothing, stepping in pace beside her and fingering her compass. Dainy stole a glance at the instrument, and saw they walked due west.

"Mac," muttered Jon, after a time. "Are you still detecting no shelter?"

Their brother shook his head, looking apprehensive.

The moon took its place above as snowflakes drifted ceaselessly around them. They now treaded a thick white carpet underfoot, although their tracks were concealed by more flurries. How could Dainy begin to apologize? Because of her stubbornness, they were stranded in the mountains during a snowstorm, with no shelter to take for the night. She was almost in tears by the time the men halted, and she heard the clang of iron against iron.

"Dainy." Mac's shadow turned to her. "I…I think we found the gate."

Feet throbbing, she traipsed forward to greet an imposing barred door topped with towering, spindly pikes. She gripped the gate and jiggled it, but it was locked. "A match, Jon," she requested, her breath visible in the icy moonlight.

The man reached into their shared satchel and extracted a matchbox. He lit a small flame, illuminating snowy columns of iron and a black keyhole. Indi gasped, pointing to a succession of characters engraved over the gate. *"One-six-six-one Tsongii,"* she read.

Dainy's heartbeat quickened as Jon shook out the racing flame before it should reach his fingertips. He extracted another and struck it. "Your key, Dainy."

She reached into her pocket for the silver triangle that had traveled with her for so long. Jon's match lit her view once more, and the girl raised the key to the lock, hand trembling.

It fit perfectly. She gave it a turn, and the gate opened with a deep, dull groan. Heart drumming, she stepped inside of the fence's vast confines, her companions tailing curiously behind her.

They explored the snow-covered grounds for several minutes, but in the dark, there was not much to see. From all Dainy could tell, it was naught but a lonely stretch of acreage, with shadows of what she imagined were more rock formations looming above them. She couldn't help but feel increasingly underwhelmed, even as Mac led them forward, thankfully spying an open cavern.

So this was all her key had led to? A gate to nowhere?

"There's no kindling for a fire," Mac noted. "All rock, no wood. Our coats shall have to suffice for warming us."

At last, they crawled into the covered cave, glad to at least be dry, if not particularly warm. Mac ran his hands around the archway, emitting a baffled noise. "Peculiar." His voice echoed around them. "This appears to be a manmade opening."

"And how exactly does man make an opening in rock?" Dainy asked for the sake of asking, although she wasn't truly interested.

"Dynami," said Jon and Mac together.

She snorted, seeking a place to lie down. "And why would anyone wish to go to all that trouble out here?"

Indi knelt, feeling the floor. "There are tracks."

Puzzled, Dainy turned. Jon struck another match as Mac knelt beside Indi, patting the barely-visible rails on the ground. "What is this place?" Mac glanced around the circular room.

Dainy lowered herself, growing numb with cold and disappointment. Her key had merely led them *there*? To a desolate mountain, with an abandoned project in some cave? For *this* she and her friends had risked their lives and traveled all the way to Asiotica?

"This is it, then?" she whispered, her back against the wall. "This is what my parents left me? Some deserted wasteland?" Had she the energy, she might've cried.

"My love, it is dark, and we are all very weary," came Jon's placating voice. "I am sure there's more to it. Come daylight tomorrow, after we're all rested, we'll figure this out, I promise you."

"Maybe our fortune's down that tunnel," Mac teased, pointing deeper into the cave, where the iron tracks disappeared.

Or maybe that, too, has been looted, thought Dainy glumly, recalling her vacant treasury vault.

38

MACMILLAN

COSMITH WAS LAUGHING. AT FIRST it merely sounded like one of his smug, knowing cackles. But it evolved into something more—a hearty, delighted outburst.

Macmillan opened his eyes. He was lying on a cave floor, staring at a row of rails crossing into a tunnel. They were far more visible in the morning light. Carefully, he sat up, moistening his cracked lips, and glanced over at his companions. Indi rubbed her eyes beside him, and Dainy stirred as well, obviously disrupted by Cosmith's rowdiness.

"What, may I ask, is so funny, Jon?" Macmillan grunted, clearing sleep from his throat and massaging the feeling back into his face.

"This is brilliant." Cosmith was breathless. "The Ducelles," his face glowed, "were *brilliant*." He knelt down beside Dainy. "My love, time to rise. You must come and see what your parents have left you." His voice trembled with excitement.

Dainy yawned tiredly, but Cosmith was unrelenting, pulling her to her feet before she even had the chance to bid anyone a good morning.

Curious, Macmillan and Indi followed them out of the cavern, examining in the daylight what they'd failed to see the night before. Tucked between the surrounding mountains were a series of snow-capped buildings and other strange wooden towers. More iron tracks poked through the snow at their feet, lined with empty carts. Macmillan removed his hat and scratched at his matted hair. What the...?

"It's a *colliery!*" bellowed Cosmith, tossing a black stone into the air.

"A what?" Dainy's voice was drowsy.

"These are *col mines*, Dainy. Acres upon acres of them." Cosmith turned to Macmillan, brown eyes alight under the morning sun. "You two are the wealthiest children in all of Halvea!"

"I don't understand," said Dainy, before Macmillan could say the same.

Cosmith gave another bout of exuberant laughter, shaking the girl by the shoulders. "Do you not realize what you can offer Jordinia with col?"

Dainy only looked at him.

"Why, the nation could be as prosperous as Asiotica! Jordinians can scarcely afford firewood. Their resources are dwindling. They're hungry and cold, homeless and out of work. Think of the use they could make of this col, the thousands of jobs created through its import and implementation! Think of the thriving economy we could build together with the technology, just like what they've done here in Shaomiin."

His eyes glowed. "Darling, if you're bringing col to the table, the citizens of Jordinia will eject the New

Republic and reinstate you as Empress faster than you can say *counterrevolution*."

The man was positively quivering as he beamed at her, while Macmillan's pulse quickened. But surprisingly, Dainy appeared less than enthusiastic.

She looked down at her boots. "But I'm just an innkeeper from Heppestoni. I don't know the first thing about col mines or counterrevolutions, politics and economies..."

"But you've friends who do," smiled Cosmith, the glint of triumph never leaving his eyes. With an air of pride, he paced before her, listing their allies on his gloved fingertips. "Boslon Visigoth, our fearsome zealot from the north. His family regularly attended royalist rallies during the Revolution. I'm sure he knows every secret royalist in Dekantor."

"But Bos and I quarreled," Dainy protested. "I dismissed him from our party, I ordered him to leave!"

"You are his Duchess; he will forgive you." Cosmith shrugged, unconcerned. "Seluna Campagna. The woman's father was in the Emperor's Guard, for heaven's sake. And, last she told me, her mother is still on the streets of Pierma. Trust me, the city is swarming with royalists who've been homeless and jobless since the Revolution was won, all for their ties to your father. If we spread the word, we can round up an underground following in the capitol."

Dainy stared at him. "You are mad, Jon."

"Maxos Maxeos, the Third," he went on. "I know he worked for your uncle, Gatspierre. But if it wasn't for Maxos, we'd never have known you were trapped in that vault. Let us not forget, the man is a trained political advisor. He's on the lam somewhere in Häffstrom, but I know we can find him."

He paused, drawing nearer to her, eyes interlocking with hers. "And then, my sweet, you've one friend in particular," he grinned, "who boasts a seven-year career in Intelligence, who knows the inner-workings of the Republic." He dropped his voice. "I can personally infiltrate Jordinia, speak to the people, plant the seeds of resistance—"

"No," Dainy cried, looking suddenly stricken. "That would be far too dangerous."

Cosmith laughed. "And everything we've done 'til now was not?" He took her hands. "Dainy, your parents were visionaries. They were clearly in on Asiotica's developments with col. They foresaw that our present resources would run low, and planned for their children to usher in the next era of industry. This was to be your inheritance all along." He studied her face. "It is your destiny."

Macmillan listened, stunned.

His sister only looked away. "I thought," she whispered, "that we were coming here to…find some chest of gold, or a trunkful of valuables. Something to carry home with us. And then Mac would take his portion, and I'd take mine, and you and I would settle down someplace, and have—"

Cosmith shook his head. "It is bigger than that."

"Bigger than us?" She scrunched her brow. "I care not about an empire, Jon. I want only you."

"What about Jordinia?" he demanded. "There are thousands of people whose worlds you could better, whose lives, frankly, you could *save*—"

"And what do I care for the nation that murdered my family and exiled us all?" She tossed up her fur-clad arms. "I am no empress. I do not wish to start an industry, a war. I want only you, Jon, every day and night; I want to feel my womb swell with your children. Nothing more, nothing less." She met his eyes. "*That* is my destiny."

"Eludaine." Cosmith stroked her chin. "Make no mistake, I will give you more children than you can count." He smiled tenderly. "But if you abandon your legacy now, then you rob them forever.

"Yet, if you use this—" he gestured to the mines around them—"incredible gift from your family, then our sons and daughters for generations shall be dukes and duchesses of Jordinia. How can you deny them their birthright?"

He jabbed his head in Macmillan's direction. "And what about Mac, here? Our faithful brother? Is he not a duke of Jordinia? Does he not deserve to return to something more than a cottage in the Knights' Forest, when all of this is through?"

"Give it to Mac, then," said Dainy, to Macmillan's astonishment. "Let him become a wealthy mine owner. He'll take care of us, and send us whatever funds we need. I've no interest in running this place."

Cosmith dropped his head into his hands, and Macmillan knew it was time to intervene. "Don't sell yourself short, Dainy," he urged her. "Listen to Jon. This isn't just about you or me, or him. It's about a nation, a future, all of our descendants to come—"

"I cannot do it, Mac!"

"What are you so afraid of?" he finally asked her. "War? Exile? Execution? In case you've forgotten, you've survived it all! You cannot quit now. Not when the stakes are so high and we've made it this far."

"But I can't garner thousands behind me," she argued. "I'm just a girl! People will never follow me."

Macmillan snorted. "You are the Duchess of Jordinia! Your survival alone will enthrall the whole world! Not to mention, you enchant everyone you meet." He grinned. "Even your own brother, once."

He thought he saw a trace of a smile playing at her fey-like features. Alas, it was overshadowed by a grimace of doubt.

Macmillan did not retract his grin. "The people will fall in love with you, Dainy. Just like everyone does." He laughed. "Damn it, if you can capture the hardened heart of a depraved scalawag like Jon Cosmith, and transform him into a halfway-decent human being," he gave the man a wink, "then you can easily win over Jordinia."

She finally cracked a reluctant smile, just as Macmillan detected movement behind him. He turned to see Indi gawking at them. In the excitement with his siblings, he'd entirely forgotten their guide.

"Who *are* you three?" she breathed, incredulous.

Macmillan exhaled. "It's a rather long story."

Indi cocked a thin eyebrow. "Well, it's a rather long walk to the foothills."

39

COSMITH

"BUT CAN'T THERE BE SOME other way?"

"Someone's got to stay here and get these mines running."

The Duchess plunked down her teacup. "First Selu, then Bos, now you. Our whole team is crumbling apart!"

Cosmith lifted his eyebrows. "And what am I, a side dish?"

"It's not forever, sister." Macmillan patted her hand. "Everything's already been set up for us. Jon will leave me plenty of blue silver to hire miners, line up freighters for export, and compensate an adept translator to assist me in doing so." He shot an appreciative glance at Indi, and the Asiotican girl inclined her head.

"But you *are* coming back?" Dainy asked yet again.

"Soon as I hire someone trustworthy to oversee our mines," Macmillan avowed, "I will sail back to West Halvea."

Cosmith watched as Dainy's pout deepened. He'd

never realized how attached she'd become to Macmillan. It was rather endearing, although he couldn't help but feel a twinge of pique. "And is it so dreadful that you must continue with only me?" he asked her.

She studied the floor. "Of course not."

"Left alone together, you two will cause more trouble than our group of five ever had," Macmillan teased. But the corners of Dainy's mouth raised only slightly.

The market was crowded when they exited the tea house and parted ways with Indi. Dainy pulled her wool hat overhead, looking forlorn as she watched Cosmith select items for the journey home. Meanwhile, Macmillan ambled behind, clearly brewing in his own thoughts, making his own preparations.

"We'll need to purchase you a weapon," decided Cosmith, fingering a particularly fine blade.

Dainy watched him, her eyes conveying her intrigue.

"I think the moons during our voyage back to West Halvea shall be the perfect opportunity to begin teaching you."

"Teaching me what?"

Cosmith met her eyes. "Everything I know."

For a moment, Dainy looked touched. Yet, she suddenly turned, lifting a bulb of fruit from a produce stand. "You mean, outside of the bedroom?"

Cosmith folded his arms, amused.

"Cor, Dainy." Macmillan came up behind them. "You used to be such a nice girl. Now you're beginning to sound like Cosmith."

Cosmith laughed. "I've still much to teach her."

"Beg pardon?" Dainy set the fruit back onto the

cart. "I'll have you know, I can gut a crab in five seconds with my bare hands. I'd like to see you try that, Agent Cosmith."

Cosmith squeezed her. "No disrespect, my lady," he purred, "but no one in Intelligence refers to each other as *agent*. In the New Republic, the only title exchanged is *comrade*."

She twisted her lips, watching the cobblestone street beneath her boots.

"Case in point, Dainy." Macmillan elbowed her. "Apparently, you do have a thing or two to learn."

40

DAINY

THE S. S. *ISLA* TRUMPETED her foghorn in the snow-speckled waters of Shaomiin Harbor. Dainy clung to Mac, refusing to let go of his warm leather jacket, his comforting freckled grin.

"They're boarding now." He gave her a sad smile. "Time to go."

Dainy ached. All this way she'd come with Mac, since the very beginning, yet they were to leave him behind in a faraway land. Her sole surviving brother, with whom she'd only just been united, would no longer be part of her daily affairs for the foreseeable future.

"Promise you'll write."

He ruffled her hair. "I will."

"Send our post to the Omar Village inn, in Häffstrom," Jon told him, "until further notice."

"You're returning to Häffstrom, then?" Mac looked confused. "I thought you said the *Isla* was sailing to—*Ouch!*" He released his sister abruptly, glancing down at where Jon had stood on his foot. Dainy did not miss the glowering look Jon gave him, and she glanced suspiciously between them.

Mac cleared his throat. "Right. I'll send your letters to Omar, then. And you've the Chows' address, where I'll be staying. I want to read all about your wedding. I'm sure it will be quite special." He winked at Dainy.

He stepped up to Jon, and the two men embraced. They said nothing, only slapping each other on the back irreverently, the way men do to avoid sentimentality. The foghorn blew again, and another wave of passengers pushed past, lining up to ascend the congested steamship.

"Take care of yourself, Cosmith," Mac told him.

"Likewise." Jon hitched his and Dainy's satchel over his shoulder.

Dainy wiped her eyes. Sailors shouted in Sen over the buzzing crowd, and she knew it was time to leave. Taking Jon's hand, she stole one last glance at their lone brother on the dock before joining the queue at the boarding ramp.

41

BOS

THE ONDRIGAN VESSEL ON WHICH Bos sailed home was dark and rat-infested. The weeks had been long, and his heart had never felt colder. After docking in Häffstrom, he rode horseback to his empty farm in Solomyn, arriving by nightfall the following evening. He'd no choice but to return; he still owned property there, and a neighbor was caring for his livestock. He half-expected the place to feel accursed, haunted for what had befallen him there. But he found the wooden house merely looking serene under a fading layer of snow.

His boots crunching on the ground, Bos made his way up the dirt drive to see his neighbor hurriedly approaching, dressed in plaid flannel night robes.

"Evening, Mr. Winebrenner," Bos grunted. "I've only just returned."

"Mr. Visigoth." The neighbor inclined his head. "I hope your travels went well." He reached into his pocket and extracted a small scroll. "I promised her I'd give you this, soon as you returned. I swear, I've not read it."

Bos took the scroll, confused. "Promised whom?"

"*Her,*" said Winebrenner. "The woman who used to live here with you."

The giant furrowed his brow. He could not possibly mean Selu?

"A good night to you, sir," Winebrenner bade him, retreating across the lawn, clearly eager to return to the warmth of his own home.

Bos glanced down and unfurled the scroll. *My dearest Boslon,* it read:

M C. would know to find me here. Otherwise J'd have waited here for you. He is not my husband. J am going to the place where we last left our friends. Meet me there, and J'll explain everything. J will wait however long it takes. Hagja Laende. —S.

Bos stared down at the parchment, rereading it several times to ensure he wasn't imagining it. *M. C.* stood for Montimor Campagna, that much he deduced. But could it really be that the man was somehow *not*

Selu's husband? How? Had she committed an act of utmost blasphemy, and severed her marriage?

As for the place Bos and Selu together had last left their friends—well, that was the Omar Village inn. But was she truly there now, waiting for him? Or was someone playing a cruel joke?

He gazed at the runes again. The script certainly looked like Selu's. And no impostor would know about the engraving on the nuptial bracelet he'd carved for her.

The man heaved a sigh, trying to work through his conflicted heart. When Selu had gone, he was shattered. But then there was Eludaine. Somehow, the girl had become his diversion. She'd given him a sense of hope, of purpose. Indeed, he'd even felt something sweet and new stirring within him when he'd kissed her…

But was he in love with the Duchess? Or had he merely confused his loyalty to the Ducelles with the type of affection he fostered for Selu? Was Cosmith right—had Bos merely gone after Eludaine as a replacement?

The man dragged a hand across his brow. If Selu was truly unmarried and awaiting him in Omar Village, then there was no question he would meet her at once. For in the racing of his heart and the sudden lightness of his spirit, Bos hadn't a doubt that he still loved her, just as he knew he always would.

42

COSMITH

"EXCELLENT, DAINY." COSMITH WIPED HIS brow. "Now, try it again. And this time, with all your strength. Do not go easy on me."

Her chest heaved. "All right."

Cosmith grabbed her wrist, and she flung it through the gap between his thumb and forefinger. With one hand, she grabbed his throat, while whipping out her new dagger with the other.

"No, no." He pushed the dagger down. "You forgot to block my hands. Look." He raised his grip to her neck. "I could've throttled you while you tried that maneuver. It would've been better had you seized my wrists in turn, and thrown me down beneath you."

Dainy nodded, perspiration glistening at her temples.

"Go again." He took her by the waist, and the girl instantly kneed him in the groin before raising her palm to his nose in threat. Cosmith buckled down, his lower body throbbing.

"Oh." Dainy blushed. "Sorry, Jon."

"No," he grunted, waving her off, though he was still keeled over, reeling from the blow. "That was very good. Go for the manhood, then the kill. Perfect." He straightened, exhaling uncomfortably. "Perhaps that is enough for today."

Dainy chewed her lip.

"What?"

She hesitated. "It's just…you don't expect I'll actually have to use these techniques, do you?" She scratched her ankle with her bare foot. "Is anyone really going to attack me?"

"I'll try my hardest to prevent that, I assure you." Cosmith adjusted his shirtsleeves. "But I'll not have you thrown into this war defenseless. You must be prepared for anything."

Her expression softened, and she nodded trustingly.

He glanced out the stateroom window. "Are you hungry? The hour is almost nigh for dinner."

"Famished." She slipped her jade bracelet back on and smoothed down her dress. "You know, this combat business would be far easier wearing trousers," she remarked, extracting a comb from their satchel, which she began to run through her hair.

"My, but it's gotten longer since we first met." Gently, Cosmith took the comb from her, and continued the job himself. She gazed up at him with those glowing eyes, and he laughed self-consciously. "You are staring as though you've never seen me before."

"Am I?" she asked, still staring.

He lowered the comb.

"You've never brushed my hair before." She seemed touched by the simple gesture.

"It was never long enough to brush," he teased.

"I wonder how long it shall be," she hinted carefully, "on my wedding day."

Cosmith smiled. "Not much longer," he promised.

43

WILQEN

"DAMNED JORDINIANS."

His Royal Majesty Horatio Wilqen, King of the Bainherd Plains, sat at the head of the table, slamming down the posts his councilors had brought in. "Who in hell gave those infernal comrades the right to exploit the Knights' Forest? The woods are just as much ours as theirs. They rest on *our* borders, for God's sake!"

"Infuriating," muttered Councilor Maccob.

"I'm surprised it hasn't happened sooner," sneered Councilor Bell. "The New Republic takes whatever they please. Of course they'll drag their axes into the forest soon as they run out of their own trees. And who's to stop them?"

"We are," growled Wilqen, "that's who."

"We cannot *afford* a war, Your Majesty," bemoaned the Financier.

"Neither can the Republic." Maccob shrugged. "Perhaps they'll step aside at the threat."

"The New Republic never steps aside," insisted Bell. "Insufferable bastards."

Elder MacParsons frowned, white hair standing on end. "This would never be happening if the Ducelles still reigned."

"Well, the Ducelles are all dead, MacParsons," grumbled Maccob. "No use crying about it now."

"That's not what they're saying in Häffstrom," the Elder whispered significantly, and the table at large sighed.

"The little Duchess is *not alive*," insisted Maccob, as though telling the old man for the hundredth time. "That was just a cockamamie rumor started by her lunatic uncle, Hessian Gatspierre. I heard he's since been locked up in prison."

Bell smirked. "Are you sure it was not an asylum?"

"Back to subject," barked the King. "Marten Hoste is out to claim the forest. Not only that, but I know he's trying to spread his dratted Republic south. And then what's to stop our own citizens from rebelling against us?" He shook his sandy head. "We've got to end this before it begins."

Maccob peaked his fingers. "We cannot begin with outright confrontation…"

Bell interrupted him. "But if we're friendly, we'll not be perceived as a viable threat!"

"Being perceived as a viable threat will most *certainly* guarantee us a war we cannot afford," moaned the Financier.

"Elder?" Wilqen turned to the old man. "You are my senior councilor. What do you suggest?"

MacParsons shrugged his withered shoulders. Bell exhaled loudly, and the King turned to him. "Well, Councilor? Can you think of something?"

"I say we call them out." Bell looked between

them. "Warn Hoste that, if he tries to usurp the forest, we shall beat him to it. And then we follow through, and stake our claim of the woods. The New Republic and our citizens alike must know that Bainherd is not a kingdom to be trifled with."

The King ran a hand through his hair. "I second that," he murmured, and both Maccob and the Financier heaved enormous sighs.

"Well, gentlemen," Wilqen pushed back his chair, "sorry to cut this short, but my lovely daughter is awaiting my presence at her harpsichord recital. We shall resume this conversation after dinner." He rose to his feet.

"Please give our regards to Lady Eponina, Your Majesty," said Maccob, inclining his dark head.

The men bowed, and King Wilqen departed them, flanked by his guards.

44

DAINY

THE *ISLA* WAS A LUXURY passenger ship, but Dainy was rarely granted opportunity to enjoy its luxuries. For Jon was all work and no play, each day training her in combat, teaching her history, and drilling her endlessly on Jordinian politics.

"What is the capitol of the New Republic?"

"Pierma."

"How much are its citizens taxed?"

"Forty-nine point eight percent."

"Who led the War of the Revolution?"

"Jothann von Sparx."

Jon took it all quite seriously, leaving little room for much else, and Dainy wished for at least a few days' leisure. She tried to lighten the mood once, during a rather physical bout of defense practice, where she let Jon pin her to the ground, then playfully wrapped her legs around his waist. He only pulled away, snapping at her to concentrate. Feeling spurned, she did not try for intimacy again.

"You are dreadful at undetected extraction, Dainy,"

the man drawled presently, catching her reaching into his vest once more.

Dainy huffed, yanking out the matchbox with which they'd been practicing. "Perhaps because you always know what I'm about to do."

"Or perhaps because you aren't employing any methods of distraction, like I taught you." He took the matchbox back, and returned it to his pocket.

"How's this for a method of distraction?" purred Dainy, unbuttoning the top of her blouse.

Jon merely frowned. "You are not taking this seriously."

"And you are taking everything too seriously." She scowled, dropping down into a chair.

"Get up."

"No."

Before she knew it, Jon was pulling her by the elbow. She flung her arm from his hold and grabbed his, twisting it back and pressing into his chest. With all of her might, she heaved him away. He stumbled back. "Excellent!" he praised her, brushing off his sleeves. "Go again."

"No," cried Dainy. "Damn it! I am tired, Jon."

"Again," he repeated, taking her arm once more. But she went limp, refusing to react.

He crossed his arms. "You were right. You are just a girl." He shrugged. "Clearly, you fail to grasp the gravity of what we're doing. You stand not a chance if you refuse to fight, to learn—"

"Excuse me?" Dainy felt the heat climb up her neck. "Since setting foot on this ship, I've done nothing but work my tail off to please you!"

"This is not about pleasing me! Do you not understand? I am preparing you to counter a revolution, to lead a war. So focus!" He snapped his fingers in her face. "And give me more than half your heart."

She was shocked. "You own my whole heart, body and soul!"

"Oh, Dainy." He gazed down at her with emotion. "I worry for you every day, damn it. I want to see that my little Duchess can defend herself. Now get over here," he pointed to the floor in front of him, "and prove to me that you are more than just a stubborn young woman."

With determination, Dainy rose and marched up to him. Forcefully, she swung her leg around and struck him behind the knees, sending him toppling down. Jon grabbed the desk to pull himself up, but she swooped down and kissed him thoroughly, meanwhile subtly slipping the matchbox from his pocket.

She gave the man a firm pat on the cheek, dangling the matchbox before his eyes. Jon stared.

"Perhaps we ought to break for lunch," she suggested, straightening his collar.

He swallowed. "The dining deck isn't serving lunch for another hour."

"I didn't say anything about going to the dining deck," she grinned.

SHE'D NEVER SEEN A CLEARER sky. The air was crisp, perfect for star-sighting. Swathed in her white furs with her fiancé beside her, Dainy stood at the frosty rail of the promenade, gazing up at the crystalline constellations.

"Have you ever heard the ballad of Felix Strong?" asked Jon, brushing a gloved finger down the nape of her neck. "He was the greatest hero in Old Jordinia."

Dainy's lips pulled into a smile. "You say that about all the characters in your ballads." Her breath was a cloud in the frozen air.

"Ah, but Felix was particularly capable."

"I'm listening." Dainy gripped the rails as Jon wrapped an arm around her and began to sing. She watched the tranquil black waters as the man wove a colorful yarn about a man called Felix Strong, who climbed the highest mountain to rescue a sultan's daughter from a pride of vicious, winged lions. Felix cleverly tamed one of the fearful creatures, and flew the woman to the moon on its back, the lion's forked tail burning a trail of fire through the sky as they went.

...And there they remain, Felix Strong and his dame
In the garden of moon rocks they grow
And their children fly by, throwing stars in the sky
So that all of us down here will know.

Dainy rested her head against his chest as he finished the last note. "Wherever did you learn so many ballads?"

"I write them," he replied plainly.

"You *write* them?" Dainy startled. "The one you just sang? What about the others you sung to me in Al-Habar?"

Jon shrugged, as though it were so simple. "I make them up as I go along."

Dainy gaped at him, and he gave an uncharacteristically bashful laugh, his cheeks somewhat pink—although it may have only been from the cold. "What?" he asked. "Does it impress you so much that I can string a few impromptu rhymes together?"

"Your mind is beautiful." She brushed her fingers across his brow. "Why ever do you waste it with drink, petty thievery and lewd jokes?" She shook her head. "You are capable of brilliant things, Jon Cosmith."

"That is what you and I shall accomplish together." He squeezed her hand. "Brilliant things."

Dainy leaned in and tasted his lips. They felt cooler, firmer out there in the frigid evening. Wrapping her arms around his shoulders, she planned to warm and soften them before the night was through.

45

COSMITH

THE SHIP MADE PORT IN West Halvea at last. Cosmith could hardly sit still as he watched Dainy washing and dressing methodically with the rising sun, none the wiser that the *Isla* was not docked in Häffstrom, as he'd led her to believe. He'd waited moons to see the look on her face as he finally escorted her out to the deck. His satchel over one arm with Dainy gripping the other, he led her down the boarding ramp.

"Hang on." Dainy gave a start, eyes round as she took in the sandy shores, shady palms and black-skinned people waving from the docks. "*Jon!*" she squealed. "This—this is Heppestoni!"

He tried not to look too pleased with himself as he wove her through the crowd.

"How far are we from Beili?"

"A few hours by wagon." He grinned openly at her.

"Can we go there?" she pleaded. "I want to see Aunt Priya and Aunt Paxi, and the bungalow!"

"That was the plan." He winked.

They hailed a wagoner and rode to the Beili Dunes, Dainy chattering happily the entire way. Cosmith held her hand, watching her tenderly, though not without a trace of guilt, for he knew they wouldn't be staying long.

As they neared their destination, however, it struck him that something was not quite right. Dainy grew significantly quieter, peering out the window with confusion, her delicate eyebrows kit together. When the wagon finally stopped, she shook her head. "This isn't Beili."

Without waiting for Cosmith to open her door, she jumped down and called up to the driver in Heppestonian. At the brown-skinned man's response, her hand flew over her mouth.

"What's wrong?" demanded Cosmith, hurrying down with their satchel. He placed a hand on her shoulder.

"He says a tremendous hurricane hit Beili last autumn." Her voice threatened to crack. "Oh, gods," she breathed, taking in the empty, flattened land around them.

Cosmith looked down, and only then did he notice the shards of wood, glass and other debris in the sand at their feet.

Looking apologetic, the driver turned his wagon around, leaving them to wander the dunes by themselves. Dainy gasped at the sight of her neighbors' modest homes flooded or collapsed along the wintry shore. Tears flowed freely down her face as she led Cosmith up the familiar path to her home, both of them dreading with each step what they might find—or fail to find—there.

Eventually, they came across the inn's wooden sign lying in the weeds. The bungalow no longer stood. Cosmith felt sick as he watched the young woman fall to her knees, head in her hands.

The man dug his fingers into his hair, sighing with regret for having taken her there. But how could he have known? And what would have been more romantic than to wed her on the shore where they'd first met, maybe even finally make love to her in the dunes, as he'd so longed to do on that magical summer's night, when he'd first held her in his arms?

He knelt at her side, resting a hand on her back as he looked out to the roiling waves and filmy sun. He knew not what to say. Surely, she wouldn't wish to wed him here, now. And if anything had happened to her aunts, would she be too distraught to marry him at all?

Poor Dainy—as if her family's execution, Pascale's murder, and Gatspierre's betrayal had not been enough. Was there no justice for the girl?

He didn't know how long they'd been kneeling in silence when they heard female voices in the distance.

"…But Hattie swore she seen a white woman weepin' where the inn used to be."

"Hattie is so ancient, she cannot tell a white woman from a pineapple."

"Neither can you, Priya."

"I can still see shadows, Paxiamma, thank you…"

Dainy slowly rose to her feet, her face paling with disbelief. Brushing sand from his trousers, Cosmith stood up beside her. Together, they met the stunned gaze of a familiar, stout black woman guiding a brown-skinned lady across the beach.

46

DAINY

"DAINY-GIRL?" AUNT PAXI SHRIEKED, HER rich voice carrying over the waves. Dainy could make out the elated smile on Aunt Priya's lips, although the woman's eyes wandered upward, unseeing.

Her heart slamming in her ears, Dainy treaded sand at top speed and threw herself into their embraces. Aunt Priya's hands frantically felt their way over her face, her hair. "It's you!" She pulled her in, and Dainy wanted to cry at the beautiful, familiar scent of her perfumed skin.

Aunt Paxi roared with delight, lifting her from the ground.

"What—what happened?" Dainy wiped her eyes. "Your vision, Aunt Priya…"

"Priya lost her sight in the hurricane," Paxi told her. "She—"

Priya interrupted. "It's not a story for such a happy time as this. Worry not, Dainy, for I can still discern light from shadow."

Dainy ached with guilt. Her aunts had already lost

Pascale; they didn't deserve to lose their home and Priya's vision, too. But Paxi's hinting voice broke through her mournful thoughts. "I see you've not returned alone."

Of course. Dainy had nearly forgotten Jon lingering behind. She beckoned him.

"I don't believe it," Paxi murmured to Priya. "You'll never guess which one she picked."

Dainy cleared her throat as Jon approached.

"Which one?" demanded Priya.

"The handsome one."

"The one about whom we both said that, if we were far younger women, we'd not hesitate to—"

"That's the one," muttered Paxi, stepping on Priya's foot.

Priya gasped. "The dishy one with the dreamy eyes, and the nice, tight—?"

"Aunt Priya," sang Dainy between her teeth. "He's standing right here, listening to every word you say."

"Ah." Priya smiled. "Mr. Cosmith, right?"

"*Shoha*, Priya," he grinned.

"I see Dainy has taught you some Heppestonian." Priya wrapped her arms around him. "Hard as a rock," she observed shamelessly, slapping his shoulders, and Dainy rolled her eyes. The woman brought her bronze hands over his face, and pecked him on the lips.

"Aunt Priya!" Dainy scolded her, while Jon laughed in surprise.

Her aunt smirked contentedly. "My apologies. I thought I was only kissing his cheek." She shrugged, pointing to her sightless eyes. "I cannot see what I'm doing, after all."

Dainy shook her head, watching as Jon embraced

her other aunt. "Miss Paxi."

"That's *Aunt* Paxi to you now." The black woman beamed, eyeing Dainy's jade bracelet. "So, you two are—?"

"Engaged." Jon took Dainy's hand. "I was…hoping we could marry here in Beili, with you as our witnesses."

Dainy's pulse skittered as she looked up at him. "You were?"

He met her eyes, nodding, as the older women wore sentimental grins. "Only, I feel horrible for what's happened here," he added somberly. "Your home, your village…"

"And Uncle Pascale…" Dainy fought back the threat of tears, remembering her dear uncle, Paxi's brother and Priya's betrothed.

"It was no fault of yours, child," Aunt Priya assured her. "The gods' plans are often different than our own. As I've come to learn." Her blind eyes glistened mournfully, and Dainy was far from comforted.

Jon glanced down. "Perhaps it is inappropriate for us to wed here."

"Nonsense," declared Paxi. "Something good's well overdue to happen in this place. Let me see that," she added, indicating Dainy's bracelet.

Dainy extended her wrist, allowing Paxi to finger the green stones. The woman looked at Jon knowingly. "Like her eyes," she nodded. She took her friend's hand, pressing it to the piece. "Here, Priya. Feel."

"Unusual," complimented Priya. "It's unique as you are, Dainy."

"And you'll be happy to hear that our girl's hair is at least past her chin now," reported Paxi.

"Yes, because my short haircut so deterred me from attracting any worthy suitors," Dainy joked, earning a wink from Jon.

"Well, let's get out of this chilly weather, and get on home." Paxi tightened her shawl about her.

"Home?" Dainy blinked. "But the inn is gone."

Her aunts laughed. "You didn't think we've been homeless since the storm, did you?" Priya grinned. "Do you recall my nuptial bracelet from Pascale?"

Surprised, Dainy nodded. She then remembered that her aunt couldn't see, and answered, "Yes, I recall."

"Well, we sold it." Priya reached for her hand. "We've a nice little spot downtown now. Come."

47

SELU

HER MOTHER HADN'T BEEN LYING. The New Republic was at it, plotting to seize the Knights' Forest. And the Bainherd Plains—according to Häffstrom's bulletins—were rightfully upset. The great woods had belonged to no nation since time immemorial. Whose right was it to suddenly profit from its resources?

Shivering in the winter wind, Selu turned from Omar Village Square, heading back for the inn. She re-entered the parlor, warming herself before the crackling hearth, when someone cleared his throat in the shadows behind her. She went rigid, peering into the fire as a deer stares down the archer's bow.

"Hello, Seluna."

She forced herself to turn. There he stood, blond head towering to the ceiling, a full beard at his face, his blue eyes conveying a hundred silent emotions.

"You came," she said simply, steadying her breaths. Why did they have to issue so sharply, as though she'd been sprinting?

Bos watched her expectantly, and so without preamble, Selu launched into the story of her so-called husband's deception. The man listened without questioning, until she'd finished. Afterward, he stared at her for a time, sharing no thoughts of his own.

"So, what've you been doing all this time?" she inquired. "Did you go to Asiotica?"

"No." His expression hardened. "At least, I did not make it that far."

"But Winebrenner said you'd gone away. Did you meet up with our friends?"

Slowly, he nodded.

"And what happened?" Selu laughed at his sluggishness. "Did Dainy find her inheritance?"

He shrugged his massive shoulders. "I know not. The Duchess asked me to depart her company."

"Why?"

Bos sighed, running a hand through his beard. "You must understand, I believed you to be married. I thought I was never to see you again—"

"Just spit it out, Bos; I'm sure I can handle it," said Selu, though she was unsure for what to brace herself.

He hesitated. "I grew rather…fond of Eludaine."

Selu had not been expecting this. At first, she felt a stab of betrayal. Bos had fallen for someone else in her absence? And not just anyone, but Dainy, their friend? The girl was eighteen years young, royalty, and large-chested, for God's sake. How was Selu supposed to compete with that?

Then again, she reminded herself, she was the one who'd gone back to Ferro with her alleged husband, where she'd been forced to share his bed and endure his groping every night. "And does the Duchess reciprocate your affections?" she asked, careful to keep her tone even.

"Of course not," grumbled Bos. "As always, the girl is irrevocably moonstruck over Cosmith."

Selu was relieved to hear this. And yet the bite in his tone unsettled her. "But you still care for her?"

He glanced around the empty parlor. "Perhaps like a sister," he sighed at last. "But now that I'm once more face-to-face with you, Seluna, the swelling of my spirit is unlike anything I've ever felt for another."

Her heart softened. "May we begin again?" She stepped nearer.

He stooped down to kiss her brow. "Let us say we never ended."

48

COSMITH

JON COSMITH MARRIED THE DUCHESS quietly, on a morning when the temperature was mild. Her Aunt Paxi had gone through the trouble of seeking a priest of the Eternal God to marry them, as was the cult of Dainy's ancestors.

Before the priest, a local legislative official and the two witnesses, Cosmith and Dainy crossed hands and exchanged vows of devotion, their eyes interlocked with meaning. His withered voice straining to be heard over the rolling tides, the priest gave the traditional Blessings of the Bride in Old Jordinian, first upon Dainy's bracelet, then over her womb, before blessing their two hearts as one.

At last, Dainy came forward, her bare feet pressing tracks in the sand as her simple sage dress fluttered in the morning breeze. Never had Cosmith dreamed this day should come for him. Yet, there she was, the woman who'd disarmed him, sweeping him from his senses yet again as she wrapped her arms around his neck and gazed lovingly into his eyes.

To a tiny but enthusiastic smattering of applause, Cosmith brought his mouth to hers and kissed her deeply, his hands roaming across her back, caressing her. The priest pronounced the couple man and wife, and the two signed their names in ink on the Certificate of Marriage: Jonwal and Eludaine Cosmith.

Afterward, the newlyweds paced hand-in-hand through the remains of Beili. The afternoon sun was just warm enough, and Cosmith searched the dunes for a deserted spot, which was, fortunately or unfortunately, not too difficult to find, given the damage done by the recent storm.

The man slowed to a stop on an empty stretch of shore, reaching longingly for his bride. He began to untie the back of her dress, but she steadied his hands. "Jon, it is broad daylight."

"So?" He kissed her. "No one is here. And I want you now."

With more gentle kisses, they knelt down on the cool, abandoned beach and undressed, the waves frothing rhythmically behind them, and the occasional cry of a lone gull carrying over the tepid sky.

She would never know how perfect she looked, and he would forever be unable to articulate her loveliness as she lay down on the damp sand, her flawless flesh puckering in the most beautiful places from the damp breeze.

Breathless, his heart hammering as though this were his very first time with her—nay, with any woman—he gathered the girl into his hold and made vigorous love to her, tremulous and overeager as a virgin. The mounds of her breasts were so round beneath his chest; her fingers so hypnotic, dragging down his back;

the heat of her, so warm and inviting; her sweet, alluring voice repeating his name so erotically, he had no choice but to relinquish all control.

Losing himself in the shared rapture, he released within her. Her stunned gasps beneath him only served to heighten his pleasure, prolonging it until he finally collapsed at her side, both of them panting wildly, her raven hair sprawled out and speckled with sand.

"Dear God." He smoothed back her hair. "But you truly are a fantasy fulfilled, my Eludaine."

She exhaled his name. "I henceforth wish for it to always end this way."

"Then you will most certainly conceive my son," he murmured, his lips at her ear, "and perhaps now is not the time."

"Nay," she insisted, "would that I could beget you a son every time we make love, husband."

The man emitted a low chuckle. "Well. I am flattered, to be certain, Mrs. Cosmith," he intoned, pulling her back into his arms. "And now, I'm afraid you are arousing me all over again."

49

DAINY

IT WASN'T EASY FOR DAINY to leave her aunts. Although they now owned a charming flat in downtown Beili—or at least, what was left it—she still worried for them. Aunt Priya was optimistic about regaining her vision, but was unable to afford a doctor; and without the inn, the women had no income.

The morning of her departure, Dainy tearfully hugged them farewell. Then, most unexpectedly, Jon poured out more than half his remaining blue silver, wordlessly offering it to her aunts. They tried to decline, but he'd not relent. Dainy's heart soared when they finally accepted the gift.

Weary of travel at sea and not wishing to sail with the vernal rains approaching, the couple took their time by wagon, horse, and foot on the now-familiar route from Heppestoni to Häffstrom. It was a dreary, blustery evening when at last their wagon rolled into Omar Village. Already missing Heppestoni, Dainy stared glumly through the rain-studded window at the gray streets. Why could they not have simply shelved their lofty ambitions, and remained by the sea to begin a life together?

"The village inn is our base for now," Jon explained, resting a hand on her leg. "It's a safe place in neutral territory, where our friends shall know to find us."

Dainy nodded, reluctantly descending the vehicle. Jon donned his hat to shield from the pelting rain, and Dainy held her shawl overhead as they dashed across the wet lawn, charging for the door. They headed straight to the glowing hearth in the parlor, shaking rainwater from their clothes as they awaited the innkeeper's greeting.

Dainy gave a start, however, as her husband's hat was plucked from his head. The couple swiveled around in search of the thief, only to spy a slender figure encircling them, spinning the hat in her hands. "Fancy meeting you here," came a familiar velvety voice.

"*Selu!*" Dainy flung herself onto the woman. "What are you doing here? How can this be? I thought I'd never see you again!"

Selu returned her embrace, laughing, as the innkeeper's assistant approached Jon. "Your names, sir?"

"Mr. and Mrs. Cosmith." He handed the young man a piece of currency. "One room, please."

Selu's eyebrows disappeared into her hairline. "Did I just hear what I thought I heard?"

50

Bos

"YOU DO REALIZE BAINHERD AND the New Republic are embarking upon a dispute?" Selu pushed aside Cosmith's stacks of notes and diagrams. "Our timing could not be worse."

Bos glanced over at the newly wed Duchess, and she smiled at him. Thankfully, it had been a warm reunion, and she'd forgiven his indiscretions.

Selu went on. "The whole mess with the Knights' Forest…"

"Is perfect," interjected Cosmith. "Hit the Republic when they're already weak, while they're distracted elsewhere."

Selu frowned. "But how is Dainy going to wedge into all of this?"

Cosmith stared at her with an obnoxious expression only he would wear. "Am I the only one who sees it?" He laughed incredulously, earning an eye roll from Bos.

Pompously, the man rose to his feet and paced the empty parlor. "The entire continent's wood supply is low. The Duchess has inherited an exorbitant amount of col." He crossed his arms. "Now, Bainherd's economy is as poor as the New Republic's. Do you not think they could prosper from the Ducelles' col mines, as well? Make the connection, Selu, you are an intelligent woman…"

"What are you saying, Jon?"

"I am saying we go to the King of Bainherd for our ally. We offer him a contract with any number of our mines to prosper his nation, so he need not worry about a measly wasteland of trees. And in turn, we ask for his mercenary support in our endeavors." Cosmith looked between them. "Wilqen has plenty of trained, able-bodied soldiers to enlist in our cause. Otherwise, how in the blazes are the four of us going to build an army from scratch?"

"The rebels did it," grunted Bos.

"The rebels were led by Jothann von Sparx, who was a military mastermind," countered Cosmith.

Bos smirked. "And you are not?"

"Very funny," said Cosmith dryly, aptly detecting the giant's sarcasm. "Look, we need an ally with troops to lend. If the King of Bainherd agrees to back our cause and enlist his men, coupled with the three of us—" he indicated Bos, Selu and himself— "building our cases on the streets of Jordinia and rounding up coups where we can," he took a breath, "then we might just stand a chance."

Bos and Selu exchanged heavy glances.

"From what I understand, Bainherd can hardly afford to fight," said Selu. "And they definitely cannot afford to lose." She dropped her voice. "But that is beside the point. What concerns me most is invading Jordinia. You know the Republic has eyes and ears everywhere, Jon."

Cosmith sputtered with laughter. "And who in hell do you think you're talking to? I have *been* those eyes, those ears. I know the business and everyone in it!"

"And they know you," Bos reminded him.

"I managed just fine for four years after abandoning my post, without ever being caught." Cosmith shrugged, content.

"Well then, you are fortunate to have never set foot in Jordinian prison," muttered Selu. Bos took her hand.

A rare trace of pity passed over Cosmith's features. "I'll not ask you to go, then." He shoved his hands into his pockets. "But I will ask for names and information. We need all the help we can get."

Selu looked away, momentarily unable to speak, and Bos held fast to her hand, guessing at what traumatic memories must be haunting her. At last, she straightened. "I will go, if you believe it to be our best tactic."

"Good." Cosmith nodded approvingly. "But we still need a strategy for approaching the King of Bainherd. His alliance is crucial. Luckily, I know of a political advisor who may be able to help us. In fact, he's the very reason I wished to return to Omar."

"Oh?" asked Selu, while Bos and the Duchess watched him with interest.

"Maxos Maxeos, the Third."

"Gatspierre's former advisor?" Bos stroked his beard, skeptical. "You trust the man?"

"Of course," Selu interjected. "Maxos helped to rescue Dainy, remember? The only question is, where has he gone?"

"Leave the scouting to me." Cosmith grinned smugly, brushing off the cuffs of his sleeves. "That is, after all, my area of expertise."

51

GATSPIERRE

THE PRISONER SAT SLUMPED AGAINST the cold wall of his cell, long legs arched before him. The sores on his back and arms itched terribly, but he knew better by now than to scratch them.

"Hessian Gatspierre," barked a guard, accompanied by impending footfalls. Gatspierre squinted through the meager light. "You've a visitor."

The man blinked. Had he heard properly, or had the solitude of prison addled his brain at last? He didn't rise, but remained on the stone floor, watching as the green-clad guard stalked forward, followed by a second, more robust figure.

Gatspierre recognized the visitor. Why, it was Jonwal Cosmith, one of the volunteers who'd returned his niece, Eludaine, to him the previous summer. He swallowed. He'd heard the girl had somehow escaped the vault in which he'd locked her, although he never did find out the details. And it was clear, judging by the hard set of Cosmith's jaw and the icy glint in his eyes that Eludaine's ordeal had been neither forgiven nor forgotten.

The guard stepped away, returning to his vigil at the gate. Slowly, Gatspierre rose, wincing. "And to what do I owe this honor, Mr. Cosmith?" he managed to rasp.

Cosmith wiped his brow. "The stench in here is unbearable. I know not how you endure it." Gatspierre raised an eyebrow, and Cosmith exhaled, clearly breathing from his mouth to avoid inhaling the putrid air. "I need information. And you are to give it to me."

"Oh?" Gatspierre suppressed a grin at his arrogance. "Or else what?" He gestured to the dank cell in which he stood. "As you can see, I'm already in prison."

"Aye, and a foul one it is," muttered Cosmith. "Which is where you belong, if you ask me." He shrugged, fidgeting with his cuticles. "Pity you aren't more cooperative."

"Go on."

Cosmith glanced up, feigning ignorance. "Hmm?"

Gatspierre sighed, his curiosity giving him no choice but to play into the man's game, whatever it was. "I sensed you were prepared to give me some incentive to talk."

"Incentive?" Cosmith blinked. "Have you no guilt for what you've done? Attempting to murder your own sister's daughter…" He shook his head. "Never you mind. You are a cold-blooded crook, Hessian Gatspierre. I should never have been so foolish to assume you might consider any small gesture of apology, no matter how far it might get you." He shoved his hands into his pockets and made to depart, but Gatspierre uttered a sound of protest. Eyebrows raised, Cosmith turned back.

"You've not even asked me what you wish to know." Gatspierre gave him a pained smile.

Cosmith appraised him. "I need the whereabouts of one of your former staff."

"Even if I wanted to help you, I'm afraid I cannot. They've all fled. I know not where they've gone."

Cosmith clucked, clearly not believing him. But Gatspierre was, more or less, telling the truth. "Come now. You must have some idea where they are," murmured Cosmith coaxingly. "Nay?"

Gatspierre shook his head.

"Shame." Cosmith sighed. "I was going to offer to transport you to someplace a bit more...*palatable*. Alas..."

Gatspierre snorted. "And what leverage would you have to arrange that, boy? Aren't you no more than a Jordinian outlaw yourself?"

Cosmith stretched his lips into a wide smirk, as though sharing a private joke with himself. "You've no idea the leverage I am about to possess, old man," he growled. "But seeing as you clearly have no idea where Maxos Maxeos might've gone—"

Gatspierre emitted a woof of laughter. "Well, why did you not tell me it was *Maxos* you sought?"

Cosmith appeared taken aback. Instantly, however, he smoothed his expression, and Gatspierre had to give him credit for a game well-played. "I cannot guarantee anything," the prisoner disclaimed. "I can only give you my best guess."

Cosmith grinned, gripping the iron bars of the cell. "Guesses are good enough for me."

52

SELU

THEY LEFT WITH THE SETTING sun. The carriage wheeled up the rainy streets of Omar as Selu sat with Bos and the Cosmiths, reflecting on the stout, unassuming man who was once Hessian Gatspierre's advisor. She was surprised that Cosmith had visited the Duchess's abominable uncle in prison, but hoped that his findings would yield fruit.

Up they rolled to a stone house atop a frightful pier. Candlelight glowed in the windows, and Selu shivered. She felt uncomfortable, intruding on a stranger, uninvited, in the middle of the night. She and Dainy followed as the men descended the vehicle and proceeded up the walkway, barely making out an array of hedges through the rainy darkness. Cosmith stepped up to the door and thumped the knocker.

After a minute, the wooden door slid open, revealing a dark-haired man with heavy-lidded eyes. "May I help you?"

Rain pelted down the brim of Cosmith's hat. "Are you Franz Diego?"

Cautious, the man nodded.

"Then we are your friends," said Cosmith. "Please, may we come in from the storm?"

Franz looked reluctant, but stepped aside and permitted them entrance, as though he'd no other choice. Selu looked round as their host closed the door behind them. His home was warm and tidy, filled with richly-finished furniture and cheerfully glowing candelabras.

"May I offer you something hot to drink?" Franz led them to the parlor.

"No, thank you," replied Bos. Franz glanced up at his towering height and swallowed.

"I'll cut to the chase, Mr. Diego." Cosmith met his anxious gaze. "We seek a man called Maxeos."

Selu did not miss Franz Diego's uneasy expression. "May I ask why you seek him here?"

There came an uneasy silence.

"We were told you are…a friend of his," said Cosmith delicately.

Franz cleared his throat. "And were you also told that Mr. Maxeos, wherever he may be, is at risk of deportation back to the New Republic of Jordinia, where he is wanted for royalism?" He fixed Cosmith with a defeated frown. "Or is that why you are here?"

They shook their heads hurriedly. "No, sir."

"What do you want from me, then?"

"We need only his whereabouts," insisted Cosmith.

Their host remained silent, clearly not trusting them.

"Please," came Dainy's voice, and Franz glanced at her. "Maxos helped save my life last summer. I am indebted to him. And it's because of me that my friends have come tonight, for I need his help once more. I swear, we mean him no harm."

"And you are?"

"Eludaine Cosmith, sir. Née Ducelle."

Franz sucked in a breath and immediately bowed, tucking his head between broad shoulders. "*You* are little Lady Eludaine?" Selu heard him whisper, his voice drastically warmer. "Well, why didn't you just *say* so?" He laughed, embracing her. "You are even cuter than I expected!"

He kindly relinquished her, a newfound sparkle in his eyes. "*Max!*" he called at the top of his voice. "It's our dear friend, the Duchess!" There came scrambling upstairs, and Franz looked round at them apologetically. "Forgive me. Given the climate of things, you understand why I couldn't be so quick to—"

"Lady Eludaine," came a breathless voice. Selu looked up to see a balding man descending the staircase, wearing a knitted sweater. He seemed to have lost a bit of weight over the past several moons, his face more angular and his gut narrower than Selu recalled.

"Maxos!" Dainy embraced him.

He bowed to her before looking to Cosmith, Bos and Selu. "Ah, but of course." He smiled. "Your valiant escort. Although someone is missing, no?"

"Mac is in Asiotica," Dainy informed him, following him to the hearth.

"Maxos." Cosmith shook his hand rigorously. "We've a proposition for you."

"Oh?" Maxos exchanged glances with Franz. "Of what sort?"

"Become the Duchess's advisor," said Cosmith succinctly, "and help her recapture Jordinia."

"What the devil are you talking about?" Maxos gasped, while Franz looked positively thrilled.

Cosmith grinned, removing his hat. "Where to begin?" he sighed, wiping rainwater from his brow.

53

DAINY

"THE VILLAGE *INN*?" FRANZ WRINKLED his stout nose. "Why should you ever wish to stay there? But of course, you'll stay with us."

"Franz is a tremendous chef," Maxos contended.

"Are you not weary of weak stew from the inn's kitchens? And what about business? You've scandalous aspirations to dominate West Halvea's largest nation." Franz grinned devilishly. "Would your classified discussions not be better suited here, in the safety and privacy of my humble home?"

Dainy turned to her friends. Bos and Selu shrugged, deferring to her, while Jon raised his eyebrows as if to say, *he has a point.* "Very well," she decided, and Franz clasped his hands delightedly.

They presently enjoyed a sumptuous dinner of their host's making, and it wasn't long before the men were deep in conversation.

"If we're going to approach the King of Bainherd, then we ought to do it soon, before he becomes too involved with the forest dispute," Maxos told them, spectacles resting in his breast pocket. Without them, he looked a bit younger, and perhaps less stuffy.

Jon laughed. "There will *be* no more forest dispute once we've offered Wilqen a portion of our col."

Maxos swished the wine in his goblet thoughtfully. "The col is somewhat tributary, Your Grace."

At the formal title, Selu and Dainy sniggered, and Jon shot them a lazy grin. Although he'd insisted on being called by name, Maxos was intent on addressing him in the manner of a duke, as he was now a duchess's husband.

The advisor went on. "Here's the deal with Horatio Wilqen: Bainherd's economy has been nearly as poor as Jordinia's for two decades. Ever since the Jordinian rebels overthrew their emperor, Wilqen has feared his own citizens doing the same to him. Indeed, there's been talk…" He paused to sip his wine. "Of course, he wishes to prosper his people. But maintaining his kingship is his prime concern, I can tell you as much."

"Ah." Jon smiled knowingly, making a connection that was lost upon Dainy.

"Well, is this not ideal?" boomed Bos, helping himself to another goblet. "If Wilqen helps us overthrow the New Republic and reinstate the Ducelle Empire, then he'll most certainly secure his kingship. For who of his citizens shall wish to rise against him after such an assertion of monarchy's power?"

Maxos nodded. "Precisely."

"Mmm," intoned Jon, the corners of his lips raised.

"But we can't just show up at Pon Castle unannounced." Maxos entwined his fingers. "We must first write to Wilqen and await his invitation."

Selu looked up. "Surely, we cannot put the details

of Dainy's survival in a letter?"

"Why not?" asked Bos. "Hoste has met her; he knows she lives."

"Yes, but should the Republic catch us corresponding about the Duchess with a foreign king, Hoste will know we're up to something," said Jon shrewdly.

"Therefore, we keep our message veiled," agreed Maxos. "But we assure Wilqen that our revelation, which cannot be named in writing, very much pertains to his interests. Namely that of preserving and prospering his kingdom. He'll not refuse us."

"Very well; has anyone a quill?" Jon glanced about eagerly. "I should like to pen this scroll forthwith."

Franz went to fetch one, and Maxos looked to Dainy. "Do you feel prepared, my lady?"

"Oh, yes," she replied. "Jon spent two moons aboard the S. S. *Isla* teaching me all about combat and the politics of the New Republic."

Maxos gave her a weak smile, looking unconvinced. "What about the *old* Jordinia, though? Know you anything of your family's empire, life at court, or your royal duties, should the land someday return to you?"

Jon and Dainy turned to each other, their faces faltering. Why, she realized, the man had been so preoccupied preparing her for the war itself, he'd neglected to properly educate her on the very empire they were seeking to restore.

"Not a problem." Franz hurried back into the dining room, cradling a heap of writing supplies. "Max can teach you all about the royal family. He even managed to salvage a few royal relics from Gatspierre's estate. Say, have you ever seen your family's etchings, Eludaine?"

Dainy's eyes widened. "You have a likeness of my family?"

Franz dumped the parchment, quills, and inkwell unceremoniously in front of Jon before dashing from the room. Seconds later, Dainy heard him hurrying up the staircase.

"So, you shall present the Duchess to King Wilqen, request his mercenary help, and offer him a contract with her mines in turn," Bos recounted in his baritone voice. "What of the Jordinian people?"

"Indeed, they must be persuaded that Dainy can do a better job than the New Republic," Selu pointed out. "Otherwise, they'll simply revolt at another transfer of power."

Dainy grew nervous at her words. *Could* she do a better job of governing a nation? She wasn't so sure. She wasn't even nineteen springs old yet. Despite her blood, she hardly felt qualified to be an empress. Besides, what poor timing for such matters, mere moons after her wedding day! Why, other young brides would still be on their honeymoons, cementing their marriage bonds with no other cares in the world. Why was she forced to contend with such a weighty predicament now?

Jon spoke to Maxos. "Thus is why I shall return to the streets of Pierma, and speak to the citizens in person."

Maxos looked alarmed. "That would be quite a dangerous undertaking, my liege, and one which I'd strongly advise against—"

Jon waved him down. "Supply is low," he insisted, "and demand high. The Ducelles' col will bridge that gap. We'll provide more resources," he held up his index finger, "and more jobs," he added a second finger, "restoring the economy, not to mention guaranteeing the lowering of taxes." He held up a third finger. "It is crucial we spread this information to the people. And I intend to do it myself."

"Much as I understand you are well-practiced in the art of persuasion," said Maxos nervously, "returning to Jordinia now is a grave risk, especially for the Duchess."

"The Duchess is not to go with me," snapped Jon.

Dainy looked up, her heart jolting. "What?"

Her insides chilled to match the unusual iciness in Jon's tone. "You did not actually think you were coming to Jordinia with me?"

Dainy couldn't help it. With a loud scrape of her chair, she rose to her feet. "I did not agree to be left behind."

Jon stood as well, looking severe. "It is for your own safety. And it's a decision I've already come to. You've no say in the matter." He pointed to her chair. "Now sit back down, and cease your protests."

Dainy's neck burned. "No. I am going with you, or the whole plan is off."

Jon glared at her. "*Sit*."

"What about us?" Her voice shook. "You wish to be separated for moons, possibly years? I…I do not think I can bear—"

"This is war, Eludaine!" Jon shouted over her.

"It does not have to be," Dainy bellowed back, taking a massive step towards him. "I never asked for any of this! This was all *your* idea!"

Jon emitted a growl of frustration. "I am warning

you, wife, I've not the patience for this…"

Dainy scoffed. "Funny. You've no patience for me, yet you've unlimited patience for scheming how best to seize a nation using *my* wealth and blood." Her anger bubbling, the words frothed out even as she knew she did not mean them. "It's true, then! You are only using me to become Jordinia's next emperor."

His hand arose before she could blink, hovering midair just before her cheek. For a moment, the only emotion Dainy could register was shock, until the man seemed to recover his senses, and slowly lowered his arm.

Dainy stared at him in disbelief, her pulse galloping as his anguished eyes shifted downward. Had her spouse truly been about to strike her?

He clenched his jaw. Furious, he stormed from the dining room, boots pounding over the stone floors, until Dainy heard the thunderous slam of the front door.

54

COSMITH

JON COSMITH STARED ACROSS THE dark lawn, despising himself. His wife was stubborn. And perhaps he'd imbibed too many beverages. But how could he have come so close to imitating his loathsome father? How could he have contemplated, if even for a moment, raising a hand to the one he loved?

All the same, her lashing words bruised him. Did Dainy truly believe he was feigning his love for her, merely for the sake of political gain? After everything they'd been through, the myriad ways he'd imparted his heart to her, and how hard he'd striven to redeem himself, she would pronounce his devotions disingenuous?

The audacity of the accusation tormented him. He had married her, for God's sake! Dainy was the only woman Cosmith had ever dared to love. Yet, she would throw it all back in his face, simply because he sought to do right by her, and restore her to her throne? Not to mention, he sought atonement for the wrongs he'd committed during his stint in Intelligence.

Cosmith sighed. That was another matter. But he'd still never confessed to his wife or their friends what, exactly, he'd done for the New Republic—and they had never asked. Yet, who did they think was the target of his former surveillance?

He'd had one job. And that was to hunt the only known enemies of the state: its own disloyal citizens. Secret royalists were heavy among them.

Jon Cosmith had reported it all: women discreetly tracing circles over their brows; a man carrying an etching of the royal family; someone he'd heard grumbling about some law or another, which he believed the Emperor had upheld more competently than Marten Hoste. For seven years, Cosmith had been responsible for the arrests, floggings, and in some cases hangings of numerous royal devotees. Dainy's devotees. Too many to count.

Not that he'd ever held anything personal against the royal family. It had all been strictly business to him, a way to put bread to mouth. The New Republic had recruited him as a vagrant youth, after all. He'd have done anything, should he not have had to sleep in a grimy, freezing alley under the wintry sky any longer. But his guilt now unhinged him, both for losing his temper with his wife that night, and for persecuting her advocates in years past.

Indeed, it was a dark day when Cosmith had uncovered the truth, that prominent politicians of the Republic were hoarding citizens' tax payments for their own accounts. With the nation's taxes three times higher than ever, one would think the government held plenty of funds to invest back into its people and cities. Alas, the land was at its most impoverished, and declining still. And Cosmith finally understood why.

Disgusted, he'd lost heart in his work and abandoned his post, eventually losing himself in drink and frivolous women. He applied the skills he'd acquired in Intelligence to elsewise get by and ensure his next meal was seen to. He had no one to care for but himself. And that was the way he'd preferred it.

Until Dainy.

She changed everything. As a result, Cosmith had become arguably the greatest royalist of all, his own bride the Duchess, his half-brother the ill-begotten Duke. The pair deserved their rightful empire. And Cosmith planned to help them seize and prosper it, despite the measures he would have to take to regain Dainy's trust and earn forgiveness for all of his wretchedness.

If he had to beg of her, then so be it.

55

DAINY

HER MOTHER'S FACE STARED UP at her from the parchment. Dainy examined the slender, sloping nose, the almond-shaped eyes and darkly-shaded hair, startled by her own resemblance to the woman. In her mother's stout arms rested a small infant, her round face poking out from beneath the swaddling blankets.

Beside them stood an imposing figure with a strapping chest. He wore an elegant suit, recalling military regalia, heavily decorated with medals on a sash adorning his front. His hair was an inky black that matched his moustache. There was no question that he was the former Emperor, Dane Ducelle—Dainy's father.

Her gaze lingered over the three young men seated before her parents. The eldest who, in this likeness, could have hardly seen fifteen years, was rather handsome. Like their father, he was sturdily built, while something in his posture held the promise of strength, a conviction to lead.

"Hegren," said Maxos, following her eyes. "Your eldest brother. He was to inherit the throne." He pointed to the other two boys, possibly around eleven or twelve years old, and Dainy was taken aback by how much they resembled Mac. In fact, she felt sure this was exactly what her half-brother must have looked like in his own childhood.

"The twins. Guy and Willem. Although no one but your mother could tell them apart." Franz smiled sadly.

Dainy wiped a tear from her eye. Her family had been beautiful, had looked so affluent, powerful and capable. Even the youths, whose unsmiling faces gazed at the artist so solemnly, had clearly been trained in dignity and propriety since birth. How had the Ducelles been overthrown and murdered by a faction of their own people?

She traced her fingers across the etching, careful not to smudge the ink, although it had long since settled into the parchment. Much as she wanted to remember them, she simply could muster nothing from her memory.

Meeting her eldest brother's demanding gaze, she began to feel inadequate in comparison. She shifted her eyes from the image of her family. In spite of sharing their blood, Dainy did not much feel like royalty. Unlike Hegren Ducelle, she had not been expressly raised to rule an empire.

The front door slid open noisily, disrupting her thoughts, and brusque footfalls sounded in the foyer. Dainy went rigid.

No one acknowledged Jon's entry. Selu was curled up in Bos's lap, the couple poring over old bulletins that Franz had unearthed, while Maxos and Franz began to converse quietly. From the corner of her eye, Dainy spied Jon watching them with uncertainty, as though deliberating over whether he felt welcome to join them.

Careful not to meet his eyes, she set her family's portrait aside and reached for her mug.

"I remember this," Jon said softly, lifting the picture from the table. "I was ten when they posted it all over Pierma, the first portrait of the royal family together with their newest addition." Was that tenderness in his voice at those last few words? Dainy grimaced. So Jon would be sweet on her now, would he?

He extended the portrait to Bos, who gave him something of a cool look before extending his giant paw. "Ah, yes." His cheeks pulled into a smile. "I recall this."

"What a cherubic babe you were, Dainy," Selu cooed, eyes crinkling at the bundle in the Empress's arms.

"How diplomatic of you," replied Dainy. "I was rather chubby."

Selu chuckled. "You were well-nourished."

"And I'm sure it won't be long," sang Franz, taking up the empty mugs, "'til our lady cradles a fat little baby of her own."

Dainy stiffened as Jon looked down, his expression indiscernible.

SHE LINGERED AT THE STAIRWELL, her back against the wall. But the others had already retired, and Dainy knew she could not avoid her husband forever. Resigned, she climbed the steps.

Approaching their room, she detected a rim of candlelight glowing beneath the door. So much for hoping he might already be asleep. Reluctant, she entered the chamber, barely glancing inside as she took her time securing the door.

"There she is," came his gentle voice, and Dainy cursed the tremors rippling down her arms. How did he never fail to have that effect on her, merely by speaking?

She turned, and her heart fluttered. But heavens, he always looked so effortlessly incredible. With his blouse half-buttoned and rolled up at the sleeves, his hair carelessly brushed back, Dainy was ruthlessly reminded of all the times he'd made love to her. Oh, she knew how firm those arms felt around her, and she wished she could stop recalling the sweetness of his mouth…

Stop, she urged herself. Could she not resist the charms of Jon Cosmith for one night? Then again, as she well knew, a woman did not simply resist Jon Cosmith. Least of all, his wife.

"My kitten." His voice was more baritone than usual, and Dainy begrudgingly quivered at the cloying endearment. Those brown eyes appraised her with such trepidation until at last, he sorrowfully intoned, "I am so very sorry, love."

"Whatever for, husband?" Her voice was remarkably steady for the cavalcade of competing emotions within her.

"I didn't mean to…lose myself back there. I'd never hurt you."

She said nothing.

"I—I've been w—working on something for you," he announced, and the hopeful stammer accompanied with the childlike earnestness in his eyes was too pitiful for Dainy to withstand. Don't you dare smile, she begged herself, though she watched curiously as he went to the bureau. A quill dripping with fresh ink lay beside a leaf of parchment. Jon snatched up the page and handed it to her.

Dainy barely glanced at it. "What's this?"

He mumbled in response.

"*A poem?*" She brandished the page with a withering look, unimpressed. "And you think poetry is going to compensate for the way you treated me tonight, do you?"

Jon remained silent, and Dainy pursed her lips. Very well. If he would speak harshly to her, even consider lifting a hand before her, then she would mock this feeble attempt at reconciliation. She took a breath, and in her most scathing voice, read his cramped, angular scrawl aloud:

Before her was dusk and immeasurable despair
A smothering casket with no hope for air
Yet somehow, an angel hath rescued me there:
The woman who sovereigns my soul.

Transgressor I am, yet she summons from me
The man whom I thought I never could be
My need for her rages perpetually:
The woman who sovereigns my soul.

Her tone lost its mockery. She continued to articulate the runes, swallowing back the lump in her throat:

Forgiveness is something I'll never deserve
For lo, I've disgraced what I ought to preserve
That radiant dove whom my heart vows to serve:
The woman who sovereigns my soul.

Her resolve crumbling, she came over to the edge of the bed, and sat down beside him.

"I am not my father," he whispered, and Dainy couldn't bear the agony in his eyes. "It won't happen again. You have my word."

She sat still, allowing him to lean in, her lips merging with his, her spine tingling at the path of his tongue along hers. His arms enfolded her, returning her to the safe, familiar place where she knew she was loved, and she held him close, wracked with guilt for her thoughtless words.

"I didn't mean it." She shivered as he brought his mouth down her neck. "About you using me. I know not why I even—"

"Hush." He nestled his face into her hair. "It is behind us."

Dainy frowned, even as she yearned for him. "But you won't actually go into Jordinia without me?"

"I must."

"*No.*"

Jon made to embrace her again, but she ducked away. "Don't be impossible," he cajoled.

Dainy shot to her feet. "Goodnight, Mr. Cosmith," she said curtly, climbing into bed. A heavy silence befell them.

"Dainy." He spoke with his back to her. "I know how you're feeling. It tears me apart as well, to go away from you. But Jordinia is far too dangerous for you right now."

"What about for you?" she demanded. "What if you're caught or arrested?"

"That is my problem."

Her jaw fell. For a moment, she stared at his back, speechless. "How can you be so aloof? We are one now, Jon. There is no part of this that is only you."

He snuffed out the lantern, and Dainy watched his shadow enter the bed beside her. She did not protest when he groped for her beneath the blankets. "Forgive me," he begged. "All that I know of love, I am learning from you."

She sighed. "Then if you love me, you will preserve yourself from harm. For should anything befall you, darling, I'd be inconsolable."

He grunted. "This, coming from the woman who leapt before a flying dagger."

She squeezed him. "I had to protect you."

"And so must I protect you." His eyes found hers in the darkness. "The answer is no, Dainy. I must go alone."

56

MACMILLAN

THE VERNAL EQUINOX CAME AND went, and springtime in Asiotica was a vibrant affair. While the city of Shaomiin had been bustling in wintertime, the crowds and activities seemed to triple since temperatures had warmed and the snows melted.

Even so, Marley Macmillan endured a sense of aloneness there. It wasn't that he still pined after the woman Donatela—nay, that fruitless infatuation had finally surpassed him—but he often wondered after his siblings back home, and found himself missing their company.

Yet, his stay in Shaomiin was not in vain. With Indi's assistance, Macmillan had garnered the consideration of a promising partner to run his and Dainy's col mines. Dr. Andre Chen was a doctor of the law, and savvy about the mining business. They were currently in negotiations, and it appeared an agreement was nigh. If all went well, Macmillan would sail back to West Halvea by summertime.

Presently, his chamber door bowed open. "You've

a letter," came his translator's even voice. Indi handed him a scroll and, with a courteous bob of her head, left him to read in privacy.

Macmillan laughed as he unfurled the parchment to see the sender's name inked gracefully across the heading: *Mrs. Eludaine Cosmith.* Why, they'd done it—they had wed! Jon Cosmith, a bona fide married man. The thought struck Macmillan as inexplicably hilarious.

He began to read. *Dearest Mac*:

How we miss you! We constantly wonder how you are faring. How's business? Have you found someone trustworthy to manage our affairs?

She continued to inquire of his welfare, and that of their mines, before relaying the details of her and Jon's seaside matrimony in Heppestoni. Macmillan read on, sad to learn of the calamity that had befallen her hometown, though charmed by the quaintness of the wedding.

We leave for the Bainherd Plains soon, so please address our post to Pon Castle hereon. I wish I could tell you why, but Jon says I cannot put such information in a letter. (Jon is, in fact, extremely bossy with everything; he presently hovers over my shoulder, supervising every rune as I write. It is rather annoying.)

Good, now that he's gone, I can spill my heart in lamenting how I miss you more than I can bear. So please do hurry up over there, and sail back to us posthaste. We eagerly await your return, and continue to think on you daily.

Your loving sister,

Dainy

Smiling, Macmillan reread her letter, feeling warmer than he had in moons.

57

COSMITH

"I CANNOT BELIEVE WE MISSED your birthday, my lady! It says right here," Franz Diego brandished an old document: *"The Duchess of Jordinia, Eludaine Cecinda Ducelle, was born during the fifth waxing quarter moon of the seven hundred and forty-fifth year of the Ducelle Empire.* The nineteenth anniversary of which surpassed us just days ago!"

"Interesting." Dainy glanced up from her breakfast. "So that's my real birthdate."

"The fifth waxing quarter moon." Selu dug a spoon into her grapefruit, looking contemplative. "This is good luck. It means you were born to grow and gain, to build something that will endure past your lifetime."

"Come, Selu, *lunology* is just a heathen superstition," Bos chided her, poring through the morning's bulletins. "The practice is abhorred by the Eternal God."

Selu shrugged, taking another bite of grapefruit.

Maxos looked up, spotting Cosmith. "Good morning, Your Grace."

"Morning." Cosmith took a seat beside the Duchess. "Happy belated birthday, then." She grinned at him, and he petted her hand, regretting that all too soon, he'd no longer greet her warm smiles each day, at least for a time.

Maxos checked his pocket watch. "You'll be ready to leave soon as the carriage arrives, I trust?"

Cosmith nodded. After breakfast, he returned upstairs to secure his and Dainy's satchel in preparation for the journey to Bainherd. Though his back was to the doorway, he sensed her presence before she spoke.

"I saw a carriage heading up the hill. Is everything packed?"

"Aye."

She fingered the doorframe, her hair now at a beautiful shoulder length. "We're very fortunate that the King of Bainherd has expressed his willingness to receive us."

"He is the fortunate one," replied Cosmith.

Dainy's eyes radiated like the jade at her wrist, and she surprised him with a peck on the cheek. "*I* am the fortunate one."

Cosmith traced his thumb under her chin.

She swallowed. "I suppose this is the last journey we'll be making together. At least for some time—"

"Shh." He hushed her, dropping their satchel to run a hand along her flawless face. "No sad thoughts. We're off on another exciting adventure, no?"

"Mr. and Mrs. Cosmith," Franz's voice rang up the stairwell. "Your chariot awaits, my dears."

Dainy cleared her throat. "You have your materials?"

Cosmith nodded. Her eyelids dropped as he brought his mouth to the base of her neck and traced his lips up to hers, reveling in her mouth that tasted of nectarines, her hair smelling of sweet sunshine—

"Oy! Cosmith," Selu's irreverent call interrupted them. "Are you going to pay your driver, or shall I have to use my own gold?"

He rolled his eyes, retrieving the satchel, and Dainy grinned. Arm in arm, the pair descended the stairwell.

"Two carriages," his wife observed confusedly, looking out the front window as they reached the ground floor. Cosmith turned to Bos inquiringly.

"Seluna and I have no place at Pon Castle," explained the giant. "We depart for Jordinia today."

Dainy looked stunned. "Already?"

"Are you sure you know what you're doing?" Cosmith furrowed his brow. "Don't you need my help?"

Selu and Bos looked to one another. "We feel it safer for us all this way," the woman replied carefully. At first, Cosmith thought her to be insinuating distrust of him. But taking in the haunted shadow in her eyes, he realized that it wasn't him she distrusted, but herself.

"They have ways of making you talk in prison," she said, affirming his suspicions. "Best we not know your exact business, nor you ours. One cannot tell what one doesn't know." She shrugged.

"We'll be working toward the same goal," Bos assured them. "You three in Bainherd, Seluna in the capitol, and I in the north."

Cosmith's pulse quickened as he watched Dainy hug them goodbye. They were really doing it, then. The outlaws were infiltrating the country from which they'd been banned to round up conspirators for the Duchess's cause.

The five finally took to their separate carriages, Bos and Selu to one, Cosmith, Dainy and Maxos to the other. The advisor wasted no time in consulting his notes as they rolled down Franz's drive, briefing Cosmith yet again on their strategy with King Wilqen.

The discussion eventually subsided, and Maxos presently snoozed in his seat. Dainy stared out her window, and Cosmith gave her hand a squeeze. "Why so quiet, sparrow?"

"You think they'll be all right?"

He did not have to ask to know she meant Bos and Selu. For a moment, he chewed the inside of his cheek, before deciding to answer candidly. "I know not."

Dainy watched him. And then slowly, she nodded, as though thanking him for his honesty.

58

HOSTE

MARTEN HOSTE, LEADER OF THE New Republic of Jordinia, ran his fingers through his wiry white hair. The evening had been long, yet he was still in the office, meeting with his cabinet.

"The Knights' Forest is virtually ours, and Heppestoni will be child's play." Comrade Boaz brushed his quill across the map. "But what really intrigues me is Bainherd. The Wilqen dynasty shall soon be going the way of the Ducelles. Why stand idle while its citizens form their own republic, when we could be expanding ours?"

Hoste shrugged, examining his cuticles. "More mouths to feed, more aid to dole out…"

"More citizens to tax." Boaz grinned.

Hoste concealed his smirk.

"And the Häffstrom Guard are entirely inept," drawled Heywood. "Not to mention how they pride themselves on being *neutral*. They would do nothing to prevent us."

"Comrade, if I may," came Rew's musical voice,

and Hoste politely turned to the old man. "We could be well on our way to fulfilling Jothann von Sparx's vision to command all of West Halvea."

"And beyond," agreed Boaz. "Look at our progress in a mere sixteen years. There's nothing to stand in our way, nothing to stop our momentum." His turquoise eyes glinted. "We must seize the occasion."

Hoste shifted his eyes away. None of the men present that night had been informed about the Duchess's survival. Of course, she was only a girl. And she'd given him her word that she had no intention of starting any trouble. But it wasn't necessarily her that he worried about.

It was the people.

With few men, Jothann von Sparx had led the War of the Revolution, striking the monarchs during a rough bout of famine, and the New Republic was born in a relatively brief span of time. Yet, the majority of today's citizens had grown up under the Ducelles' reign, just as their ancestors before them. While they'd been collectively discontent about the famine, most were mortified when the royal family was put to death.

Marten Hoste would privately admit that von Sparx's leadership (before his untimely death) was rather a reign of terror. For over a decade, the warrior persecuted anyone with even the remotest royalist ties. But still, there remained many who revered the royal family. They had simply learned to keep silent. And Hoste had a distressing suspicion there were far more than Intelligence could ever round up.

Therefore, if word got out that a Ducelle still lived, he knew there could be an uprising. Yes, those persisting royalists would come crawling out of the woodwork, too many to bridle. They would worship the girl, demand her back on her throne, in her family's abandoned palaces.

Hoste was no fool. He knew the number of homeless and destitute among his citizenship was unprecedented. Intelligence reported to him the grumblings of the dissatisfied on a daily basis. And he was the one they blamed. Seizing wood from the Knights' Forest seemed his best tactic to revitalize the economy. But then, it was liable to cost him an expensive war with the rest of Halvea which, he was sure, would further remove him from the people's favor.

"Comrade Hoste?"

He blinked, realizing the members of his cabinet awaited his response to a question he'd not heard.

"It is rather late," admitted Rew. "Perhaps we ought to call it an evening, gentlemen."

Hoste rose to his feet, bidding them a good night. When the last had finally departed, he massaged his temples with a fatigued sigh. Perhaps he was too weary to think properly. But of course, a nineteen-year-old girl, regardless of her blood, would have no power to overthrow him. Who would follow her, a penniless orphan with nothing to offer? There was, after all, nothing left of her family's empire.

Shaking his head as if to clear it, the man donned his navy jacket and bowler hat and snuffed out the candles on the table. His guards awaited him in the hall with lanterns alit and, flanking him in perfect form, escorted him from Capitol Tower.

All would be well, Hoste assured himself. Indeed, the New Republic of Jordinia had nothing to fear.

Part 2

Revival

59

WILQEN

KING HORATIO WILQEN TRIED TO reserve judgment as his guards escorted the guests into his meeting room. "To His Majesty, King of the Bainherd Plains," announced the steward, "I present Misters Jonwal Harrington Cosmith, and Maxos Maxeos the Third."

The men bowed.

"Well." Wilqen leaned back in his chair, fiddling with the ruby on his middle finger as he took in the two strangers, with whom his scribes had been corresponding. "Here we are, face-to-face." He grinned, lifting a sandy eyebrow. "Judging by your most intriguing letters, gentlemen, I believe you've something rather significant to share. Let us do away with gratuitous preamble and get straight to business, shall we?"

The balding man, Maxeos, dutifully popped open a case.

"We've come on account of my wife, sir," began Cosmith, and Wilqen turned to him with interest. This was not the sort of introduction he'd expected, nor did the attractive fellow look the sort to be married. "She owns an expanse of col mines in the Tsongii Mountains of Asiotica. Are you familiar with col, Your Majesty?"

Wilqen stroked his chin. "Aye, I've read of the curious technology."

"It propels the future," proclaimed Cosmith, as Maxeos extracted a pamphlet of parchments. "As you can see," Cosmith indicated the pages, "the resource can be used in unlimited ways: to power steamships, mobilize wagons without livestock, and create heat and light for the household hearth, stove and lantern."

Wilqen examined the diagrams.

"The magnitude of untouched col on my wife's property is such that Bainherd and the Wilqen dynasty will greatly prosper, should you choose to pursue a contract with us."

Wilqen grunted. "So, that's what you want? An investment?" He brushed the diagrams aside. "Unfortunately, son—and it's no secret—my kingdom has accrued a bit of debt over the years. I haven't much left to invest in ventures like yours."

"All due respect," Cosmith gave a tiny bob of his head, "but we do not seek your wealth, sir. Rather, your alliance."

"Alliance?" Wilqen eyed him, bemused. "Of what sort?"

"One against the New Republic of Jordinia," supplied Maxeos. "You already intend to battle them over the Knights' Forest, do you not?"

"Who told you that?" the King demanded.

"Forgive us." The men bowed. "Only, it's implicit in the posts we've read abroad, regarding the infamous dispute."

Wilqen scowled, suspicious. "And what have the

pair of you against the New Republic?"

"A tremendous weapon," came Cosmith's indirect reply.

Maxeos cleared his throat. "Your Majesty, perhaps you've heard the rumors about the Duchess of Jordinia, Eludaine Ducelle?"

Wilqen gave a start. This conversation continued to take one unexpected turn after the next. "Just rumors, are they not?"

Cosmith shook his head deliberately from side to side, a grin spreading across his lips, as Maxeos extracted another leaf from his case. "We've witnesses in the Häffstrom Guard from the Omar Treasury who can attest that an eighteen-year-old woman opened a Ducelle Littemuse Lock with her own blood last summer. The signatures are here."

Astonished, the King examined the roster of autographs. "And you're sure it was Eludaine Ducelle?"

"One hundred percent," declared Cosmith.

"Sire," said Maxeos, "we desire to restore the young royal to her throne."

"By means of eliminating the New Republic," muttered Cosmith, shuffling through more papers.

Wilqen laughed, though not derisively. "Restore an empire? It has never been done before. Monarchies are not simply reestablished, gentlemen. And from what I understand, there's nothing left of the Ducelle Empire to speak of, anyway."

"Ah, but respectfully, sir, that is where you are incorrect." Cosmith passed him a new sheath of parchment, and the King glanced down to see none other than a likeness of the last Empress of Jordinia, Néandra Gatspierre Ducelle.

"This might help refresh your memory," said Cosmith. "As you'll see, there is no mistaking that the woman you're about to meet is her daughter."

Wilqen looked up. "*Meet?* You mean, she is *here?*"

"Waiting just outside this door," said Maxeos. "Shall we bring her in?" He looked to the guards.

Wilqen gaped between them. He then set the Empress's likeness down, his head spinning. "Just a moment." He massaged his brow. "You have failed to explain how your wife's col mines have anything to do with the Duchess of Jordinia, Mr. Cosmith."

"Ah." Cosmith smiled, clasping his hands together. "Your Majesty, the Duchess of Jordinia is my wife."

60

COSMITH

"TO BE CLEAR THEN, LORD Cosmith," Councilor Maccob arched a thick eyebrow, "you wish for us to enlist our soldiers in exchange for a portion of your wife's mines? You do realize it'll take more than just our army to overthrow the New Republic, assuming it can even be done?"

"The Jordinian people will demand it," insisted Cosmith, as a servant lit the last of the lanterns in the darkening window. "Once they learn of the resources she can provide, they'll revolt against their government. Only, they cannot do it alone. We need your troops to back them."

"You're asking us to wage war against Jordinia, my lord."

"Were you not already encroaching battle with them over the Knights' Forest?" countered Maxos.

"I think it's brilliant," interjected Councilor Bell. "Who needs the forest's wood when we could have col? Rather, we may redirect our efforts against the enemy themselves: the blasted Republic."

"Exactly." Cosmith looked to the King. "The New Republic's goal is to eventually govern all of West Halvea. Come, men, we know this was von Sparx's ultimate vision. Your kingdom is at risk. Yet, I offer the opportunity to vanquish all threats of your own subjects rebelling against you."

Maccob looked as though he were about to object, but Wilqen held up a ringed hand. "Go on," he entreated Cosmith. Bell's grin widened.

"To be blunt, this land is one rebellion short of becoming the New Republic of the Bainherd Plains. To dance politely around the matter does naught but insult us all." Cosmith took a draught of wine. "What we need is *revival*. For the Ducelles of Jordinia, and the Wilqens of Bainherd."

"Your Majesty," said Maxos, "if you help take down the Republic and reinstate Ducelle sovereignty, then so you assert your power. *The Republic is dead! Long live the Empire!* Think of the message you'd send to your people! Never again shall the sanctified institution of your monarchy be questioned."

"Not to mention," added Cosmith, "we will give you the wealth to back it up, and the resources to abolish the scarcity that has embittered your citizens against you in the first place."

Bell nodded vigorously.

"And likewise in Jordinia," continued Cosmith heatedly. "Col will revitalize the nation." He indicated the diagrams in the center of the table. "It'll lower taxes, create industry...my wife's inheritance can offer tremendous improvements to the Jordinian way of life that the New Republic simply cannot."

"It sounds like every bit of a win-win to me,"

shrugged the elderly MacParsons.

"Indeed it does, Elder." Wilqen sighed. "Which begs the question: what is the catch?"

"There is no catch." Bell smirked. "We cannot lose."

"And if we win?" inquired Wilqen. "How do we know Lord Cosmith here intends to uphold the Ducelle legacy, and will not simply become another tyrant? Let us not forget, the Duchess, whom he wishes to instate as Empress, is his wife. Thus, he seeks to enthrone himself beside her as Emperor. Do you not, Cosmith?"

The calculating gaze of the council fell upon him. "No, Your Majesty," Cosmith replied, making every effort to hide the offense in his tone. "I've only my wife's interests at heart."

"And yet, you are the one who's here," Wilqen pointed out, "appealing on her behalf."

"Forgive me." Cosmith inclined his head. "Due to the patriarchal customs of our land, I thought it only proper that I speak for her tonight."

"And will you not speak for her, then, were she to become Empress?" Wilqen was smirking now.

Cosmith met his copper eyes, and knew the only way to answer was honestly. "Of course." Dainy was, after all, a girl of nineteen springs. She'd need his guidance for a time, until her own experience awarded her the discretion to make political decisions on her own.

Wilqen cackled. "Ah, so *that's* it. I am onto you now." He grinned, and Cosmith gave an uneasy smile in return. "That's what this is really about. You married Eludaine Ducelle, acquired her wealth, and have come to enlist my help in overthrowing the New Republic, all so that you may be crowned Jordinia's Emperor."

Cosmith said nothing, his fingernails digging into his palms.

"A man of opportunity." Wilqen beamed. "Shrewd, ambitious. I like that." He stood to his feet, beckoning for him to do the same. Cosmith stood, his eyes never leaving Wilqen's.

The King encircled him. "Eloquent. Good-looking. Surprisingly savvy for one so young," he appraised him. "You wish to become a king, like me?" With a flourish of his hand, he gestured to his councilors, servants and guards in the chamber around them. "Assets to manage, masses to command...not to mention, all the women you desire." He chuckled. "It's all right, son. You can admit it."

Cosmith swallowed.

Wilqen swatted him on the back. "It only makes me like you more. In fact, I've half a mind to help you, if not only to see whether you can really do it." He addressed his men. "For I believe this man would make for a formidable emperor. And his is an allegiance I should like to have.

"Besides," the King added, settling back into his chair, and Cosmith resumed his seat as well, "if we don't take his tempting offer to prosper our lands and reinforce our monarchy, I've a feeling this cunning young duke will seek someone who will."

"A wise decision, sir, if you don't mind me saying," piped Maxos, dabbing a kerchief at his brow.

"Not at all," boomed Wilqen. "We shall meet with my General on the morrow then, to devise a stratagem. In the meantime," he grinned at Cosmith, "to the Revival."

61

DAINY

FAREWELL WAS NOT A TERM Dainy had ever associated with her husband, Jon. Since the two had first met, a year earlier, she'd not spent a single day apart from him. Yet, after a mere week at Pon Castle, he was already packing his satchel, preparing to leave for the risky mission up north.

"You don't have to do this," she told him for the dozenth time, resting her hand over the mouth of his bag.

"Stand aside, wife."

Dainy stepped away, allowing him to add his spare blouse and razorblade. "I shall worry for you every day." She sighed as he sheathed the sword at his belt. "Why must you do this to me?"

He looked up, his expression unreadable. Dainy couldn't bear the notion that she'd no longer behold that handsome face, nor fall under the gaze of those captivating brown eyes indefinitely.

"I am doing this *for* you." He fastened the bag with a note of finality. Despondent, she watched as he tossed his hair from his eyes and slid on his jacket, wishing she could find another way to tell him that she didn't want him to do this, had never asked him to do it for her.

He came to her at last, tucking her hair behind her ears. "Sometimes I forget how very young you are. But someday, Eludaine," he nodded, "you will thank me."

"Do not patronize me," she snapped.

Jon grinned. "Do not lose your spark, little fire-cracker," he whispered, honing in to kiss her. Dainy remained rigid, not kissing him back. He wasn't leaving. He couldn't be.

"There, there." He thumbed aside the tear she'd not realized she'd shed. "I shall think on you every moment. The memory of your angelic smile and the knowledge of your love shall be my constant companions."

"Please don't go." Perhaps if she begged, he would stay.

Alas, he made for the door. "Care to see me out?" he asked, eyes smiling. How could he possibly seem cheerful?

"How long until I see you again?" Dainy asked, following him down the stone hallway.

"You know I cannot answer that, love."

They reached the ground floor, where the rising sun cast a colorful kaleidoscope on the tapestried walls. Dainy's heart grieved. "I suppose this is where you leave me, then." She realized now more than ever that she didn't want an empire, a war. Why, everything she wanted stood right before her, preparing to walk out the door with the brightening dawn.

"I'll write, if I can," he promised, raising her hand

to his lips.

"You'll remain faithful to me up there, won't you?" asked Dainy, remembering all the occasions on which her husband had garnered the attention of other women, from Jano to Asiotica.

"What is this nonsense?" He took her into his arms, and Dainy clung to him. "You are my one and only; my empress. Never forget that." He gave her one last affectionate pinch on the arm before turning for the front doors, leaving his wife staring helplessly after him.

62

SELU

HER FIRST NIGHT BACK IN Pierma, and already someone had his hand in her trousers.

Selu gripped the pickpocket by the wrist and swiveled around to face him. In the black alleyway, she could just make out the young face blinking up at her. "Who in hell are you?" she demanded beneath her bandana, in the deepest rasp she could muster.

"Sorry," chirped the lad, backing away with a rather Cosmith-like grin.

"Not so fast, thief." She took in the youngster's curly hair, tattered clothing and sooty face under the waning moonlight. "You live out here on the streets, don't you?"

"What's it to you?" He yanked his hand away.

She let it go. "I'm looking for someone."

"Friend or foe?"

She pulled down her bandana. "Friend, of course."

The lad took in a breath. "You are female!"

Selu smiled. "I seek a woman called Betine Toustead."

"*You're* her daughter," the boy gasped. "Hey, haven't you been banished?"

"*Shh.*" Selu held a finger over her mouth. "You know her, then?"

"Of course." He blinked. "She's my street mum."

Selu appraised him with some sympathy. She well remembered the practice on the streets of Pierma to form familial-like bonds with fellow homeless. Of course, she and her mother always had each other. But those whose families had been killed by the New Republic, or else imprisoned, often forged connections with "street" parents or siblings to look after them.

"Carlo DiGyle." He held out a hand, grinning. "You must be Seluna."

She followed him through the winding lanes, keeping to the shadows as young Carlo scanned for food or coins on the grimy ground. They stepped over several sleeping men and bypassed a few destitute young women offering up their companionship for a fee, until Carlo led her up a desolate, rickety stairwell and entered what appeared to be an abandoned shop.

Stepping into the dingy parlor, Selu noticed a glowing fire. Huddled around it were ragged folks, who glanced up in greeting. "Where's Bet?" Carlo asked them.

Someone pointed down a hall. "Tending Clemsen. It appears he's sprained his ankle."

While Selu was sorry that someone had been injured, she appreciated that her mother was putting her skills to good use. Before the Revolution, Betine Toustead had been a nurse.

"Just keep off it a few days, there's a good lad," Selu heard her mother clucking as she followed Carlo into the kitchen. Bet glanced up from her patient. "Seluna!"

"Hello, Mother."

"Montimor said you left." The woman lowered her voice. "He's stopped sending me funds. I knew not where to find you…"

"May we speak in private?" Selu glanced covertly at Clemsen and Carlo.

Bet rose and guided her daughter down yet another dark hallway. "What is this place?" Selu asked, peering around at the old brick walls.

"Abandoned baker's apartment." Her mother steered her into the bedroom. "And the bakery's down below. 'Tis one of the best-kept secrets in Pogue District. We've been squatting here for moons, ever since the last shop on the strip closed. No one can afford to stay in business any longer."

Alone with her mother, Selu cleared her throat. "You've a street son," she remarked.

Bet nodded. "Aye. He had a street brother once, but the man up and disappeared on him, 'bout a year ago. I've been looking after him since." She shrugged. "What choice had I? He's only just come of age."

Selu nodded, empathetic.

"But I s'pose you did not wish to convene in private just to talk about Carlo?"

"Indeed, no." Selu met her mother's violet eyes with her own identical pair. "I've come to tell to you the reason I've been banished from Jordinia."

Bet's eyes shifted. "Do I truly wish to know this, daughter?"

"Trust me, everyone must know. I take it you've heard the rumors by now, about Eludaine Ducelle?" Bet gasped at the name, but Selu ignored her. "They're true, Mother."

The older woman raised a hand to her mouth.

"That is where I'd gone last spring. To participate in the quest to find her. And we did." Selu's voice deepened with excitement. "We found her."

"No," whispered Bet.

"Aye. And she intends to restore her father's empire."

Her mother let out a long breath. "This is outrageous, Seluna. Do you realize the danger in which you've placed yourself? If you had any sense, you'd flee Jordinia tonight and stay put elsewhere, before your knowledge gets you killed—or worse."

"The time for fleeing is behind me," declared Selu. "I'm going to help the girl. She has resources—"

Bet shook her head, fearful.

"What've we to lose?"

Her mother's face was pallid. "You're going to get yourself hanged."

"Mother," Selu implored her. "I know you're still a royalist! And I'd be willing to wager everyone in this apartment is!"

"What is it you want from your old mum, then?" Bet demanded.

"I want you to spread the word to your friends, and help me gather support for the Duchess. I wish to form a coup."

"Selu." Bet took her daughter's face between her hands. "You are talking treason."

"Dear woman," replied Selu, placing her hands over her mother's. "I am talking *revival*."

63

Bos

BOS HAD ALL BUT FORGOTTEN the comfort of home. The familiar stone streets lined with wooden cottages held the echoes of his youth, while the pines and evergreens welcomed him back like old friends. But his first destination was the place he'd missed the greatest, where he'd most longed to return.

With a surreptitious glance over his broad shoulders, Bos tucked his massive form into the narrow passage concealed behind the apothecary, and felt for the hidden stairwell. Once his large boot distinguished the first step, he descended into the earth, beneath the quiet street.

At the base of the stairs, he heaved open the old, unassuming door with relative ease. Nostalgia washed over him as a heady draft of incense flooded his nostrils. Any remnants of sunlight were muted with a careful closing of the door, and the sanctuary was enshrouded in solemn silence.

Bos came up to the sacred candles burning at the altar. After tracing a wide circle over his brow, the giant knelt onto his substantial knees, bowing his head in prayer. Detecting movement, however, he looked up in time to see a black-robed priest emerging from the sacristy. The man gave a start as his eyes widened behind gilded spectacles. "Boslon Visigoth?"

Bos rose to full height. "Father Asa."

"So good to see you," the priest whispered, embracing him. "I thought they might've taken you away."

"Not yet," rumbled Bos. "Although nothing about my presence here in Dekantor is exactly legal."

"Nor is mine," muttered Asa, and both men chortled, their sniggers echoing off the cavernous walls.

Bos glanced about at the makeshift pews. "Have you still many parishioners?"

The old priest shrugged. "Some brave souls still risk everything to venture down here and worship the Eternal God. Not many. But not too few, either." He craned his head to meet Bos's eyes. "You've been gone some time, Bos."

"I've been banished."

Father Asa looked mildly surprised, but remained silent. After all, as a priest of the cult of the Eternal God, the holy man was forbidden from Jordinia as well. But that didn't keep him from remaining concealed, administrating an unlawful underground chapel.

Bos dropped his voice even though, apart from them, the sanctuary was empty. "The winds of change are about to blow over this nation. And I intend to add my breath to them."

Asa lifted his silver eyebrows. "This isn't about the Ducelle girl, is it?"

Bos was taken aback. "But how did you know?"

The priest smiled. "Rumor has it, the Duchess of

Jordinia lives, and has been sighted abroad in the company of an immensely tall man."

Bos broke into a grin of his own. "The rumors are true."

Asa brought his hands together. "*O Almighty Eternal God,*" he incanted. "*Thy plan is unfolding. Our gratitude is Thine.*"

"Father," Bos whispered. "I am wondering whether your parishioners might be willing to help in my cause to restore the girl's throne."

The priest looked up, his thinning mouth agape. He then glanced about the chapel, shrugging once more. "I suppose we are already defying the New Republic," he admitted. "What more have we to lose?"

64

COSMITH

HOME WAS JUST AS BAD as Cosmith remembered, if not worse. The streets of Pierma were filthier than the people (which was saying something), and even more shops had closed since he'd left. Deliberately, the man paced the city, trying his best to avoid notice, all the while scanning passersby for familiar faces.

He spent the night alone at a rundown inn, although he promptly abandoned his mat for the floor when he discovered the hay to be crawling with large beetles. He hardly slept that night for the stifling air, his mind anxious and hands restless. It took him some time to realize it was Dainy he missed, her warm form beside him, her steady breaths lulling him to slumber.

The following days came and went uneventfully, and Cosmith wondered whether he was losing his touch. Surely, during his career in Intelligence, he'd managed to gather information far more adeptly. Yet, he was unfocused now, restive and uncharacteristically nervous.

Another evening descended upon him, and he

could keep neither his mind nor his feet still. Despite the fact that Wilqen's Guard had pledged to protect Dainy in his absence—not to mention, it would've been unthinkable to have brought her with him—Cosmith couldn't suppress his constant worry for her.

He was approaching Pogue District when, at long last, he spotted someone he recognized. The silhouette of curly hair and the childishly clumsy yet charming gait gave the boy away. "*Carlo.*" He took a step from the deserted alley in which he'd been lingering.

The lad turned. The moment Carlo DiGyle spotted him, a tremendous grin spread across his youthful features. "I'll be damned. Jonny-boy!"

Cosmith glanced around. "Keep your voice down, kid."

"It's quite all right. Pogue District is virtually abandoned, but for us homeless." Carlo looked him up and down with an air of insolent amusement. "Where in hell have you been?"

"Later," muttered Cosmith. But he took in the boy's hopeful grin and tattered clothing, and pulled him into a gruff embrace. "How are you?" he asked, apprehensive. "Did you—did you manage all right without me?"

Carlo snorted. "As if I cannot take care of myself, Cosmith. You know I've just come of age?"

"Congratulations," said Cosmith flatly, eyeing the boy's emaciated stomach beneath his ratty tunic. He felt another pang of guilt. "How many meals a day are you getting?"

"I'm fine," contended Carlo. "I've a street mum who looks after me now. Ever since my street brother up and ran out on me…" He feigned a pout.

Cosmith sighed, making his way out of the alley. "I'd told you I was leaving."

"But you still never said where."

"*Later,*" repeated Cosmith. "In the meantime, please let me buy you a meal. All right?"

"And a pint?"

Cosmith gave him a sideways glance. "Sure."

"Fifth Street Tavern it is, then."

Cosmith walked alongside him for several blocks, barely listening as Carlo prattled on about girls and food and close encounters with the authorities. The lad had matured some since Cosmith last saw him—over a year ago, now—but was still grossly malnourished.

That was Cosmith's fault.

It had happened seven years ago, when he'd overheard a man in a pub calling Jothann von Sparx a "sadistic pig." Cosmith had promptly reported the remark, and the fellow was sent to jail without a trial. Little had Cosmith known, however, the man he'd imprisoned had a young son, whose mother was dead from the fever epidemic. With his father suddenly imprisoned, young Carlo's future was condemned to homelessness.

Cosmith knew what it was to be a youth on the streets of the capitol, starving, shivering… He'd had to learn how to steal, to be resourceful. He never had a mentor. Perhaps if he had, things might not have been so difficult.

And so, he'd seen it his duty to look after the boy. He would visit him regularly, bring him food and clothing, teach him skills… Carlo never knew that Cosmith worked for Intelligence, or that he was the agent who'd jailed his father. To the boy, Cosmith was simply his "street brother." And that he had remained, until he'd departed the city to participate in Hessian Gatspierre's quest.

At present, they approached the tavern on Fifth Street, where the stench of pipe smoke and liquor assaulted them. The hovel was noisy and crowded with people in various stages of drunkenness, engaging in all manner of card games, senseless debates and shallow flirtations.

"Order whatever you want," Cosmith told his companion, stealing a stool at the bar. He rested his face in his hands, his stomach roiling. He had no appetite; the place was disgusting.

Carlo settled down beside him. "Two pints," he told the waitress. "And serve me whatever dinner you have on special," he called at her retreating back.

When the drinks and a platter of roast chicken were served, Cosmith frowned, watching the ravenous boy devour his dish and lick the juices clean from the plate. "You may order another," Cosmith told him, taking a sip of ale. He promptly gagged on it. It tasted like bathwater.

"Cheers, mate," beamed Carlo, just as Cosmith felt a most startling grip at his shoulder.

A lithe hand slid suggestively down his forearm and back up again, proceeding to stroke his hair. "My, my. Jonny *darling*," a seductive voice breathed at his neck. "It's been quite a while since I last saw you around here."

He shuddered uncomfortably as the woman pressed her lips too near his ear, her heavy blonde hair falling unwelcomely into his face. "My husband is out of town again. Fancy another go?"

His skin crawled. "No thank you, comrade."

She shrugged, returning to her full height. "No matter," she drawled, tossing back her hair. "You are probably not as a good as I remember."

"And fortunately, I do not remember you at all," replied Cosmith smoothly, taking another sip of watery ale. This earned him a vicious slap from the woman, and several onlookers chortled as she sauntered away.

"That cannot possibly be Jon Cosmith I hear?" came a new voice, and Cosmith groaned as a second woman stomped over. "Well, well," she greeted him crossly, hands upon her broad hips.

He looked into his glass. "Hello, Shoshanna…"

He braced himself as she flung back her wrist and walloped him in the face. "That was for me." She struck him again, black eyes flashing. "And that was for my sister!"

She stalked away, leaving Cosmith to massage his cheek, while the group behind them laughed openly at him. "S'pose I deserved that," he muttered.

Carlo gawked at him. "What is this?" He pounded Cosmith on the back as the waitress returned with a second platter. "Why did you decline Mrs. Stokes? And why aren't you on your feet, sweet-talking yourself back into Shoshanna's good graces?" His eyes glinted mischievously. "This is most unlike you, Jonny-boy."

Cosmith clenched his jaw.

"Ah, but I know what this is all about." The young man gasped. "There's another woman, isn't there?"

"Hush."

"There is!" Carlo laughed in disbelief. "My God, Jonny, you are in love! I can see it in your eyes. Who is she?" he demanded. "Have I met her?"

Cosmith sighed. "Nay, you've not met her."

"Ha! You admit it!" Carlo slammed down his fork with a resounding clang. "I do not believe this. Jon Cosmith, gone soft!"

"Shut it, Carlo…"

"Who's the lucky girl then, Jon?" asked the red-headed barmaid bitterly, scrubbing the bar with needless vigor. "I thought you said you would never commit."

Cosmith blinked up at her. "Sorry, but do I know you?"

She huffed, flinging her washrag down, and stormed into the backroom.

He finally rose and plunked a handful of silver coins beside Carlo. "Eat until you are full," he told him. "When you've finished, I should like to speak with you elsewhere." He glanced around, uneasy. "Apparently, I have trifled with every woman in this place."

Carlo laughed. "It'll be much the same at any other tavern in Pierma, comrade. '*Ladies, ladies,*'" he imitated his friend, outstretching his arms gregariously. "'*There's plenty of me to go around…*'"

Cosmith cringed. Had he really said that? What sort of scum had he once been? Disgusted, he went outside to wait. His stomach curdled to imagine what Dainy would think of him, had she been there. He felt both very grateful and quite guilty that she was not.

After a time, Carlo emerged, holding his stomach. "I think I overate," he moaned.

"Let's walk it off, then." They turned down an empty lane beneath the sallow moon, Cosmith slowing his steps in time with Carlo's.

"This gal's really gotten to you, Jon. I can tell."

"What do you know of it?" Cosmith grunted.

They headed up another block. "Will you not say who she is?"

"Eventually, perhaps," replied Cosmith vaguely, realizing that the boy was leading him back to Pogue District. "But for now, I should like to inquire of your father."

"What about him?" The young man frowned. "I've not seen him since he was locked up. You know that."

Cosmith eyed him furtively. "Do you never visit him?"

"Why would I? The man is an unabashed royalist. Can't be seen calling upon him now, can I?" Carlo snorted. "Unless I want to join him behind bars."

Cosmith followed him down a quiet strip of abandoned shops. "Carlo." He halted at last. "There's something I must say." He took a breath, looking around. The street was eerily empty, darkness creeping at them from every angle. "I am a royalist," he confessed, as Carlo emitted a sharp hiss.

"*Good God*, Jon." The boy grabbed his arm, dragging him into a shadowy pocket behind a forsaken milliner. "After all this time, you tell me this now?" He glanced about, no doubt ensuring they weren't being overheard. "Is *that* why you've always sought to look after me?"

Cosmith swallowed. No, that was not why. But it made for a rather useful alibi. "Yes," he lied, meeting the boy's eyes squarely. "And now I must know if your father kept any friends like me. Royalists," he clarified, "who've avoided arrest."

"But *why*, Jon? Your cause is dead, the empire gone. Why remain loyal to the royal family?" Carlo shook his head, incredulous. "It'll only get you killed!"

"Listen to me," Cosmith breathed. "Eludaine Ducelle is *alive*."

They boy's face blanched under the misty moonlight. "The rumors are true?"

Cosmith nodded. "And she's going to recapture Jordinia, and revive the nation. Only she needs the help of people like us, and anyone your father might know, who'd be willing to back her."

"But how do you know all this?"

"I've met her," said Cosmith. "That is where I've been all this time. D'you recall Hessian Gatspierre's crazy duchess quest?"

The boy stared at him.

"I won it."

65

DAINY

DAINY HAD TO ADMIT, SHE'D never been treated better. To the royal family and staff at Pon Castle, she was still a princess, regardless of being stripped of her title. As such, she was given her own private quarters, with maids who insisted on helping her wash and dress; chefs to prepare her meals, which she took in the dining hall with the Wilqens themselves; and other staff who ensured she lifted not a finger in her own mending or tidying. Needless to say, she was most unaccustomed to it.

King Horatio Wilqen was a rather busy man, despite Bainherd's decline in wealth (and admittedly, significance), so Dainy did not see much of him. But his wife, Queen Tara, and their children served as most delightful companions.

There were three royal children in all, each with fine, gossamer hair so blond it was nearly white, like their mother's. The eldest was Lady Eponina, who had recently celebrated her fifteenth birthday, followed by the Crown Prince, Lysander, at age eleven. Last was wee Blanchette, the youngest princess at six years old. While each was courteous to Dainy, it was Eponina who tailed her everywhere she went.

"Is it warm in Heppestoni? Do you miss it there? Are you going to acquire Heppestoni for Jordinia when you become empress? Have you actually *eaten* a shellfish?" the keen girl wanted to know.

Dainy laughed. "Surely, I appreciate your passion for knowledge, my lady. But I can only answer one question at a time!"

"Sorry." Eponina's youthful face flushed. "It's just so exciting to speak with the future Empress of Jordinia!" She sighed, digging her suede heels in the dirt. "If only I could become an empress like you someday. I'm quite savvy with politics and figures, you know," she declared proudly. Yet, her fair features fell. "Alas, Lysander says I shall end up married off to some trumped-up prince in a faraway land, who shall neither permit me to speak my mind nor make use of my skills."

Dainy gave her a sidelong glance. "Would that you could take my place," she confessed. "For you are far better at this royalty business than I."

Eponina laughed. "You are funny, Lady Eludaine."

Dainy's smile did not reach her eyes. She wasn't jesting.

After their walk, Dainy retreated to lie down in her chamber. She awoke with a cramp, however, and was dismayed to find her thighs sticky. The young woman heaved a deflated sigh, thrusting her raven head back into the pillows. Her blood of the moon had come yet again.

She knew that she and Jon had not been expressly trying to conceive. But as the man had ceased withdrawing from her during lovemaking ever since exchanging their marriage vows, Dainy had been secretly hoping that perhaps he'd left some part of himself within her, that she was carrying his son in his absence. Alas…

Was there something wrong with her? She began to wonder. Was her womb closed up? Was she unable to bear children for her husband? The idea devastated her.

A knock at the door interrupted her worries. "My lady?" It was her handmaid, Sheila.

Dainy sat up, pulling the sheets to her waist. "Is it dinnertime already?" It didn't seem so late.

"Not quite yet. But a letter for you has just arrived."

Dainy's heart thrummed. A letter? Could it be from Jon? "Please enter."

The door slid open. Dainy reached forward to receive a scroll from her maid, and curiously unfurled it, skimming over the runes. Her spirits brightened. It wasn't from Jon, but from someone equally special.

"*Mac.*" She beamed up at Sheila. "My brother has fulfilled his business abroad, and is returning to West Halvea."

Sheila looked up, startled. "Your brother, my lady?"

"MY FATHER SIRED A SON out of wedlock," Dainy explained delicately. Perhaps it was not the most appropriate dinner conversation, but King Wilqen had asked, and so she was obligated to answer.

"Ah." The man sighed. "These things tend to happen." He cast a furtive glance at his wife, Tara, and Dainy suspected the King sired a few illegitimates of his own.

"He is very dear to me," she went on, slicing her mutton. "And I intend to instate him as Duke of Jordinia when I am Empress."

"How diplomatic of you," said the Queen serenely, pearly eyes placid as moonlight. "But illegitimate children cannot inherit a duchy."

"The future empress can do as she pleases," snapped the King, waving a forkful of carrots in his wife's face. He shoved the utensil into his mouth. "Besides, Jordinia's nobles are gone, anyway. She's got to rebuild her courts somehow."

The Queen merely imbibed a sip of tea, as the children looked curiously between their parents.

Wilqen tore off an enormous bite of mutton. "Well, then. Your brother shall stay here with us when he arrives."

Dainy's head jerked up. "Truly, sir?"

"Of course." He took a hearty draught of wine, even as he ground the sheep's meat between his teeth. "Any son of Dane Ducelle's is a friend of mine."

66

SELU

"*MOVE OVER, THIS AIN'T A damned atrium.*"

"The fire needs more kindling."

"Has anyone seen Sofie?"

"Quiet, all of you," barked Cosmith, his face indiscernible beneath his hat as he pushed through the gathering. "If you continue making such a racket, you're going to get us all hanged."

"He's been so pleasant since his return." Carlo winked at Selu.

The violet-haired woman rolled her eyes. Ever since she'd come to stay with them in Pogue District, the boy had not ceased in his constant advances towards her, regardless of her age and the bracelet she wore. Selu believed him wholeheartedly when he claimed that Jon Cosmith had taught him everything he knew.

Bet bustled into the room, clapping her hands. "All right, everyone, listen up," she called over the din. "My daughter has something to say."

"*Me?* I thought Jon was doing the talking." Selu indicated the hatted man who peered through the windows to ensure their privacy.

Bet shrugged.

Selu turned to the numerous faces staring at her. A wave of silence washed over the crowd of three to four dozen people, and someone shushed a pair of chattering men in back. She swallowed, her back warm against the hearth.

"Er... My name is Selu," she began uncertainly. "I'm here tonight because my father, Ignatius Toustead, was a member of the Emperor's Guard, slain in battle. Likewise," she inclined her head, "each of you is here because you, or someone you love, has had some connection to the royal family."

Somebody coughed.

"I was twelve," she continued as all eyes, even Cosmith's, were upon her. "First came many moons on the streets, until my mother and I were thrown into prison for my father's occupation. I need not tell you what the rebels did to their female prisoners, young and old."

Her audience frowned, and one middle-aged woman nodded grimly.

"Then, when Hoste finally permitted us leave, we'd no place to go. For who would hire or lease to us, or have any business to do with us whatever, the wife and daughter of a royal guard?" Her voice rose as the gathering looked her over with mounting sympathy. "Likewise, who will hire you, or lease to you? Are you not homeless for whatever your former royalist ties?"

One man in a fraying tunic stepped forth. "My father fought on the Ducelles' side during the Revolution. The New Republic tortured him, and starved my mother to death. My home has since been the streets of Tremblay District."

An older couple raised their hands to be seen. "My sister was tutor to the Crown Duke, Hegren Ducelle, before his death," proclaimed the wife. "Her head was found, but her body..." her voice faded, and Selu felt fairly sure she was crying.

To her surprise, Carlo stepped up, blond curls glowing against the firelight. "My Pa was jailed for making one stupid comment about Jothann von Sparx. Some Intelligence filth overheard him and reported it." He spat onto the floor. "Pa remains in prison to this day. As a result, I have grown up orphaned."

At Carlo's mention of Intelligence, Selu shot a discreet glance at Cosmith. The man remained stony, his hat concealing his expression.

More attendees came forward to share their stories, and soon women were weeping, men cursing the New Republic, and Cosmith had to issue a shrill whistle to silence them. He cocked his hatted head in Selu's direction.

With the eyes of the heated congregation back upon her, Selu wasted no time. "What if I told you things could be different? That you could return to your homes, your professions, your lives as they once were?"

A woman furrowed her brow. Nobody looked convinced.

"What if I told you that your royalist ties could not only be accepted, but favored—rewarded, even?" She stole a quick glance at her mother, who was biting her lip, although watching her somewhat proudly. "What if Jordinia could prosper once more?"

The man in the tunic looked skeptical. "What are you peddling then, Comrade Selu?"

"A brighter future."

But to Selu's surprise, her mother intervened. "There will be no use of that unwelcome title here, sir. None us are *comrades* of the New Republic after all, are we?" She looked around, as if challenging someone to argue.

"If I may," interjected Cosmith, removing his hat, and Selu eagerly stepped aside. "The Duchess of Jordinia is alive."

At this bald proclamation, an eruption of chatter spilled through the room.

"But how do you know?"

"That's just a fairy tale."

"You lie," said the man in the tunic.

"Easy," snapped Carlo. "I've known Jon Cosmith since I was a boy. He is many things, but a liar isn't one of them."

Selu cast another furtive glance at Cosmith. Clearly, Carlo didn't know his "street brother" as well as he thought.

"We've no reason to risk our necks lying to you all about this," said Cosmith over the murmuring. "You can believe us, join our ranks in support of the girl, and help her revive Jordinia; or you can go on with your miserable lives, and continue permitting the Republic to beat you and your families into the ground. The choice is yours."

An older man in back removed his beret. "But how can the Duchess—if she truly lives—revive Jordinia?"

"This one's all you, Cosmith," Selu muttered.

"Ladies and gentlemen," Cosmith flourished his hat in the air. "Is anyone here familiar with *col*?"

67

BOS

"*COL?*"

Father Asa nodded at Bos, who felt somewhat sacrilegious standing at the pulpit. But far more men showed up that night than expected, and the priest insisted Bos address them from the front.

"To be clear," piped Tuck Henn, one of Bos's neighbors, "it can replace firewood?"

Bos nodded at the villagers crammed in the pews, as a fellow in back ejected, "We could avoid the whole forest dispute with the Bainherd Plains!"

Bos pointed to him. "Precisely. Listen to the lad. Who wants a war with Bainherd that we cannot afford? Rather, let Bainherd fight with us, *for* us, to reclaim the nation we once knew and loved."

"Mr. Visigoth." The butcher's wife clung to her husband's meaty arm. "Pray tell, what's she like? The little Duchess who survived?"

Bos pondered how best to describe the young woman who had become something like kin to him over the past many moons. "She is kindhearted," he answered, and his audience collectively leaned forward. "In appearance, she's the very likeness of her mother, though with the Emperor's spirit of fire." He nodded, smiling to himself. "But above all, she is among the most compassionate and loyal souls I've ever met."

"Brethren." Father Asa stepped forth. "The ways of the Eternal God are often not our own. But now and again," his silvery eyes shone behind his spectacles, "we may but catch a glimpse of His master plan."

Bos took in the earnest faces of his hometown neighbors, with whom he'd been acquainted since childhood. Would he truly ask them to risk their lives? Then again, were they not already doing so?

The holy man spoke again. "It can only be the will of God that the girl survived her family's execution. And as is professed in our Tradition," he glanced at the sacred candles flickering upon the altar, "every king and queen, emperor and empress has been ordained by the Eternal God Himself."

Tuck Henn rose to his feet. "Then what would God have us do, Father?" he inquired, as a hiss of whispers erupted through the tiny chapel.

68

COSMITH

COSMITH ASKED THE GUESTS TO stagger their departures, in order to avoid suspicion. When the last of them had finally dispersed and the baker's apartment was left to its usual squatters, he went into the kitchen. "Is there anything to eat?" he grumbled at no one in particular, flinging open an empty cabinet. "Or must I go and purchase victuals for you all again?"

Selu's voice startled him from behind. "There are still some plums in the icebox."

"To bed with you already, Carlo!" Bet Toustead called, as the lad traipsed over and wrapped a long arm around Selu. She sighed, shoving him off.

"You heard your mother, love," Carlo purred. "It's off to bed with us."

"*Ugh.*" Selu grimaced. "As if I would ever."

"Leave off her," Cosmith told him sternly. "She's taken."

Looking amused, Carlo pointed between Cosmith and Selu, but they hurriedly shook their heads. The lad only smirked.

"Heed my mother, DiGyle," barked Selu. "Go to sleep."

He sidled up to her. "Only if you kiss me good-night first."

Cosmith massaged his brow. What sort of terrible influence had he had on the child?

"Nice work with this one, Cosmith," snapped Selu, her thoughts apparently mirroring his own. "Were you always this big of a jerk, or only when showing the ropes to Carlo?"

Cosmith turned away. It was bad enough he'd imprisoned the boy's father, but now he could see he'd imprinted his own rogue mannerisms onto the youth himself.

For the sake of busying his hands, he knelt down and dug into the cobwebby icebox. There were indeed several plums left, and he slowly ate one, avoiding the others who bade each other goodnight and retreated to their various rooms.

After he'd finished eating, he found Selu still watching him. Carlo had finally gone elsewhere, and Cosmith was alone with the woman. He could tell from her tense stance and the asking look in her eyes that some sort of confrontation was forthcoming, although regarding what, Cosmith could not surmise.

She dropped her voice. "Some 'Intelligence filth' ratted out Carlo's royalist father, eh?"

His stomach dropped.

The shrewd woman continued. "I wonder if that same agent might've felt rather sorry afterwards, putting a little boy out on the streets like that. Perhaps for this reason, he might've adopted the kid as his 'street brother'?"

Cosmith made to push past her, but she blocked his way, despite her meager frame. "But if that were the case between you and Carlo, you'd have come clean by now," she whispered. "After all, he insists that Jon Cosmith is no liar." Her glare was accusing.

"Goodnight, Selu."

She finally let him pass. But Cosmith could feel her eyes on his back as he did.

69

Bos

"TO LOWER TAXES!"

"To industry!"

"*Long live the Ducelle Revival!*"

The pub owner stamped his way over to Bos and his companions, and clasped Tuck Henn's shoulder. "Comrades." He looked more frightened than angry. "I was as conservative a royalist as any northerner back in the day. But you boys better cease this ruckus before you get my pub shut down, and all of us thrown behind bars."

"We tell the truth, Silas," Bos contended.

The owner glanced up at him. "Then tell it elsewhere." He jabbed a thumb at the door. "I've a wife and four children to feed."

Bos, Tuck and the others from Father Asa's parish had no choice but to leave as requested. They were pleased, however, to find a handful of fascinated patrons following them out.

70

COSMITH

"BE CAREFUL."

"Relax, Selu." Carlo grinned. "Jonny can hold his own."

"You're going to get yourself killed."

"What is *she* doing here?" Cosmith indicated the familiar brown-haired, broad-hipped woman who'd just spoken, and was joining them at the Square.

"I'm sorry." Selu frowned. "Have you met Shoshanna?"

Shoshanna smirked. "I suppose you could call it that," she muttered, strutting back to the gathering crowd.

"Great." Cosmith glared at Selu. "The woman hates me. She's probably here to turn me in."

Selu held out her hands. "How was I to know who she was? She overheard me recruiting at Fifth Street and volunteered to come today, of her own accord."

Cosmith only shook his head. Just what he needed, and now of all times: a shrew he'd scorned, come back to haunt him, if not outright punish him for his transgressions.

Selu lowered her voice. "She says her aunt was hanged for circling her brow and praying in Old Jordinian over a meal at a dining hall."

"Yes, I know," replied Cosmith, before he had the sense to stop himself. He immediately winced, covering his mouth, though not before Selu's eyes went round with shock. The man looked away, trying to avoid the now livid woman glowering at him.

"Let me see if I cannot piece *this* one together," she hissed. "You had a woman hanged, then used the occasion to take advantage of her mourning *niece*?"

Both nieces, in fact—as Shoshanna had previously made sure to remind him of her sister, Savanah… But Cosmith was not about to share this with Selu. "I never claimed to be perfect," he mumbled, evading her eyes.

"You predator," she breathed. "Sometimes I forget how disgusting you really are. For Dainy's sake, I pray for your atonement."

It was as though the breath had been struck from him. Did Selu not realize that he was tormented by his own mistakes, that no one regretted his past more than he? And as if he needed yet another reminder of how wretched he'd been, and how undeserving he was of the clement, regal Eludaine Ducelle for his bride.

"Cosmith." Someone nudged him. "They're waiting for you." He was promptly handed a tarnished speaking trumpet. Inhaling, he took one last glance around Capitol Square.

Permitting himself no other thoughts, Cosmith leapt onto the ledge of the posting wall, raising the trumpet to his mouth. "*You are being lied to,*" he called out, and was startled by the amplification of his voice.

He waited as the eyes of his friends and passersby alike rested in his direction, their voices dropping or else falling silent to hear him.

"You are being swindled, exploited." He looked around significantly. "Each and every one of you." He pointed to a middle-aged man emerging from around a corner. "You, sir, are being robbed this very moment. And you, ma'am." He caught a young mother off her guard as she pushed a pram up the sidewalk. "Is that your son?"

She nodded.

"Would you like me to tell his future?" He took a step toward the swelling crowd, squinting as though extracting a vision. "I foresee he shall grow up hungry, just as you and your husband are, no? How many meals a day is your family down to now? Two? One?"

The mother shuffled her heels.

"The cost of food is only rising," Cosmith lamented. "As is the cost of wood. What are you to do? Take up a job yourself?" He shrugged. "Good luck finding work." He addressed the growing gathering. "Aye, all your sons will meet an equally dim fate." His heart thumped. Exactly how much time did he have before he was asked—forced—to desist?

"But it doesn't have to be this way." He paced the ledge. "We can rise against those who exploit and deceive us, who rob and starve our families. Because they were never meant to be in power in the first place. It is not their right.

"The famine was not your enemy," he declared, tearing down a random posting from the wall for effect. "The economy is not your enemy," he added, ripping off another. "Rather," said Cosmith, pointing over his shoulder at the stony Capitol Tower behind him, "*they* are your enemy. The New Republic!"

His newest onlookers gasped. The mother pushed her pram away, hastily retreating up the street.

"They tax you at fifty percent," Cosmith went on, noticing that, for every person hurrying away, several more approached to hear him. "Yet, look at our cities." He threw up his free hand, indicating the grimy, crackling streets, the boarded-up buildings in disrepair. "With half of every citizen's income, one would think our government possesses the means to clean this place up, support our businesses and feed our children, no?"

He took heart in his enraptured listeners, their furrowed brows and convicted nods. "Indeed, that's what the New Republic *claims* to be doing with the taxes they force from you, year after bloodsucking year. But it's clear, my friends, that they are not. Yet, the coin has to be going somewhere. Can you guess who's pocketing your hard-earned wages? *Are you going to stand for this?*"

Silence.

At first, he feared he'd garner no response, that his speech had been thus far ineffective. But to his utter relief, it was Selu, Bet, Carlo and surprisingly Shoshanna who stepped forward together, insisting, "*Nay.*"

After a cautious pause, a few more dared add their own protests.

Cosmith scanned the crowd for any sign of authorities. Miraculously, there were still none. He had to go on. He had to make use of every moment he could to convince the crowd, to start the conversation in Pierma, before he was made to stop.

"Are you going to work your arses off, only to

see your children starve, while those greedy crooks—"
he pointed again at the Tower—"dine on delicacies by
your coin?"

"Nay," came more voices.

"Are you going to watch your families shiver from
cold this winter, because your government fails to provide you basic firewood, without accruing some costly
war for which *you* shall be made to pay?"

"Nay," replied the crowd at large, and Cosmith's
heartbeat skipped.

"Is this the great Jordinia of our parents and grand-
parents? The fair, prosperous country we all knew and
adored?"

"*Nay!*" boomed the most resounding call of all, as
boots stomped and fists were raised.

"Nay, indeed," agreed Cosmith, chest heaving as
he jabbed a finger in the direction of Capitol Tower yet
again. "Because they should not be in power. After sixteen years, the New Republic has proven to be pretty
damned incompetent, wouldn't you say?"

His friends cheered with enthusiasm, while others in his ever-expanding circle covered their mouths
in shock.

Cosmith waited, staring back at them, building
their anticipation with his silence. "You've heard the
rumors by now, I trust," he finally continued. "Have
you not? The Duchess Eludaine Ducelle *lives*." He
jumped down from the ledge as a ripple of chatter
erupted among his audience.

"And with your help, she will bring industry and
innovation of unprecedented magnitude to prosper this
great land. For she possesses an inheritance so magnificent, she cannot possibly keep it all to herself. Incomes

will rise, taxes will drop—!"

"All right, people, break it up," snarled a startling voice. A hundred heads swiveled round to spot a slew of blue-uniformed officials marching into the Square, hilts of their swords glinting threateningly at their belts.

Cosmith swore, pulse smacking as he threw down the speaking trumpet. It landed with a clang onto the pavement. Amidst the shouts of the officials, the congregation dispersed, people darting every which way.

Cosmith lingered for just a moment too long, watching to ensure that no one was being seized or elsewise harmed, when a hand clasped his upper arm with an iron grip.

"Nice little speech there," came an angry hiss at his ear. "You're coming with me."

"Let him go," a soft voice issued behind them. They turned to meet a middle-aged man, dark brown eyes gazing up at the guard beseechingly.

Cosmith's mouth went dry, and his throat constricted as he took in the familiar face that looked so alike his own, albeit more worn. He'd not seen that face in over fifteen years. "Father," he breathed, his breast swelling in anguish.

"Please," begged Kormac Cosmith, still addressing the guard. "J-Jonny's a good boy. He means no harm…"

"Get away from me, you filthy drunkard," growled the guard, making to steer Cosmith away, but Kormac took his son's other arm.

"I've not touched a drink in three years." He met his son's gaze, and Cosmith stared back at him, the villainous father who'd tormented him in his youth. He feared he might become ill.

The guard only tightened his hold. "Out of my way," he commanded, but Kormac slowly withdrew a small knife from his belt.

Cosmith's eyes widened. "Father, what are you doing?" he cried, as the guard released him to reach for his sword.

The old man gave his son one last imploring look, his eyes speaking a magnitude of sorrow and apology. He whispered his final words, "*Flee, Jonwal,*" before lunging at the official with his little knife. The guard flung out his sword and sliced the older man's neck with such ferocity, Kormac's head was swiftly severed from his body.

"*Father!*" screamed Cosmith in horror, bile rising to his throat as his eyes seared with tears. People cried out at the decapitated corpse bleeding in the murky street, while the young guard, trembling at the work of his hands, glanced about the Square in shock.

Jon Cosmith had only one choice. He obeyed his father, and fled.

71

HOSTE

FIRST HAD COME THE WHISPERS. Hoste knew they were about the Duchess. A secret current was passing through the capitol city, peasants discreetly huddling in corners, suspicious gatherings in abandoned buildings, covert murmurings on the streets between passersby.

Then came the previous night's news. An ultimate act of disloyalty had been committed, though by whom specifically, they'd yet to discover. The prized gold statue of Jothann von Sparx had been overturned into the Kempei River. At last, those traitorous northerners were confessing their true sentiments.

Not that Marten Hoste hadn't known all along. But it was rather a mess trying to keep *that* story out of the posts. The last thing he needed was copycat acts sprouting around the country.

And, of course, there was the recent fiasco in Capitol Square. Some charismatic character was working quite a crowd, Hoste was told, riling them up about taxes and other nonsense, before outright announcing

Eludaine Ducelle's survival.

The leader glanced out his carriage window as they rolled under a bridge. Whoever the delinquent speaker was, Hoste wanted him found and tried before the populace. Let his citizens see exactly what happens when one of them dares speak out against his government.

Hoste grasped his chest as they emerged from the tunnel.

"Everything all right, Comrade?" called the coachman from his bench.

No, everything was certainly not all right. Hoste swallowed, making a mental note of the offensive graffiti between Twelfth and Miller Streets. He would need to send someone to clean it at once. For under the bridge, in enormous black runes for all to see, Hoste had read the Old Jordinian declaration: *VIVEKEI DUKESA.*

Long live the Duchess.

72

DAINY

THEY WERE DEPARTING THE DINING hall when a voice carried up the stone corridors. "*Your Majesty!*"

Dainy turned, watching Maxos Maxeos hurry up the hall, with several young pages following. The fellow dabbed at his balding crown, quickening his steps as King Wilqen halted to await them.

Maxos bowed, holding out a sheath of parchment. The King snatched it up, and Dainy and Lady Eponina watched as his copper eyes scanned the runes imperiously. Slowly, he broke into a crooked smile. Eponina gave Dainy an inquiring look, but Dainy shrugged. She couldn't read the post from where she was standing, either.

"Call my councilors to my meeting room at once," ordered Wilqen. The pageboys scurried off. He then beckoned Maxos and, unexpectedly, Dainy. "You two, come with me."

His daughter appeared hopeful. "May I come too, Papa?"

"Nay," the King dismissed her, without so much

as glancing at her. He made to head down the opposite corridor, and Eponina's countenance fell.

"Please, sir," Dainy intervened. Impatient, the King turned. "I'm uncomfortable being the only lady in a room full of foreign men," she lied. "I should feel far more at ease if your daughter accompanied me."

Wilqen sighed. "Very well," he relented.

Eponina bounced on her heels, pearly eyes aglow. "Thank you," she mouthed to Dainy, and Dainy grinned. She knew how much the Bainherd princess longed to witness one of her father's meetings. Eponina had blushingly relayed her secret fantasies of leading such conferences, formulating brilliant ideas that astonished the council, and saving the day with her shrewd intellect. Dainy wished she shared the girl's passion for matters of state.

The young women entered the meeting room in the King's wake. "Nina, you are to sit beside the Duchess and remain silent." Wilqen indicated a pair of chairs.

"Yes, Papa," the girl obeyed.

They waited as the room filled with members of the council: first, a spindly elder with wispy white hair, followed by a brooding-looking fellow with thick black eyebrows and mopey eyes. After came a man sporting a stout nose and a rather pinched face. Last, it was clear that the bespectacled gentleman cradling tomes of parchments was some sort of bookkeeper. It wasn't long before each was staring openly at Dainy.

"You act as though I've not told you the Duchess of Jordinia has come to stay with us," barked the King, taking his seat at the head of the table. "Bring ale," he ordered a servant, and turned back to his councilors. "This meeting concerns the Duchess. As her husband isn't here to speak for her, her presence this evening is necessary."

Dainy watched as the men took their seats opposite her. She'd never much favored the idea of being spoken for, but now that she sat alone among these strange and stately figures, she wished more than ever that Jon could be beside her.

She felt Eponina tense excitedly at her left. To her great comfort, Maxos then sat down at her right, giving her hand a reassuring pat. "This is good news," he whispered, as Wilqen flourished the post he'd received.

"It has happened." Smugly, the King passed the parchment to the elderly councilor. The old man made a fuss at fishing for his spectacles. When he couldn't find them, the man with the eyebrows snatched it from his withering fingers.

"Let me see that, MacParsons." He and the stout-nosed man pored over the article.

"What does it say, Councilor Bell?" inquired old MacParsons.

"Jordinians are revolting in the north," grinned the pinched-faced Bell with delight. "Some gang overturned a statue of von Sparx into a river. And then," he glanced back at the page, "a flag bearing the Ducelle crest was seen hanging in Dekantor Village."

To Dainy's surprise, the men turned to her with warm smiles. She tried to grin back, yet her mind was stuck on the town Councilor Bell had named. Was Dekantor not Bos's hometown? Was the giant there now, and responsible for displaying this flag? Surely, he'd have gravely endangered himself by doing so.

"Strange." MacParsons scratched his white head. "One would think every artifact bearing the Ducelle insignia had long since been destroyed by the rebels. Is that not so, Councilor Maccob?"

"Those bullheaded northerners," muttered Maccob, though he appeared pleased.

"Actually," said Maxos, "it is rumored the flag was newly sewn."

Wilqen cackled as his servants returned with mugs for the table. Dainy sniffed hers, and was put off by its bitter odor.

Eponina took a small sip, and promptly returned her mug to the table. "It tastes like diluted vomit," she breathed into Dainy's ear, and Dainy had to suppress her laughter.

"Even better," declared the King to Maxos.

Dainy leaned over, prodding her advisor. "Maxos," she whispered, "I don't understand. Why is it important if the flag was newly sewn?"

Unexpectedly, it was Eponina who answered. "It means you presently have active supporters in Jordinia, my lady," the girl informed her in a low voice. "If it's not some mere relic drudged up from the past, then someone recently took the time and great risk to create it."

Dainy nodded, although she felt rather foolish for not having reached the conclusion for herself.

"It's clear, then," said Maccob. "Lord Cosmith and his men are succeeding in rallying support. So, what's our next step?"

Wilqen gulped his ale. "The time to march is not yet nigh. However, awareness is certainly spreading." He cast a thoughtful look around the table. "For now, I believe we ought to reveal her to our own people. They will be awestruck by her survival. They'll demand her return to her rightful throne. There is no better way to garner much-needed sympathies for this impending war."

"Respectfully, Your Majesty," Maxos interjected, "but Eludaine's safety concerns me. For, if we go about flaunting her presence all over Bainherd, would the New Republic not issue a bounty on her head?"

At first, Dainy thought he was merely being hyperbolic. But she was startled by the solemnity of his expression. "By all means," Maxos continued, "they've already made multiple attempts to assassinate her."

"It's true," Dainy admitted. "The only reason they've left me alone is because I promised Marten Hoste I'd not seek to reclaim my empire."

A shadow panned across the King's features, and Councilor Bell's face appeared, if possible, more pinched. "But why would you make such a promise, my lady?"

Before Dainy could formulate a response, Eponina rounded on him. "And what other choice would she have had, Mr. Bell?" Her eyes narrowed. "I imagine Hoste came at her surrounded by his guards, intimidating her into compliance. How could she have challenged him to his face, without being seized or elsewise attacked?"

Wilqen held up a hand. "Enough, Eponina. I told you to remain silent. If you speak again, I shall have to order you to leave."

"She's right, sir," Dainy insisted.

Wilqen grunted, lowering his hand. Impatient, he banged his empty mug on the table for more. As his servants refilled it, he turned back to Maxos. "And you think my guards inept, Mr. Maxeos?"

"Of course not, sire."

"The New Republic shall not touch Lady Eludaine under my watch." The King reclined in his chair. "Besides, the citizens of Bainherd would not allow it. Not after the revelation of her *miraculous* survival." He grinned.

"How romantic," simpered Bell.

"The girl will need an opportunity to enchant the people, should we wish to win their favor," wheezed MacParsons, "for the renaissance of both our monarchies."

Dainy swallowed. She was unsure whether she'd be able to enchant much of anybody.

"What do you propose?" Maccob's dark eyebrows furrowed. "Shall we issue an announcement in the posts?"

The King shook his head. "To take proper effect, she must be revealed in person."

Bell eyed him. "Are you speaking of some sort of press release, or public festival?"

"*Oh!*" gasped Eponina, but quickly covered her mouth as her father shot her a sharp glare. The princess gave Dainy a pained look, clearly desperate to share her idea.

The men continued to muse and bumble on for several minutes about conferences, county fairs and village visits, until Eponina could evidently stand it no longer. "Please, Papa," she finally burst. "Let me speak my thoughts, and then I promise, I will leave."

Wilqen ran a hand through his hair, looking severe, but made no objections.

"Why not unveil the Duchess at *Carnivalle*? Autumn is right around the corner!"

Maccob shook his head. "Respectfully, my lady, the festivities of the seasons are no longer practiced among the public as they once were."

"So?" retorted Eponina. "Mama said our family used to host *La Maskérada* at the castle every year!"

"The Masquerade?" said the bookkeeper dubiously. It was the first time Dainy had heard him speak. "My dear, gold and resources are very scarce. If we were to throw some lavish ball, the citizens might think your father frivolous."

"Or they might be *enchanted*," countered the princess, "and reminded of our court's romantic splendor and glorious past, as we all agree we need them to be, in order to—"

"*Out*, Nina!" commanded Wilqen, pointing at the door.

She did not need telling twice. In one fluid movement, Eponina rose and departed the meeting room, white-blonde hair flapping at her back. A servant secured the door shut behind her.

Her fresh absence and empty chair unsettled Dainy, until the King set down his mug, proclaiming, "My daughter has a point. And I rather fancy her suggestion."

Dainy's eyes widened. The King *liked* Eponina's idea? Then why had he just rebuked her before the council, and banished her from the meeting room?

"Leave it to a teenaged girl to propose a ball," chuckled Bell somewhat snidely, although he seemed to be considering it. "It just might work," he admitted.

Dainy leaned over. "Maxos," she whispered again. "What is *La Maskérada*?"

"It means *the Masquerade*," replied the man quietly. "It was the custom of the Halvean courts to throw a masked ball for Carnivalle, the annual autumn festival."

"A masked ball?"

He nodded. "Literally." He passed a hand over his face, suggesting the donning of a disguise. "A dance to which guests wear masques."

But why? Dainy wanted to ask, for she'd never before heard of such a ridiculous notion, a roomful of prominent adults costuming their faces. However, the King and his men addressed her advisor.

"I confess, it'd be the most talked-about event in West Halvea." Maxos chuckled, removing his spectacles. "What drama! Hundreds of nobles in the crowd, and from them, we ask our featured guest to step forth. She does so, slowly removes her masque, and—"

"*Voila!*" howled Wilqen. "The Duchess of Jordinia is unveiled before their very eyes!" His voice grew louder as he hammered down his mug for yet another refill. "I love it, Maxos."

Dainy frowned. The Masquerade had been Eponina's idea, not Maxos's.

"We'd invite the press, of course," said Maccob, whose leery demeanor was giving way to evident amusement. "Imagine the headlines after such an evening: *The resurrected Jordinian Duchess, unmasked at Carnivalle!*"

"Why, we'll be receiving scrolls left and right from peasants and nobles alike, requesting we do something for the girl, and not simply stand idle while the New Republic ravishes the entire continent," said Bell.

The King grinned, cheeks ruddy with mounting intoxication. "A most intriguing plan, gentlemen. That is, of course," he nodded to Dainy, "if the Duchess approves."

"I trust Lady Eponina's judgment, Your Majesty," replied Dainy coolly. She simply could not permit either of these men, King or not, to claim credit for the princess's clever proposal.

She almost thought she saw Wilqen wink at her.

But she may have only imagined it, for the man resumed conversing with his council.

The conference endured for some time more, until it was decided that the Queen would coordinate the event. Balls and fêtes were, after all, a woman's domain, with which the men could not be bothered. To them, La Maskérada was naught but a potent strategy for announcing Dainy's survival in a striking way, one which would evoke sentimental nostalgia for both royal families of West Halvea once more.

Dainy could not have been more relieved when the meeting finally concluded, and she was free to leave the drafty chamber full of scheming, semi-drunken men. She wasted no time in escorting herself through the doorway without so much as a second glance over her shoulder.

At the sound of her name in the King's sonorous voice, however, she halted in the candlelit corridor. What now? She wondered, as Wilqen approached.

He stopped just before her, looking her up and down. "You think lowly of me," he growled, cornering her by a decorative suit of armor, "for my treatment of my daughter tonight."

Her heart flounced. "Surely not, sir."

Wilqen ignored her. "I can see it in your eyes. You think me a heartless father, admonishing Eponina, humiliating her, dismissing her, only to steal her very apt idea."

Dainy swallowed. She could not argue with that.

"My daughter is quite precocious," the man declared, and only then did Dainy realize the pride in his voice. "*Too* intelligent, one could say. For, unlike you, Lady Eludaine," he prodded her shoulder, "she is not to become an empress, but merely wife to some prince or another, who shall expect her to possess no opinions of her own and keep her mouth shut."

The King dropped his voice, his face apologetic. "It's for her own good, see. I know her mind is capable and bright. But there is no place for it." He shook his head, regretful. "Therefore, you see why I cannot encourage my daughter. For, were she permitted to speak her mind here, think how unhappy she'll be someday, to find herself in a setting where it's no longer tolerated. Nay, I should much rather acquaint her to the way of her future now."

Dainy knew not how to respond. In fact, she was beginning to feel rather sorry for both the King and Eponina, the former for having to veil his admiration of his astute daughter, and the latter for continuously suffering her father's seeming disapproval. She wished there was something she could do. Alas, she comprehended the King's position.

After bidding the man goodnight, she resumed to her bedchamber, only to collide with the princess herself. "You must tell me everything that happened after I left," Eponina besought her.

Weary as she was, Dainy marveled at the girl's enthusiasm. Why, she'd have just as soon left the meeting room when Eponina did, had she so been permitted. But she kindly took the girl's hand. "Why not come to my chamber then, Nina, and I shall tell you all about it?"

73

SELU

"FROM BAINHERD," MURMURED BET, DISCREETLY passing over a folded card. Selu shoved it in her pocket.

The two women rounded the familiar corner into Pogue District, making their way back to the abandoned baker's apartment. Upon entering, Bet was summoned to examine a welt a fellow squatter had acquired, while Selu, fingering the card, took up a candle and retreated to the bedroom to read it.

She startled, however, to find Cosmith pacing by the window. "What are you doing?" She set down her candle and saucer. "You are in hiding, Jon. You should not be parading before an open window."

The man ran his fingers through his lengthening hair, which was looking uncharacteristically greasy and unkempt of late. "I'm going stir-crazy, Selu. I cannot remain cooped up in this dratted place. I've got to—got to…"

He proceeded to murmur incoherently to himself. That was another thing he'd been doing a lot of: muttering to himself like a madman. Nay, confinement did not suit Jon Cosmith at all.

A shrill giggle emitted behind them. Carlo emerged through the doorway, steering the brown-haired lass, Shoshanna, on his arm. The couple stopped, however, to discover the room already occupied. "Oh." Carlo grinned. "Sorry."

Cosmith pushed past them. "I was just leaving."

"Jon." Selu grabbed his sleeve. "You cannot go anywhere."

"Speak for yourself." He slipped from the room.

Shoshanna watched him go, clutching Carlo's arm more tightly. "Trust me, dear," she drawled to Selu. "He's not worth it."

Selu snorted, snatching up her candle. Why did everyone there seem to conjure the revolting notion that she and Jon were a pair? "You need not tell me he is worthless, sweetheart. I figured that for myself the instant I met him."

"Funny." Carlo eyed her, suspicious. "For a man and woman who claim to have no interest in each other, you two sure spend a lot of time together."

"Oh, for crying out loud." Selu tossed up her candle-free hand. "Jon is married, Carlo!"

He and the young woman exchanged glances. "Married?" repeated Carlo, bewildered.

"To whom?" demanded Shoshanna, and despite her hold on Carlo's arm, she almost sounded angry.

Selu ignored her, speaking to Carlo. "I thought he already told you about the Duchess quest."

"He only said that he won it."

Selu rolled her eyes. Of course, Cosmith would claim to have won the competition singlehandedly.

Meanwhile, Bos and Macmillan had probably done most of the work.

But comprehension dawned upon the young man's face. "*Eludaine Ducelle?*"

Selu nodded. "Only it's Eludaine Cosmith now."

She departed the bedroom to find Cosmith downstairs in the old bakery, tightening his bootlaces as if intending to go someplace. He hummed to himself, although there was something rather frantic about the sound of it.

Selu took a tentative step. "Jon?" Her candle's light accentuated the heavy lines beneath his eyes. When had he last slept? "Where are you going?"

He didn't answer, only continued singing under his breath as he fastened his vest.

"Are you all right?"

It was as though he'd only just noticed her. If Selu hadn't known better, she'd have thought him at the drink. Alas, the anguish in his eyes spoke of something deeper, and arguably worse.

"All right?" Cosmith blinked, as though unacquainted with the word. "I've only been quarantined in this godforsaken hovel for the better part of a moon after witnessing my father's head rolling off before my very eyes; other than that, I am perfectly all right!"

Selu inhaled. The man was in shock. She well understood the feeling. But she had to calm him before he should do something reckless. "I've a note from Bainherd." She reached into her pocket. "Perhaps we can read it together?"

The prospect of news seemed to recall his senses to him, and he held out a calloused hand. She gave him the card, and together they scanned the runes, realizing that it was no ordinary bulletin, but rather, a formal invitation from the King's courts.

"For whom is this intended?" he whispered.

"Mother didn't say. I think it's merely a copy, meant to keep us informed."

The man glanced up, and Selu could tell from the familiar glint in his eyes that the gears of his sharp mind were churning again. "Wilqen is reviving La Maskérada for Carnivalle?" His hand rose to his chin. "In order to make a '*most exciting announcement,*'" he read from the parchment.

"Featuring his '*special guest of honor, to be unveiled at the event,*'" read Selu.

"Eludaine," he breathed. The faraway look returned to his face. Abruptly, he began to pace. "Wilqen wishes to reveal her to his populace this autumn." His brow creased. "This must be his tactic for garnering support. He's preparing to march, and her unveiling is the first step."

He glanced back down at the card. "While I understand the necessity, I cannot have her exposed without my protection. I must go to her. I must be present for this—this Masquer—"

"It's dangerous enough that you leave this apartment, Jon," Selu argued. "You could easily be recognized, captured…"

"I must go to her," Cosmith repeated, and Selu knew by the determined set of his jaw that the matter was not eligible for negotiation.

"Then you'd better not try to return," she warned. "It'll be a miracle if you make it out of Jordinia." She folded her slender arms. "Do not tempt fate by attempting to infiltrate again. And especially not now, when you are more wanted than ever."

Cosmith made no indication of hearing her. "I must go to her," was all he iterated, tucking the invitation into his breast pocket.

Selu watched as he made for the door. "Keep to the shadows," she called, although she shook her violet head. She wasn't entirely confident that the man was in his right mind. And she didn't even wish to contemplate how devastated Dainy would be, should something happen to her husband on his way back to her. Alas, there was nothing Selu could do. "Tread carefully," she added, a sense of dread overtaking her.

"And you, Seluna." Cosmith gave her one final blank look and slipped outside, disappearing before her eyes.

Sighing, Selu took up her candle to retreat upstairs. She gasped, however, to collide with someone who'd been perched, clearly listening, on the step. "Carlo," she growled, recognizing the curls.

"I was just—"

"Eavesdropping?"

He laughed uneasily, and Selu gripped his collar. "Whatever you heard, you are to repeat to no one," she hissed, her heart drumming furiously. "Are we clear?"

The lad's chest heaved, eyes darting about as if seeking an escape. Yet gradually, a most unpleasant smirk overtook his lips. "All right," he relented. "I'll keep my mouth shut for you, love." He leaned in. "If you open yours for me." He made an obscene gesture.

"This is for Jon's safety, you maggot," she snarled, shoving the boy aside and pushing past him up the steps.

74

COSMITH

AIR. NOT JUST ANY AIR, but fresh air outdoors. And sky. Not a breeze through an open window, but the true night sky, speckled with stars as far as the eye could see.

It was chillier than when Cosmith had last been outside. The moons were passing, the next more quickly than the last, and the cooler seasons were approaching. He was grateful that summer was nearly over. Anything to push the recent past as far away as possible.

He folded down the rim of his hat, shielding his face. He spent his first night on the road in a stone lane, and the following day, he only walked. While his feet did the work, his mind was all but absent from the rest of him. If only the images would leave him. If only the confusion and conflicting emotions would go away.

The terrain gradually rolled into countryside, and Cosmith lost count of the nights passed in green meadows and wooded groves. His pounding feet exhausted, he paid a farmer with an ox and cart to haul him to the border of Bainherd, where the land smoothed, and flat plains overtook the hills. All the while, as yellowing fields stretched endlessly before him, he could envision only one thing: the look of surrender in his father's eyes as he leapt at the uniformed guard in Capitol Square.

Kormac Cosmith had clearly known he'd not stood a chance. The old man had only a small knife, for heaven's sake. And at his age, he surely knew he was incapable of fighting. Yet, he'd stood up to defend his son, willingly giving his life to grant him time to flee.

The apology, the anguish clearly wrought upon his father's aging face haunted Cosmith hour after hour, week by week. For, while his boyhood memories consisted of naught but the terror the man wreaked on him, the same father had sacrificed his life for him. He did not know how to feel.

Autumn approached as he took to the road by foot again, and the rains descended over the fields of Bainherd, a threatening purple haze overwhelming the sky. He gazed over his shoulder, taking in the eerie stillness of the sparse treetops. Something wasn't right. He didn't much like the way the clouds in the north seemed to bind together, growing blacker by the minute.

As cool raindrops soaked his sleeves, a vein of silver lightning pulsed through the clouds, accompanied by a rushing breeze. The wind picked up, blowing dust and gravel into his eyes, as though suctioned up by the sky itself. Cosmith's heart drummed as he lifted his tired feet into a jog, while reminding himself that only a fool attempts to outrun a storm. He needed to take shelter, and soon. Only, there was no place to go. The plains extended limitlessly before him, with nary a valley in sight.

A heavy, grating whistle sounded in his ears as

he carried on, rain and wind whipping at his face. He glanced back again and sucked in a breath. The black clouds conjoined and rotated, hovering in the air as they encroached upon him.

He ran in earnest, boots pounding the paved road. The sky darkened as he gasped for air. The cyclone drifted nearer, the funnel's tail toying with the crowns of the tallest crops, scattering grass, hay and all manner of debris in its wake.

He darted west. To his tremendous relief, he spied a small chapel. He squinted through the rain, making out a slew of arched stones dotting the field in which it stood. He ran to them, not knowing or caring what they were, only hoping for a cellar, a dip in the land, anything to help him survive the storm. As he neared, however, he realized he was headed for a cemetery.

Cosmith jiggled the chapel's doorknob, but it was locked. The windows were too high to break. Desperate, he turned to the graves, eyes darting between headstones. "Dear God," he whispered. He'd finally spotted a safe place to take cover, but it did not bode well for him.

A fierce whistle such as he'd never heard rang through the sky. He looked east, watching in panic as the cyclone touched down at last. Glancing down into a freshly-dug open grave, the man jumped in, landing with a thud atop a crude wooden coffin that had recently been lowered there.

Cosmith could only wonder at the identity of the corpse reposing beneath him, separated by naught but a pinewood lid. But it wouldn't be the first time a dead man saved his life.

75

BOS

BOS STAYED WITH TUCK HENN and his wife, Mahla, in their Dekantor cabin. The Henns opened their home to revivalist meetings, as did Father Asa his underground chapel. There were other places as well; the back of the butcher's shop, for instance (although no one much fancied the odor there).

Their ranks were rapidly growing, and they had to break into factions, with appointed leaders in separate districts. In this way, their cause spread throughout northern Jordinia, until Bos heard news about a statue of von Sparx overturned into the nearby Kempei River. To celebrate, Mahla Henn and the butcher's wife hung their latest project in the center of Dekantor Village: a flag bearing the Ducelle crest. Of course, the women promptly removed it. But not before making their statement, evoking whispers, and even, Bos heard rumored, being mentioned in foreign posts.

But the men were growing restless, eager to take more than just symbolic action with statues and flags. They were acquiring and refurbishing weapons, steadily building an arsenal between them.

"We set dynami to Capitol Tower."

Bos glanced up as the Henns' kitchen fell silent, everyone staring at Rolf Lymston, who had spoken. Rolf stared back, shaggy hair concealing his expression.

The arguing began, their voices collectively rising, and Bos held up a great hand. "Cease." They quieted. Mahla Henn looked up from her stovetop. "We cannot simply march to Pierma and accomplish such a feat. This sort of thing takes careful planning." Bos stroked his beard. "And frankly, we've still not enough men."

"I'm aware of this, Visigoth," Rolf grunted. "But I say that's our plan. We collect the dynami, recruit more revivalists, and then convene with your friends in Pierma to take down the Tower."

"What about Bainherd?" inquired a young man from the next village over. "Bos has been saying for moons that their troops are poised to help us."

"And we've yet to see hide or hair of them," muttered Samuel Crane.

Bos swigged his wine, shrugging. "I only said my friends are enlisting King Wilqen's aid. That is all I know." He turned to Rolf. "I don't dislike your idea. I simply suggest we ought not to be hasty."

Rolf grinned. "I can be patient."

Tuck Henn set down his goblet. "What are we saying, then? Are we to blow up Capitol Tower with Hoste in it? We plot to assassinate the leader of the New Republic?"

"Why not?" Rolf growled. "They assassinated our Emperor."

"I'm not objecting. So long as we realize that if

anyone divulges a word of this to the outside," Tuck glanced around the table warningly, "we will all be killed."

"And wouldn't we be for holding this meeting in the first place?" asked Rolf. "What's your point?"

"Something must be done," agreed the butcher.

"Patience," Tuck assured them, though the others grew louder still. He raised his voice to be heard. "We must first involve the leaders of our branches in Kempei, Harborton, Greygørn—"

"Ah, to see that Tower blasted until it should topple over, bringing down those damned rebels with it," mused Rolf with relish.

"Rolf." Bos nudged him, grinning as he knocked the mouth of his goblet against the other man's. "We are the rebels now, my friend."

AUTUMN

76

MACMILLAN

AFTER DAYS OF BUMPING AND bustling along paved and dirt roads alike, the man finally slowed his wagon at the gates of Pon Castle. He could hardly see the building for the black sky and torrential downpour, when a cluster of imposing-looking guards approached, demanding his name and business thereabouts.

"Marley Macmillan. I'm here for the Duchess Elu—" He'd barely finished his sentence when the guards immediately drew the gate.

"Our apologies." They beckoned him through. "Go right along, Your Grace."

Macmillan paused at the strange title, but said nothing, urging his oxen up the drive, until a hooded stable master came to relieve him of the animals. Macmillan took up his bag, descending the old wagon at last.

Thunder groaned in the distance, and the rain tittered noisily as he followed a pair of guards to the front doors. An old steward ushered him inside, while a pair of matronly maids made to help him from his cloak.

"I can manage, thank you," Macmillan assured them, clutching his bag, which contained the remainder of the blue silver his brother had given him. "I don't wish to be of any further inconvenience," he added, so as not to sound impolite.

"Of course not, sir," the steward insisted, offering him a towel. "We have long been expecting you."

Macmillan blinked. He'd not been anticipating such a reception.

"Shall we show you to your room?" asked the steward, after Macmillan had dried off. "There, the maids may draw your bath, and bring you anything you should desire to eat." Macmillan shivered at the notion of a hot bath and food as he followed the man up a stone stairwell. "I shall inform His Majesty of your arrival on the morrow."

"And the Duchess?" asked Macmillan. "She is here with her husband, yes?"

"Her husband left moons ago. But she remains." The old man led him down a hall garnished with tapestries, and Macmillan could discern a spidery bolt of lightning through one of the rain-spattered windows. At last, they came to a spacious guest chamber. "And what do you crave from our kitchens?"

Macmillan's stomach gurgled. "You haven't any meat pies, have you?"

"Every sort. Which do you prefer?"

Macmillan grinned. "All of them."

The steward departed, and Macmillan rummaged through his bag, seeking a clean change of clothes. Alas, none of his garments had been washed in a great deal of time, and all were hardened by—not to mention, stank of—the salt of the sea.

When more servants arrived with pails of hot water for his washtub, he indicated his pile of clothing. "Is it possible to have these laundered?"

A maid dutifully scooped up the pile into her arms. "Sure thing, Your Grace. Have you need of somethin' else to wear in the meantime?"

He nodded.

"Briggs is about 'is size," remarked another servant, pouring the last of the buckets into his bath. "I'm sure he's got somethin' to fit the Duke."

Macmillan stared at the women, wondering whether the whole castle knew of his identity as the illegitimate son of Dane Ducelle.

Once they'd left, he bathed, combed his hair, trimmed his newly-grown goatee and, after toweling himself, received his borrowed clothing and meal from the manservant at the door. He dressed in the plain white tunic and trousers of the King's staff, and finally consumed his dinner.

Satisfactorily fed and groomed at last, he reclined on the bed. He didn't bother snuffing out the lantern as he dropped his eyelids, hands resting behind his neck. Breathing deeply, he listened as the rainfall tapped peacefully at the window. The song of the storm rose and fell, soft echoes of melodic notes, pressing a familiar succession of chords onto his window pane…

Macmillan abruptly sat up, opening his eyes. Why, that sound was not the rain, but true music. And a song he knew, no less. But who could be playing an instrument at that hour?

Unable to help his curiosity, he slipped from the lush mattress, bare feet cold against the flagstone floors, and opened the door. The notes drifted down the corridor, and he recognized the sharp, string-like quality belonging to the harpsichord.

He followed the wafting music as it grew louder, until he could make out the chamber from which it issued. Intrigued, he pulled back the door, ears dancing as he stepped into a room filled with song. A single lantern rested on the instrument's ledge, illuminating the face of a very young woman with a perfectly straight veil of white-blonde hair spilling down her back.

Macmillan couldn't help himself; she played one of his favorite melodies. His voice simply itching to join her, he stepped into the room, singing:

I found the Harper's Meadow, her music called to me
For I'd wandered days through the hills and mazes
of dreams...

The girl gasped, her sheet music toppling down to the pedals at her feet.

"I'm sorry," he apologized automatically, retreating as she looked up at him in alarm.

"What are you doing here?" she demanded, eyes like opals as her posture tensed.

"I mean no harm." Macmillan held up his hands. "I only heard such pleasant music from my chamber, and—and wished to seek its lovely source."

She gave no response, her budding breast heaving

somewhat as she stared at him.

"I can go now, if you wish," he offered gently, making for the door.

But to his surprise, she called him back. "Wait." She straightened. "Forgive me. I was merely startled. I did not mean to be so rude."

"And I should've knocked." He gestured toward the opulent instrument. "Please, continue playing."

The girl made to reach for her notes, but Macmillan took another step forward. "You don't need those."

"Yes, I do," she insisted, grabbing at the fallen parchments. "I play by sight, not by ear."

He came to stand beside her, and dared to softly stay her hand with his own. "Why not play by feeling?"

She looked at his hand on hers before slowly raising her gaze to his face. His pulse trembling, he allowed his fingers to linger, meeting her unusual iridescent eyes before finally pulling away.

She hesitated. Carefully, she pressed down the keys of the first chord.

"Very good," he encouraged her, and she scrunched her brow to recall the next chord. After a slight delay, she found it accurately. Macmillan praised her again. "You see?" He folded his arms. "You can play without notes."

She beamed, sounding out the next keys. All the while, Macmillan admired her, her skin creamy as milk, pale hair like gossamer, her delicate lips parted in concentration. Who was this girl?

Boldly, he took his seat on the bench beside her. And the maiden, perhaps equally as boldly, did not inch away. "You may sing," she commanded him unexpectedly.

Macmillan grinned at her. He took a breath, and resumed:

I found the Harper's Meadow,
and so renewed my soul
For I'd wandered lost with the albatross of my woe
She strummed her chords so sweetly,
her angel voice so soft
Where I once was buried, her music carried me off...

The girl descended into the chorus, and together they sang:

O Harper's Meadow, where I'm joyful once more
For there is no ailment that her harp cannot cure.

She turned her glowing face to him, setting a hand over his wrist. "You have an incredible voice."

As incredible as those otherworldly eyes, or your radiant smile? Macmillan longed to reply, when she drew in a sudden breath.

"Oh, but it's very late." She shot to her feet, slamming the lid over the keys rather unceremoniously and gathering her sheet notes. "My guards are going to scalp me." She tightened her silken robe about her petite waist and took up her lantern.

Macmillan rose, bemused. "Your guards?"

"Yes. I must go." Her eyes, however, shone like moonlight. "I will be here again at midnight tomorrow," she whispered, and disappeared through the door, leaving behind a mild flowery fragrance and the echoes of her music, which had ended all too soon.

The man was left in silent darkness, with naught but the hall's torchlight to illuminate the path back to his chamber—if he could even remember which one it was. Feeling strangely lightweight, he ambled up the long corridor until finding the door he'd left ajar.

He lowered himself back onto his mattress, finally appreciating his exhaustion. His heart drummed to accompany the rainfall outside, and he wondered how he'd ever failed to notice just how romantic rainstorms were.

He suddenly heaved a sigh of dismay. But *how* could he have been such a fool to neglect to ask the girl her name? Then again, weren't they both staying in the same castle? Surely, Macmillan would see her again.

77

DAINY

THERE CAME A RAUCOUS KNOCKING.

Dainy sat up, blinking in the darkness. It couldn't be breakfast time already? The sun had hardly risen. She heard squabbling, and had barely uttered the word "enter" before her door burst open and Eponina bounded in, long hair flying behind her.

"I tried to stop her," apologized the maid.

Dainy rubbed her eyes. "What is the hour?"

"A quarter to sunrise," proclaimed Eponina. Embarrassed, the maid shook her head and departed them. The princess secured Dainy's door shut and leapt atop the edge of her bed. "I've barely slept a wink all night. I've just been bursting to tell someone!"

"For someone who's hardly slept a wink," remarked Dainy, "you sure seem quite energetic."

"Eludaine," Eponina leaned in, her face alight, "my head is in the clouds. I hold the stars in my fists."

"Indeed, the moon is in your eyes." Dainy smirked. "This wouldn't happen to be about a *man*, would it?"

The princess looked both parts awestruck and

mortified. "But how could you possibly know that?"

Dainy laughed, holding up her left wrist, where her jade bracelet glittered. "Have you forgotten I'm a married woman? I know how it feels to be in love." She grinned sadly at the thought of Jon. It had been moons, and the season had already changed to autumn. But still, she'd received no word from him.

"Is that what this is?" Eponina clutched her heart, long hair entangling in her fingers. "*Love?*"

Dainy twisted her lips. "Hmm, let's see. You cannot sleep, you're wound up with boundless energy, you feel as though your head is in the clouds..." She ticked the items off her fingers. "Have you an appetite this morning?"

"Nay," replied the maiden cheerfully.

"Do you feel as though you're falling down a flight of stairs every time you picture him?"

"Aye!" Eponina bounced from the bed. "How did you articulate it so perfectly? That is exactly how I feel about—about..." But she wrung her wrists, agitated. "Argh, but I never learned his name. Though I told him I'd meet him again, this evening at midnight!"

"Midnight?" Dainy was suddenly concerned. "Surely, the Princess of Bainherd is not sneaking off alone so late to meet strange men?"

The girl gave her a cool look, and Dainy felt wracked with hypocrisy. After all, had she not snuck off to sea with Jon the night she'd first met him, regardless of all better judgment? But that had been different, hadn't it?

Dainy frowned. At least she'd been of age, unlike Eponina. And she and Jon were now wed, weren't they? But who was going around Pon Castle at night, trying to woo the young royal?

"Sorry," said Eponina curtly, making to leave. "I can see you were the wrong person to tell."

I'm only concerned for your virtue, Dainy wanted to attest, but stopped herself. Her brother had said that to her once, and she'd not appreciated it. Certainly, Eponina wouldn't either. "Nina," she said at last. "I am glad for you."

The girl stalled.

"Perhaps I shall feel even better," Dainy added, "once I learn who he is."

The princess frowned, nodding. "So shall I." She gazed through the curtained window, looking as though she wished to say more.

"What is it, dear?"

"It's just…he was dressed in servants' clothes," Eponina murmured so quietly, Dainy had to strain to hear. The girl appeared as though she might cry. "Papa would never permit…"

"People aren't always what they seem," Dainy assured her, sliding down from the bed and resting a hand on Eponina's shoulder. "Take my brother and me, for instance. We were something of peasants, you know. We'd no idea we were the children of an emperor."

Eponina shrugged her off. "The man I met last night is about as likely to wind up an emperor's son as I am to become an empress," she grumbled. "These are just useless fantasies, Eludaine. Already, love has cursed me."

"Oy." Dainy wrapped her arms around her. "It'll be all right."

The girl relented, embracing her.

After dawn, they departed to break their fast in the dining hall with the Wilqens. Dainy's mind strayed as her shoes clacked down the corridor, when a familiar voice startled her, singing out across the way: "*Love, it so tears me asunder when I am apart from thee.*"

Both Dainy and Eponina froze at the opening line of The Lover's Ditty. It was the song Dainy had once sung with…

"*Mac!*" Forgetting all inhibitions, she ran toward him with the enthusiasm of a small child and catapulted herself into his hold, squeezing him with all of her might in a rollicking embrace. Her brother wrapped his arms around her in turn, and Dainy couldn't help but notice they felt sturdier than she'd remembered. "A goatee," she laughed, examining his chin.

"Don't make fun." He grinned.

"Nay, it becomes you," she insisted breathlessly, gripping his hands as if he might slip away. Oh, what joy to see Mac again after so many moons, and to have her own family with her at the castle! "You look…more robust." She examined him further.

He shrugged. "I suppose frequent hikes to our mines in the Tsongii Mountains will do that to a person." He took the ends of her hair between his fingers. "So long now! I can't seem to get used to it."

Dainy beamed at him, when the King himself stepped out of the dining hall. "Ah." The imposing man gave Mac a hearty smack between the shoulder blades. "The siblings have been reunited." He turned to Dainy. "I had the pleasure of meeting your brother this morning, my lady. Henceforth, I insist he join us at mealtimes." He beckoned them into the room. "Shall we?"

Dainy was about to respond when Wilqen snapped his fingers. "*Nina,*" he barked. "What are you doing, lingering back there like a wallflower? Don't be shy. Come and meet the Duke of Jordinia."

Dainy could just make out the princess's stunned

expression until, with an air of determination, she finally marched forward.

"My eldest daughter, the Princess Eponina," King Wilqen introduced her proudly, as Eponina gave a graceful curtsey. "Daughter, this is Marley Macmillan, the Duchess's brother."

Dainy did not miss the look of intrigue on Mac's features. "Enchanted to meet you, my lady." He bowed politely. Was that a smirk he was concealing?

Eponina stared at him, her face reddening. It was the first time Dainy had ever seen the girl rendered speechless. And then, as the King rounded back into dining hall, Dainy finally comprehended the look of recognition passing between them.

Eponina turned at last, following her father, and Dainy grabbed Mac's forearm, pulling him from the others' sight. "Let me guess," she hissed. "You and the princess have already become acquainted."

Mac glanced over his shoulder. "I'd no idea she was the princess," he whispered. "I thought Eponina Wilqen was supposed to be a little girl!"

"She *is*, Mac. She has seen only fifteen summers."

He craned his neck for another glimpse of the young woman. "Are you sure?"

"Positive," snapped Dainy. "And she is my friend. So you'd better not have any ideas about her *a la* Donatela—"

"Whoa," interrupted Mac, his brow creased.

"Or else you shall have me to answer to." Dainy grabbed his hand. "Now, let us go and eat," she gave him a look, "before we are missed."

78

DuBerre

DAMON DuBERRE'S FOOTMAN HAD SELDOM been an excitable man. This rainy afternoon was no different. Thus was why DuBerre, suspended Head of Jordinian Intelligence, thought nothing of it when he was summoned to his study to greet a visitor.

"Comrade Hoste, sir," pronounced the footman placidly, opening the door. Before DuBerre had time to react, the old man drifted, leaving him facing none other than the leader of the New Republic.

The white-haired yet youthful man removed his bowler, and held it against his rain-streaked cloak. "Damon," he greeted.

"Comrade Hoste." DuBerre ran his fingers self-consciously through his oily hair. He'd not yet bathed, his usual routine of things crumbling since he'd been suspended from his position. "To what do I owe this honor?"

Hoste smiled, though DuBerre could tell something troubled him. There were more lines on his brow than DuBerre recalled, and his fingernails appeared bitten down to the quick. "I'd like to offer you back your post."

At last. "You mean, you are withdrawing my suspension?" he asked, just to be certain.

"If you'll return."

"Ah." DuBerre fought to conceal his grin. "Is our favorite little *dukesa* causing enough trouble simply by breathing?"

"I know not how it all happened," Hoste whispered darkly, "and so quickly. One moment, the girl is vowing to cause no trouble. The next, her followers are felling statues, painting graffiti, and preaching against us in Capitol Square." He shook his head. "How did she even *acquire* followers, Damon? No one but a tiny group of individuals—all of whom I've banished, mind you—knows she exists!"

DuBerre lowered into an armchair, glancing at the stacks of bulletins piled up on his desk. Although he hadn't been working, he'd kept abreast of current events, especially those concerning the dreaded Duchess. "If I may," he offered, "I suspect it might be those same individuals behind these occurrences."

Hoste sighed, flustered. "Then I should've offed them when I had the chance."

"Precisely the favor I was suspended for trying to do for you, Marten," DuBerre laughed.

"Forgive me."

DuBerre merely shrugged.

"The man in Capitol Square," began Hoste. "Do you reckon—?"

"Jonwal H. Cosmith. Tolohov identified him as such."

Hoste blinked. "Tolohov?"

"Quixheto, my assassin. Whom you also suspended."

The leader frowned. "And who exactly is Jonwal H. Cosmith?"

"Former Intelligence," replied DuBerre. "Rounded up a good deal of traitors for us some time ago before suddenly going AWOL. No one knew where he'd disappeared to. 'Til now. Not to mention, he was a participant in Gatspierre's quest."

"Gatspierrie's quest?" Hoste gaped at him. "Why, I *met* the bastard! Thinks he's a double agent, does he? Damn him," the leader spat, the color in his usually friendly face darkening. "I want this Cosmith person found, publically tried, and hanged."

DuBerre smirked. "Why bother bringing him to trial, Marten, if you've already decided upon the outcome yourself?"

Hoste cast him a look. "You know why."

Indeed, and that was all he needed to say. The citizens of Jordinia had to be given the illusion that they still held some degree of control over the justice system, that it was still *their* Republic.

"No matter. Now that you've reinstated me, I will see to it that your man is found." DuBerre met Hoste's gaze. "I assure you, Comrade, Cosmith will hang."

79

EPONINA

THE CLOCK TICKED SOUNDLY AT her bedside. Quietly, Eponina arose from her linens and lit a lantern. It was almost time. On the tips of her toes, she traipsed to her wardrobe, brandishing the light before an array of gowns. She subsequently frowned. But none of these would do.

She sighed. When she'd first met the man of her dreams, she was merely wearing her night robe. Nothing special or revealing. She'd certainly not expected a handsome man to discover her at that hour. Had she known, why, she'd have worn her most flattering attire.

The question was: exactly which attire would that be? Her mother, the Queen, had provided her with naught but the high-necked, knee-length frocks of youthful girls, since Eponina was still technically not of age. She didn't yet possess anything low-collared, tight-fitting, womanly…

She twisted her rosy lips, finally deciding upon a garment and dressing hurriedly. All the while, her heart palpitated. What if she were caught wandering through the corridors fully dressed at midnight? What would be her excuse? Or worse: what if the Duke did not show?

Silently as she could, Eponina crept to the music room, careful to keep her lantern dim and steps gentle. When at last she met her destination, her heart fell somewhat to find the room still dark.

Hopeful, she made her way to the harpsichord, onto which she set the lantern. She was adjusting the collar of her frock, desperately willing her breasts to appear a morsel larger, when she finally heard footfalls.

In he stepped, and there he was—all black hair, dark goatee and warm green-brown eyes. Why, he was even handsomer than on the night before, now dressed in what could only be his own clothing, a pressed tunic and trousers, with a brown jacket.

"You came," she declared excitedly, before remembering that a woman should never take the first word in a conversation.

He seemed not to notice her error. "Of course."

He said nothing more, so Eponina assumed her seat at the harpsichord bench, perching her fingers over the keys. "So, what song shall we share tonight, Your Grace?"

"Perhaps I've not come tonight for a song."

"For what have you come instead, then?" she dared ask. A kiss, she prayed inwardly. Please let him say he has come for my kiss…

"A word," the Duke of Jordinia replied rather casually, leaning against the doorframe. "For I owe you an apology. You see, I'd no idea who you were last night."

Eponina's hopes fell to her soles. "Oh." She didn't bother concealing her underwhelmed tone as she closed the harpsichord's lid. Apparently, there would be no music that night.

"Had I known you were the King's daughter," he went on, "I certainly would've never—"

"And I knew not that you were the Emperor's son." She rose to her feet. "Rather, I mistook you for a manservant. So we are even, Your Grace."

He looked taken aback. "You know," he said, inspecting a flake of paint on the wall, "you don't have to use those titles with me. My friends just call me Mac."

"I have few friends," Eponina admitted. "But my father sometimes calls me Nina."

"Well," the man glanced at his hands, "I cannot presume to address you in the manner of His Majesty. Though, perhaps I may bestow upon you a more suitable title of my own?"

Eponina blushed. He was inventing a pet name for her? What sort of endearment would he assign? And what might it reveal about his sentiments, if any, towards her?

She waited until he offered, smirking, "How about *moppet*?"

Her features contorted at the irreverent epithet. "I beg your pardon?" So he would call her juvenile, would he? "I'll have you know," she huffed, "I have already seen my fifteenth summer."

"Really?" The Duke stroked his goatee in mock fascination. "Why, you are even older than I thought."

Eponina scrunched her brow.

"You do not look a day over twelve." He laughed even as he uttered the burning words, and Eponina's jaw fell.

"And you have no manners." She folded her arms. Oh, why had she been such a fool to hope the mysterious man she'd encountered the night before had found her as alluring as she'd found him?

But he only laughed more, tickled by her pique. "Come now, moppet, I only jest."

"Do not call me that."

"Why not?" He inched nearer, stopping just short of their toes touching. "For the record, I find the moniker rather endearing." His hazel eyes connected with hers. "Like you."

Her pulse trembled as she gazed into his face, memorizing the defined cheekbones, the kind smile beneath his goatee, the map of freckles on his brow…

"Pity you're still such a tyke," he added cavalierly, and Eponina groaned. But to her utmost surprise, he took her chin between his thumb and forefinger, and gently lifted it. "Why, with that spirit of yours, my lady," he intoned, "you are bound to win the heart of some grand Continental prince someday."

"Or a Jordinian duke?" she countered swiftly, unflinching.

The man was clearly not expecting so brazen a response. It was his turn to blush.

Satisfied that she'd rendered him speechless at last, Eponina gathered her breath. "Unless you were raised by wolves," she declared, "you might know that sixteen is the age of betrothal in Bainherd."

The Duke of Jordinia slowly lowered his hand. "I did not know."

"Well, now you do." Her pulse smacked against her breast. And then, because she simply could not permit the conversation to go any further, Eponina reached for her lantern. "Goodnight," she saluted him, marching to the doorway, "*Mac.*" She gave him a final parting glimpse before hurrying back to her quarters.

80

CARLO

FIDDLERS AND STRUMMERS PLAYED AT Fifth Street that evening. Carlo DiGyle had salvaged a few pieces of silver—never mind without their owner's consent—to drop by the tavern, where he presently sat enjoying a pint with his friends.

The front door opened, letting in a draft of cool air, and the lad huddled closer to the hearth, barely listening to his companions' stories. Peering into the flames, he sipped his drink when he heard a hoarse voice rasp: "Jonwal Cosmith?"

Several barmaids rolled their eyes, and Carlo glanced around the dingy room. Surely, Jon couldn't be there. He'd left ages ago.

He watched as two cloaked strangers approached the bar. "We seek a man called Cosmith," the hoarse one told the bartender.

"He's not here," Carlo informed them.

They turned. "You know him?"

Carlo nodded.

"Then you are coming with us."

Carlo drew another sip. "No thanks." Whatever deal these shady blokes were up to, he wasn't interested.

But the larger of the two loomed over him. "You don't understand, comrade," he uttered in a deep voice, flashing something gold for only Carlo to see: a badge imprinted with a sword-crossed diamond. *"You are coming with us."*

Carlo swallowed. These men were with the New Republic. And their summons had been a command, not an offer.

He set down his glass. His companions, deep in conversation, barely noticed him departing, as he had no choice but to follow the officials out through the backdoor. Once behind the building, Carlo held up his hands. "Look, whatever this is, I don't—"

The large one interrupted him. "What is your connection to Cosmith?"

Carlo's breathing weakened. It was too late to lie; he'd already confessed he knew the man.

"Hmm?" pressed the official, as the other cornered him against the brick wall.

"H-he is my friend."

"Do you know where he's gone?"

"No." Carlo made to push past them, but they blocked his way. "Look, he left Pierma some time ago. I know nothing else, I swear."

The larger one reached into his pocket and extracted a sack. "Perhaps this might recall his whereabouts to your memory?"

Carlo gazed at the bag bulging with silver. Surely, those coins could rent him a room for a time, and fill his stomach for a number of weeks. He promptly felt disgusted with himself. "Bribery?" He shook his head. "You comrades are worse than I thought."

The other official cackled. "Protecting Jonny, are you? Why, we're not his enemies." He grinned. "Rather, his colleagues."

Carlo furrowed his brow.

"Know you not that Jon Cosmith is an agent for Intelligence?" He laughed softly at Carlo's stunned expression. "Why do you think he hangs around with royalist filth? He *spies* on them."

These men were out of their minds. "You lie," said Carlo. "If Jon worked for you, why would he risk his neck promoting Eludaine Ducelle in Capitol Square? That's why you're after him, isn't it?"

"Come, boy, are you truly so dim?" The larger man dropped his voice, hair shining silver in the moonlight. "How else was Cosmith to round up so many royalists in one gathering? And who do you think summoned the authorities on them?"

Carlo stared, feeling dizzy. Not Jon.

"Think now. How d'you suppose Cosmith was able to escape the whole ordeal unscathed?"

"Because he works for us," supplied the hoarse one. "The whole event was pre-planned."

Carlo felt ill. He wished they'd stop. "It's not true. I've known Jon for years. He is like a brother to me. If he ever worked for you, trust me, I would know."

The men scrutinized him a moment, until one finally inquired, "What is your name, son?"

It was no use lying to the New Republic. And Carlo would very well find himself in deeper trouble if he did. "Carlo DiGyle, sir."

"DiGyle?" The official fell into a thoughtful silence. "Are you any relation to Havier?"

The young man winced. Even after seven years, the mention of his only parent, who remained in prison, pained him. "Aye, Havier is my Pa."

The men laughed throatily, the sound eerie, sinister. "Oh, dear. But Jonny has certainly been playing you. Would you like to guess the identity of the agent who turned in your father?"

It felt as though the brick walls were caving in on him. Carlo shook his head numbly.

"In fact, Comrade DuBerre possesses Jon Cosmith's original reports on Havier DiGyle. Don't you, comrade?"

"Indeed, I do, Comrade Quixheto."

Carlo looked away. Could Jon truly have had something to do with his father's arrest?

Then again, when had Jon first entered his life? The man had seemingly appeared out of thin air one day, just after Carlo's father had been jailed. He'd always assumed Jon to be a fellow street-dweller. And yet, as Carlo was coming to realize, Cosmith dressed well, always possessed some money, even supplied Carlo with food and garments...

"Why?" He stared into the evening sky, his mind racing. "If Jon is the man who saw to my father's arrest, then why would he have befriended me?"

"To uncover more royalists, no doubt," supplied the one called Quixheto, and Carlo startled. Why, when Jon had first returned to Pierma that summer, was his first inquiry not after Carlo's father, and whether the man knew of any persisting royalists who had, until then, avoided arrest? Carlo said nothing, gaping at the ground in disbelief.

The other, DuBerre, rested a meaty hand on his shoulder. "I am sure this comes as rather a shock to you. How difficult it must've been to grow up without a father. You have Jon Cosmith to thank for that."

Carlo looked between them, fighting back the overpowering urge to break something. "Why do you seek him?" he pried, his anger mounting.

"That is classified."

"Suffice it to say, it would behoove you to help us locate him."

"Perhaps," added DuBerre, "we might even consider a pardon for your father, should you willingly co-operate."

Carlo's pulse quickened. He could have his father pardoned? His blood seared at the thought of Cosmith. Whatever these officials wanted with him, Carlo clearly didn't owe him his protection—rather, his vengeance.

"He's gone to the Bainherd Plains," spat the boy. "Something about an invitation from the King, to an event on Carnivalle."

DuBerre and Quixheto exchanged glances. "What else?" DuBerre's eyes bored into Carlo's.

"I think he said the King of Bainherd plans to un-veil his wife to the populace there."

"Whose wife?"

"C-Cosmith's wife."

Quixheto looked surprised. "Since when is Jon Cosmith married?"

"Since he won Hessian Gatspierre's quest for the Duchess Eludaine, sir, and took her for his bride." Chest heaving, Carlo watched as the officials' eyes narrowed.

Quixheto flashed him a dangerous grin. "Apparently, you did know a thing or two." He hurled a fist into Carlo's stomach.

"*Tolohov,*" grunted DuBerre, as Carlo doubled over.

"That is for withholding your knowledge when we first inquired of you," growled Quixheto. He offered a hand, helping Carlo up. "In the future, you'd best be forthright with any information Mother Republic would command of you. Consider this your only warning, Di-Gyle."

DuBerre tossed the sack of silver at him. "For your troubles."

"Wait." Carlo clutched the sack to his breast. "What about my father?"

"Should your claims prove to be fruitful, we will consider it." Lifting their dark hoods overhead, the men disappeared into the crisp night.

81

CAPITOL TOWER

"LET ME GET THIS STRAIGHT." Marten Hoste ran nail-bitten fingers through the snowy hair at his temples. "The King of Bainherd is throwing an event for Carnivalle, at which he intends to reveal Eludaine Ducelle to his citizens?"

"According to the boy, sir."

"And Cosmith is her *husband,* you say?" Hoste's face reddened. "This whole ordeal is becoming more ridiculous by the minute. I've a forest to appraise, firewood to acquire for my country. I've not the time to deal with some vengeful ex-royal and her traitorous husband."

His voice dropped. "I made an agreement with her. I permitted her amnesty outside our borders, so long as she left us be. But she's going around flaunting herself abroad, stirring things up. She is forging some sort of alliance against us with Bainherd, I know it. This has gone far enough." He slammed a fist onto his desk. "It stops here."

"We'll take care of it," DuBerre assured him, while

Tolohov Quixheto nodded beside him.

"Good. Then send your men to Pon Castle for this event on Carnivalle, when we know the girl will be present. I want you to get rid of her, once and for all. And do not cause a scene," Hoste went on, rising from his chair. "Seize her alone, and off her quietly. I don't want a press circus surrounding this.

"As for Jon Cosmith," he added carefully, "I want him captured and brought back to Pierma, alive." He gave a curt nod, affirming this to himself. "I will make an example of him."

"Yes, sir."

"And comrades?" Hoste fingered his cravat. "This time, there is no room for error."

82

DAINY

IN ALL HER TIME THERE, Dainy had never seen Pon Castle as lively as it became during the weeks leading up to Carnivalle. Each day, Queen Tara and her ladies oversaw some new order of props and décor, flowers and furnishings. The cooks and every scullery maid were already preparing to feed the multitudes that should attend the event, while the grand ballroom—which had been defunct for the last few decades—was diligently cleaned, refurbished, and redecorated for the impending event.

The Duchess could not help but wonder, as she watched a parade of servants carrying ornate vases up the hall, how all of this could possibly be for her. Then again, it was for the Wilqens, too. For the occasion was meant to grant the two royal families opportunity to join together in solidarity, and resurge affection for monarchy in Halvean hearts—or so, at least, they hoped.

Presently, she and Mac walked side-by-side through the courtyard, lightly discussing the Queen's musical selections for the ball, as well as their own costume ideas.

"…or I may go as a greenman," mused Mac, referring to the mythical plant spirits of lore.

"I so dread being presented before all," bemoaned Dainy, golden leaves crunching beneath her shoes. "Why can I not simply keep my masque on and remain in disguise?"

Mac laughed, retrieving a long branch from the ground. "By all means, Miss Future Empress, you'd better get used to greeting crowds," he reminded her, using the branch for a mock walking stick.

"Ugh." Dainy's stomach twisted at the thought when her name rang through the brisk air. She turned to see Eponina hurrying across the lawn, blue frock billowing up at her knees. She was alarmed to see the girl's pink face streaked with tears. "What's the matter, dear?"

"She says I cannot go," Eponina cried. "The whole event was *my* idea, yet Mama says I am too young!"

Dainy took the distraught princess into her arms.

"After all this time, everything I've contributed, she says it is improper for me to attend La Maskérada, for being a measly eight moons short of my sixteenth birthday!" Eponina clung to Dainy's sleeve.

Once again, Dainy wished that she could trade places with the princess. Indeed, she would gladly spend the upcoming evening alone in her bedchamber, rather than face such an enormous gathering in her honor.

She happened to glance at Mac, who twirled the walking stick, looking thoughtful. "And what if you had a chaperone?" he inquired evenly. "Would Her Majesty permit you attend then?"

Eponina slowly lifted her head.

Mac's eyes were fixated upon her. "I shall approach your parents after sundown, and specially request your accompaniment for myself, if you'd like."

"Really?" she squeaked, wiping her eyes. "You would escort me?"

"That's right." He folded his arms, and Dainy's brow lifted. Since when did her brother so resemble Jon?

"Oh, Mac," sighed Eponina, a grin brightening her features. "You are so kind, I could just kiss you!"

"Then why don't you, moppet?" He smirked, and Dainy's mouth fell agape.

Eponina's cheeks raged scarlet before she turned on her heel and darted back across the courtyard.

"Mac!" Dainy whacked his arm. "I told you, she is only fifteen!"

"So?" He smoothed down his goatee, smiling after the girl. "Sixteen is the age of betrothal in Bainherd. Or so I've been informed."

"You'd better be serious," whispered Dainy. "Eponina has become like a sister to me. If you are flippant with her, or break her heart, I shall never forgive you."

Mac turned to her. "And why would I break the heart I intend to win?"

Dainy blinked, taking in his words. And then, she could not help but soften.

83

COSMITH

COSMITH LOST TRACK OF TIME, of the days. All he knew was that he was exhausted, famished, and aching with thirst by the time he arrived to the outskirts of Pon Castle.

People were everywhere. It was disconcerting. Mules trudged by, hauling carts, while children chased mangy dogs up the lanes. He cast his gaze about, vaguely recognizing that the entire village seemed to be decorated for some occasion, with street vendors and artisans lining the block, peddling all manner of masques, veils and scarves.

"Last chance to purchase your costume for La Maskérada! The event of the season," one merchant shouted. "Don't miss out. Show up to court in style!"

"Forty percent off my handcrafted masques," called a woman. "Come on, folks, I've got to evacuate my wares by this evenin'."

"Excuse me." Cosmith approached a passerby. "Is Carnivalle tonight?"

The man laughed in his face. "Where've you been

living, son, in a cave?" He strode off, shaking his head. *"Is Carnivalle tonight…"*

Cosmith watched him depart, barely aware of the mob bustling around him. He glanced down at his own clothing. It was filthy, muddy, ragged in places. That would not do.

Slipping his hand into his pocket, he fingered his money pouch. A new purchase was in order, and immediately.

84

MACMILLAN

THE VIOLINISTS WERE ALREADY PRACTICING.
Macmillan could hear the harp as well as the harpsichord, and a line of percussionists. He stepped out of
his chamber, dressed in a suit of forest green, but the
masque was his true costume. Careful not to wrinkle
the papier-mâché leaves so carefully adhered to it, he
lifted the dyed leather to his face and fastened the strap
round the back of his head.

Stealthily, he stalked to his sister's quarters. Grinning behind the leather, he leapt into her chamber with a
mighty roar. Dainy shrieked, and Macmillan dissolved
into laughter.

"Very funny, Mac," came a dry voice, where
Eponina was seated at the vanity. His hilarity subsided
as he took in the pale tresses of gauze and silk cascad-
ing down her lithe figure, her fine white-blonde hair el-
egantly wrapped atop her head.

Dainy sighed as he removed his masque. She was
dressed entirely in white, her sleeves belling out at the
wrists and her hem studded with tiny pearls. "Where

are your wings, ladies?" he inquired.

"Unlike *some* who plainly lack maturity," sniffed Eponina, "the Duchess and I are not running around the castle in full costume hours before the ball."

She and Dainy burst into giggles, and Macmillan checked the clock on the wall. "I suppose there is still time to practice our footwork," he proposed, extending a hand to the girl.

Eponina remained seated. "So eager to get your hands on my waist, are you, Your Grace?"

"Nina," Dainy gasped, while the princess barely concealed her smirk.

Macmillan's heart murmured as he took a seat on the edge of Dainy's bed. "Let's see your masques, then."

Eponina held hers up. It was painted stark white, with round spritely cheeks and an abundance of flowers glued along the sides. A little wood nymph, to go along with his greenman. Although Macmillan doubted whether any of the woodland fairies of legend were as beautiful as the eldest Princess of the Bainherd Plains.

His sister displayed her own masque, the saintly, porcelain face of the Angel of Loch, just as the maids bustled in.

"I'd best be going," Macmillan decided.

"Oy," Eponina called. "Are we still meeting on the stairwell at a quarter 'til?"

Would that we were meeting in the courtyard now, Macmillan thought longingly, gazing at the ethereal maiden. He still could not believe his luck, that the King and Queen of Bainherd had honored his request and permitted him to chaperone their daughter to the Masquerade.

He cleared his throat. "Of course." He winked at her. With a nod to his sister, he departed the chamber, his steps unusually light.

85

DAINY

THIS WAS IT. DAINY GRIMACED, tripping over her shoes again as she descended the stairs on Maxos's arm. She was already a poor enough dancer; now she had these cumbersome slippers to contend with. How was she to have any hope of appearing graceful tonight, when the art of dancing seemed to despise her as much as she despised it? The only time Dainy had ever enjoyed dancing was on her Uncle Pascale's boat, when she'd first danced with…

Do not think his name, she commanded herself, her nose already burning as she shoved the thought away. For the most painful part of the night—even worse than having to dress up and dance—was that she would be without her husband.

Oh, Jon. It'd been far too long since she'd last seen him smile, last fell asleep to the sound of his heartbeat, or awoke with his arms around her. What if he never came back? But do not think that way, she reprimanded herself.

She and Maxos followed Mac and Eponina into the

ballroom, where a deafening symphony poured through the open doors. Maxos bid her adieu, and Dainy, now alone, glanced around the enormous hall, her eyes large behind her angel masque. The room was dimly lit with intriguing star-shaped lanterns, while masked guests adeptly took to the dance floor.

Attendees arrived by the droves, most looking rather macabre in their strange costumes, and Dainy hurried out of their way. Unsure what to do with herself, she kept to the far wall, watching as castle staff orbited the room with trays of wine glasses and infinite hors d'oeuvres.

She adjusted the swan-feather wings at her back. They were perhaps not as delicate as Eponina's wax fairy wings, but at least they looked classier than the bizarre tails or sets of horns the other guests sported.

She was unfortunate enough to overhear a group of nearby men recounting a rather crude joke. Turning away from their coarse laughter, Dainy heaved a sigh and removed a glass of wine from a servant's tray. It was going to be a long evening.

86

COSMITH

COSMITH HAD NOT NECESSARILY CHOSEN his costume. There was little left to choose from, really. It was merely the only one left that still retained some semblance of subtlety and style. And so, dressed as an infamous viscount, Cosmith took his place in line outside of Pon Castle, awaiting permission to enter. Soon, however, a dismayed outcry drifted down the queue.

"They're saying the ballroom is full!"

He stepped aside and marched up to a patrolling guard. The man held out a halting hand, but Cosmith removed his masque. The guard's eyes widened. "Apologies, Your Grace. Right this way." He wove Cosmith past the queue and in through the front doors, as hundreds of masked faces watched curiously.

Once inside, Cosmith bade the guard return to his duties, and made his own way to the ballroom. He could barely hear the music, hardly perceive the aromas of hot meats, ripe wine and fresh flowers, so single-minded was he to find his wife.

But which one was she? He wondered, side-stepping an oddly-dressed man who staggered with a mugful of mead. There were gowned women everywhere, some sporting cloaks, others in hats, all with their faces disguised. He glanced at the orchestra, before which multitudes of couples twirled gracefully across the floor. Well, he could be certain she wasn't one of them.

He paced the room's perimeter. It was stuffy behind his masque, but he could not remove it yet. Seek her figure, he told himself, now looking past the taller, skinnier lasses. Surely, if anyone was familiar with the shape of her, it was him, so many times had he stroked and caressed her every last curve…

The man shivered with yearning. It had been much too long. How could he have ever thought leaving her behind would be easy? He'd been anticipating another adventure, but the whole ordeal had instead become a nightmare.

Dainy would make it better. She always did.

Cosmith was beginning to wonder whether Wilqen was keeping the woman hidden, preserving her until her designated hour of unmasking, when he spotted someone gowned in white at the opposite end of the hall. She stood by her lonesome, a glass of wine in her gloved hand, a small pair of feathery wings at her back. He could just make out the strands of black hair tumbling from her crown and—as his eyes trailed downward—her jutting bust.

Breathless, the man lifted his feet and pushed his way through the masses, his watchful eyes never leaving their lovely destination.

87

QUIXHETO

"THIS HAD BETTER BE A damned joke," hissed agent Josef Hasmond furiously. "And if it is, it's not funny."

Quixheto sighed, gazing down at the hundreds awaiting entry into Pon Castle. An event was certainly taking place that evening for Carnivalle. But the Di-Gyle boy had failed to supply one important detail.

"They're all wearing masques!" cried Hasmond. "How in hell are we supposed to tell which one is the Duchess, and which is Cosmith?"

"Silence, Josef," Quixheto muttered. He could not concentrate with the young agent bumbling in his ear like a horsefly. "Our informant claimed the Duchess was to be revealed tonight. She will remove her masque." He watched from their perch atop the roof. "As for Cosmith, he is her husband, no? He'll likely be found at her side."

Hasmond huffed. "Bloody brilliant. A bloody Masquerade. You'd think DuBerre would've *told* us."

"DuBerre did not know," snapped Quixheto, his

patience diminishing. "Nor did I. Our informant didn't say this fête was a revival of *La Maskérada*." He spat the term with disdain.

The men squatted in silence under the darkening sky, the air chilling as the sun disappeared beneath the horizon. "We cannot seize them in plain sight of the multitudes, anyway. Hoste does not want a scene." Quixheto glanced around. "There is only one way to go about this."

Hasmond cast him a perplexed look.

"We determine where she sleeps. No doubt the King is hosting her. Filthy monarchs and their extravagant castles…" He backed into the shadows as an armed guard cast an arbitrary upward glance.

"How?" whispered Hasmond, crouching beside Quixheto.

"By stalking the servants, of course. We hide in the dark of her chamber and await her there. When she and her husband retire for the evening, they shall walk right into our hands." Quixheto shrugged. "Simple enough."

Hasmond exhaled. "Now, why didn't I think of that?"

88

DAINY

DAINY WAS FORMULATING HOW best to subtly lift her masque to taste her wine when a figure draped in midnight black drifted hungrily toward her. She backed out of his way, assuming whoever it was to be headed elsewhere. But instead, the phantom stopped just before her, arching out a hand.

Dainy shook her head. She was not an available maid to be courted. Did he not see her bracelet? But the man cocked his head toward the dance floor. She turned away; she would not dance with a stranger.

He suddenly seized her hips. Dainy gasped, tearing away from his crude touch. "Excuse me," she hissed. "I'll have you know, I am a married woman!"

"Is that so, firecracker?" came the intimate purr behind the mustachioed masque.

Dainy nearly sloshed purple wine down her snowy front. "*Jon?*" Was she mistaken, or had she just heard her husband's voice?

"The one and only, my pet." He wrapped his hands around her middle again, and Dainy could only fall into him, her spirit singing as those strong arms contained her at last.

"Now, put this silly thing down," he cooed, reaching for her wine glass, "and have a dance with your husband."

She let him guide her to the crowded floor. The orchestra was playing a slower number, and the pair wedged themselves between the other couples. Dainy tripped over her new shoes as Jon took the first step, although he didn't seem to mind, only holding her closer as he steered her in a graceful circle.

"When did you arrive?" she asked him, her skin tingling beneath his touch.

"Tonight." His answer was succinct.

She stumbled over his foot. "What is happening in Jordinia?"

"Dainy. Let me lead."

"I *am*." Her masque concealed her flushing cheeks. "I'm just…not very good at this."

Jon merely continued to move her in time to the music.

"You didn't answer my question. What is happening in—?"

"My dearest," he sighed. "I've come a long way, and it's been a trying journey. I finally have you back now; I do not wish to think on anything else at the moment."

Dainy watched her clumsy feet. What had happened in Jordinia that Jon did not wish to discuss? Would he now be keeping things from her?

"Oy." He gave her a little shake. "Let me guess: you are the Angel of Loch?"

"Yes. Although I cannot quite figure who you're

supposed to be." She eyed his rather sinister-looking garb.

"Come now. You don't recognize the demon Viscount of Svatzlund?" He chuckled, taking a series of complicated steps, which Dainy struggled to match.

"Never heard of him," she admitted, stubbing her toe on his boot. "Ouch."

Jon paused, allowing her to collect herself. "The Viscount is one of the most notorious literary figures of the last century."

"And for what is he so notorious?" inquired Dainy, who had never been exposed to much literature. A Heppestonian innkeeper had little time to read novels, after all.

"Ah, but perhaps that is not a conversation for such a refined setting as this," said Jon, though Dainy could hear the smirk in his voice. "However, if you really wish to know…" He leaned in and proceeded to whisper a most alarming account of an irresistibly handsome yet wicked killer, who lured countless virgins to his bed, only to murder them with his poisonous semen.

"Jon!" Dainy chided as he cackled darkly. "Why ever would you dress as a villain so vile?"

"I'd few choices, darling." He was still laughing when a second voice issued behind them.

"I don't believe it," whispered Mac behind his masque, leading Eponina to dance parallel to them. "That cannot be Cosmith I hear?"

For once, Jon fell out of time with the music. "*Macmillan*? When the devil did you return to West Halvea?"

The men lifted their hands from their partners'

waists for a subtle handshake. "Good to see you, brother," murmured Mac. "Albeit in costume. Yet, how fitting for the two of you." He sniggered. "A demon and his angel."

Dainy was about to tease him in turn, when the music abruptly ceased, and the crier's voice issued through an enormous gilded mouthpiece. "Ladies and gentlemen, we interrupt the festivities to bring you a most exciting announcement. But first, all hail Their Majesties, the King and Queen of the Bainherd Plains!"

A procession of red-uniformed guards preceded the royal couple into the now silent ballroom, and Dainy spotted Wilqen, flanked by a dozen armored knights and lavishly costumed as some ancient god. Queen Tara stepped gracefully beside him, dressed as what could only be the god's consort goddess, a horned helmet painted with the crescent moon over her white-blonde braids, her magnificent golden gown tailing several feet behind her. Soon, every knee had descended to the floor, while every masked head bowed.

The King bade them all rise. Collectively, the crowd straightened, watching as the opulent man climbed the platform and took up the crier's trumpet.

"Beloved citizens," Wilqen addressed them, his sonorous voice magnified as he beamed at his guests. "Welcome back to our wondrous courts!" The people cheered, and Wilqen nodded encouragingly. "I regret to confess, it has been far too long since our kingdom last opened its doors for you all to bask in our proud glory."

Another outcry, even more enthusiastic than the last. Dainy glanced at Jon, meeting his eyes behind his masque. He squeezed her hand.

"My dear people," said Wilqen, and the starry lanterns glimmered majestically off of his vibrant costume, "I know you've toiled and suffered much in these times of economic strain." He took a step forward, crimson robes folding with his movements. "And yet, here we still stand. Here we proudly proclaim: we are the Kingdom of the Bainherd Plains!"

There came heavy applause at this, and Dainy swallowed. It was only a matter of time...

"While others would knock us down," Wilqen continued, "attempt to overtake us with their foreign ways, we stout-hearted citizens of Bainherd have stood fierce in defense of our kingdom. For indeed," he lifted his voice, "we are indestructible, invincible.

"You know, the institution of monarchy is indestructible," he said thoughtfully. "Would you not say? It shall not be silenced, cannot be killed. In fact, my special guest of honor, who stands masked among you tonight, can attest to that."

Dainy's pulse thrummed while hundreds of masked faces glanced about the ballroom.

"Aye, the gods are on our side." The King nodded. "For while it might've once seemed as though the winds were changing, blowing in new regimes and crumbling the empires of old into oblivion, one brave, young soul has miraculously, by the will and power of the holy ones, crawled out from beneath the ruins, arisen from the ashes to stand here among you tonight. Perhaps you know of whom I speak. Or perhaps this might come as rather a shock to you.

"And now," said Wilqen, and Dainy took a shuddering breath, "it's time I ask my special guest to step forth, and join me on the platform. My dear, where are you?"

Dainy's slippers were sealed to the floor. Jon and Mac nudged her. "Go on, Dainy," Jon whispered, as hundreds of guests swiveled around, a wave of murmurs overtaking the room.

At last, Dainy willed her legs to move. Every pair of eyes watched her from behind painted masques as she moved. After several excruciating moments, she climbed the platform to join the King.

"Ladies and gentlemen, behold," bellowed Wilqen, "I present Eludaine Ducelle, the once and future Duchess of Jordinia!"

Just as they'd practiced, Dainy tore off her masque and bowed deeply to the people of Bainherd.

The reaction was instantaneous. The room collectively gasped, followed by a thunderous roar of applause. Her stomach leaping, Dainy shot a glance in Jon's direction, but could not discern his masked face from the many others at this distance.

"Yes!" shouted the King over the din. "The rumors are true. The Duchess lives!" He took Dainy's arm and lifted it, beaming as the room rang with a deafening symphony of cheers. Everyone bowed, glasses were toasted, and Dainy could not help but grin, even as her heart lolloped in her chest.

89

QUIXHETO

"I DON'T BELIEVE THIS," WHISPERED Hasmond, gaping at the multitudes wildly saluting the former Duchess. "The place is swarming with press, too. Look at everyone with quills, writing…" He shook his head. "Good God. Hoste is going to have a conniption when this turns up in the posts tomorrow."

"The girl will be dead by tomorrow," Quixheto muttered. "In the meantime, let's get out of here."

The two slipped by the guards, silently departing the great ballroom. Their faces, thankfully, were concealed behind the masques they'd borrowed from a pair of inebriated guests.

Quixheto peered down the corridor as a pair of maids carrying baskets of linens veered around a corner. He beckoned Hasmond, and the agents set off behind them, keeping at a shadowy distance.

90

MACMILLAN

SHE MOVED LIKE CLEAR WATER trickling over stone, her soft skin like warm silk. Macmillan clung to Eponina, resting his chin on her shoulder as they slowly turned on the floor. Presently, he did not much care that the rest of the room had fallen enamored under the spell of his sister's revelation, nor that he and the princess were one of the few pairs remaining on the dance floor. For now, all he wished to do was hold her, rocking her gently to the music.

After hours of ambushing and interviews by skeptics and fascinated supporters alike, Macmillan's poor half-siblings had finally been escorted away, their expressions of relief tangible even from the distance. At least the Masquerade was proving to be taking its desired effect.

"I'm parched," came Eponina's voice. Macmillan led her to the refreshments, pointedly aware of her many guards watching them. Once the princess had satisfied her thirst, she grabbed Macmillan's hand and steered him to the far wall.

"Eponina—?"

She shushed him, motioning for him follow. "Here it is," she whispered. "Lysander and I discovered this when we were small."

Bemused, Macmillan trailed behind her through a narrow opening in the wall, which led to a tiny hallway. "What the—?"

"It's a servants' passage. It has long been out of use." She laughed at his hesitation. "Come on! It merely leads to the kitchens."

He tried to stop her, but she evaded his grip, trudging forward. "Eponina," said Macmillan, very seriously. "I cannot just disappear in here with you. Your guards, your parents—they will think the worst. Do you understand? My sister and I cannot afford to lose their trust now."

She paused, her back to him. "Is that the only reason you wished to chaperone me tonight, then?" She sounded suddenly frosty. "To earn my family's favor at every angle, in order to fund your sister's war?"

Macmillan would not stand for that. He took the girl by the waist and spun her around. "You retract that accusation," he demanded. "And do not pretend you don't know why I chaperoned you tonight."

She trembled in his hold. "Tell me why." Her eyes glowed up at him like white lanterns. "I want to hear you say it, Mac."

He inhaled the flowery fragrance of her hair, relishing in the press of her sprouting breasts against him. "Eponina Wilqen," he murmured, running his hands down her flawless spine. "The things I wish to say to you…" He restrained himself, taking a pained step back. "Alas. You are still too young."

Eponina's breath heaved, and Macmillan felt much the same. He hated to spurn her, but could not be irresponsible. Nothing about his sentiments toward her was exactly proper. At least not for another eight moons.

He reached for her hand, and she allowed him to steer her back up the passage, until they both saw the light of the ballroom once more.

91

DAINY

DAINY KNEW THE WAY TO the fishpond. No one typically ventured that far on the castle grounds. And certainly, nobody would be there tonight. Squeezing each other by the hand, the couple dashed across the dark acres to the swampy brush, the air chilly on their faces as moonlight glistened behind a film of fog. Between the barren tree stumps they collapsed, the abandoned pond overgrown with algae and smelling mildly of fish, while crisp leaves crackled beneath their weight.

Jon took Dainy by the back of her neck and pressed his lips over hers. Her pulse vibrated as she kissed him back, tasting the salt of his tongue, reveling in the softness of his mouth. Her head spinning, she climbed atop him, wrapping her arms and legs around his. "No ladies in waiting," she murmured. "No maids bidding me sleep and rise. No watchful bodyguards." She exhaled unevenly. "Just us."

His breathing was heavy as he lay beneath her. And that was when she noticed the strange melancholy, the disturbed distance in his eyes. "What's wrong?" she asked at once.

"Nothing," he replied, after a beat.

"There is something." Dainy backed away, straightening. "You do not seem yourself tonight, Jon."

He didn't speak at first, and Dainy looked away, crestfallen. But what was the matter? What had happened while he was away? And why had she ever let him go?

He took her back into his arms. "Dainy." He smiled. "I'm right here." He slid his hand up her thigh, stroking her tantalizingly, and she quivered with pleasure.

She lifted her gown overhead, her flesh pebbling in the moonlit draft, and he slipped from his own clothing, his eyes hungrily scanning her. At long last, Dainy joined herself to her spouse beneath the foggy stars, drinking him entirely in, so warm and real beneath her, just as she'd dreamed of him for many lonely moons.

She could hear the torrent of emotion in his voice as he professed his love to her. All too soon, she felt the familiar pulse of his release within her. She held him close, rocking against him to accommodate his pleasure.

Jon dropped his head onto the grass, and Dainy showered him with kisses. "Sorry." He draped a hot arm over her back. "Only, it's been so long, and you look so beautiful…"

She laughed intimately. "Do not apologize."

He gave her a tender grin, tracing circles on her shoulder with his fingertips, until looking concerned. "My dear, you are freezing," he fussed. "We ought to retire. Never mind the ball; it's been a long enough evening for both of us."

Dainy allowed him to help her back into her gown, now undoubtedly stained with grass and earth. She knew that Jon had journeyed far and wide, and must be fatigued. At the same time, however, she'd not quite had her fill of him yet.

She was glad to take him to her bed. But she did not much plan on letting him sleep.

92

COSMITH

COSMITH SIGHED WITH RELIEF AS they rounded the final corner to Dainy's quarters. To take to his wife's bed at last, to lie beside her, holding her throughout the night…it was the prospect of heaven itself.

"Curious," she remarked upon finding her door ajar. "The maids must've visited."

Cosmith stayed her hand. Something did not feel right, yet he couldn't quite explain.

But he was becoming delirious in his weariness, was he not? The man stepped back, allowing her to enter the dark room. Holding up a lantern, he followed suit, when Dainy gasped, hands flying to her mouth. He nearly dropped the lantern to see one of the castle maids lying on the floor, dead.

Dainy shrieked as she fell to her knees, cradling the woman's head between her hands. "*Sheila!*" She shook her. "Sheila, wake up!"

Cosmith's eyes followed the pool of blood issuing from the woman's heart. "Step away, Dainy," he commanded tremulously. "My darling, leave her be. She's dead. There is nothing more we can do."

Shaking, Dainy rose to her feet and clung to him, tears streaming down her face. His blood rushed painfully as he steered her back to the door. He had to act immediately. For it was clear that Dainy had been the intended target, and not her hapless maidservant.

But she slipped from his hold. Cosmith turned, about to inquire what the devil she thought she was doing, when his breath caught in his lungs. A dark figure had emerged from the shadows, and was forcing the girl back by her arm.

"*Dainy,*" cried Cosmith.

She freed her wrist and swung her leg behind her attacker's knees. The shadowy figure fell to the floor, and Cosmith crashed his lantern over the man's head. Numb with fury, he repeatedly bashed the stranger's skull.

So overpowering was his instinct to protect his wife, it was several moments before he realized that Dainy was shouting and clawing at his sleeve. "*Enough, Jon!*" She was sobbing. "I think—I think you've killed him!"

Cosmith glanced down, panting. The blunt end of the lantern and his hands were now coated in blood. Dazed, he slammed down the sticky lamp and took his wife's elbow, pulling her out of the condemned chamber. "*Guards,*" he bellowed down the hall, while Dainy repeated his summons.

There sounded the responsorial stomping of heavy boots as a team of sword-clad men dutifully rounded the corner. "Come quickly," Cosmith commanded them. "Someone has tried to assassinate the Duchess!"

The head guard clutched the hilt of his sword.

"Did you see his face?"

Cosmith swallowed. "I think he's dead."

The guard's expression darkened, and the men poured into the room to investigate. Cosmith and Dainy remained in the doorway, staring at each other. By the look on her face, he knew they shared the same thought: what if they'd gone straight to bed that evening, instead of first being intimate by the fishpond?

A guard emerged with a gold badge bearing a familiar insignia. "This was found on the deceased man's person."

"The New Republic?" Dainy looked to her husband, stunned.

A current of rage coursed through Cosmith. "*Damn it!*" He smacked the doorframe. How in hell did the New Republic know that Dainy would be there? "Summon the Duke Macmillan immediately," he ordered, and the guard set off.

The head guard approached him grimly, and Cosmith rounded on him. "You must evacuate the guests and search the castle. The assassin may have a partner still at large."

The man appeared somewhat miffed at Cosmith telling him how to do his job. But he only inclined his head. "Very well, Your Grace. With your pardon, I shall obtain His Majesty's permission to do so."

Cosmith saw him off before pulling Dainy into his arms. "My darling," he whispered, "just know that, no matter what happens, my heart is forever your—"

"Jon," she interjected, uncertain. "Why do you speak like this? The assassin is dead. Shan't everything be all right now?"

While he knew his spouse's would-be assassin had

indeed been defeated, Cosmith could not shake the inexplicable dread that someone else was lurking in the castle. Neither of them was safe.

"What's going on?"

Cosmith looked up to see Macmillan striding briskly up the corridor. His half-brother had certainly changed since they'd left him in Asiotica. The man seemed somewhat older, stronger, his facial hair and confident gait granting him an air of maturity that had not quite been there before.

Cosmith placed Dainy's hand into Macmillan's. "You must get her out of here."

"Jon?" Dainy looked fearfully between them.

Macmillan clasped her hand, his expression even. "And where am I taking her?"

Cosmith met his eyes significantly. "To the place we agreed to."

"What?" demanded Dainy. "Where? Why must I go? Aren't you coming with me?"

"You are no longer safe at the castle, Dainy. Nor would you be safe with me." Cosmith looked up at their brother. "The New Republic is after me."

Dainy jerked forward, gripping his hand. "And they are after me as well. We're both fugitives; we flee together."

Cosmith could only shake his head at the woman he loved, and gently pry her fingers from his wrist. The Republic well knew his face. She would be far safer without him. His heart tore as her eyes pooled. Oh, how she loved him. But heavens, how little he deserved it.

He turned back to Macmillan, his chest aching. "Take her," he implored him.

Macmillan wrapped an arm around his sister's

shoulders. "Come, Dainy," he ordered, hurrying her away. Cosmith could hear her protests all the way up the corridor. They were gone by the time the head guard returned.

"His Majesty does not wish for the guests to suspect anything. However, the crier has announced the conclusion of the festivities, and the ballroom is evacuating." The guard dropped his voice. "Only thing is, if the suspect has any partners in crime at large," he inclined his head toward the dead agent in Dainy's chamber, "they could easily escape with the rest of the guests."

Cosmith massaged his brow, tormented with regret. "I have endangered us all. For all I know, it is I whom the Republic followed here. I must leave at once."

"Would you like an escort, sir?" The guard indicated his men uncertainly.

Cosmith shook his head, proceeding down the corridor. Stealth was in order for escaping unscathed that night.

Had it somehow been his fault that the Republic knew where to find them? It had to be, although he couldn't fathom how. He clearly remembered being utterly alone throughout his journey, especially during that dreaded cyclone. Surely, he'd have noticed someone tailing him.

At least Dainy was being seen to safety. So long as he could trust Macmillan to spirit the girl away from any further danger Cosmith could cause her, he hardly cared about himself. He rounded a back stairwell and found a series of passages which, after several minutes of jogging, led out to a courtyard. He glanced around, regaining his bearings. The stables rested just ahead in the foggy distance.

A horse was in order. Surely, Wilqen wouldn't mind him escaping upon one of his many steeds. Urgently, Cosmith darted across the courtyard, just as a gravelly voice issued his name.

"Jonwal Cosmith?"

He never should have stopped. He never should have permitted that voice to halt him for the fraction of a moment. Alas, he slowed, and gasped as something struck his leg. An arrow stuck clean from his calf. It hadn't gone in deep, but was enough to slow him down as he struggled to remove it.

It was too late. His attacker swooped over him and bound his wrists. Cosmith tried to fight back, but the cloaked man brought a steely fist to his temple. Cosmith saw white starbursts, his head throbbing.

"It's about damn time," the man growled, and Cosmith recognized the raspy voice, the aging face beneath the black hood.

Tolohov Quixheto flashed a sinister grin, square teeth glinting as he extracted a needle from his cloak. Cosmith struggled to pull away, but Quixheto yanked up his sleeve, exposing the blue veins of his forearm. He jabbed the needle in, pushing God only knew what substance into Cosmith's blood.

The man felt himself slip away, his limbs going limp, brain turning fuzzy. Within moments, all he could comprehend was the vague sensation of being tossed onto the floor of a moving vehicle, and his abductor's hoarse cackle, repeating: "*It's about damn time.*"

93

Bos

IT WAS HALF PAST MIDNIGHT when Bos was awakened by incessant pounding on the Henns' front door. "Flee with your wife, should you need to," he whispered, meeting his host on the stairwell. "Let me handle this."

"Nay," insisted Tuck, descending the steps alongside him. "Whatever this is, we face it together."

Bos pulled back the door, prepared to see the blue-uniformed officials holding out warrants for their arrests, or else rope with which to bind them. But when he and his host peered onto the porch, they met only the frightened faces of their young neighbors from Kempei. "Boys?" Tuck looked bewildered. "What brings you here at this hour?"

"You're next," cried a red-haired lad, who could not have been more than fourteen. "All of you! They're headed for Dekantor Village as we speak!"

"Who?"

"The New Republic!"

Bos and Tuck turned to each other.

"They set fire to our village, in retaliation to what our fathers did to the von Sparx statue," the lad declared, and that was when Bos noticed the youths' faces were gray with soot. "And they're headed here now, because of your flag with the Ducelle crest." The boy swallowed, nervous. "As well, someone squealed about Father Asa's chapel."

Bos pointed to the skinniest of the lads, who would most easily be able to shimmy up a belfry. "You," he grunted. "Hurry downtown and sound the emergency bell." He faced the rest of them. "Once he returns, you're all free to flee. Thank you for the warning." He turned to fetch his boots, but the boys stood staunch on the porch.

"We intend to stay and fight, sir. Our fathers are gathering their weapons."

Bos wished they'd not involve themselves; it did not bode well for them. Then again, had he not once dreamed of joining his cousins in the Emperor's Guard when he was younger than the least of these? Although, once Bos had come of age, there was no longer any emperor left to guard.

Relenting, he turned back to the house to arm himself. He was not about to watch his home village go up in flames, nor allow any of his unsuspecting neighbors to die in their beds. Nay, when the Republic came for them, they'd be prepared.

94

MACMILLAN

THEY RODE LIKE HELLFIRE THROUGH the night. Macmillan had seized a horse from the stables, and off he'd set with his sister seated behind him. "But *where* are you taking me?" she continuously demanded, her teeth chattering in the night's chill.

"Just try to rest," Macmillan advised her, although he knew that would prove impossible atop a galloping horse. Once several hours passed, however, and Macmillan still persisted, Dainy fell silent, her head resting upon his shoulder, bouncing slightly with the rise and fall of the horse's hooves.

The terrain thickened with the promise of trees when the sky first began to lighten, the black horizon giving way to midnight blue. Soon, he heard chirruping birds in the distance. Eyes sagging, Macmillan urged his horse forward, even as the sun illuminated the eastern sky.

At long last, they reached village of Bearn, Bainherd. Just twelve more miles, Macmillan assured himself, begging his eyelids to stay open, his numb fingers to retain their hold on the reins. Only a dozen miles…

The sun revealed its luminous face by the time he slowed the horse, weaving it through the familiar path of trees. He was startled by the sudden lump in his throat. Why, all of this time, he'd never realized how homesick he'd been.

One more mile… Dainy stirred behind him, his poor horse snorting furiously under the strain of the night's exercise. The tiny cabin loomed nearer, enshrouded beneath the pines, its sides crawling with moss and vines.

His sister heaved a yawn as he finally halted the spent horse, and the two siblings stretched their arms overhead, preparing to dismount. "Mac?" Dainy glanced about their woodland setting. "Where exactly are we?"

"In the Knights' Forest," he replied, sliding down from the animal's back. He stretched his sore legs and helped his sister descend. She stumbled as she reached the leaf-covered earth, and Macmillan took her by the shoulders, balancing her. Her eyes darted about until she spied the little cabin, and comprehension dawned upon her features. Silently, Macmillan led her up to the front door which, without any preamble, he opened.

"What the—?" They heard a startled voice, accompanied by the thudding of bare feet. A familiar mane of brown curls emerged around the corner. "Marley?"

Macmillan embraced his mother.

Marlena squeezed him in return. "What are you doing here? Have you—have you come home for good?"

He sighed. "Nay, Mother." He was simply unable to explain all that had transpired since he'd last seen her, over a year ago. "I cannot stay. But I must ask you to do me one vital favor." He placed a hand on Dainy's back. "Behold, your daughter. You've met the Duchess once before," he reminded the woman. "She is your son's wife now."

His mother gaped between them, looking horrified. "But Marley, she is your sister…"

"Your *first* son," Macmillan clarified impatiently. "Jon's wife."

At the mention of Jon's name, Marlena's eyes dimmed.

"We need you to look after Dainy awhile. She must be harbored here, hidden from sight. No one must know where she is. Do you think you can help us, Mother?"

Marlena did not immediately respond, and Macmillan's breathing slowed. If his own mother turned them down, if their harrowing flight through the night had been for naught…

"All right," she agreed.

Macmillan heaved a relieved sigh. "Thank you." He headed into the kitchen. "In the meantime, we're ravenous. Have you anything to eat?"

His mother smoothed her curls self-consciously. "There's some venison drying in back. But nothing fit for a princess." She looked down.

"Dainy's not a picky eater," Macmillan assured her. "Trust me, I've seen her eat things even I would not touch. Squid, oysters…"

"Would you care for a seat, my lady?" he heard his mother ask.

"Erm… No thank you," came Dainy's polite response.

Macmillan didn't blame her. After a night of rigorous riding, he'd no desire to be seated again upon his raw backside, either. "After we eat, I'm going to sleep," he informed the women. "And then, I'm afraid I must leave."

"Already?" His mother clutched his arm. "But you've only just returned!"

Macmillan shook her off. "Nay, Mother, war is coming and I cannot stay."

95

COSMITH

A ROPE JOINED COSMITH'S WRISTS while another constricted his ankles, its sharp fibers digging into his skin like briars. They had stripped him of his costume, and there he sat, bound to a metal chair, wearing the prisoners' uniform: a gray tunic and trousers of the identical dismal shade, two sizes too large. Lanterns glared in his face, although the room was dank and freezing, and Cosmith blinked up at his captors.

It was startling, although not necessarily unexpected, when Damon DuBerre's fist collided with his jaw by means of introduction. Cosmith gasped in pain, but would not cry out. They were not to glean that satisfaction.

DuBerre walloped him again, this time in the stomach, and Cosmith inhaled, battling the unbelievable urge to holler in pain. When DuBerre gained no reaction, he struck Cosmith again and again, until Cosmith could taste blood running from his nose into his mouth.

"Beat on a man bound with no means to defend himself?" he managed to utter, struggling to keep his voice level. "How very brave of you."

This earned him a mighty kick in the shin from Quixheto. Cosmith winced, wanting nothing more than to shout every obscenity in his vocabulary.

"Where is the Duchess?" DuBerre demanded.

"I know not."

DuBerre smacked him again. "I am only just getting started, comrade," he growled, his voice unsettlingly low. "Now, I will ask you again. And this time, you'd better give me an honest answer." He bent over, his face sagging over Cosmith's bleeding one. "Where is the Duchess?"

"I know not," repeated Cosmith. DuBerre subsequently stood on his victim's bare toes with his boot, crunching down with the capacity of his hefty weight until Cosmith finally grunted in pain.

DuBerre raised a bristling eyebrow, and slowly lifted his boot.

"Either tell us where she is," rasped Quixheto, "or die."

Cosmith shot them an insolent grin. "Then you will have to kill me."

"Oh, we will, comrade. Only, not before we beat her whereabouts from you. Isn't that right, Tolohov?"

"Then you are chasing a dead end, my friends," contended Cosmith. "For truly, I know nothing."

Quixheto clicked his tongue. "You know nothing of your own wife? We find that rather difficult to believe."

Cosmith willed his breath to steady. But how the devil did they know the Duchess was his wife? "I've no idea what you're talking about," he bluffed, palms perspiring.

Quixheto's bloodshot eyes shone. "Ah, but surely Mr. DiGyle does."

Cosmith's heart jolted in confusion.

"Don't you, son?" Quixheto added.

A slender figure stepped forth from the shadows. Shocked, Cosmith took in the blond curls, the bony, tapering limbs. The happy-go-lucky boy seemed entirely displaced here in this dreary, sinister prison, although his usually mischievous blue eyes were narrowed menacingly.

Quixheto placed a spidery hand on the youth's shoulder. "Carlo," he addressed him conversationally, and Cosmith wondered wildly how the pair had become acquainted on a first-name basis. "Is there anything you'd like to say to your old friend? Any parting words, before justice is exacted upon this despicable traitor?"

Carlo peered into Cosmith's bewildered face. "Only that he is a coward and a liar. And that he's been nothing but a curse to me and my family."

"Carlo," whispered Cosmith. "How can you—?"

"You are the agent who reported my father! You are the reason I grew up orphaned and homeless!"

"And that devastated me," cried Cosmith. "Do you not understand? That is why I took care of you!"

"Oh, bull, Cosmith! You only befriended me to uncover more royalists to turn in!"

"That is *not true*," growled Cosmith, but his friend only turned away. "Carlo," he implored him. "I'm sorry about your father. I really am. But I was only doing my job."

"Oh?" The youth glared at him. "Well, now I have done mine."

96

HOSTE

HOSTE STIRRED ANOTHER TEASPOON OF cream into his tea when there came a knock at the door. "Enter," he commanded softly.

The door slid open. "Sir? A message from Intelligence."

The leader glanced up with interest.

"They say it's been days now, but the suspect still refuses to speak."

Hoste continued to stir his tea placidly. "Tell them I sanction any degree of experimentation they wish to use. If he still refuses to divulge anything of consequence in his next interrogation, he shall have no trial."

"Yes, Comrade."

Hoste frowned, contemplating the insolent renegade, Cosmith. He could no longer bear the fury coursing through his blood. The leader dropped his teaspoon onto the saucer with a clang. "Either way, he will hang," he decided. "In fact, I want you to run that post, Latimer. Plaster Jonwal Cosmith's sorry likeness all over Capitol Square, headlined: '*Hanging of royalist activist to take place on winter solstice.'"*

The lad dutifully jotted down his request.

"Let them see what happens when you lay a hand against Mother Republic." Hoste leaned back in his chair. "She will have your head."

97

MACMILLAN

MACMILLAN FINISHED LACING HIS BOOTS, and met his reflection in the looking glass. A pair of hazel eyes stared determinedly back at him. He was ready. He took up his bag and departed the guest chamber, joining the guards who awaited him in the hall. Surrounding him, they marched up the corridor.

After seeing his sister to safety, Macmillan had returned to Pon Castle, only to discover that the worst had happened: Jon had been seized. Wilqen's men could only assume it was the New Republic who'd abducted him, seeing as it was a Jordinian assassin who'd tried to murder Dainy. And their suspicions were confirmed by a subsequent post from Pierma.

Macmillan swallowed, thinking on the ominous bulletin recently brought in by the King's messengers. Macmillan's elder brother sat in Capitol Prison, condemned to execution on the solstice, suffering God only knew what in the meantime.

He descended the stairs, guards following suit. In his bag was a letter from King Wilqen, which Macmillan would personally deliver to Marten Hoste, requesting Jon's pardon. If Hoste declined (which, Wilqen's councilors agreed, he likely would), then Wilqen would order his troops onto Jordinian soil, commencing the war at last.

They emerged into the fresh sunlight of the castle lawn, prepared to depart. This would be Macmillan's first journey to Jordinia. Oddly enough, he'd visited every nation on West Halvea, except for the one his birthfather had governed.

"Mac!"

Her sudden call startled him, so little had he been expecting to hear her on the lawn at the early hour. He turned to see Princess Eponina, her ladies-in-waiting stringing behind her.

She stopped before him, gazing up at him with those ethereal eyes. Deliberately, she reached into her pale, gossamer hair and tugged on the silvery blue ribbon that held it back. No longer bound, her hair slid down her lace-clad shoulders and curtained her face, glowing majestically against the rising dawn.

"For you," she said evenly, extending a slender arm as she offered him the ribbon. "A token of mine to remember me by, while you are away."

Touched, Macmillan received the favor, not caring that their guards and maids gawked at them. He tucked it into his breast pocket. "I shall ever carry it close to my heart."

A thought occurring to him, he stooped down and extracted his knife. After measuring a length of his bootlace, he sawed off a portion. He rose again, taking the fair maiden by her hand. "And this is for you." He tied the string around her left wrist and knotted it. "It's not much now. But when I return by your sixteenth birth-day, it shall be replaced with the most opulent nuptial bracelet ever forged. For I will have you as my bride, Eponina Wilqen," he declared, ignoring the gasps of her ladies-in-waiting.

He kissed the stunned princess's hand and made to depart, when she called out after him: "Then I will wait for you! And I'll accept no other suitors!"

He did not suppress his grin. "Good," he told her, and set off with the King's men.

98

COSMITH

ANOTHER MORNING. ANOTHER RUDE AWAK-ENING by the creaking of his barred door and a cold bath of water tossed over his clothed person. Afterwards, he was led, shivering, into the interrogation room, and forced back into the metal chair.

Quixheto and DuBerre waited as the guards strapped him in, purposefully stepping over his bare feet with their heavy boots on their way out. Cosmith winced, hanging his head. He was exhausted, deprived of sleep (for who could sleep on a freezing floor skittering with rats?), parched and starving.

"Good morrow, Jonwal," DuBerre greeted him, beefy hands tucked behind his broad back. "We were hoping today shall be the day. For our most equitable leader, Comrade Hoste, has said that if you don't comply with our questioning this morning, then you're not to have a trial."

"You hear that, Cosmith?" Quixheto set a plain black box on the table between them. What it contained, Cosmith could not fathom. "Speak now or hang."

"Go to hell," Cosmith rasped.

DuBerre and Quixheto exchanged glances. "Very well." DuBerre sighed. "I've done all I can to avoid these measures, but you leave us no choice."

"And now," Quixheto popped open the box, "things are about to get...rather ugly." The man extracted a corked tincture. It appeared empty, until he held it up to the light, and Cosmith realized it was filled with clear fluid.

Quixheto made a show of slipping on a pair of rawhide gloves before uncorking the vial. The liquid emitted a hissing vapor, punctuated by a pungent chemical odor. Why, was it poison they would force Cosmith to drink? He would simply refuse to open his mouth, even if Quixheto held his nose. Even if he had to bite the man's fingers off.

"You know, Damon," Quixheto broke into one of his revolting leers, "I think it rather unfair that such a two-faced turncoat happens to be so naturally good-looking. Wouldn't you agree?"

DuBerre grunted.

"I think it high time your appearance finally reflects your duplicity, Cosmith." Quixheto appraised him. "The right side ought to do," he decided. Without any further warning, he splashed the contents of his tincture onto the right panel of Cosmith's face.

Cosmith howled. His cheek seared, the skin peeling, sizzling, melting. Desperate, he made to grab at his flaming flesh, hold it, massage it, anything to distract from the insurmountable agony tearing through the right hemisphere of his face. Alas, his hands were bound together, and then to the chair. He was trapped with nothing to do but endure the misery, and pray for it to end.

DuBerre clucked his tongue unsympathetically. "That'll leave permanent scarring. Shame. You used to be such a handsome boy."

Tears spilled down Cosmith's cheeks, burning his raging skin.

"Anything you'd like to tell us, comrade?" DuBerre softened his voice. "After all, we could stop with just your face."

Cosmith trembled. No matter what he did, the debilitating pain would not subside. His face was on fire. Yet, his voice ragged, he hurled a slew of curses at his attackers.

DuBerre let out a low whistle. "You kiss your wife with that mouth?" He grinned cruelly, and Quixheto extracted a second vial.

"No," Cosmith begged. "Please."

Quixheto grabbed a tuft of his hair and forced his head back, spilling the tincture onto the right half of Cosmith's lips. They were now ablaze, singeing, blaring with torment.

"Well," sighed Quixheto, "I don't suppose the fair little Duchess should long to be kissed by such a grisly mouth any longer."

DuBerre leaned in. "Where is she?"

Cosmith would never tell him.

"Where is she?" DuBerre repeated, shaking him by the shoulders. But the movement only exacerbated the pain, and Cosmith whimpered, turning away.

"Can you not hear me?" DuBerre bellowed into his ear. "Are you deaf? *Where is she?*"

Still, Cosmith did not respond, resting his eyes and entertaining a vague sensation of floating from his body. They'd already done their worst, hadn't they? They could not, at this point, harm him any further. Could they?

DuBerre huffed, flustered. "Right, then," he muttered, as Cosmith re-opened his eyes. "If the scoundrel refuses to hear us, Tolohov, then we shall give him a reason not to hear us."

Quixheto returned to his black box, and Cosmith's eyes widened in terror.

"No. *No!*" He thrashed about, twisting in every possible direction as Quixheto tried to steady him. But DuBerre seized his head between his meaty hands and turned it, exposing Cosmith's right ear. Quixheto uncorked a third vial, and emptied its contents down his struggling victim's ear canal.

Jon Cosmith's screams could be heard throughout all of Capitol Prison.

99

MARLENA

ELUDAINE LOOKED JUST LIKE THE former Empress. Marlena had thought so the moment she'd first met the girl. There was something in her upright posture, the way she kept her elbows pointed, and the dignified lift of her royal chin that intimidated Marlena.

Yet, despite her young daughter-in-law's lineage, the Duchess was a rather unassuming girl, and quite industrious. She put herself to endless tasks day after day, sweeping the floors, pruning the mats and canning preserves without needing to be asked. Much as Marlena fancied her a pampered princess, it was clear she was accustomed to hard work.

At first, things felt rather strained. The two women had little to say to one another. And Marlena did not miss the accusing looks the girl often threw her way whenever Jonwal's name was mentioned. But how could Eludaine begin to understand Marlena's past?

Marlena Harrington had never pretended to be a saint. As a young entertainer, she'd traveled the land, passing through the arms of more young men than perhaps she should have. Her own mother and grand-mother had been much the same; they were *gipsia*.

She had never learned the identity of her father. She was raised by her mother and grandmother, along with the ladies in their traveling caravan. From child-hood, she'd been trained in music, song and dance, to make her living entertaining gentlemen. Along with fortune-telling, this was the trade of her women. They did not marry, nor take to households; they were no-mads.

Things changed, however, one spring equinox in Pierma. After her performance at the city festival, she was wooed by the handsomest man she'd ever laid eyes upon. Kormac Cosmith was all passionate brown eyes and umber hair, muscular shoulders and strong-jawed grin. His hands were like lumber, hot from the bonfire, warming her skin, his mouth freshly-churned butter melting into hers. She conceived his son that night, and despite her mother's protests, returned to Pierma to in-form him. She'd always longed to know her father, and would not deny her own child the opportunity.

To her astonishment, Kormac offered to wed her. Marlena agreed, and thus was how she came to be dis-owned by her gipsia mother, and shunned from the car-avan. It was a heartbreaking ordeal, indeed. But it did not prevent her from continuing her career as a min-strel, even after Jonwal was born.

Jonwal.

She'd deeply loved her son. How could she not have? The little boy was flawless, a perfect replica of his father. Yet, while her new husband was at first dot-ing, Marlena eventually came to discover him rather possessive. He'd no longer permit her to dress up and perform for other gentlemen as she always had. And she was unaccustomed to having a man tell her what to do. By the time she found herself secretly expecting the Emperor's child, Marlena was terrified. She'd been away at the Garden Palace for weeks; Kormac would know the child was not his. Not to mention, general sentiments towards the Emperor were just beginning to sour in those days. She did not know how to face her fate. And she feared for the safety of her unborn babe.

Her first thought had been to flee with Jonwal, of course. But then, she'd reprimanded herself guiltily, what of her poor husband? Kormac would be abandoned by both wife and child, with nary an explanation. The man did not deserve to be left entirely alone, she'd decided. He loved their son as she did; she trusted he would take care of him.

Presently, she lowered herself into a kitchen chair, her face in her hands. She'd simply no idea what a mistake her choice would have been. She could not envision her husband laying a hand on the little boy they had both adored. Yet, apparently, he had.

She ran a sleeve over her dripping eyes. It was all her fault. Her own son despised her. And for good reason.

At first, she barely noticed the gentle hand smoothing down her curls. She lifted her head to find Eludaine standing over her. "I have failed as a mother," Marlena confessed.

"You've not failed," came the Duchess's quiet reply. "There is still time to befriend your eldest son."

But Marlena did not feel that she deserved his friendship, now or ever.

THE SEASON WORE ON, AND the air only grew more bitter. The soil hardened, the trees turned bare. Mornings were kissed with a dusting of frost, and Marlena was soon unearthing the victuals she'd buried in the ground in seasons past.

She was showing her daughter-in-law how to lay a trap for rabbits, when the girl clutched at her brow. "Is something the matter?" Marlena asked.

"Dizzy spell." Eludaine's cheeks glowed pink. "I must've crouched down too quickly."

Marlena leaned in and placed a hand on her forehead, but it did not feel warm. Perhaps the forest elements were too harsh for the young royal. Her sons would never forgive her if the Duchess fell ill under her watch.

"Perhaps you'd better lie down," she suggested, offering the girl a hand up. They could finish erecting the traps later. She helped her back into the cabin and onto Marley's mat, where Eludaine squeezed her eyes shut.

Marlena draped a blanket over her. "Rest a while, and call on me, should you need anything." She left the girl to sleep, though it was not long before she cried out in a high voice, *"Marlena!"*

She found the young woman scrambling to her feet, her blanket askew. "I'm going to be sick," she gasped, cupping a hand over her mouth. Indeed, her face had gone pallid.

Marlena hurried to fetch a basin and brought it to

the girl, who was promptly ill into it. "My lady, what've I done?" She wrung her wrists. "Have I fed you something rogue?"

"I'm sure it shall pass," Eludaine croaked weakly.

But whatever her malady, it was not passing through, as she only seemed to worsen as the days wore on. Hour after hour, Eludaine lie on her mat, moaning in displeasure at the odor of food, or else regurgitating any meals she tried to consume. Were it summer, Marlena would've ventured into the deep forest to gather medicinal herbs. But winter was nigh, and vegetation scarce. She'd have to hike the twelve miles into Bearn, Bainherd on the next market day, and purchase supplies from the apothecary's cart.

And so, one blustery morning, the woman arose with the dawn, saw that Eludaine rested soundly, and braved the icy wind. Her feet chafed in her boots as she wove through the naked trees, the hood of her fraying cloak continuously blown back by the billowing wind. But onward she traveled, determined to find a cure at market for whatever ailed the Duchess.

She came into Bearn's village square, where vendors displayed their wares in wooden carts. The smell of barnyard and donkey reeked through the air, while Marlena's eyes were assaulted with colorful squashes and legumes, hanging antelope carcasses, and rows of pricey woven blankets.

The apothecary's cart contained an array of dried herbs and tinctures. Marlena had learned a bit about the healing sciences from her grandmother, but that was long ago, and her memory was dim. She perused the stand until discovering an extract of ginger root, which bore on its label: *For the nausea.* She bartered a basket of tubers and a can of preserves in exchange for it, and tucked it safely into her pocket.

Setting back down the square, she half-glanced at the posting wall, when she was startled to a halt. Her eyes must've deceived her. Her former husband, Kormac, and their son had been on her mind lately, was all. She'd not just seen an etching of one of them in the posts. Had she?

The woman slowly cycled back, scanning the wall until finding the bulletin that had caught her off-guard. It bore the seal of the New Republic of Jordinia, her eldest son's full name stamped prominently above his likeness. It was an announcement of his pending execution by hanging.

Marlena grabbed her chest, backing into the stone wall behind her. It could not be. Yet, there it was, the news having spread all the way to Bainherd. Her son had been caught and condemned by the New Republic, on account of "treason" and "royalism," she read.

Pulse throbbing, Marlena glanced over her shoulder, ensuring no one was watching, and ripped down the post. She'd not have her son's face plastered all over town like some coarse criminal. She shoved the page into her pocket alongside the ginger root tincture, fretting her entire march home over Jonwal's fate, and that of his ailing wife.

100

SELU

DAINY'S FACE WAS EVERYWHERE. AND apparently, the New Republic was powerless to stop it. For each post they tore down, several more cropped up. Selu scanned page after page of the sensational reports from Bainherd, each proclaiming the Duchess's miraculous survival.

She shuddered, though she left the parchments hanging prominently as she turned out of Capitol Square. It was bad enough that she'd come across multiple signs bearing Jon Cosmith's image and announcing his pending execution. But now, with the reports from Bainherd, the New Republic would certainly know where to find Dainy. Selu prayed that the girl had had the sense to flee Pon Castle, and remain in hiding elsewhere.

How far had Cosmith gotten, Selu wondered, as she walked back to Pogue District feeling sick with dread, before he'd been captured? Had the man even made it out of Jordinia? And what on earth were they doing to him in Capitol Prison?

She was so distraught with worry, she hardly noticed she was about to collide with something solid. The woman gasped as her face met an enormous chest, while two mammoth hands steadied her.

"Best watch where you're going, ma'am," grunted a familiar voice.

"*Bos!*" She launched herself into his mighty embrace.

He held her in turn. "I've been seeking you for days."

"Days?" She took his arm. "How long have you been in Pierma? What are you doing here?"

Bos steered her down the opposite street, and she glided eagerly alongside him. It was as though no time had passed, as if they'd never been apart, so natural did he feel beside her, all bulky arms and loping strides and full blond beard, newly grown.

"There was a battle in Dekantor, between us and the authorities. We won. Although the New Republic is doing quite a job covering it up." He lowered his voice. "After that, we determined it time to march south. The time is not yet ripe for our attack. But soon, Seluna."

She stared at him. Attack? "Where are you taking me?" she asked, bemused as they crossed another street, nearing one of the less-populated, albeit wealthier districts.

"Headquarters," Bos murmured. "Dr. von Schultz is hosting us."

"*The* Dr. von Schultz?"

"Aye."

Selu was impressed. Pabol von Schultz, the once-prominent physician, had personally tended the royal family. She could only wonder how the man had managed to evade arrest for all of these years. However, eyeing the posh villas by which they strolled, she had a sneaking suspicion the doctor must've paid handsomely in exchange for his freedom.

"You've heard about Cosmith?"

He nodded discreetly.

"It devastates me," she confessed. "If anything happens to him—"

"I've a plan to help him. Only we'll need to convince the others to reallocate some of our weaponry for the cause."

"Oh?" They stopped before a towering villa at the rear of a cul-de-sac.

Bos bent down to whisper in her ear, and Selu listened as he recounted his companions' plan to blast down Capitol Tower with dynami. "We've acquired nearly enough explosives. But if the others agree to spare a few, we can take down the prison, as well."

"Take it down? But would we not harm everyone inside?"

"We'd only blast an opening," he explained, "at the base. It'll be enough to make our statement and release the inmates, including Cosmith."

"Assuming he can even walk," snapped Selu, and Bos hushed her. "Have I not told you what goes on in Capitol Prison?"

The man continued around the back of the villa. Selu followed him down a curious flight of steps, which led below-grade. "If he cannot walk, then I will carry him out myself," Bos declared, pulling open the cellar door.

101

MACMILLAN

HE'D MET MARTEN HOSTE ONCE before. Indeed, Macmillan perceived a flicker of recognition in the man's eyes. Back then, the leader had seemed mild-mannered, albeit stately. Yet now, Macmillan sensed something tenser, more disgruntled about him.

Hoste's scowl deepened as he skimmed over Wilqen's scroll. Once he'd finished, he gave Macmillan a cool, silent glare. Macmillan stared back. Eventually, the leader made to move, and the Bainherd guards bristled. But Hoste merely crossed his legs, unspeaking.

Macmillan waited. The man was clearly trying to intimidate him with his silence. But Macmillan would not be the first to speak. He would stand wordlessly for however long it took.

At last, the leader relented. "And why, exactly, does His Majesty request Cosmith's release?" He tossed the scroll aside. "The man is not a citizen of his."

"Because he is innocent," said Macmillan, earning himself a pointed snort from the Jordinian guards.

"Unfortunately, Comrade Macmillan, you—whoever the hell you are—and the King of the Bainherd Plains are not the judges of who belongs in my prisons and why." Hoste rose to his feet. "Furthermore, I am aware of the identity of Mr. Cosmith's *spouse*," he annunciated the word with emphasis, and Macmillan's pulse quickened, "and that Wilqen is clearly scheming something with the pair of them. I'll not stand for it. My answer is no."

Macmillan chanced a glance at his guards, who gave him the smallest of grins. This was, of course, the response they'd been expecting. "No?" he repeated innocently, just to be sure.

Hoste's face flushed, the contrast stark beneath his white hair. "Absolutely, unequivocally *no*."

"Very well, sir." Macmillan beckoned his men. "We shall inform His Majesty of your decision at once."

102

DuBerre

"COSMITH, YOU USELESS VERMIN," MUTTERED Quixheto, cigar between his teeth. He had pressed the flaming tip repeatedly up the length of Cosmith's arm, but to no avail. The man still would not talk.

DuBerre frowned at their prisoner. He was bound half-naked to the metal chair, his head drooping limply over his shirtless chest, blood dripping crimson from his nose and mouth onto his ragged trousers.

"Why does Bainherd wish for your pardon?" DuBerre demanded. "What are you and your wife conspiring with Horatio Wilqen? *Speak!*"

Cosmith only hung his head, and DuBerre heaved another smack at his bruised and torn face. He had never encountered anyone more stubborn, never subjected a captive to so much torture who still would not divulge a word.

Quixheto rummaged through his box and extracted his signature vial of flammable oils. He doused Cosmith's right arm and half of his front.

"Tolohov?" DuBerre watched him uncertainly.

"What are you doing?"

Quixheto tossed his cigar into the prisoner's lap. It swiftly went up in flames, engulfing the man's bare skin as he screamed and thrashed in terror. "*Put it out!*" bawled Cosmith hysterically, his right arm and part of his chest burning alive as his trousers began to singe.

"Tolohov," barked DuBerre. "Hoste wants him alive until the solstice! He is to be made an example of, to the populace!"

Quixheto shrugged, and emptied a bucket of water onto the suffering man, whose continued screams were deafening.

"Damn it," exclaimed DuBerre, examining their prisoner's bubbling skin. Hoste was set on Cosmith's public execution. The leader would be furious if Du-Berre was to let him die of wounds or infection prior. "You idiot," he growled, glaring at Quixheto, even as Cosmith continued to writhe and wail in agony.

"Well, Jonwal," he announced loudly, for the man was now deaf in one ear, and a bit hard of hearing. "Look at you. The prince of vanity, a mutilated beast. I suppose it's a good thing your wife shall never see the monster you've become. I do not think your weak heart could bear the sight of her cringing away from you."

He leaned in. "Although you need not suffer any-more. Simply tell us where to find her, and we are hap-py to bring in the medics, clean you up, administer *lau-danium* for your pains…"

Cosmith remained speechless, gushing with tears and shaking his head in refusal.

"Do you weep, Jonny?" said Quixheto, as the mangled man before them trembled with sobs.

DuBerre surveyed him with disgust. "Come, Tolohov. Let us give those eyes something to truly weep about."

"Right eye?" Quixheto removed a small decanter from his black case.

DuBerre nodded grimly, frowning at their unfortunate captive.

103

DAINY

SHE WAS FEELING A BIT stronger from her teas laced with ginger root, although her appetite had still not returned. Marlena coaxed her to eat at least twice a day, but even the faintest aroma of food caused Dainy's stomach to roil. Indeed, her new mother-in-law must've unwittingly fed her something spoiled, although Dainy had not the heart to hold it against her. The woman was clearly trying to help. And she had, after all, gone to market and found a useful bit of medicine.

It was early afternoon one day when Dainy recovered enough strength to walk about the cabin. Marlena had gone into the woods to see to her rabbit traps, and Dainy thought she'd help with dinner. She stoked the hearth and heaved a bucket of water into the cauldron, to bring to a boil. The weather was frigid, and a pot of stew seemed in order.

The young woman chopped and peeled roots and tubers and scooped them into the cauldron, along with some carrots and a jarful of beans. She searched the cabinets for flavoring spices, but found none. Running her hand along the interior of the wood, however, something papery pricked her finger.

"*Ach.*" She brought her fingertip to her mouth to lick the blood trickling forth. Curious, she reached back into the cabinet and extracted the culprit: a sheath of parchment. A familiar face stared up at her from the page. Frantically, her eyes scanned over the devastating headline that promised her husband's pending execution.

Dainy trembled, horrified. She had to be dreaming. Or else, her illness had made her delirious. Jon was not in danger. He couldn't be.

She picked up the fallen bulletin, which she'd dropped in her initial shock, and gaped back down at the runes. He was to be hung on the winter solstice? Why, that was mere weeks away! How long had Marlena known? And why had she never told Dainy?

As if her thoughts had summoned the woman, she heard the crunching of boots over snow. "Eludaine," Marlena remarked upon entering the cabin, clearly surprised to find her out of bed. She glanced at the bubbling cauldron on the hearth, her brow knit with concern. "I hope you are not overexerting yourself, dear."

Dainy hardly heard her, so aquiver was she with rage and resentment. Her weak stomach heaved in agony as the fate of her spouse, her darling Jon, grew weightier and more real with each passing moment. "Is this true?" She raised the accursed post. "Has my husband, your son, been captured by the New Republic?"

Marlena did not respond.

Tears streamed down Dainy's cheeks, but she did not bother to wipe them. "Why would you hide this from me? How could you not have told me?"

"You've been ill," the woman explained, her voice shaking. "I did not think you fit to handle—"

"And what were you planning to do for him?" Dainy waved the bulletin in her face. "Will you not try to help him, save him?"

Marlena shook her head in despair. "He is beyond saving."

This only enraged Dainy further as she stared at her mother-in-law in disbelief. Furious, she threw down the parchment, a fire roaring in her chest. That a mother would yet again dismiss her son to a horrific fate, and not even attempt to rescue him, was simply unimaginable.

Livid, Dainy stormed into Mac's bedroom and tore down his old cloak from a peg on the wall. "W-what are you doing?" stammered Marlena, hurrying after her.

Dainy slipped on the cloak and buttoned it up to her neck. She fought off another wave of nausea as she slid into her white shoes from the Masquerade ball— they were the only pair she had—and headed for the door.

"Eludaine," Marlena pleaded, chasing her out of the cabin. But Dainy only marched onward. She could see her breath in a haze before her, and her feet were already freezing, but she cared not. She would walk to Pierma if she had to.

"Where are you going?"

Dainy spun around. "It's me they want, not him." Her fury at the New Republic had never been greater. They could murder her parents, her siblings, even her. But they were not to lay a hand on Jon. "I am going to offer myself in his place." She raised Mac's hood overhead.

Marlena's eyes widened. "B-but I promised to protect you."

"And who will protect Jon?" Dainy glared at her. "He has already been abandoned once, Marlena. I am not about to let it happen again."

The woman remained in place, silent as she watched Dainy press her way up the hill and through the naked trees.

104

WILQEN

"A PAGE JUST IN FROM Jordinia, sire."

Finally, thought Wilqen, glancing up from his desk. "Send him in."

A young man entered, still cloaked from his travels. He bowed deeply, his gangly figure swooping over the stone floors, before informing the King: "I bear word from His Grace Marley Macmillan, sir."

Wilqen raised an eyebrow.

"Hoste refuses to release Lord Cosmith."

Wilqen interwove his fingers. "You may leave."

It was time. On the morrow, he would order his troops to commence their march into Pierma and force the aspiring emperor's release. Of course, as anticipated, the New Republic would fight back. But it was far more than a single prisoner over which the battle would prove to be. For little did the Republic know, the monarchs of West Halvea planned to collapse their entire regime.

Indeed, the war had begun.

105

COSMITH

THERE WAS ONE WINDOW IN Cosmith's fifth-story cell. A tiny one, high up, near the ceiling. He lay on the hard, filthy floor in a pool of his own blood for many hours, staring up at that window. Only one of his eyes illuminated the world for him; the light in his right eye had been brutishly extinguished. He believed his tormentors when they said the damage would be irreparable. He'd not likely be seeing out of his right eye, or hearing from his right ear, ever again.

He thought he was hallucinating when soft white stars began to pass by the window. Was he dying at last, and the cosmos were descending to carry him unto the ether? Alas, he could still feel the freezing floor at his back, still writhed from the burns mauling his arm, shoulder and leg. His right foot, as well, was in unspeakable pain, for they'd ruthlessly broken it, and he was unable to stand or walk.

Snow, he finally understood, watching the white flakes floating by. It was the first snowfall of the season. Or at least, the first one he'd seen. And that meant he had now seen twenty-nine winters.

It would be his last birthday, he realized. Although he could not quite decide whether this saddened or comforted him. Surely, he should not wish to live like this for very much longer: half-deaf, half-blind, with a lame foot and disfigured body. And DuBerre was right; at least his wife should never have to witness the hideous creature he'd become.

Instead, she would evermore remember Jon Cosmith as the handsome fellow he once was, and would never be again. Aye, her last memory of him would be making love to him in the autumn leaves when he was attractive and whole. Good—that was what he wanted.

He could not necessarily complain of his fate. After all, he had lived long enough to experience love—true love—and real forgiveness. He'd been fortunate enough to marry a beautiful young duchess, and be adored by her. And he'd finally discovered what it was to care for someone beyond himself, to give his whole heart entirely to another.

He only hoped there would be some deific being awaiting him on the other side. That way, he would have someone to eternally thank for Dainy, his lovely wife, his darling girl.

106

DAINY

DAINY HAD BROUGHT WITH HER no food (she hadn't an appetite, anyway) or money, neither had she thought about where to take shelter during the snowy nights. Jon was the only thing on her mind when she left Marlena behind in the Knights' Forest.

By her first evening, she'd made it into Bainherd by foot, although her illness particularly troubled her. The young woman lost much time crouched down on the side of the road, heaving into the dead, snow-laced grass. When she could stand it no longer, she took a detour into the nearest town.

Evening had fallen, and unsavory characters prowled the dark avenues, peddling outlawed goods or else offering illicit services. Dainy tightened Mac's hood over her face. She was only seeking the local barber. She had sold her hair once before; she would simply have to do it again, to earn coin for passage. But when, at last, she found the barbershop, she was dismayed to find it locked. She rattled the door again to be sure, and peeked into the window, but all was dark.

Hopeless, she turned away. That was when she spied the lone wagon parked innocuously in an alleyway. Could it be? Blankets, quilts, and rugs of all sorts were rolled up and bundled in twine, with a great leather tarp loosely folded on top. But where was its driver?

Either way, it was perfect, she thought, climbing into the wagon bed. She'd not be too long; just a nap was all she needed. Nestling beneath a wool comforter, she closed her eyes. It was the last she recalled, until a bump jostled her awake, and she let out an involuntary yelp.

"Whoa," cried a male voice. The wagon jolted to a halt.

Dainy's heart pounded. She heard the squeal of a mule, followed by the sound of boot steps. Off came the leather tarp, exposing her to the harsh glare of sunny daylight, and a pair of bewildered blue eyes peered down at her, clearly as startled as she.

She blinked, looking around. It appeared to be many hours past sunrise. How could she have slept for so long? Judging by the open fields of frosty, dormant grass stretching on for leagues, the man had driven her quite far.

He shook his hatted head, emitting a low whistle. "Well, Siggy," he announced in an accent Dainy somehow identified as western Jordinian. "Looks like we got ourselves a stowaway."

She frowned. To whom was he speaking?

The man removed his straw hat, revealing a head of dark blond hair and a tan line creasing his brow. "Question is," he muttered, "what to do with 'er?"

She sat up, rolling a woven rug from her legs. "Please, sir. I didn't mean to—stow away. Only I haven't any money, and need passage into Pierma."

"Pierma?" He laughed in surprise. "No one in their right mind is headed up there now, doll. There's some weird skirmish going on with Bainherd, a bunch of royalists swarming around like angry hornets. All hell's breaking loose." He scratched his head. "And I don't understand the half of it.

"Anyway." He jabbed a thumb over his shoulder. "Out you get. I can't be caught smuggling hitchhikers cross-country. It'll look suspicious. Besides, it's against company policy."

Dainy wanted to ask which company he worked for, but thought better of it. "Please, at least bring me to the border. I've been ill, and it's rather difficult to walk—"

"Hey," the man interrupted her. "You look sort o' familiar." He squinted. "Have we met?"

Dainy hurriedly shook her head.

To her dread, his eyes lowered to the nuptial bracelet on her wrist. "By golly," he whispered. "But is that genuine Asiotican jade?"

"You've heard of it?" she asked in spite of herself. It was a rather exotic stone, after all.

He laughed, a flowing sound as big as a river, and his smile revealed dimpled cheeks. "Well, of course, honey! I work in the merchant business." He pointed to her bracelet. "And I'll trade you just about anything for that."

She clutched her wrist. There was no way she'd sell her nuptial bracelet. It did not matter how destitute she was. "It's not for sale," she said stiffly.

"All right." He shrugged. "Y'hear that, Siggy? She says it ain't for sale."

Dainy couldn't help herself. "Who are you talking to?"

The driver blinked. "The mule, of course." He chuckled, flashing his dimpled smile again. "His name's Sigmund Odin. Pretty serious name for a donkey, right? That's why I call him Siggy, for short.

"You think I'm crazy now," he added, replacing his straw hat atop his sunny hair. "But wait'll you spend weeks on end traveling the road by your lonesome. You'll find yourself talking to mules, too."

Dainy didn't doubt it.

"Look." His expression was not unkind. "I'd love to help you, sweetheart. But I can't risk my job." He frowned. "A job ain't exactly easy to come by these days, and I'm grateful to have mine."

A shiver passed through Dainy. She never dreamed it would come to this. But her husband was trapped in prison, condemned to death, and she was determined to offer herself in his place, whatever it took. Though a few years older, and his skin certainly ruddier, the man's physique resembled Jon's enough. Perhaps if she kept her eyes shut the whole time, she could pretend it was him.

Hands trembling, she unfastened her cloak, detesting herself, unable to believe her own pathetic desperation.

"What're you doing?" he asked, bemused. "It's not exactly springtime yet."

Dainy ignored him. "Would this change your mind?" She slipped off the cloak, revealing the red dress she'd borrowed from Marlena. It was a bit long for her, but hugged her chest and hips snugly, accentuating her shape.

His face flushed scarlet to match her gown. "Whoa. Hang on there." He held up his palms. "Out of the question. Now, you go and find yourself some honest way to get to Pierma, y'hear?"

Dainy stared at him disbelievingly, experiencing every range of emotion from exasperation to relief. She was even surprised to feel a twinge of pique that he'd spurned her. She began to weep with abandon, so weary and ill was she. Why could he not simply permit her passage in his wagon?

His face fell. "Well...hey, now. Don't do that."

Dainy choked with sobs. "Now I'll never make it in time, and my husband is going to die! He's locked up, and they'll hang him if I don't stop it!"

The driver stared, and Dainy hiccupped, nose streaming. "Did you say your *husband* is to be hanged?" he asked.

She nodded, and he gave a self-deprecating snort. "Of course," he mumbled to himself. "Just your grand fortune, Felix. The one time I find a beautiful girl hiding in the back of my wagon, and she's already married." He scratched his neck. "I never did have much luck with women..."

But Dainy was stuck on the name he'd uttered. "Felix?" She wiped her eyes.

"Aye, that's my name, ma'am. Felix Gavins."

Dainy tried to recall where she'd heard the name before. And then, she remembered: Felix Strong was the hero in one of the ballads Jon had composed and sung to her, that night on the S. S. *Isla*. She looked into the wagoner's face, feeling an inexplicable sense of comfort. It was almost as though some part of Jon had sent him her way, the name like a providential reassurance.

Felix's broad shoulders fell slack, and he offered her a hand. "Come on, then," he relented, helping her down from the wagon bed. "If you're going to ride with me, it won't be as a stowaway. You can sit up front, like a proper lady. And if you're *really* nice to me," he added, "maybe I'll let you steer the reins once in a while."

He stalked ahead, and Dainy followed, stunned. "You mean, you'll take me?"

"I s'pose. If it were me, I'd want the chance to rescue my love from the gallows." He gave her a lopsided grin. "Don't be shy, comrade." He hopped into the driver's seat, patting the bench next to him. "Come and sit a spell."

"Oh, Felix, you are a very good man indeed," breathed Dainy, climbing up beside him.

"Yeah, yeah." He waved her off, egging Siggy into motion. But the dimples in his cheeks betrayed his smile.

107

Bos

HER HAIR WAS VELVET RUNNING through his fingers. Selu grinned up at him, and Bos smiled back. He liked having her there with him, hearing her smooth voice calling order over the men's rowdiness.

She suddenly swiveled around. "I just heard the front door," she whispered. Bos followed her down the stairwell, taking care not to bump his broad elbows against the bannisters. They recognized the top hat of Dr. von Schultz passing through the checkered foyer. A maid tended him, taking his cloak as Bos and Selu reached the ground floor.

"Did you see him?" Selu asked the doctor, anxious.

Von Schultz removed his hat. His sideburns connected with the tips of his connoisseur moustache. Silent, he nodded.

"And?" demanded Selu.

"Seluna." Bos placed a hand on her arm. "Let the doctor remove his gloves."

Indeed, the man was prying leather gloves from

his fingers. Bos and Selu waited, while von Schultz adjusted his cravat and pointed his chin toward the cellar.

He led them down, glancing surreptitiously behind his shoulder, until they reached the expansive base of the house, where a camp of revivalists was currently dwelling. Bos watched his footing, careful not to step on anyone's bedding as he wove between his card-playing, flask-sipping companions.

Selu clapped her hands together. "All right, listen up!" she hollered, and several dozen heads lifted. "The good doctor has an update for us!"

Von Schultz waited until the din died down, and the group in back stopped sharpening their knives to look up. "Good evening," he greeted them. "As you know, I was summoned to Capitol Prison this afternoon to treat an injured guard. Before leaving, however, I honored your requests to locate the Duchess's husband and report back on his condition."

To Bos's dismay, the doctor frowned. "I found him on the fifth floor. Alas, I'm sorry to inform that, from what I could see, the man is near death. He has been tortured beyond recognition."

Selu sucked in a breath, and Bos reached for her hand. The others folded their arms. They did not personally know Cosmith, but far as they were concerned, the Duchess's husband was, in essence, their emperor.

"Did you speak with him?" Selu whispered, mortified, but the doctor only shook his head.

"He was unconscious." Von Schultz's eyes were sincere with regret. "If the poor man has any hope of recovery, then he must be removed from the vicinity immediately. However," he sounded uncertain, "even still, there's a chance Mr. Cosmith would not survive past the New Year. It appears his wounds have gone too long without treatment."

Selu buried her face into Bos's chest, and Bos wrapped his arms around her. Perhaps Cosmith was not a perfect man. But no one deserved such a fate. Poor Eludaine, wherever she was, would be devastated.

"I hope this answers your questions," said the doctor, and retreated back upstairs.

Bos turned to the grumbling group. "We must get him out of there. The Duchess has lost enough. The New Republic is not to murder yet another of her relations."

"It appears they already have, Visigoth," argued James Briar, looking disheartened. "You really want us to waste our ammunition to break a dead man out of prison?"

"You heard the doctor." Selu wiped her eyes. "If we get him out soon, there is hope for recovery."

"That's not exactly what he said, sweetheart," murmured James.

"We need not use all our dynami." Tuck Henn stepped forward in Bos's defense. "We're not trying to detonate the entire prison. We'll only blast our way in and wipe out the entry guards. It'll be enough to rescue the man."

"When do we take action?" growled Rolf Lymston.

A pregnant hush settled over the room, and Bos met Selu's apprehensive face. "Tomorrow night," he decided. "So be ready."

108

MACMILLAN

MACMILLAN REMAINED CAMPED WITH WILQEN'S men outside of Pierma. They'd since sent a pageboy to deliver their message to the King, and now awaited the rest of Bainherd's soldiers to join them.

It was evening when Macmillan wandered back into the city, heading for the prison. He felt compelled to be near his brother, unable to shake his profuse worry for the man. He gazed up at the stone tower, wondering which of the windows might be Jon's, if any, when the sound of wagon wheels startled him.

He inched back so as not to be seen. Silently, he watched as a cloaked figure wrapped its arms around the coachman and descended the wagon. Funny, thought Macmillan, squinting through the darkness. He'd once owned a cloak that looked an awful lot like it…

The strange figure lowered her hood, and as the city lanterns reflected off of her glistening black hair, Macmillan realized that it was no stranger at all. "*Dainy?*"

She spun to face him. "Mac?"

He grabbed her arm, dragging her out of the

streetlamps and into the shadow of the towering jail. "What in hell are you doing?" he hissed. "Let's get you out of here, before you are seen."

"I intend to be seen." The girl did not bother to keep her voice down. "They want me, not Jon." She pointed to the prison. "I'm going to hand myself in, in exchange for his freedom."

"Oh, no you are not," Macmillan growled.

"My mind is already made, Mac."

"Dainy. This whole war is *for you.* Everything for which we've worked so hard, all this time, shall be undone if you do this! Bainherd's troops are coming, if you can just hold off a bit longer—"

"What's this, a family reunion?"

They gasped at the familiar new voice. A black-clad figure strode forth, a bandana concealing her face. Macmillan recognized the slender limbs and lithe gait at once. "Selu? What are *you* doing here?"

"I should ask you the same." The woman pulled down her bandana, looking concerned. "Should you not be in hiding, Dainy?"

Macmillan grimaced. "My sister seems to have it in her head that she's to turn herself in, in exchange for Jon's release."

"No, she's not," snapped Selu.

"That's what I said." Macmillan gripped his sister's arm.

Dainy glared between them. "Have either of you any idea what I've been through to get here?" she demanded. But, rather unexpectedly, she brought a hand over her mouth.

Macmillan raised an eyebrow. "Erm, Dainy? Everything all right?"

"Just...dizzy again. I—I think I ate something wonky in the forest. Either that, or I'm suffering some persistent bout of influenza. I'll be fine."

A new light bobbed their way, accompanied by boot steps flapping down the cobblestone. Macmillan made out the silhouette of a patrolling guard with his lantern aloft. Selu lifted her bandana, while Dainy raised her hood, and the trio edged away from the prison, Selu in the lead.

Macmillan allowed her to guide them through the winding streets of northeast Pierma, where the homes became steadily posher. He and Dainy asked no questions as they approached the final residential street, coming to an expansive villa at the rear of a cul-de-sac.

Selu placed a finger over her veiled mouth and steered them to the back of the house, proceeding down a flight of stairs. At last, she led them into an enormous cellar packed with squatters. Men of all ages were scattered everywhere, some sleeping, some shaving, most engaged in card games or conversation. Macmillan glanced around in surprise, when a frighteningly thin woman hurried over.

"Seluna, where have you been? I thought something might've gone awry—"

"Peace, Mother." Selu removed her bandana. "Everything looks fine. We're ready to blast."

Someone shouted, and there came a bout of laughter from a dozen men. Macmillan stared at the impressive arsenal housed in the cellar, from daggers and swords, to sticks and balls of pure dynami.

Selu whistled between her fingers. "Are we ready for tonight?"

"Aye," the men roared.

"Good." Casually, she slipped a bundle of dynami into her pocket. "The folks from Pogue and the other districts are meeting us in the Square at midnight. In the meantime, why not greet your Duchess at last?" She beckoned Dainy, and the men scratched their heads.

Macmillan watched as his sister slowly stepped forth. Every pair of inquiring eyes rested upon her. With a hesitant look at Selu, Dainy carefully lowered her hood, revealing her porcelain face to the room at large. Someone whistled softly.

"Behold," announced Selu. "Lady Eludaine, alive and in the flesh."

At first, Macmillan thought that every occupant of the chamber had tumbled over simultaneously. But he realized the entire room had fallen prostrate before his sister, as if her throne were already restored—nay, as if it'd never been abolished. It was much like her unveiling at the Masquerade ball, only this time, they were in Jordinia's capitol.

Macmillan was moved to see an older man dabbing at his eyes. They love you, Dainy, he wanted to tell her. But she graciously insisted they return to their feet, and so they did, murmuring excitedly amongst themselves.

Dainy turned back to Selu. "Is there a water closet?" she whispered urgently. "I think I'm about to be sick."

Selu gave her a strange look. "Mother," she called, after a slight delay. "Care to escort the Duchess to the privy?"

Selu's mother assented with an incline of her gray-violet head, taking Dainy's elbow.

"My mother, Bet, is a trained nurse," Selu told the

girl. "She'll assist you, all right?"

Dainy nodded and disappeared upstairs with Bet. Selu and Macmillan watched them go before exchanging glances.

109

BOS

THEY DEPARTED THE DOCTOR'S CELLAR in groups, each taking differing routes to Capitol Square. Macmillan, who had rejoined them, summoned his guards from Bainherd, while the Duchess, whom Bos was dismayed to see in the capitol at that time, was made to remain in the doctor's home.

"Somebody ought to smuggle her out of here." Bos sheathed his borrowed sword. "She shouldn't be here."

"Guards are surrounding the villa, and my mother will see that she remains safely in bed." Selu tailed him out to the winter's night where snow blanketed the ground. "She's a woman grown. We cannot force her away."

"Not even if it saves her life?" He cut through a grove, steering clear of the main streets as they headed southwest, boots crunching over the ice.

They arrived at Capitol Square to spy scores of shadows converging from every path and corner. There were nearly ten times more people than they'd been expecting. Selu was taken aback. "So many?" Her oblong eyes shone curiously at Bos.

"Visigoth," someone whispered, clearly recognizing his height. Bos turned to see his friends. "We must hurry. The patrolling guards have been spotted making their rounds. A few pounds of explosives have already been laid."

"Slay the guards," Selu ordered them unexpectedly. "The bastards."

Bos's jaw stiffened. It was time to ignite.

110

COSMITH

COSMITH GASPED IN HORROR. A pair of gray eyes watched him soundlessly through the iron bars of his cell. He attempted to roll away, but his tormentor's gravelly voice rang through the dismal chamber. "No need to fret, Cosmith. At least not presently." Tolohov Quixheto continued to watch him, looking merely thoughtful.

What are you doing here? Cosmith wanted to ask, but his throat was dry as sand. Yet, was it not the middle of night? At least, all was dark. What series of sadistic tortures could the man possibly wish to inflict upon him now? He was already at death's threshold.

"The solstice is mere days away." Quixheto blinked down at him. "Clearly, you fear death no more than I." He sighed. "I simply felt compelled to come by tonight. For I noticed a certain Dr. von Schultz made a pointed effort to visit you before leaving the premises yesterday. What do you know of the old doctor, Cosmith?"

Cosmith closed his eyes, his head thrumming. It

ached every night, lying upon that cold, dank floor. He hadn't the faintest idea of what Quixheto spoke. He hadn't the faintest idea of what anyone spoke these days.

"Are you aware that Dr. von Schultz was physician to the Ducelles?"

Cosmith could only shrug, knowing the movement was barely perceptible.

"Curious. Even so, I suspect the man may be a knee-bending, brow-circling royalist. I've informed DuBerre of my suspicions." Quixheto contorted his face. "I know not how von Schultz managed to slip us by all these years…"

There came a sudden, enormous crash, and the floor beneath them quivered. Terrified, Cosmith tried to lift his head. Had he just imagined it, or was the earth quaking?

"What in hell?" Quixheto had fallen to the ground and was climbing impatiently back to his feet.

A rising wave of shouts crested from the ground floor, four stories below, as another deafening explosion sounded. Cosmith thought he was reimagining the pirate attack on the *Evangela*, until a roar of footsteps pounded throughout the prison, accompanied by a cacophony of loud voices, hundreds of voices.

"What is the meaning of this?" spat Quixheto, his footsteps trailing away, when boots thundered up the stone stairwell.

"*You,*" growled a familiar voice, and Cosmith wondered whether he'd not lost his mind at last. "Jon was right. I should've killed you when I had the chance."

He turned in time to witness a massive, bearded shadow plunging a sword into Tolohov Quixheto's gut.

Quixheto shrieked and hurled a dagger at the man, but it merely grazed his brawny arm. An army of men blazed up the stairwell, and one swiftly finished Quixheto off with a blade to the throat.

"Key ring," the deep voice bellowed.

A match was ignited as more explosions sounded beneath them. Cosmith shut his eyes against the light, listening vaguely as the men deciphered which of the keys on the ring (which they must've stolen) matched the numerals on his cell. He was numb with shock when his cell door finally opened, and a torch on the wall was lit.

"Good lord," someone gasped, and Cosmith winced.

"My God, Jon, what have they done to you?"

He wanted to speak, to move, but was incapable. And then a miracle, like lifesaving elixir, a pair of enormous hands scooped him up from the floor and carried him down the stairwell, away from the hellish nightmare of his torment.

"Is he even alive, Bos?"

"Hush," grunted the one who held him, his voice a vibration in his massive chest.

A pair of hands checked for his pulse, and someone draped a blanket over him. Cosmith felt the icy sting of winter as they emerged through what appeared to be a tremendous hole in the wall, surrounded by mounds of rubble.

"Hang on, Jon," his friend whispered, as Cosmith shivered uncontrollably. "Don't let go. Your wife needs you."

Cosmith exhaled hollowly. His wife?

The crashing and cracking sounds continued, riding on the air with the shouts of men and women alike, battle raging all around him. With his left eye, Cosmith cast his gaze into the midnight sky, only to see a green streamer lighting its way to the heavens. The firework exploded into a thousand emerald stars reflecting in his pupil, and that was the last he saw, before consciousness slipped away.

111

BET

AS BLASTS OF DYNAMI SOUNDED across the city and fireworks illuminated the night sky, the Duchess paced worriedly by her chamber window. Bet Toustead immediately closed the drapes.

Eludaine wrung her wrists, plainly agitated as she held her ear to the papered walls, listening to the goings-on outdoors.

"My lady, you are fretting," chided Bet, guiding the plump youth to sit on the chaise lounge. Her dinner remained on the bureau, barely nibbled, and the broth she'd managed to drink had quickly come up again into the floral chamber pot.

Bet pressed a palm to her forehead once more, but she was not warm in temperature. Emotional, though. Could it be her woman's cycle? "Perhaps it is your moon time, dear?"

The Duchess shook her head. "It's been some time, actually. I do not recall my last…" A resounding *bang* issued outside, and the glowing glare of firecrackers momentarily brightened the chamber.

"Yes, well." Bet smoothed her skirts absently. "Worry can delay a woman." Soon as she'd spoken, however, she glanced back up. Why, had the girl not been vomiting and suffering the nausea, as well? "Forgive me," she said slowly. "But when did you last embrace your husband?"

The Duchess's complexion turned rosy. "*Carnivalle.*"

Carnivalle was the last night of the tenth moon. Bet worked the sums in her head, her eyes widening. "My dear, I really ought to check you."

"Ch-check me?"

"Remove your undergarments and lie down."

The girl gave her a strange look, but did as told, rolling down her stockings and reclining in the chaise lounge.

"This might hurt a bit." Bet folded up her hem and coaxed her thighs apart. "But try to relax."

The Duchess cried out as Bet slipped a hand into her. "Ah. High and soft." She swiftly removed her hand, and the girl gasped, clutching herself. "Put your stockings back on. I'll be right back."

Bet hurried down to the kitchen, where she plunged her hands into the soapy basin, just as the backdoor swung open. Men poured in, faces black with ash and clothing reeking of smoke. "Quickly," came the worried voice of her daughter, and Bet sighed with relief. Seluna was safe.

The bulky figure of Seluna's fiancé, Boslon, squeezed through the doorframe, carrying something limp in his arms. The men cleared the great table, knocking bowls and all manner of cutlery haphazardly to the floor. As the giant lowered his cargo onto the surface, Bet took in a breath, recognizing the man lying unconscious before them.

She swallowed, eyeing Jon Cosmith's mutilated features, the warped, scarred skin on his right-side torso and face; his right eyelid, which appeared to be sealed shut; and ear, melted against the side of his head. But most concerning was the state of his foot. It was broken, and clearly infected.

"The doctor's on his way," Seluna informed them, her voice tremulous, and the others circled their brows, as though Cosmith were already a corpse. She then spotted Bet. "Mother, aren't you supposed to be tending Eludaine?"

"Seluna." Bet drew nearer, whispering her suspicions about the Duchess into her daughter's ear.

"That's what I thought," Seluna muttered. "Confine her to her bedchamber. *Do not* let her in here." A shadow passed over her face. "This is not something a woman in her condition ought to see."

Bet returned upstairs, only to find the Duchess making to leave. "You are to stay here," Bet told her, steering her back into the chamber.

Eludaine frowned. "But, I hear people—"

"You must rest."

The Duchess gave her an indignant look, pushing past, but Bet barred her way. "It is imperative," she insisted, "that you take to your bed and not distress, my lady." She guided the girl to the mattress and turned down the quilt, inviting her to lie down.

"I'm not tired," the Duchess objected. But even as she spoke, she stifled a yawn. Bet gave her a stern look, and at last, the girl relented.

112

SELU

MACMILLAN WAS HYSTERICAL. THE OTHERS averted their eyes as Bos restrained him so that the doctor could examine his patient. "Keep it together, Mac." Selu rubbed her friend's back bracingly.

"My God, brother, what have they done?" Macmillan sobbed. "*I'll kill them!* I'll kill every last one of them with my bare hands!"

Bos tried to hush him, but Macmillan only lunged away, joining von Schultz at Cosmith's side. Desperate, Selu watched the doctor, praying he would pronounce some hope for the man.

"Looks like his entire side has been doused in chemical fire," murmured one bloke, and his companion nodded gravely.

"I can tell you that foot's infected," said another voice, as Cosmith stirred in delirium.

The doctor spoke. "Indeed, his foot must go. But first, a narcotic. Joya," he addressed a maid, "fetch the tincture of *laudanium* from my wife's boudoir."

The woman bustled off, and Macmillan held

his stomach, gazing upon the scorched figure of his half-brother. "Dear God." He rocked on his heels, turning to the doctor. "Is he invalid?"

Von Schultz pursed his lips. "Burned, poisoned, badly beaten… We can figure out his mind later. For now, let us determine whether we cannot salvage his body." He slipped on a pair of gloves, and it occurred to Selu that her mother might be useful in assisting him. She departed the kitchen.

"Mother." She rapped at Dainy's door.

After a moment, Bet's tired face was revealed in the darkness. She held a finger to her lips. Dainy was resting.

"You are needed downstairs," Selu whispered. "I'll trade posts."

Bet stepped out, and Selu entered the chamber in her stead. In the dying candlelight, she viewed Dainy's form reposing beneath the linens. Gently, Selu ran a hand through the girl's raven hair before lowering herself down onto the chaise lounge, and resting her eyes. It wasn't long, however, before both women were awakened by a lusty shriek. More ungodly screams followed, and Dainy jolted out of bed, running for the door. Selu rose to hold her back.

"Jon," Dainy whimpered. "Please let me go, Miss Bet. That sounds like my husba—"

"Dainy, it is I."

"Selu?" Dainy blinked. "What's happening? Is Jon down there? Did you break him out of prison?"

Selu hesitated. "Yes."

Dainy's eyes lit up, and she raced for the door again.

"Dainy, *no.* You are not to see him. Not yet."

Dainy clawed past her. "Let me go!" she screamed. *"I must see him! I must—!"*

"Dainy, calm yourself!" Selu finally cried. "Your distress may harm the baby!"

The girl sucked in a breath. "What baby?"

"You are with child! That is what ails you! Now lie back down," Selu pointed to the bed, "and relax your nerves. You must think of your son now."

Stunned, the young woman slowly lowered herself onto the mattress, resting a hand over her navel.

113

DAINY

DAWN WAS APPROACHING WHEN THERE came a knock at the door. Dainy rubbed her eyes.

"The surgery is complete," came Bos's hushed voice. "His foot has been fully remov—"

"*Shh,*" whispered Selu, and Dainy sat up. Whose foot?

"Capitol Square is flooded with protestors," Bos went on quietly. "The good news is, they protest alongside us. The bad news is that New Republic soldiers are on the march."

"And so are Bainherd's, according to Macmillan." Selu shook her head. "We need to transport the Cosmiths out of here. Neither is in any condition to be present for this."

"My thoughts exactly. The doctor, as well. We've just been informed they're coming for him. We all must evacuate."

Selu swore under her breath as Dainy climbed out of bed.

"Eludaine," Bos greeted her, his bearded face wan

as Dainy embraced him. "A carriage awaits you."

She followed him down the hallway. "Is Jon still here?" Her head was strangely light. She did not feel thoroughly awake yet, still recoiling from the shock of discovering, mere hours ago, that she wasn't ill, but carrying Jon's child.

Bos halted at the stairwell. It was still dark out, and the house was eerily silent despite the number of men Dainy knew the doctor hosted. "Yes," he responded at last, and Dainy's heart fluttered. "But you must understand," he looked pained, "we're unsure if he shall be the same man he once was...the man you knew...ever again."

Dainy would not be swayed. "I wish to see him at once."

"You shall." Selu sighed. "But we're warning you, Dainy, he's been badly disfigured. Therefore, if you think seeing him like this may alarm you, then for the babe's sake, we really ought to transport you separately—"

"What is this rubbish? Of course I will travel with my husband!" Dainy proceeded down the stairwell, trembling with anticipation to be reunited. She cared not what they said. No matter how he looked, or what the New Republic had tried to do to him, Jon would always be her Jon. Nothing could deter her, nor diminish the magnitude of her love for the man she'd wed, whose son she now carried within her.

They led her through the backdoor to a cobblestone alley, where an unmarked carriage sat parked beneath a bitter sunrise. Bos opened the carriage door, revealing an older man sporting a top hat and silver-black moustache.

"Dr. von Schultz will go with you," Bos explained. "His wife already left to be with her family."

Dainy embraced her friends and slid into the carriage opposite the doctor. She turned to watch as two men emerged from the villa carrying a shrouded figure. Her breaths fell short. Could it be...?

She recognized Mac, his black hair and goatee steadily gathering snow, as he lowered the limp figure into the carriage. At last, she received her husband, his head gently placed to rest in her lap.

"Jon," she whispered, horrorstruck as the dawn's light illuminated his torn and battered features, the rippled skin on the right half of his face, his disfigured ear, his scarred eye. She stifled a tearful gasp to see that one of his ankles ended in a bloody tourniquet, and she held him ever closer, wildly thankful that he still breathed.

Anxious, she glanced between Mac and the doctor. "Does he sleep?"

"He remains bewitched by the laudanium," supplied von Schultz. "It will eventually wear off."

"This is how he shall look from now on, sister," said Mac softly. "That is, if he lives."

"Of course he will live," snapped Dainy, although her and Mac's glistening eyes reflected each other's tears.

She kissed her brother goodbye, and the carriage rolled forth, keeping to the backstreets. Dainy and the doctor pulled the shades over their windows, apprehensive to depart the city. All the while, she cradled her husband's head, running a tender thumb down the flawless skin left on his face, careful not to touch his wounds, for fear of hurting him.

More than an hour passed, and Dainy dared to

lift her shade and peek outside. She recognized the snow-flecked countryside from the wagon ride with Felix Gavins. For a moment, she reflected upon the kindly wagoner who'd made it possible for her to be with her husband now, fleeing together to safety. For Dainy's sake, Felix had driven his mule at top speed through day and night to deliver her to Capitol Prison. He hadn't asked for anything in return, and she wondered how she could ever repay him.

At the sound of the doctor clearing his throat, Dainy glanced up. "Know you not, Lady Eludaine," he inquired, "that I was your mother's physician?"

She was surprised. "You knew my mother?"

"And you." He smiled. "I delivered you from her womb."

Slowly, Dainy grinned. "Well." She rested a hand on Jon's brow. "Then perhaps you shall deliver the babe I'm expecting as well, Doctor."

114

Bos

"THEY'RE HERE!"

"Bainherd's soldiers are marching in!"

And not a moment too soon, thought Bos. He and his companions were back at the Square, distributing spare weapons among the freed prisoners and rioting commoners who had none.

"Macmillan!" Bos turned to see a Bainherd guard cupping a hand over his mouth. "The General wishes to speak with you."

Macmillan went with him, and Bos glanced apprehensively at the shadow of Capitol Tower. Rolf Lymston followed his gaze. "Rumor has it," the man grunted, tossing his shaggy hair from his eyes, "we nearly exhausted our dynami supply on the prison last night."

Bos swallowed. Indeed, it'd taken more ammunition than they'd anticipated to blast through the stone fortress of Capitol Prison. But it had been worth it to save Cosmith, and free more supporters. Hadn't it?

Before Bos could respond, a trumpet sounded, and a storm of blue marched through the foggy distance.

Bos peered over the hundreds—nay, thousands—of heads in the rioting crowd, his height granting him the advantage to be seen and heard by all. Making up his mind, he brought two enormous fingers to his mouth and whistled. Those around him hushed, while scores of faces turned to him.

"It is time," Bos pronounced at the top of his voice, "for the oppressors to fall. Time for Jordinia to return to its rightful monarchs." Although he'd not slept in days, he felt oddly invigorated. "We know not what shall befall us, but we fight for something greater than ourselves, as the Ducelle legacy promises better days to come, and a brighter future for those who come after us. *To the Revival!*" he bellowed.

More than a thousand voices echoed his call.

115

Selu

"WHERE HAVE YOU BEEN?" SELU eyed Macmillan as he emerged through the crowd, clad in the red jacket of Bainherd's army and swinging a shining sword by its ornate hilt.

"To see the General," he replied smoothly, not bothering to sheathe his new weapon, as more blue-garbed Republic soldiers bounded ominously towards them. "They thought they were to help us storm Capitol Prison this morning. I explained that Jon has already been broken out, and is en route back to Pon Castle with the Duchess."

"And what did the General say?"

"He asked if they'd wheeled their cannons all the way up here for nothing." Macmillan smirked. "And I replied no, they may aim them at Capitol Tower."

Selu smiled as a formation of Bainherd soldiers poured into the misty Square, surrounding them.

"Marley!"

Selu turned inquisitively. She spotted a tuft of sprightly brown curls, as the woman she recognized as both Cosmith's and Macmillan's mother shoved her way through the masses.

"*Mother?*" Macmillan gaped. "What are you doing here?"

"Did your sister make it?" she asked breathlessly, and Selu examined her, taking in the creamy skin, high cheekbones and delicate jaw. She almost reminded Selu of the gipsia women. How fitting for Jon Cosmith's mother…

"I let her go, Marley." Marlena sounded stricken. "I should not have. And it took me 'til the morning after she'd left to realize I ought to go after her, and help her save Jon. Only I never found her on the road—"

"Peace, Mother," insisted Macmillan. "Jon and Dainy are safely gone from here."

"Both of them? Safe?" Her hazel eyes were round.

"Aye, but you must get yourself away at once. We are about to go to battle!"

"I know this, son." His mother extracted a crude dagger from the folds of her skirts.

"You cannot be serious."

"Please, Marley." She wiped what looked like dried animal's blood from the blade onto her tatty cloak. "Have I not passed the last twenty-two years in the wilderness? If I can take on horned bucks and wild boars, I can slay a New Republic soldier." She frowned. "They murdered your father, and imprisoned my son."

Macmillan made to protest, but Selu stayed his arm. "Plenty of women are fighting today, Mac. Your mother has as much right to be here as they."

116

COSMITH

COLORS, FADED. LIGHTS, DIM. PAIN, dull. Blurry ceiling. A room he did not recognize. Windows, bluish black…

Cosmith blinked his left eye several times, wondering why he could not seem to open his right along with it. The memory then recurred to him like a returning tide: the acid. The eye was blind.

But where in the world was he? He looked down, surprised to register how brightly white his linens shone in the candlelight of the spacious chamber. There were empty cots beside his, and a wooden cart bearing all manner of bottles and tinctures. Someone stirred to his left, and he startled. Who could possibly be lying beside him in a strange cot in the middle of the night, if not—?

"Dainy?" he whispered, an ineffable warmth flooding him as he took in the almond-shaped eyes, the familiar roundness of her face, the crimped sheet of midnight hair trailing down her neck.

"*Jon!*" He exhaled with unspeakable comfort as she cupped his face between her hands and kissed him on the mouth. "You're awake! A-are you lucid?"

He stroked her skin, so supple, tender and real beneath his fingertips. "I think so," he replied, although he seriously wondered whether he wasn't dreaming. "Where are we?"

"The infirmary at Pon Castle."

Cosmith furrowed his brow.

"In the Bainherd Plains," she clarified, mistaking his expression for one of confusion.

"I remember where Pon Castle is, Dainy." He grinned somewhat with the portion of his lips that he could still move. "But why are you here? Please don't tell me you've been injured as well?"

"Nay, darling." She slipped her arms around his neck. "I am only here because the nurses could not pry me from your side."

His heart quivered as he received her embrace, trapped in a state of disbelief. "My love, I feared I was never to see you again."

"As did I. They kept saying you may never fully awaken, that your body might soon expire, if your mind hadn't already. But I knew they were wrong." She pulled him closer, burying her face into his neck, her tears wet against his skin. "I knew you were stronger than that."

They held each other for a time, and Cosmith repeatedly kissed her, praying that his fantasy was real, or else that he'd never awaken from it.

"Does it hurt?" she eventually asked. Gingerly, she stroked his right cheek.

He shook his head. The skin had since hardened into a sort of hide, and while he could still perceive some feeling, it was no longer painful. He gave her another half-smile, then leaned over to the wooden cart.

"It's not time for your medicines," she told him. But he was not looking for medicines. His hand fell upon something smooth and cool. He lifted it, bringing the glass over his face.

The man cringed and made to hurl the mirror across the room, but Dainy removed it from his grip. "I am hideous." His stomach roiled with humiliation.

Dainy shushed him. "You are beautiful."

"For a dragon."

"Oy." She met his eyes. "You are still the most handsome man in all of Halvea. Even more so."

Cosmith made to sit up when a shooting pain met his right ankle, and he realized he couldn't feel his toes. Panicked, he threw the linens from his leg, only to see the stumped conclusion to his calf. *My foot*, he wanted to cry out, but couldn't formulate the words as the horrors he'd endured in prison assaulted his memory. He began to convulse.

Dainy murmured in Heppestonian, smoothing back his hair and hushing him. It was not until she began to sing, however, that he relaxed, and his mind, permitted to wander into her melody, was somewhat placated.

Yet he couldn't help but fear, even despite her gentle reassurances, that perhaps he was damaged beyond repair.

117

BOS

FOR FOUR DAYS AND NIGHTS the battle raged, while Marten Hoste remained barricaded in Capitol Tower. Many had fallen, while those remaining exchanged haphazard shifts, gaining mere minutes of fleeting rest before returning to the front.

The cannons had long been aimed at the Tower, but the Bainherd General's strategy involved persuading Hoste to voluntarily surrender first. When no such resignation came, however, they ground their teeth and prepared for the final act: the attack which, they prayed, would champion them the victors. For without Hoste, his soldiers were sure to abandon their cause. They were barely paid their dues as it was, and hadn't been for years. As well, mutiny had already occurred among their ranks, as Bainherd offered victuals and warmer clothes to any Republic soldiers who dared switch sides.

Presently, Bos had arisen from another ill-timed rest, only to find Macmillan on his knees sobbing openly in the street, where blood ran like a creek. His mother, Marlena, was among the dead that morning.

Selu turned away. The slain also included countless northerners, including many of Bos's neighbors, along with a young couple Selu identified as Carlo Di-Gyle and Shoshanna Levyn.

The afternoon was late by the time rumors of the unthinkable penetrated the air: Marten Hoste planned to emerge from the Tower with the sun's descent. The soldiers retreated, calling a temporary armistice, and all of Pierma waited anxiously until dusk.

At long last, the front doors at the base of Capitol Tower rolled open, and a string of guards issued out. Bos recognized the upright stance and white-haired crown of the Jordinian leader among them.

Marten Hoste faced his battle-worn audience, looking uncharacteristically ragged. He was handed a speaking trumpet, but merely fingered the piece, apparently deliberating upon his thoughts. Bos watched as he finally brought the instrument to his mouth. "I have just been held hostage," he began, voice limp as it rang across the darkening sky, "in my office for four days."

Bos could not help it. Above the crowd, he cried out: "That is nothing, compared to the nine months the royal family spent quarantined at the Garden Palace!"

A resounding applause broke through the masses, and Hoste raised a hand to silence them. But the people would not be silenced, as voice after voice—young men, old women—hollered out their sentences and that of their loved ones who'd been murdered, imprisoned, or else forced into lives of hiding during the last sixteen years.

Despite their angry faces, bloodied wounds and tears of despair, Bos's heart somehow, absurdly, began to lighten. For only then did he realize just how many others had remained royalists, like him. All this time, he'd never been alone...

"See reason, people." Hoste was clearly losing patience with the railing crowd. "You don't really want to do this, do you? After all we've worked for, all our progress—?"

He was interrupted by a collective hiss of scorn, while others laughed coarsely at the notion of his socalled progress. The leader howled over them. "You really wish to unravel the last sixteen years, all for some delusional young woman who *thinks* she's the Duchess Eludaine, and her conman husband?"

"She *is* the Duchess!" Macmillan shouted, and thousands of heads turned in his direction. Bos was alarmed by the glint of madness in the man's eyes, but was quick to sympathize. The lad had, after all, just lost his mother.

Others shouted, and if Hoste was speaking, he could barely be heard. More rioting was underway, and Bos gripped Selu's hand when he noticed Macmillan had vanished. The giant looked around, but could not find his friend. Why, the man had been there only moments ago.

Chaos overtook the streets again, and Hoste's guards drew their swords. Soldiers in red and blue reemerged in all directions, and Selu suddenly gasped. Bos followed her gaze as she pointed to the Tower steps, where Hoste was standing.

Had been standing.

The leader's body toppled down the stone stairs in a pool of scarlet, a glistening Bainherd sword having sliced through his throat, cleaving his white head clean from his neck. The guards in blue flew after the red-clad murderer, brandishing their fearsome swords. But the killer deflected them with the fervor of a madman, as scores of others rushed to his aid.

"Blast the cannons!" bellowed Marley Macmillan, charging from Capitol Tower, his sword dripping crimson with Marten Hoste's blood. "Take down the Tower! *Long live the Ducelle Revival!*"

118

DAINY

"GOOD MORNING, MR. COSMITH!" DR. von Schultz spoke far more loudly than necessary, and Dainy twisted her lips. Just because Jon was deaf in one ear did not mean he needed people to yell.

"I'm glad to see you awake. I am Pabol von Schultz," he introduced himself, at Jon's vague expression.

"Jon?" Dainy rested a tentative hand on his arm. "This is the doctor who saved you. By amputating your foot, he kept you from dying of infection, or poisoning of the blood—"

Jon shook off her hand and turned away, bitter. Dainy looked down. He was still in shock, she knew. He'd awoken last night expecting to find himself whole as he remembered, to recognize his own face in the looking glass. It would simply take some getting used to.

"Regretfully, there was little I could do for your right eye or ear," lamented the doctor. "And I'm sorry to inform that you shall never walk again. At least not without the aid of a crutch."

Jon closed his eye, while Dainy stiffened, fixing von Schultz with a cool glare. How could the man have such little faith in her husband? Why, Jon was capable of anything! "Jon can do whatever he puts his mind to," she snapped. "If he wishes to walk, then damn it, he shall walk."

Von Schultz gave her an appraising look—was it one of admiration?—before responding with a staid, "Yes, m'lady."

Slowly, Jon reopened his eye. His hand found Dainy's beneath the blankets, and he gave it a squeeze.

"I take it, then, that you're faring well this morning, my lady?" von Schultz asked her, as a nurse entered the infirmary to draw the drapes.

Dainy nodded, blushing.

"Remember to eat plenty of fruits and vegetables. No raw meats. And best to forego that glass of wine with dinner."

"Yes, Doctor."

"Good girl." He winked and departed them, followed by the nurse.

Dainy looked down at her lap, although she sensed Jon watching her.

"Dainy?" he said carefully. "Care to tell me what that was all about?"

"Well, husband." She rested a hand over her navel, exhaling. "I suppose there is something else you should know."

119

MACMILLAN

NOTHING HE'D EVER SEEN COMPARED to the brilliant lights bursting over Pierma that night. There was mourning, yes. But also dancing in the streets, as streamers and fireworks of every hue lit up the black sky. A vast number of Republic soldiers had been slain, and the once grand Capitol Tower lay in a crumpled heap of stone, smashed down by Bainherd's cannon fire. Every last lantern burned that evening, as the celebration rang long past sundown. The war was over, and the Revival had been won.

Everywhere he went, Macmillan was praised and embraced, men thumping him on the back and shoving pints at him, women tailing hopefully behind him, or else outright kissing him on the mouth. He was recognized widely as a hero, the champion who'd slain Marten Hoste.

The following morning was time to march back to Bainherd in victory. "And now," Macmillan called out over the Square, as thousands from near and far had congregated to see them off, "we retrieve your new

Empress!"

Endless cheers erupted, and Macmillan climbed atop his horse, waving as he departed among the soldiers.

120

COSMITH

QUIXHETO'S LEERING FACE HOVERED OVER him, the promise of another unbearable torment glistening from his glass vial. From the shadows, DuBerre nodded. Quixheto uncorked the vial, the pungent chemical odor filling Cosmith's heart with dread…

With a jolt, he awoke. Violently, he trembled, his pillow soaked in perspiration. He tried to slow his breathing, but the effort only made him pant, until he had disturbed his wife from her slumber yet again.

"*Oh.*" Her moan was groggy as she took him back into her arms. "It was just another dream, darling. Just a dream. It's all over now."

Cosmith held onto her, pleading with himself to relax. He heard nothing but her steady heartbeat, his good ear buried against her breast. Once more, guilt overcame him. Dainy was with child. Did she not need her rest? Should he not be the one soothing her, and not the other way around? "I am worthless," he choked.

"Stop," she chided softly. "The doctor says the trauma shall pass, if you keep your mind strong." She tightened her hold around him. "Which you will."

Cosmith was unable to respond for the conflicting surges of hope, shame and despair welling within him. He wept openly, clinging to her, disgusted with his own pathetic pitifulness. "I cannot do it, Dainy."

"What can't you do?"

"I cannot be the Emperor of Jordinia." The realization fell over him like the sky itself collapsing. "I can hardly see, or hear. I cannot even stand and walk as a man…"

She hushed him, rocking him like a babe in her arms. He held her, for a moment appreciating how dear of a mother she was to become. Indeed, he always knew she would make a fine parent. The question was, with all of his handicaps, would he?

"You can and will do anything you wish."

"If you believe in miracles," he muttered. It wasn't as though he would ever regain his full hearing or vision, regrow his foot or, not to mention, appear any way other than ghastly for the rest of his life.

"I need not believe in miracles, Jon," she whispered. "I believe in you."

121

EPONINA

THE BUGLES SOUNDED AS EPONINA and her family were preparing to dine. Abandoning her manners, the princess leapt to her feet and dashed to the window. "Papa," she cried, recognizing the current of red jackets parading onto castle grounds from around the road's bend. "He has returned! I—I mean, *they* have returned from Jordinia! And they're waving the victory banners!"

Overjoyed, she spun around to watch her parents exchange pleased glances. Her little brother, Lysander, looked up from his plate. "We won?"

Their father sighed. "All right." He waved a hand at the door. "You may go and greet them."

Eponina checked her reflection in the windowpane and hurried out of the dining hall, though not before hearing her father murmur: "Now that her *amore* has returned, perhaps she will finally remove that blasted bootlace from her wrist."

Blushing furiously, the princess raced her siblings down the corridor.

122

MACMILLAN

THE RECEPTION AT PON CASTLE was magnificent, and the celebration endured all day and night, much as it had in Jordinia. Nonetheless, Macmillan was eager to return to Pierma and help his siblings begin the tremendous work required there.

That was why he was taken aback when his sister seemed more than reluctant to leave Bainherd, as she led him to an abandoned chamber, where the two could speak privately. Bemused, Macmillan followed her, wondering what she possibly wished to tell him that was more important than returning to the nation over which she and her husband would reign.

"You know I'm expecting Jon's son," were the first words from her mouth, and Macmillan startled.

"No one mentioned this to me." Although, come to think of it, there was something a bit fuller about her face, and her dress seemed to fit her abdomen more snugly.

Dainy beamed. "I suppose what with being a war hero and all, such a detail might've slipped you by."

"Congratulations." Macmillan grinned, genuinely moved by the news. "How is Jon taking it?"

She smiled. "Oh, he is thrilled about the child." But her expression fell somewhat as she fingered the lace curtain at the window. "Only, he deems himself unfit to become Emperor."

"He's just nervous." Macmillan shrugged. "He'll do fine."

Dainy did not look convinced. "He cannot even walk yet, Mac," she whispered, as if Jon were at risk of overhearing, all the way from the infirmary. "As for me…" She glanced down at her budding womb. "Well. Neither of us is in any condition to rebuild an empire just now."

Macmillan stared at her. "What are you saying?" he demanded, hoping he'd misunderstood. She could not turn her back on Jordinia now, not after thousands, including his own mother, had sacrificed their lives to restore her title.

"I am saying," said Dainy carefully, matching his stare with her own, "that Dane Ducelle has a living, able-bodied son to inherit his throne."

Macmillan's heartbeat quickened. "Dainy. Jordinia is *yours*."

"Then it is mine to give. Come, Mac, you know I never wanted any of this for myself."

Macmillan looked away, baffled. Was she truly trying to hand off her empire to him, a mere forest dweller, their father's illegitimate son? He tried to reason with her. "You are young. You've not yet seen your twentieth spring. Perhaps you're feeling overwhelmed now, but you might regret this decision someday."

"And why is that?" She folded her arms. "I shall

still be the Duchess of Jordinia. We will share our in-heritance. And you will take good care of me and Jon and our children to come, no?"

Macmillan nearly laughed at the absurdity of her proposal, all the while wracking his conscience for any counterpoints he could toss her way. "What of King Wilqen? He and his men helped us win this war in order for *you and Jon* to seize the land. Not me."

But Dainy smirked, and he felt his face redden even before she spoke. "And you really think the King shall object to his eldest daughter being crowned Empress of Jordinia?"

Macmillan swallowed.

"For the record," she added gently, "Eponina would make a far more capable Empress than I. Be assured, I've given it much thought. Please, Mac," she besought him. "Jon and I are asking you to be Emperor."

Macmillan was dizzy. Nothing could have prepared him for such a request. "I—I never expected this."

"Which is precisely why you deserve it." Her smile was kind.

"Right, then." He ran a hand over his chin. "How shall we do this? How do we explain—?"

"I'll go back to Jordinia," Dainy offered, "and speak to the people myself."

"You can travel?" Macmillan glanced at her middle. "In your condition?"

His sister exhaled with relief. "The sooner, the better."

123

DAINY

EACH STEP TO THE PLATFORM was a century of bound nerves. Every knee fell as she passed, heads bowing. Dainy nodded, wishing she could personally acknowledge each one of them. Alas, there were thousands gathered in Capitol Square, now renamed to Royal Square, that morning.

She took to the makeshift stage that had been erected for her, and accepted a silver speaking trumpet that passed along a line of guards in her direction. "Good morning," she greeted nervously, as her voice was amplified throughout the Square.

The masses rose before her, watching as she unfolded her parchment. It contained the speech Maxos had helped her write, and which Jon had made her rehearse what felt like a hundred times before her journey. "I address you today, first and foremost, in thanksgiving for all you've done and sacrificed. It is you who have made this possible."

An enthusiastic applause rang through the Square, and Dainy joined in, along with Bos, Selu, Mac and

Maxos, who stood behind her.

"Indeed," she continued, "the rumors are true. I live." She shrugged, receiving a warm chuckle from her audience. "And I do possess a tremendous inheritance, which I'm immensely excited to share with you. Rest assured, this great nation shall be restored to the thriving, prosperous land it once was under the rule of my fathers."

More applause. "*But*," she continued, "after careful consideration, I've come to a decision. The throne of Jordinia is not my rightful seat. While I am indeed Eludaine Ducelle, daughter of Dane and Néandra, an elder son of the Emperor still lives."

A gasp rippled through the crowd, and Dainy beckoned Mac. The people shifted their eyes onto him, murmuring curiously to one another as he stepped up beside her.

"You know him as Marley Macmillan. But he is also my half-brother, the son of Dane Ducelle. This has been proven by blood, to which several eyewitnesses, including myself, can attest."

The crowd was by no means silent at this, but their excited tones encouraged her to go on. "As you've surely seen, he is a brave and fearless warrior. But above all, I believe him to be the rightful heir to my father's throne. And so," she lifted her voice, "that is why I respectfully step down from my nomination as your empress, and confer the rule of Jordinia upon my elder brother, Marley Macmillan Ducelle.

"I shall always and evermore remain your Duchess of Jordinia. Thank you, and may the Eternal God bless you." Dainy handed the mouthpiece back to Maxos, and traced a circle into the air over the crowd.

Bos took a step forward and lifted Mac's arm, silencing the chattering crowd. "All hail the Emperor of Jordinia!"

"Long live Marley Ducelle!" Selu and Maxos dropped to their knees.

Heart racing, Dainy held her breath as the entirety of Royal Square slowly knelt down. And then she, too, carefully lowered herself, and lay prostrate at her brother's feet.

124

COSMITH

"IT'S CALLED A *PROSTHESIS*." DR. von Schultz presented the strange footwear to the couple.

Dainy fanned herself in the late spring heat, her round belly swelling proudly before her. Cosmith caught her eye, and gave her navel the gentlest of strokes before returning his attention to the doctor.

"It goes on as such, if I may," said von Schultz, and slipped Cosmith's ankle and calf into a fabric cushion. He then attached a heavy leather boot, strapping his leg into the artifact.

Cosmith examined it. "Peculiar."

"Now, see if you cannot stand with this cane."

Cosmith glanced at his crutches resting against the wall, cautiously took the sturdy cane, and rose, launching gingerly from his left foot. He almost lost balance as he found himself standing on both legs for the first time in moons. But the doctor gripped him attentively, steadying him.

Cosmith rested his weight against the cane. Careful, he thrust the tip of the walking stick ahead and dragged the booted prosthesis forward with the muscles in his right leg. He took in a shivering breath. A step.

He heard his wife sigh with delight as she struggled to pull herself up. "Do not rise for me," he told her, wishing the woman would remain seated in her delicate condition.

Of course, she did not heed him, only hobbled to his side and kissed the gnarled skin of his right cheek. Cosmith held her loving gaze, and could not help but give her a small, grateful smile.

SUMMER

125

MACMILLAN

"AND TO WHAT DO I owe this great honor, Your Imperial Majesty?"

Marley Macmillan Ducelle embraced the King of the Bainherd Plains, who in turn gave him a hearty thump on the back. He indicated for his guest to be seated, but the younger man respectfully declined. This was a conversation he preferred to have standing.

The new Jordinian Emperor cleared his throat. "As you know, sire, the summer solstice is upon us."

"Aye, and so it is." Wilqen's beady eyes gleamed knowingly.

"As such, it means that your daughter, Lady Eponina, has seen her sixteenth summer, and is now of age for betrothal."

"Aye, and so it does." Wilqen did not bother to conceal his grin.

Pointedly aware of the maidservants lingering in the doorway (no doubt appointed by Eponina herself to report to her the details of the conversation), Macmillan took a breath. "And so I've come to request her hand in matrimony."

Although the King appeared thrilled, he did not immediately provide his response. "If I may, Your Majesty... Why betroth yourself to Eponina now? You are the Emperor of Jordinia." He cackled. "You can have any woman you desire. In the meantime, I am happy to keep Nina available for you."

Macmillan would not be fooled by this test. "All due respect, sir," he replied firmly, "but I desire no lady other than your daughter."

Wilqen broke into a genuine grin, the corners of his eyes creasing pleasantly. "I like your answer, Marley Ducelle." He held out a ring-studded hand. "And I believe you are going to like mine."

126

DAINY

"MY LADY, YOU MUST PUSH harder," urged the midwife, coaxing the place between Dainy's legs to loosen.

Dainy threw her head against the pillows in unspeakable agony. "I am...pushing...as hard...as I can," she cried through gritted teeth, as yet another nurse smoothed back her soaking hair.

"The babe is almost crowning," insisted the midwife, as the team of attendants pressed Dainy's swollen legs back painfully.

"Yes, I know; you've been saying that for the last two hours," she panted, lapsing into another spell of sleepy exhaustion. She actually caught herself snoring when the next seize overtook her belly, and the midwife hollered: "Push!"

Dainy screamed as a circle of fire raged between her legs, and an enormous pressure forced itself forth. "That's it," squealed the nurses, now commanding her to pause and breathe, breathe, breathe.

"On your next seize, I need the biggest push of all," ordered Dr. von Schultz, and Dainy nodded helplessly, her entire body aching like death. What choice had she?

She had already been suffering this torturous hell for more than fifteen hours.

And then, like a fatal illness, her stomach contracted again. Dainy bore down, crying out as she heaved a push so enormous, she feared her eyes would burst from their sockets. There came a piercing pain, until at last she watched von Schultz sliding a pasty, blood-covered torso out from her insides.

She gasped at the little figure writhing in the doctor's hands, her body smarting in anguish, her mind numb with exhaustion, although her heart slammed against her breast in astonishment.

Hurriedly, the midwife brought her mouth to the infant's and sucked out the fluids. The babe began to chirrup until it cried, the darling voice so tiny and thin. Von Schultz severed the life cord and pressed on Dainy's belly, coaxing her to deliver the last of the afterbirth. Meanwhile, the nurses cleansed and swaddled the child, cooing sweetly under their voices.

"Need I tell you he's a boy?" Von Schultz smiled, slipping off his gloves.

Dainy shook her head. She'd known all along she was to have a son. Her bare chest heaving, soaked in perspiration and mother's milk, she held out her arms. The nurses finally placed the little heap of warm blankets into her hold, and Dainy gazed down into the tiny face of her child, awestruck as though she were peering into the depths of the universe itself.

A powerful surge of love washed over her as she took in the handsome features, so perfectly proportioned, so beautifully formed. Carefully, the new mother brought the baby to her leaking breast, and helped him latch on to suckle.

127

COSMITH

THE DOOR SWUNG OPEN. IMMEDIATELY, Cosmith reached for his cane, and Bos and Macmillan helped him to his feet.

"Good evening, Your Imperial Majesty." Dr. von Schultz bowed to Macmillan. "Your Grace." He inclined his head to Cosmith. "Mr. and Mrs. Visigoth," he smiled at the newlyweds. "I come with glad tidings. The little Marquis of Jordinia is born to us at last!"

Selu sighed delightedly, exchanging a glowing look with her husband, while Cosmith nearly lost balance, gripping Macmillan's arm for support. "Marquis?" he breathed, his left eye wide. "He is male?"

"Indeed, you've a healthy son, Lord Cosmith. Congratulations!"

"And my wife?" demanded Cosmith, taking a lumbering drag forward.

"Fine, just fine," the doctor assured him. "She is ready to receive you all now," he added, "if you'll follow me."

"ALL OF THAT BLACK HAIR," Selu whispered admiringly. "Definitely a Ducelle."

"Looks just like his Uncle Mac, he does," cooed Macmillan, gently stroking the infant's cheek.

Cosmith looked to Dainy. "May I hold him now?" he asked, eager to take the sleeping bundle that was his son into his arms for the first time.

"Come." Bos beckoned the others, rising to his massive feet. "Let us leave the family to bond with their new addition."

"After all, it shan't be long until you and the missus are in our place, right, Bos?" Dainy teased, and the giant grinned.

Their friends left, and she handed the child to her husband. Cosmith cradled the heap of blankets, wishing he had the sight of both eyes through which to view the little boy. At the same time, he was grateful to have at least one working eye to admire his son's alabaster skin, so flawless like his mother's, the tufts of black hair peeking out beneath his knit cap, the rosy lips and button nose, so delicate, so precise.

He inhaled, overcome by an unexpected wellspring of emotion. The baby was deep in sleep, his tiny mouth and cheeks flexing with involuntary suckling motions. For several moments, all was silent. There was only Jon, Dainy, and...

"My dear?" He finally broke his gaze from the child to meet his spouse's tired yet glowing face. "But what shall we call him?"

She murmured something, but it issued too near his defunct ear. He cocked his left ear in her direction. "Sorry?"

"*Felix,*" she pronounced, eyeing him as though fearful he might dislike it. Cosmith paused at the unusual suggestion, trying to recall any significance to the name. "He was the hero in one of your ballads," Dainy reminded him. "The one you sung to me beneath the stars, aboard the S. S. *Isla.*"

He could not help but watch her tenderly. She remembered that?

"As well," she added, "it is the best way I can think of to honor Felix Gavins."

"Who?"

"The wagoner who… Never mind." She rested her eyes. "Only, I think it a very good name," she added sleepily. "Don't you?"

Cosmith glanced back down at his son. "Felix." He sounded out the name, surprised to discover how well he liked it. "Indeed, my wife, it is a good name." He repeated it once, twice more. "A very good name," he agreed, looking up at her.

But Dainy had already slipped into slumber, rightfully resting off a hard day's work.

THE END

EPILOGUE

HIS IMPERIAL MAJESTY, MARLEY "MACMILLAN" Ducelle, Emperor of Jordinia, married Lady Eponina Glen Wilqen, eldest Princess of the Bainherd Plains, on her eighteenth birthday, after their two-year betrothal.

When a blue silver mine was discovered on the royal family's property in the Tsongii Mountains of Asiotica, Macmillan took his chief advisor, Maxos Maxeos's advice, and used the precious metal to further lower taxes, invest in Jordinia's infrastructure, and renovate all three of the royal palaces, including the State Palace in Pierma, where he and his wife chose to reside. As well, he had the Ducelle family's remains exhumed from their site of execution in the Knights' Forest, and relocated to the Royal Cemetery in Pierma for proper burial.

Together, Macmillan and Eponina produced a total of four Grand Duchesses: Magdalena, Raphaela, Carmen and Benedicta, but no heir, leaving the throne to be inherited by their eldest nephew, the Marquis of Jordinia, Felix Jonwal Cosmith. In time, the Ducelles' legacy of col technology greatly prospered Jordinia and Bainherd, and eventually spread to all of Halvea.

SIR BOSLON AND LADY SELUNA Visigoth remained close friends of the Emperor and his family for life. Bos was knighted and joined the Emperor's Guard, to be appointed its captain. Injuries sustained as a youth in prison made it difficult for Selu to conceive, but the couple did manage to produce one very tall son, Bram, who eventually joined his father as a royal guard. In addition to motherhood, Selu found her calling in establishing a shelter for destitute women in Pierma.

AND FINALLY...

Jonwal Harrington Cosmith, Duke of Jordinia, and his doting wife, the Duchess Eludaine, occupied the renovated Garden Palace in peaceful Rhys, Jordinia. True to his word, Jon gave Dainy many children, including five sons: Felix, Sasha, Ludwig, Andrew and Wolfgang; and one daughter, Johanna.

Lord and Lady Cosmith enjoyed more than thirty-five years of loving, faithful marriage, until Dainy's untimely death at age fifty-four, from complications of her womb. A mere six weeks after her passing, her loyal husband, Jon, died of a broken heart. The two are buried side-by-side at the Royal Cemetery in Pierma.

PRONUNCIATION GUIDE

Al-Habar: Al Hah-BARR
Asiotica: Ah-see-OTT-ick-ah
Bainherd: BAY-nerd
Beili: BAY-lee
Betine Toustead: Beh-TEEN TOO-sted
Bos: BAWZ
Carnivalle: Car-nee-VAHL
Dainy: DAY-nee
DiGyle: Dih-GUY-al
Donatela: Doe-nah-TELL-ah
DuBerre: Doo-BARE
Dynami: DY-na-my
Eludaine Ducelle: ELL-oo-dayne Doo-SELL
Eponina: Ep-oh-NEE-nah
Gipsia: Jip-SEE-ah
Häffstrom: HOFF-strom
Halvea: Hal-VAY-ah
Hazja Lænde: Hah-ja LANE-day
Heppestoni: Hep-ess-TONE-ee
La Maskérada: Lah Mass-kay-RAH-dah

Indi: IN-dee
Jano: JAY-no
Janoan: Jah-NO-an
Jonwal Cosmith: JON-vahl COE-smith
Jophlin: JOFF-lin
Jordinia: Jor-DIN-ee-ah
Kramerik: Kray-MARE-ick
Marlena: Mar-LAY-na
Maxos Maxeos: MAX-ohs MAX-ee-ohs
Montimor: MON-tim-er
Ondriga: ON-drig-ah
Paxi: PAX-ee
Pierma: Pee-AIR-mah
Pikosta: Peek-OH-stah
Pon Castle: Pawn Castle
Priya: PREE-yah
Quixheto: Kwix-ZEE-toe
Selu: SEE-loo
Seluna Campagna: See-LOO-na Com-PON-yah
Shaomiin: Shaow-min
Solomyn: SOL-ah-min
Tröndhelm: TRONDE-helm
Tsongii: Sawn-ghee
Wilqen: WILL-kin

ACKNOWLEDGMENTS

There's a number of people I'd like to acknowledge for the creation of these books. First of all, though, to you, from the bottom of my heart, I thank you immensely for reading my books. Writers write to be read, and without readers, our stories can't fully come alive. Thank you for meeting me in my world and helping to bring life and meaning to my work. You are what keeps me going!

I extend my sincere gratitude to Juanita Samborski for believing in my manuscripts and granting me the incredible opportunity to become a published author with 48fourteen. I am so blessed to have found a wonderful and fitting home for the Books of Jordinia. Many thanks as well to the marvelous Denise DeSio for the meticulous (and often hilarious) editing, and for significantly enhancing the quality of my writing; and to Amanda L. Matthews and Lyndsay Johnson for their artistic talent. Go Team 48fourteen!

With special appreciation to Michele DeLuca for encouraging me with all the original drafts and teaching me how to wear big girl pants; Sami for invaluable guidance on Jon and Dainy's relationship; and Jeff for suggesting coal mines and teaching me all about economies. To each of my readers, family members and friends who've been unbelievably supportive of this process, especially Gloria—my "publicist," Lauren C., Becca, Erin and Jake: thank you doesn't seem adequate! You are amazing!

I've a few works of historical fiction to acknowledge in addition: first, Michelle Moran's *Madame Tussaud: A Novel of the French Revolution* (Crown 2011) and *Anastasia's Secret* (Bloomsbury USA Childrens 2010) by Susanne Dunlap, both for teaching me how and why revolutions work; and Universal's 2012 film rendition of Les Misérables for much inspiration for *The Duchess Inheritance.* Merci beaucoup!

Last, but never least, to the greatest blessings and loves of my life: my husband Jeff, our son Victor, and my savior, Jesus Christ. All that I do is only through your incredible, unending, unfailing love. Thank you all.

ABOUT THE AUTHOR

C. K. Brooke is a stay-at-home mom and author. She has lived all over the U.S., from the east coast to the southwestern desert, but her heart is in the Midwest. When not writing novels or spending time with her husband and young son, she enjoys reading, singing, playing the piano, and long walks with the stroller. Visit her at www.CKBrooke.com.

CPSIA information can be obtained at www.ICGtesting.com
Printed in the USA
LVOW07s0235240415

435922LV00001B/26/P